MURDER AT SLEEPING TIGER

C.R. Koons

CAVEL
PRESS

KENMORE, WA

CAMEL
PRESS

A Camel Press book published by Epicenter Press

Epicenter Press
6524 NE 181st St.
Suite 2
Kenmore, WA 98028

For more information go to:
www.Camelpress.com
www.Coffeetownpress.com
www.Epicenterpress.com
Author's website: www.cedarkoons.com

This is a work of fiction. Names, characters, places, brands, media, and incidents are the product of the author's imagination or are used fictitiously.

Design by Rudy Ramos
Cover Photo by Edward Scheps

Murder at the Sleeping Tiger
2022 © C.R. Koons

ISBN: 9781942078982 (trade paper)
ISBN: 9781942078999 (ebook)

Printed in the United States of America

Dedication

For my children, Woodwyn Koons, Rowan Koons,
Aaron Scheps and Dillon Scheps

Acknowledgments

The author would like to acknowledge the following persons: Gayle Frauenglass for reading the manuscript and for her map illustration, Dr. Amy Zaharlick for sharing her expertise on Picuris culture and reviewing the book for cultural errors, and Carol Butler of Butler Books for invaluable advice and support on marketing. Sara Jane Herbener, Debra Kaufman and Tara Gavin gave professional editorial advice, and Linda Hube, Kurt Hube, Amelia Hube, Karen Cohen, Bette Betts, Cindy Alford and Stephen Koons read the manuscript and gave me helpful feedback. And thanks to Jennifer McCord at Camel Press for taking an interest in my story and characters and providing a publishing home for the Sheriff Ulysses Walker series. Most of all to thank my husband, Edward Scheps, who listened to countless drafts read aloud and who provided helpful criticism, emotional support and delicious meals throughout the writing process

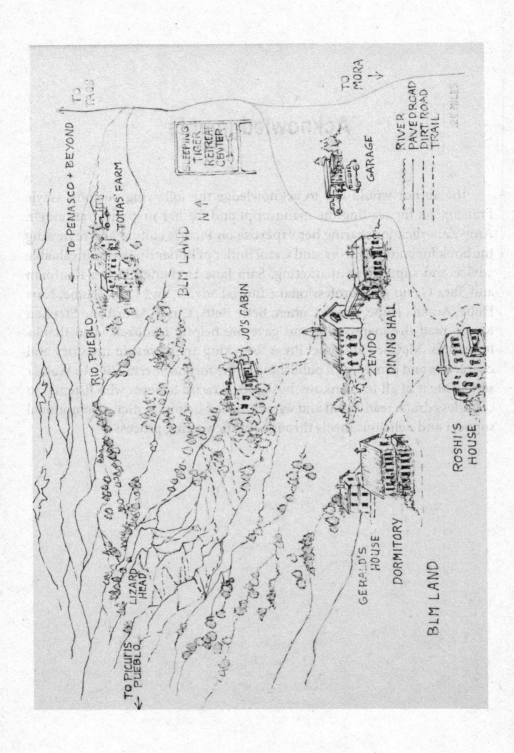

Chapter I

Why meet here of all places? Luis Duràn trudged up a snowy path as the wind blew in short, intense bursts. He had a bad history with heights and he was pretty sure this trail led to a high mesa with steep cliffs.

It was nearly sunset but the full moon had not yet risen over the mountains. Luis hated and feared the man he was supposed to meet, someone he'd known since childhood. *I have the upper hand now*, he thought with a rush of bravado. *But what if he calls my bluff?* Luis didn't want to go back to prison, especially not for murder.

Luis trembled and wondered if it was his nerves, the cold or withdrawal that made him feel so bad. He downed his last tequila mini and tossed the plastic bottle into the bushes. The week or so since he'd relapsed had been a blur. He'd been living in his truck and had caught a bad cold. He'd have to get clean before he went back to his mother's or she'd kick him out for good. Luis reached into the pocket of his jacket to check the safety on the pistol he'd stolen from her.

At the top of the ridge where the trees thinned, he saw a figure in a heavy hooded parka standing at the edge of the cliff, facing away from him. They didn't look like Gerald, the man he'd come to meet. The person turned toward him and beckoned with a gloved hand.

Luis yelled into the wind, "Who are you? What do you want?" The figure strode forward, grabbed Luis by his upper arm, and dragged him toward the cliff edge. Luis scrambled to maintain footing in his slick-soled cowboy boots. He fumbled for his pistol, but his opponent wrenched his arm painfully and struck him in the chest, knocking the breath out of him. His pistol fell into the snow at his feet. Then Luis felt something, a gun, press against the back of his skull.

The last daylight was fading and more snow began to fall. Luis looked over the cliff edge into the shadows below him. Nothing felt real. He didn't

1

feel real. He closed his eyes, gasping. Then the attacker spoke for the first time. "Jump, Luis. You deserve to die and you know it."

Luis began to beg, his words trailing off in the wind.

"Shut up and jump or I'll push you."

Luis struggled but couldn't get free. "No," he sobbed, " Please! You've got it all wrong!" He grasped at his opponent's leg but the attacker pried his hands loose. Realizing he was doomed, Luis looked up at his assailant, recognizing the face an instant before a kick to his chest shoved him over the sheer drop. In his last seconds Luis heard his own high-pitched scream, then his head slammed into a rock outcrop near the bottom. His pistol tumbled down after him, resting near his head.

A man stood on the trail just below the mesa top in the shadows of a big spruce, out of sight but listening intently. It was too dark for him to see clearly and the wind had obscured any words. But when he heard the scream, he ran down the switchbacks, stumbling in the dark, terrified.

•

Taos County Sheriff Ulysses Walker woke up to find his three-year old son, Monty, wetting the bed. The boy lay cuddled between Ulysses and his wife Rosemary, and warm urine flowed downhill toward Ulysses, who jumped up, grabbed the child and carried him to the bathroom. Monty woke up and began to cry. Rosemary, who had been up with Monty earlier, feigned sleep. "This has got to stop," Ulysses grumbled to himself. "We have got to get him to stay in his own bed." Ulysses had forgotten his dream but its disturbing aura lingered.

Wind whipped around the eaves of the old adobe house. It had started snowing overnight and it was still coming down. The full moon burnished a pewter glow in the cloud bank on the western horizon. It was five o'clock, time for Ulysses to get up anyway. He slipped off the child's soggy pull-ups and placed him in a warm bath. Monty stopped crying and began sucking his thumb. When he'd finished bathing the little boy, Ulysses wrapped him in a large towel and put him back in the warm bed next to Rosemary who groaned and opened one eye.

In the kitchen, Ulysses turned on the coffee pot and chunked a few logs of dry ponderosa pine into the woodstove. He grabbed some clean underwear and a fresh uniform and went to the other bathroom, feeling rushed and irritable. Usually he liked to meditate for at least fifteen minutes before he started the day.

The moment he stepped under the hot shower he remembered his dream.

He was late to meet someone in a dark building with many rooms and long hallways. He didn't know who he was meeting but he felt that either he would kill that person or be killed by them. He had wandered down hallway after hallway looking for the right room, a gun in his hand. At the end of one corridor, a door opened into a room that was empty except for a tall ladder leaning against a wall. Under the ladder stood a frightened-looking toddler. On the wall was a man's shadow. Ulysses stared into the room with a terrible foreboding. Then he woke up.

The message of the dream seemed depressingly clear. While he was performing the dangerous job he loved, his family was at risk. It was exactly the conversation he'd had with Rosemary the night before. "Let the deputies take on the field work, Ulys," she'd said. "You focus on running the show and live to see our kids grow up." Ulysses scrubbed his close-cropped head and lean body, but his unease persisted. He took dreams seriously even if he'd never admit it. This one was a warning.

When Ulysses got out of the bathroom, Rosemary had already made his coffee the way he liked it, with lots of half and half and a big teaspoon of honey. It stood on the kitchen table steaming, along with a plate of scrambled eggs and a buttered piece of homemade raisin toast. Rosemary was already upstairs getting Monty dressed. Amelia, their five-year-old, had quietly turned on the television and was watching cartoons, definitely a no-no, but that was not an argument Ulysses wanted to have now.

He finished his breakfast, took his dishes to the sink and prepared to leave. "Daddy, Daddy!" Amelia said coming up to him for a goodbye kiss. He picked her up, kissed her and snuggled her neck. She smelled like popcorn.

"I stayed in my bed, didn't I?" she asked as he put her down. She ran back to the television. "Today is Caterpillar Club!"

"I can't wait to hear about it when I get home," Ulysses said. "You should turn off that television before your mother comes downstairs."

"You always get home after I'm in bed, though," Amelia said.

"Not always," Ulysses replied.

"Most of the time," Amelia said, turning off the television. *It was true*, Ulysses thought, most of the time he didn't get home until both his children and usually his wife, were asleep.

"Don't worry, Ulys, I'll do the chores," Rosemary yelled from upstairs where she was getting Monty dressed. Ulysses went into the mudroom, pulled on his boots and took his gun out of the gun safe. He checked the safety and put the gun in his shoulder holster, then put a tan down jacket over his uniform and badge. As he took his wide brimmed felt hat from the peg by the door, Rosemary came in looking cross, with Monty on her hip, dressed in his snowsuit. She never liked to part without a proper goodbye.

Ulysses pushed her reddish curls aside and kissed her. "I'll be home by about seven," he said. She gave him a skeptical look.

"I'll be waiting," Rosemary said. "We're going nowhere in this weather."

"Sorry I peed the bed," Monty said.

"Okay, my man," Ulysses said. "It happens. But you need to learn to stay in your own bed."

"I know," Monty replied, "but there is something scary under my bed and I couldn't find my bear."

"What do you have going on today?" Rosemary asked.

"Performance evals, my favorite."

"At least they won't shoot at you."

"Wish I could be sure of that," he said.

"Well, come home safe. I love you," she said as he walked out the door.

"Wait 'til I go to let him loose, " Ulysses said. "I don't want him behind the Expedition when I pull out. Love you too."

Ulysses crossed the snowy driveway lost in thought about the day. He'd finished the one eval thus far, for his secretary, Lorraine Baca. Even though he rated her "fully satisfactory," she found it unsatisfactory because it wasn't the highest possible rating. Now he had to meet with four deputies and three 911 operators. At least three of them would rate "needs improvement," including his newest deputy, Josh, who was the worst of the bunch. Only one deputy, Angela Romero, had earned the highest rating, "exceeds expectations." Luckily, Angela would be unlikely to tell anyone her rating. She had the political savvy to avoid office drama.

Even though he'd been elected two years ago, Ulysses was still finding his way in this job, especially overseeing staff. The work was a far cry from being a police detective in Santa Fe, the job he'd had. Police detective work didn't pay enough for the long hours and risk involved. When he set his sights on becoming sheriff, Ulysses had imagined he'd be working in the wild, beautiful expanses of Taos County chasing down bad guys, by himself if at all possible. In the same fantasy he was less likely to get into battles with gangbangers like the man Ulysses shot and killed many years ago on the Santa Fe Plaza during Fiestas, making headlines across the state. Johnny "the Nub" Catron could have killed him had Ulysses not shot first. The incident made a powerful impression on Rosemary who was pregnant at the time, and she had pushed for Ulysses to make a career change. They compromised on him running for sheriff in Taos, the county where he'd been born. Rosemary hoped being sheriff of largely rural Taos County would be safer than policing the capital city.

Ulysses climbed into the SUV that his predecessor, Sheriff Trujillo, had bought a year before retiring unexpectedly for reasons that remained hidden. A black Ford Expedition with all the bells and whistles, it had cost the county a pretty penny. As Ulysses backed out of the garage into the snow, he felt the vehicle bump over something in the driveway. When he got out, he saw that he had run over the old handmade wooden ladder his father had used to prune their apple trees, shattering it. Ulysses pulled the pieces out of the snow and stacked them by the garage, wishing he'd put it back in its proper place when the apple season had finished. Monty, zipped into his snowsuit and clutching his recovered bear, came running out. "Daddy, what did you do?" he shouted, "Mommy's going to be mad at you!"

•

Tomàs Ulibarri was up drinking strong, black coffee just after sunrise. Thick, wet snowflakes were coming down steadily. He dressed in his cleanest pair of jeans and the new flannel shirt his daughter bought him for his birthday, then pulled on his boots. Today he had to make two trips to Santa Fe to pick up the retreat attendees. He hoped the weather wouldn't turn nasty.

Tomàs fried some chorizo and eggs, heated up green chile and tortillas, and sat down at his kitchen table. This was his mother's old house and he still felt her quiet presence even though she'd been dead for almost a decade.

Her red curtains hung in the deep-silled windows and he'd managed to keep her houseplants thriving — a jade plant, a shamrock, and three cacti. He had to stoop to get through the doorways, and the ceilings were a tad low for his six-foot-four frame. His head almost touched the bedroom ceiling. But since he mostly lived outside, hunting all fall and gardening all summer, he didn't mind.

Tomàs had returned after three tours in Afghanistan and didn't plan on going anywhere else anytime soon, especially since he'd found work just down the road at the Sleeping Tiger Retreat Center. He'd been working there for just over a year, hired at the recommendation of the cook, Carmen, who also happened to be his aunt on his mother's side. He'd thought that the army would be his career but he learned in Afghanistan that he wasn't cut out to stalk and kill his fellow human beings. He preferred hunting elk. There was one gutted on a trestle right now. He was glad the cold was holding. It needed to get cut up and into the freezer soon.

Tomàs put on his coat and went out to feed his hens in their small coop off the woodshed. He put grain in their feeders, checked the fencing to make sure no predators could get in, and took the waterers inside to thaw. Then he looked over his elk, a young doe, hanging head-down. Nothing had gotten after it yet.

Snow blanketed the garden. His mother had grown corn and beans, squash and chiles, and nursed six ancient but productive apple trees. Tomàs continued her traditions and had a bumper crop this year. He wished his daughter, son-in-law and baby grandson would settle nearby to enjoy all this bounty. But they were attached to Albuquerque, God knew why. *Oh, yeah,* he remembered: *jobs, better schools, things like that.* Also, his ex-wife Jessica would have a fit if the family moved up here. Tomàs had to acknowledge that Jessica was a good mother and grandmother even if she had abandoned him for a condo in Albuquerque and a government job, just before his third deployment.

Tomàs drove his truck a half-mile to Sleeping Tiger and parked beside the garage. Carmen was already in the kitchen/dining hall preparing food for an eight day Zen sesshin that was scheduled to begin after dinner tonight. Roshi Melanie Hirsh, Zen Master and a founder of Sleeping Tiger, always emphasized that tasty, wholesome food was central to the success of a sesshin. Somehow, twelve hour days of meditation and silence tended to make people ravenous.

Tomàs noticed that the lights were on in Roshi Melanie's house. *I'll say good morning to Carmen and then bring Melanie a cup of coffee*, he thought. Tomàs had no interest in Buddhism but he'd grown very fond of Melanie over the short time he'd worked at Sleeping Tiger. A Jewish woman from Brooklyn, Roshi Melanie spoke excellent Spanish and was the best employer he'd ever had.

Tomàs walked into the warm, bright commercial kitchen that smelled of coffee, bacon and onions. Carmen was making green-chile. She turned from the stove and wiped her hands on her apron.

"Mi sobrino!" She hugged him around the waist and laid her head below his breastbone.

"Mi tia," he whispered and hugged her back. Carmen was his mother's younger sister. She was as quick, short, round, and focused as his mother had been slow, tall, slender, and distracted. Tomàs had loved his mother but he adored Carmen.

"I've made you lunch and a snack," she said, handing him a grocery bag. "Water, a turkey sandwich, and one of my first tamales—carnitas. I also put in a few bizcocitos and some green-chile stew. And here is your breakfast." She handed him a warm plate with two eggs over easy, a tortilla, bacon and red chile.

Tomàs didn't have the heart to tell her he'd already eaten. Feeding Tomàs seemed to be the highlight of Carmen's life. Besides, Tomàs could always pack in another meal, especially Carmen's red chile. If he didn't watch out, he was going to get fat.

"How many trips today, Tomàs?"

"Two trips. One to pick up eight from L.A. at the Santa Fe airport and another to meet the shuttle from Albuquerque this afternoon, with ten. Three women are driving down from Crestone and some guy is coming over from Los Alamos."

"I've been listening to KKOB, Nephew. I've been listening to KKOB, Nephew. I don't think the group flying into Albuquerque is going to make it. They're coming from Chicago and there's a huge storm on the plains, don't you know?" She handed him a mug of coffee and filled a thermos for him to take on the drive. "By the way, the three from Crestone already cancelled. They can't make it through La Veta Pass. I also wonder about the man from Los Alamos. I hope he gets an early start!"

"I'll check the flights as soon as I can get a cell signal. I have to come back here and drop off the L.A. folks before I go get the second batch."

"You be careful. It might be icy."

"I will, Tia. Did Melanie get her coffee?" Tomàs asked.

"Oh, yes, Gerald was here ten minutes ago. But you could take her a warm-up. He never remembers she likes two cups, no?" She winked at him. Carmen didn't like Gerald, a Sleeping Tiger founder who was a Zen sensei and lived on the property. She had told Tomàs when he was hired to watch out for him. "That Gerald is a cheapskate with a mean streak."

Tomàs kissed Carmen on the cheek and went out the kitchen door with a mug of hot coffee for Melanie. He approached her two-story adobe home and stashed his lunch and thermos on her porch. He could hear Gerald's raised voice. Tomàs knocked anyway.

A lanky, middle aged man dressed in expensive charcoal slacks and a tweed jacket answered the door and reached for the coffee cup. Gerald looked like he was dressed to go to Santa Fe, a trip he frequently made on Mondays. He didn't make eye contact with Tomàs, which was part of what Carmen disliked about him. Melanie called out, "If that's Tomàs, let him in. We can finish talking later."

Gerald reluctantly held the door open for Tomàs. "How about this snow?" Melanie said, coming to hug him. Melanie was about seventy, petite, with a halo of grey curls and dark-brown eyes. She was still in her robe and slippers.

"It's not too bad," Tomàs said. "But I'm glad I got those tires replaced on the van."

Gerald said, "Did you buy all four tires? I told you to get two, not four."

Before Tomàs could reply, Melanie said, "I'm glad if you got all four. Did you have breakfast?"

"Two breakfasts, actually," Tomàs said and they both laughed. Melanie knew about Carmen's overfeeding tendencies. "Well, I should be going," he said.

"Vaya con Dios," Melanie said.

"What time will you be back?" Gerald asked.

"It depends, no? Mother Nature being as she is!" Tomàs replied.

"Well, get back soon. You have a lot of work to do!" Gerald abruptly closed the door. *As if you even know what I do*, Tomàs thought.

As he walked toward the garage, the sun came over the mountain and lit up the retreat center, twenty-six acres and seven buildings bought ten years before from the Archdiocese of Santa Fe. Tomàs was reminded of all the projects he hoped to do when the weather permitted. Retreat manager Jo McAlister's adobe cabin in a meadow to the west badly needed a new electric panel. Behind Jo's cabin, up toward Lizard Head, Tomàs planned to post some "no trespassing" signs, if Melanie would let him. He thought people should know where public land ended and private land began.

At the center of the property was a chapel built by the property's original owners, the Benedictine Order, now repurposed as a zendo, or meditation place. The zendo building included a meditation space, three VIP guest rooms and public bathrooms. It needed one of its water heaters replaced. The zendo was connected by a covered walkway to the dining hall, a large old post and beam brick building that had been remodeled when Sleeping Tiger took over. It had no current problems, thank God.

The biggest headache was the two-story stone dormitory, looming on a hill north of the dining hall. Its old, cranky boiler gave Tomàs fits. The dormitory was built in 1928 as sleeping quarters for Benedictine monks, then it was sold to the Archdiocese in the 1970's to house troubled priests sent for rehabilitation. Now it provided lodging for retreat guests. Beyond the dormitory was Gerald's house built for the superintendent of the rehabilitation center in 1970. Gerald insisted it had black mold in the crawl space.

Well, I won't be getting to any of this today, Tomàs thought as he got into the newer of the two vans and looked through his supplies: blankets, water, energy bars, chains, flares, cell-phone charger, shovel, and of course, his lunch. He liked to be well-prepared for any kind of weather, especially here at 7,500 feet of elevation where snowstorms could turn ugly quickly. He checked the glove box to make sure his pistol was there, locked and loaded. His days in the military made him more comfortable when packing a sidearm.

Tomàs looked over the manifest. His first trip to Santa Fe airport for eight passengers, all coming in on the 10:35 from Phoenix out of LAX. They included some people he'd met at previous retreats, members of the Sleeping

Tiger Board and people he didn't know. One of those was someone Tomàs had heard a great deal about, Roshi Astrid Berg. She was Roshi Melanie's former student, now a Zen roshi herself with a large following in the Los Angeles area and supposedly an attractive redhead. This sparked Tomàs's interest as he was a fond appreciator of pretty women, but Roshi Astrid also had the reputation of being "a real bitch" according to Gerald. *Should be interesting*, Tomàs thought as he backed out and headed for the airport.

•

After an early breakfast, retreat manager Jo McAlister walked the short distance from the dining hall to the zendo to complete her preparations. She was thinking over her to-do list and wondering whether she'd get help or interference from her boss, Sensei Gerald Beatty. He was second in command to Roshi Melanie. *Was that him the night before at dusk, coming down the trail from Lizard Head?* It was so unlike him to be out and about on a frigid night but Jo was almost sure she recognized his loping gait. *Why was he running?*

If it weren't for the sesshin, Jo wouldn't mind the snowstorm. She'd grown up in the Sierra Nevada. It was second nature for her to keep pantries stocked, dry wood stacked on porches, and all the kerosene lamps full and trimmed in case of a power outage. But most of the twenty-two guests registered for this retreat were flying in from out of state. A blizzard was going to ruin everything. Roshi Melanie would be so disappointed This was her ten year anniversary and she had been working on her dharma talks for months. Besides, Jo knew Sleeping Tiger needed the money the sesshin made.

Jo checked to make sure the mallet to ring the big iron Japanese bell by the front door was in its proper niche. She taped the retreat schedule to the wall beside the zendo's entrance, unlocked the double doors, came into the carpeted entry and removed her boots. The entry had pegs for coats, a shelf for hats and gloves, and a shoe rack. Jo checked the two hall bathrooms and found both clean and stocked with extra supplies, as she'd specified. She walked down the carpeted hall in her stocking feet past the three nicest guest rooms and Roshi's study, where she met individually with her students in dokusan. The bedrooms and their bathrooms were already prepared for guests. Jo was going to clean Roshi's study herself.

Jo had been a Zen student of Roshi Melanie for seven years, coming to love the compassion and scholarship of her teaching. Jo took the job three years ago, moving to Sleeping Tiger from California only a few months after her husband of thirteen years, Tim, had died from sarcoma. Against the advice of friends, Jo sold their house and possessions and moved to New Mexico. The job paid room, board, and a small stipend each month, most of which Jo saved. She had brought little with her other than clothes and a few books.

At the end of the hall was the zendo, an empty room fragrant from sandalwood incense. The room had bare white walls and a light bamboo floor but still recalled the chapel nave it had once been with its arched dark wood ceiling and large clear windows on either side that used to hold stained glass. Where the altar had been was a low stone table before a huge window facing west.

As she came into the room Jo gazed out the big window and was surprised to see Gerald again, this time walking briskly toward her cabin in the swirling snow, dressed in a light jacket and without a hat. *What on earth was he doing?*

Jo chafed at how Gerald supervised her administrative duties, alternating between being unaware of the crucial details she handled and insisting on micro-managing her. At times she thought Gerald was jealous of her relationship with Roshi Melanie. Since taking the position at Sleeping Tiger, Jo had been breezing through koan study and Roshi frequently praised her work. Recently, Gerald had given up his role as "tanto," person in charge of ceremonial aspects, saying he had too much other work. Roshi asked Jo to take over being tanto on top of everything else she did. *Yet Gerald still remains sensei,* Jo thought with a tinge of resentment.

Before setting to work she brought out her meditation pillows, a large, square zabuton of dark purple and a matching firm, round buckwheat-hull zafu that she placed on the zabuton. She sat in half-lotus position, then set her watch for thirty minutes and began to settle her mind.

Jo had discovered Zen in her twenties, when she and Tim had attended a Zen retreat. She liked the openness and informality of American Buddhism which avoided strict hierarchies and promoted first name familiarity. She felt all people, especially spiritual teachers, needed to earn the respect accorded to them in a title. Roshi Melanie quicky earned not only her respect and but her affection.

Tim soon lost interest in the retreats, but Jo found she loved the silence. She looked forward to not having to talk for days. Sometimes the noise, intensity, and complexity of her job as a paramedic left her feeling as if her mind was untidy. She loved the clean order and sparseness of Zen, which did not require one to believe in anything. Jo didn't set much store in belief systems.

After an hour of meditation, eyes half open, watching her thoughts without clinging to them, and she felt her mind was put to rights. Zen valued seeing reality for what it is, an experience of the vast emptiness contained in all form, truth perceivable only in the present moment. After the years of struggle with Tim's cancer and then the devastating grief, Jo's practice of Zen felt essential to her well-being.

The timer went off and Jo sat a few more moments before opening her eyes. She stood and stretched, stepping up to the big window. A figure, probably a man, was racing up the trail to the Lizard Head. This trail, while open to hikers, was infrequently used. In a few minutes he disappeared into the trees. There was no sign of Gerald though. Jo started to dustmop the zendo.

Rohatsu was an eight-day sesshin with unique requirements, including special incense, candles, bells, and readings. Roshi Melanie had never been a stickler for rituals, which she called "bells and smells." She preferred to focus on sitting practice, silence, and meeting with her students one-on-one for brief private teachings called dokusan. She wanted her students to adhere strictly to silence and avidly pursue an awakened mind without distractions. However, this year, with Roshi Astrid Berg in attendance, Melanie seemed anxious to make sure everything was ritually correct. Astrid observed all of the rites and rituals at her well-attended sesshins. She sometimes railed against American Zen as "Buddhism Lite", saying it cut off the roots of an ancient path to create a pleasant consumer experience. Jo knew Astrid was the youngest Zen master in the US, having received transmission from Junsu Ito, a famous and now disgraced roshi who had died four years ago. Jo had met Roshi Astrid once and wasn't impressed. Still, Jo didn't want to judge her. That would be counter to the dharma.

Jo arranged the meditation pillows in rows facing each other. She prepared seating in front of the altar for Roshi Melanie and Roshi Astrid. While Astrid would not be teaching during the sesshin, she would take over Jo's role as tanto. Jo wondered how Astrid's stern demeanor in the zendo would go over. Astrid liked the kyosaku, a stick used to wake sleepy meditators, a tradition which Roshi Melanie disliked but was allowing for Rohatsu.

Jo placed long and short incense, beeswax candles and kerosene lamps on the altar. She set the large black ceramic bell, rung at the beginning and end of each sitting, on its red satin cushion in front of where the timer, founder and board member, Dr. Anne Stein, would sit.

Jo's aversions toward Roshi Astrid returned to her mind. It was hard to imagine her as a teacher in her own right. Astrid sought a lot of attention. And Jo had heard the rumors about Astrid's ambition. Some said she had received transmission from Junsu Ito in return for keeping his secrets.

Finished with the zendo itself, Jo opened the door to Roshi Melanie's study.

The room had one small window that faced north, providing a view of the snowy peaks of the Sangre De Cristo Mountains. Roshi's desk was untidy, as always, with books, papers, teacups and a half-eaten sandwich. Several books lay open—she'd been delving into her old favorites, the Christian mystics. Jo also noted that a book on Zen protocol and *Confessions of a Buddhist Atheist*, which she'd loaned Melanie, were open facedown. Jo gently picked up each book, inserted a bookmark, and made a neat stack to the left of her desk. Underneath the books were sheets of paper covered with her spidery handwriting—new talks most likely. Roshi Melanie didn't own a computer. As Jo stacked the papers, she noticed a letter to Gerald. She resisted the urge to read it. She would never betray Roshi Melanie's trust in her by snooping, but her eye caught the sentence "You lied to me!" underlined near the bottom of the first page. Jo immediately tried to suppress what she'd seen.

She hurriedly put the dirty cups and plates in a basket to return to the kitchen and adjusted Melanie's chair in front of the shoji screen and the folding chair across from it where students sat when they presented their koans to her.

When the study was dusted and vacuumed, Jo lit a stick of incense on the altar then took her basket and prepared to go out in the snow. As she came out of the zendo, she noticed the women she'd hired to clean the dormitory leaving. *Just in time*, she thought. Tomàs was already coming up the driveway with the first van of attendees. Jo walked toward the garage to greet them.

•

Ulysses used to love snow. Growing up on a commune in Arroyo Hondo, he and his sister would gather with all the kids for sledding parties on the hill behind the geodesic dome. In those days, when it snowed they almost never had to go to school. Now snow usually just made his job more difficult. Today, though, he was glad for the invitation to postpone performance evals and get out in the field with his old friend, Raymundo Pando, War Chief of Picuris Pueblo. A tribal member had gone missing on Bureau of Land Management Land over near the old Benedictine Monastery which was now some kind of Buddhist center.

Ulysses followed Ray up the rocky trail on private land, where snow had already mostly obscured any tracks. The two men had known each other for many years, dating back to when they were both homicide detectives, Ulysses in Santa Fe and Ray in Albuquerque. Ray had retired a few years ago and returned home to Picuris. Since then he'd served on the tribal council as war chief, an elected position with both ceremonial and security roles but very little compensation.

In a couple of places Ray pointed out where boots had left slight impressions in a sloping bank. "Last night," Ray said. "Two men. I can't tell for sure if they were together." They hiked on, entering Bureau of Land Management land. After they passed a fork in the trail, Ray said, "Here's a third man." There were also fresher tracks of a man running, probably from this morning.

They climbed switchbacks through piñon, juniper and ponderosa pine. The snow was dry and packed under their boots. The wind cut into their clothes. Ulysses thought about Rosemary and the kids at home around the woodstove. Perhaps Rosemary had them doing art projects or baking cookies. Or maybe they were watching television. For the hundredth time he reflected on how his father would feel if he knew that last fall he'd put a satellite dish on the roof of the family's handmade house. His mother had taken it in stride, but she'd always been the practical one.

After half an hour of steady climbing, they stopped at the top of a switchback and Ray pointed to something in the vegetation to the right of the trail. An empty plastic mini bottle was caught in the lower branches of a bush. Ulysses bagged it and the two walked on to the top. As Ulysses and Ray stepped out onto the mesa, the wind howled. The two men walked in silence seeking signs of the missing man. "Look, Ulys," Ray shouted. Below the precipitous western cliff was a dark smudge—a body. They stood for a moment looking down. Then Ray located the trail down and the men walked carefully on the slick, steep path for twenty minutes to reach the bottom.

"Poor Luis," Ray said. The much younger member of his tribe lay spread-eagled on his back, snow partially covering his thinly clad torso, his head surrounded by a halo of blood. His face bore a prominent bruise on the left temple and his brown eyes were open as if gazing at the sky. Rigor had already passed. Ulysses thought he'd been dead more than twelve hours. Ray squatted and chanted a prayer over Luis's body while Ulysses looked around for other evidence.

Near the body under a creosote bush he found a gun, a 9 mm with the safety on. He picked it up with his handkerchief, sniffed it (not recently fired), and dropped it into an evidence bag. Murder or suicide? He couldn't be sure. Other than the gun there was nothing but snow and brush.

"I'll call the tribal council boys," Ray said, standing up and shaking his head sadly. "We'll have to use an ATV to get him out."

"I'll make sure his truck is towed off the Forest Road," Ulysses said. They started the climb back up Lizard Head. "Let's swing by that Buddhist place, too, and let them know we've had a suspicious death in the neighborhood. Do you know any of those folks?"

"No. I guess they mostly keep to themselves," Ray said. "I get that."

As they hiked back Ulysses prepared himself mentally for the visit to Luis's mother, Casimira Duràn, to tell her about her son's death. Seven years before, as a detective for the Santa Fe Police, he had been on the call that found her daughter hanging in her dorm room at the College of Santa Fe. Silvia Duràn had been about to graduate with honors. She'd left no note and the circumstances around her death remained a mystery.

When Tomàs pulled up with the retreat guests, Jo was waiting to greet them. Roshi Astrid Berg got out of the front seat, pulled her black cashmere coat tight around her and shuddered with distaste at the cold. She left her designer bag on the seat and headed toward the zendo without a word. Tomàs pulled back the sliding van door and two women Jo didn't know got out, a black woman in her thirties with braided hair and a purple down coat, and an overweight white woman in her fifties in a turquoise ski parka. Both introduced themselves to Jo: Thérèse Boisvert and Marci Kelly. They grabbed their luggage from Tomàs at the back of the van.

Jo recognized Lynne Shumann sitting in the last seat. Lynne was visibly shrunken from her robust former self, pale, without eyebrows, and wearing a close-fitting patterned cap. Her husband Gary was helping Tomàs with the baggage. Gary and Lynne never missed a Rohatsu, but Lynne looked too ill to be out and about.

Sleeping Tiger Board Chairman, Alan Wolfe, a man in his sixties with a neatly trimmed white goatee and a stern expression, got out of the front seat and came up to Jo before she could speak to Lynne. "I believe I am staying in one of the zendo rooms," he said, looking at her without recognition. The rooms in the zendo were the closest Sleeping Tiger had to VIP rooms with their ensuite bathrooms and proximity to the dining hall.

"Yes, hello, Alan. Let me get Lynne's bag and I'll walk the two of you over there."

"That would be good, " Alan said. "I can't remember your name."

"Jo. We met last year."

"Of course," Alan said. He turned to collect his bag and walked toward the zendo.

"I'll walk him over," Tomàs said, coming up beside her. He whispered, "I have to take her highness's luggage over." He winked at Jo. She hoped no one had heard him or seen him wink. Jo smiled involuntarily.

She said in a low voice "Okay, make sure Lynne gets settled comfortably too. I can show everyone else the way to the dormitory."

Jo led the way, followed by Thérèse, Marci and Dr. Anne Stein. Gary Shumann and a young man Jo didn't know brought up the rear.

Dr. Stein, wiry and silver-haired, chatted with her old friend Gary about her recently published research on PTSD, telling him how her clinical trial with female veterans who learned to meditate daily was showing promise for reducing symptoms. Gary, a tall, soft-spoken man with a ruddy complexion and thick, black-rimmed glasses, listened and asked questions. They then conversed quietly about Lynne's health. Marci, a CPA, and Thérèse, a social worker, seemed to be already acquainted. This was Marci's first retreat. The other new person, Jon Malvern, looked to be in his mid-thirties. Thin, pale and dark-haired, he carried a small suitcase and an oversize briefcase/computer bag. *I guess no one told him we frown on working during the retreat*, Jo thought.

The sidewalk to the dormitory ran alongside a gravel driveway that also led to Gerald's house. The walkway included steps at intervals where the incline was steep. Jo entered through the east door and showed the guests to their rooms, all on the more desirable southwest facing side of the building. The southwest windows looked over the whole Sleeping Tiger grounds, and, through a notch in the mountains, toward the rift valley of the Rio Grande gorge. The rooms on the northeast side were darker and chillier. They looked out at an earthen embankment where the mountainside had been carved out for the building. Deep snow and ice collected there each year, remaining until spring. There was one more southwest facing room, and Jo had saved it for Malcolm Downs, the man coming from Los Alamos. That left the rooms on the northeast side for people coming in from Chicago and Crestone, Colorado. But with a blizzard on the plains as well as the southern Rockies, their arrival was unlikely.

Jo unlocked each room and noted that all were clean and ready for the occupants. Each room had white plaster walls, one window, one or two single beds, a nightstand with lamp and an upholstered chair. A stack of white towels had been placed at the foot of each bed. The guests began to settle in, unpacking, preparing to nap or heading for the shared bathrooms, one each for men and women.

In the center of the first-floor hall was a broad wooden staircase that led to a second floor. The second floor hadn't been used since Sleeping Tiger bought the property. The door at the top of the stairs was permanently locked and paneling had been added around the formerly open staircase to keep the heat from escaping to the second floor. *It's good that the boiler is working fine today*, Jo thought. Replacing the boiler was at the top of Sleeping Tiger's financial wish list, but Sleeping Tiger always operated on a shoestring budget.

Once Jo got everyone settled into their rooms, she headed back toward the zendo building. A sheriff's car was coming up the drive. Jo crossed the gravel parking lot as a tall, fit-looking man got out of the driver's side. Another man, at least sixty, barrel-chested and dark-skinned, sat in the passenger seat with the door open.

•

"Let's make this quick," Ray said as they pulled into the Sleeping Tiger property to inform the owners about what they'd found "It's almost lunch time and I'm hungry."

Ulysses had never been on this property before but he had heard stories about it. The Catholic Church had always acquired beautiful properties like these and usually held onto them forever. He wondered how the people who bought this one got so lucky and what they paid for it. Some of the buildings, built by the Benedictines, must be on the historic register.

Ulysses knew a little about Zen from a course he'd taken on Buddhism as an undergraduate at the University of New Mexico. He recalled that it was a version of Buddhism that migrated from India, where the Buddha had lived, through China to Japan. He thought it had traits in common with Taoism, a philosophy he found intriguing even though he tended to be suspicious of anything religious.

A young woman wearing an Icelandic sweater, jeans and snow boots was walking across the driveway toward them, her tattered down coat open and a wool hat covering long dark blonde hair. "Can I help you?" she asked.

"Sheriff Ulysses Walker," he said and offered her his gloved hand which she shook. She gave him an appraising look while zipping up her coat. Ulysses was used to such looks. No one expected the sheriff of Taos County to be either young or Anglo.

"Jo McAlister," the woman said, "What can I do for you guys?"

Ray came to stand beside him. "This is Ray Pando, from Picuris," Ulysses said. Ray nodded but said nothing.

Ulysses continued. "Have you seen anything unusual in the last twenty-four hours?"

"What do you mean, unusual?" Jo asked.

"Anything or anybody not as you would expect on your property?"

Jo paused. "Not really."

"Not really or no?"

"Well…" Jo said slowly. "Last night when I was picking up an armload of wood at my cabin, I saw a man running down the switchback from Lizard Head."

Ulysses looked over Jo's head toward the trail and the exposed mesa. "Who do you think it was?" Had she seen Luis or his murderer?

"I really can't say for sure. I went inside and when I looked out my window he was gone." *For some reason this woman is holding back*, Ulysses thought.

"What time was that?"

"About five, maybe later. It gets dark so early."

"Did you know the man?"

"I can't say for sure, Sheriff."

Ulysses looked at the sky and said nothing for a moment. "Anything else you'd like to tell me?"

Jo paused as if reflecting before continuing. "This morning about 9:30 I saw a man running up the trail. Not the same man. Our trails are open to the public but we don't get many runners."

"Did you recognize him?"

"No, but I didn't get a close look either."

"Ms. McAlister, last night someone fell off that cliff up there," Ulysses said. "We are starting an investigation."

"Who is…was it?"

"I'm not at liberty to say," Ulysses said, "until the family is notified. We'll be towing his truck and removing the body later today."

"Was it an accident?" Jo asked.

"We don't know yet, but you and your staff should avoid the area. We're going to be in and out with our investigation. We'll try not to make a ruckus."

"We are starting a mindfulness retreat right after dinner tonight, Sheriff. Our guests only just arrived."

"What goes on at a mindfulness retreat?" Ulysses asked.

"We observe silence and practice meditation for a number of days. Our teacher gives talks and we meet with her for individual instruction. That's about it."

"That seems pretty serious."

"It is, but most of our attendees have some retreat experience."

"What is the schedule like?"

"We start tonight after dinner," Jo said. "Then we sit or walk in meditation for the next eight days from six in the morning until nine at night. Usually we walk outside but the weather isn't co-operating," she said and smiled.

Ray whistled under his breath.

Jo smiled. "Really, you get used to the routine. It actually becomes relaxing."

"When are meals?" Ray asked.

"Eight, noon and six in the dining hall."

"Are there breaks?"

"Yes, after each meal. Generally, the participants go back to their rooms to rest or do their work service. Oh, and did I say we also maintain silence? Insofar as possible."

"Who is in charge here?" Ulysses asked.

"Roshi Melanie Hirsh. But I manage the retreats for her and a man named Sensei Gerald Beatty is the business manager."

"Okay, well, as I said we'll try not to disturb your retreat. I'll let you know if we find anything that would be of concern to you or your guests. Probably we won't."

Jo nodded, looking worried. "Okay, Sheriff. I'll tell Roshi Melanie you were here."

"Thank you, Ms. McAlister," Ulysses said. "And if you think of anything else you can reach me at this number." He handed her a business card and touched the brim of his hat.

Ulysses and Ray drove down the snowy driveway and turned toward Taos.

"Why would anyone want to go to one of these retreats?" Ray asked.

"You heard the lady, they find it relaxing. I meditate so I know what she's talking about. You focus on your breath or maybe a mantra and it allows things to settle in your mind. But I wouldn't want to do it for fifteen hours a day, let alone eight straight days."

"Do they pray or anything like that?"

"I don't really know, but I don't think so. Maybe they chant a little, recite Buddhist scriptures, that kind of thing. But mostly they are silent."

"The silence actually sounds pretty good to me," Ray said. "There is entirely too much talk in this world. By the way, what is a roshi?"

"A Zen master."

"Like Yoda?"

"Kind of. I think the term literally means, 'old teacher.' Hey, want to go get some lunch in Taos before we go see Luis's mother?"

"Good idea, Ulys."

•

Jo walked to Roshi Melanie's house and knocked on the door. "Come in," she heard her call. Jo went into the kitchen, where her teacher sat in the breakfast nook eating a salad. She smiled. "Hi, Jo! I'm so glad you came by. I have a million details to go over with you."

"We just had a visit from the local sheriff. He and a man from Picuris found a body. Someone fell off Lizard Head."

Roshi Melanie's smile faded. "Who?"

"He wouldn't say. They just left, but people are coming back to recover the body and move the poor man's truck."

"Did the person fall or jump? Or was he pushed?" Roshi Melanie asked.

"I don't know."

Roshi Melanie pushed her half-eaten salad aside. "I'm sorry to hear this," she said and sighed. "What terrible timing." The two women sat in silence for a few moments.

"Jo, I don't think we should tell anyone about this just yet. It could keep people from settling into their practice."

"The Sheriff said we should warn people not to go up Lizard Head."

"With this weather I don't think anyone will be walking up there. Let's go over my list, shall we?"

Chapter II

After lunch Tomàs and Carmen sat in the kitchen with cups of coffee and listened to the weather radio. Twelve inches of snow were reported in Santa Fe and fifteen in Taos, with more expected.

"You'll never make it to back to Santa Fe to meet the shuttle, Nephew," Carmen said, "and if you do, you'll not get back here through the canyon!"

"I can't just leave those people stranded in Santa Fe," Tomàs said.

"Better stranded in the capital than on the side of the road."

Roshi Melanie came in, looking worried. "No one else will make it in or out of here today. They closed I-25 to Santa Fe and the flight from Chicago to Albuquerque was cancelled." She poured herself a cup of coffee and sat down.

"They always close I-25 when it gets really bad," Carmen said shaking her head. "How many were coming in on that flight?" she asked.

"Ten. All old friends." Roshi Melanie sighed.

"I was ready to try to make it down there," Tomàs said. "But if the roads are closed and the flights are cancelled, that's that."

"We'll make the best of it,'" Melanie said, trying to sound cheerful.

"Will we still have the retreat?" Tomàs asked.

"Oh, yes. We have ten here already, counting Jo and Gerald, and a few more may come if the weather breaks."

"So, you'll start after dinner?" Carmen asked.

"Yes. Silence after dinner, and meditation will be from 7:30 to 9:00, as usual."

"I'll go shovel the sidewalks," Tomàs said, "and check the boiler."

"I don't know what I'd do without you," Melanie said, patting his arm.

"He's a good boy," Carmen said.

As Tomàs went out, he saw a man with a large backpack walking up the driveway. *Must be the guy from Los Alamos*, he thought.

"Hi," Tomàs said. "You made it!"

"I'm here for the retreat. Malcolm Downs," he said, giving Tomàs a firm handshake.

"I figured. From Los Alamos?"

"Yes." The man, who looked to be in his thirties, was six feet tall with shoulder-length blonde hair. He was dressed against the cold in well-used outdoor gear and boots. "I left my car at the pullout near the Forest Road because I didn't want to get stuck in your driveway," he said.

"I'm not sure that's a good idea," Tomàs said. "People sometimes break into cars at that pullout."

"The thieves will be taking the night off tonight," Downs said, looking up at the sky. "It'll be fine."

"Have you had lunch?" Tomàs asked, changing the subject. *It's not my problem if his car gets broken into*, he thought.

"Yes, I ate in Pojoàque. I came down from Los Alamos early this morning."

"Okay, I'll get you settled in your room." Tomàs led him to the walkway to the dormitory. "Do you work at the Lab?" Tomàs asked. Just about everyone in Los Alamos worked at the Los Alamos National Laboratory.

"Why do you ask?" Downs responded.

"Just making small talk, Bro," Tomàs said. "How are the roads?"

"Pretty bad. They're going to close the canyon." The road between Santa Fe and Taos ran through a canyon made by the Rio Grande that was particularly treacherous in winter.

Downs cleared his throat. "Hey, man, I didn't mean to snap at you. I guess I'm getting ready for the retreat. I look forward to the silence, you know?"

"No problem," said Tomàs.

Tomàs took Malcolm to his assigned room, the last single room in the dormitory on the south side, next to the west door. Jon Malvern and Gary Shumann were talking in the hallway outside his door. They all introduced themselves to Malcolm.

"How do you get on the wi-fi?" Jon asked Tomàs.

"There is no wi-fi," Tomàs said.

"And almost no cell coverage," Gary added.

"Seriously?" Jon looked dismayed. "Where can you get cell coverage? I have a lot to do this afternoon."

"There's a spot near the garage where you can get it sometimes. Maybe not today because of the snow. There's a landline in the study off the dining hall," Gary offered. "If the phones aren't down."

"Do you come here a lot?" Jon asked Gary.

Gary nodded. "I used to live here."

"This is my first retreat," Jon said. "I'm not that spiritual but I've heard good things about Zen. My therapist recommended meditation for stress."

"It's a good place for a first retreat," Gary said.

"Well, nice to meet you guys," Malcolm said. "I'm going to get settled in and rest."

"Good idea," Gary said. "Sounds like you've attended other Zen retreats?"

"Yeah," Malcolm said, "One in California and another in Seattle."

"California?" Gary asked, "Do you know Roshi Astrid Berg?"

"I do," Malcolm said with a flicker of a smile. He nodded to the others, went into his room and closed his door.

•

At the other end of the hall the women attendees were chatting in Anne Stein's room.

"Have you attended a Rohatsu before?" Anne asked, rubbing lotion onto her long fingers. She'd already removed her jewelry and was dressed in a black sweater and yoga pants.

"This is my first sesshin *and* my first Rohatsu," Marci answered. "I'm kind of nervous about the schedule." Marci was still in her travel clothes. She held her cellphone in one hand and a mug of coffee in the other. "Therèse convinced me to come."

"Just think of it as meditation interspersed with activities, meals and rest," Anne said. "And remember you never have to sit longer than twenty-five minutes before you get a chance to stand up and walk for five minutes."

"Activities?" Marci said, "Therèse, you never told me about these! What kind of activities?"

"Oh, like Roshi gives a talk or you can go to have a meeting with her, or maybe we do some chanting," Anne said.

"So not like watching a movie or going out for a drink?" Marci teased.

Thérèse wagged her finger at her friend. "Hardly," she said. "We're not supposed to speak a word or have any alcohol!"

"Don't worry," Anne said. "After the first three days it will all feel like a blissful vacation from the world."

"But the first three days will feel like a sojourn in purgatory," Thérèse said. Like Anne she was already wearing retreat clothes. "This is my third sesshin, but my first Rohatsu. I'm a little nervous too."

"Don't be," Anne said, "You're in great hands with Roshi Melanie."

"Did you know we recently lost our Roshi?" Marci asked.

"I heard she had died," Anne said. "Was it sudden?"

"Yes, an aneurysm. She was only sixty. She hadn't appointed a successor." Thérèse answered. "We are all kind of struggling."

"Are you a regular here?" Marci asked. "All the way from LA?"

"I lived here for two years," Anne said. "I left eight years ago now. We used to have silent five-day retreats every month. Now I'm lucky to come twice a year."

"You were one of Roshi Melanie's original students, correct?" Thérèse asked.

"Yes, and a founding member of this sangha, along with Gary, Lynne, Gerald, and Alan and three of the folks who aren't here yet."

"Roshi Astrid wasn't a founding member?" Thérèse asked.

"No," Anne replied. "She was Melanie's student in California but never moved here full time. Eventually she became a student of Junsu Ito. She received transmission from him."

"She's young for a roshi," Thérèse remarked.

"And very talkative!" Marci said. The women laughed.

"I'm sad that so many won't make it because of the weather," Anne said, changing the subject. "I know Roshi Melanie must be disappointed."

"Surely they can come tomorrow?" Marci asked. "It doesn't really start until then, right?"

"It starts in about," Anne looked at her watch, "five hours."

"I'd better get my nap then," Marci said, returning to her room.

Thérèse looked out the window toward where Tomàs was shoveling the sidewalk. "It's really snowing now," she said.

"Northern New Mexico can have some full-on blizzards," Anne said, recalling the shock of moving to Sleeping Tiger from Southern California.

"I hope this will let up soon." She worried about what the sesshin would be like with so few participants. *Just be with what is*, she told herself, trying to put her misgivings aside as the wind gusted.

•

Gerald Beatty hadn't slept all night. He'd lain awake, sick with fear. *What had happened? Who was that on Lizard Head with Luis?*

Gerald had been late to meet Luis. He wasn't going to pay him this time; he was going to lie and say he had no more money. He was running up the trail and had to stop under a tree to catch his breath. That was when he had heard voices coming from the top, and then a scream. Frightened, he ran back, slipping and falling on the snowy trail, and locked himself in his house.

Then this morning he'd had another tedious argument with Melanie. When he came in with her coffee, he found her checking the savings and operating accounts. She'd seen where he'd taken out nearly $15,000 with no explanation. She didn't threaten him, but she revealed that she knew more of what he'd been doing in Santa Fe than he realized. She questioned his commitment to Sleeping Tiger. She even cried, begging him to "come clean." Now she wanted to go over the business accounts together, after years of letting him manage with virtually no oversight. He had meant to return the blackmail money he'd been paying to Luis. He didn't think of himself as a thief, but he had to admit now that he was.

Gerald reflected on the deeper secret he held. He had been siphoning off funds from the cash in the Center's endowment portfolio for the past quarter. He had nearly $200,000 of endowment funds socked away in Santa Fe, together with $300,000 from a former lover he'd defrauded. He could live for a long time in Mexico on that much cash. All fall he'd been focused on his escape plan, paying hardly any attention to the upcoming retreat. Alan and the board would demand to go over the accounts at the board meeting the day after the retreat ended. Gerald and Alan had always been enemies, but in the past Melanie had taken Gerald's side. Now Alan would have the upper hand. But Gerald planned to be long gone before that happened.

After arguing with Melanie, Gerald had started to go back up to Lizard Head to see what he could find, but the snow was getting so deep he thought better of it. As the first van of attendees came up the driveway, he ducked behind the dormitory and slipped into his house. He spent the next hour lying on his bed trying to figure out what to do. He had to avoid encountering Melanie and Alan alone where they could confront him. He decided to put in an appearance at lunch and changed into his freshly dry-cleaned sensei robes.

The dining hall was quiet as lunch was winding down. A few participants lingered, drinking coffee in the convivial atmosphere. Alan and Astrid sat at a table together deep in conversation. They didn't look up when Gerald came in. Gerald introduced himself to Thérèse and Marci and started making himself a plate as Jon Malvern came in from the library and approached him. *Why didn't I know he was coming*, Gerald wondered. *This is a disaster!*

"Hello, Skip," Gerald said, trying to mask his surprise. "I didn't know you were here."

"Hi, Ger," Jon Malvern said, "Happy to see me?" The younger man grinned.

"Well, I'm not sure," Gerald replied not looking at him. "Are you still mad at me?" Gerald scanned the room to see if anyone was watching their interaction. With everyone chatting and eating no one seemed to notice them.

"I'll come by your house tonight after the evening sitting," Jon said, his grin turning to a leer. "I want to hear how you plan to pay me back."

"Hey, man, keep it cool, will you?"

Melanie came in from the zendo and beckoned to Gerald from the other side of the dining room.

"Excuse me," Gerald said, "I have to go talk to Roshi Melanie."

Gerald followed her to the study off the main hall. She closed the door, looking worried.

"Gerry, the Taos County Sheriff was here. A man was found dead at the foot of Lizard Head."

"Please don't call me 'Gerry,'" he said in a tense whisper. "You know I hate that. Now, what were you saying?"

"Someone died near our property, they don't know how! Do you know anything about this?"

"What would I know about somebody dying? Who was it anyway?"

"Gerald, first I find you've taken money from the account and now this—"

Gerald interrupted her. "Melanie, this has nothing to do with me! Why are you judging me? I know nothing about this death. And I wasn't stealing. Those were errors. I told you I would fix them!"

"Well, Alan is very concerned. He is coming by this afternoon to look at the books with me. You'd better come, too."

"Calm down, Melanie. We have a sesshin to run and we are in a near blizzard! Surely this can wait. We can go through everything at the board meeting. As I've told you, I have nothing to hide."

Roshi Melanie took a deep breath and tried to calm herself. "Well, you have a lot to explain. I don't know if I can get Alan to wait. Just come by around 2:30, will you? That's when Alan and I are going to meet. I think you should be there too."

Gerald returned to his house without eating lunch. He was sweating and his mind was racing. *Luis must be dead.* He thought of the scream again and felt sure that it was him. How long before someone figured out he had been involved? He couldn't just get in his car and leave until the roads were plowed. Even with the new heavy grade snow tires he'd bought for his Volvo, the roads could be impassable. He couldn't walk out either, because he'd have to leave all his stuff behind. The only way out was to drive once the roads were plowed.

There was no way he could go through with the sesshin, trying to look mindful and sitting still in silence for hours while his mind ate him alive with visions of what would happen if all he'd been doing became known. The only option was to feign sickness and keep to his room. He already had most of what he was taking in the trunk of his car, including his clothes. He would have to leave his nicest things—art, antiques, fine furniture and Persian rugs collected over the years, but he had no choice now. He had to escape, tonight if at all possible.

Gerald considered whether to tell Melanie he was ill or just not show up. Would she believe him or confront him? He decided to write her a note and put it on his back door. He didn't think she'd insist on seeing him if he told her he was coming down with the flu.

•

Jon Malvern paced in his room ruminating over his encounter with Gerald at lunch. The worst part was the moment when Gerald first noticed he was there and Jon saw a look of disgust pass over Gerald's face. Remembering it fanned Jon's anger and shame into a self-loathing rage. He pulled the gun he'd brought out of his luggage and visualized sticking it in Gerald's face. This was the man he thought he loved, this lying, cheating abuser! This was his first true love, who'd seduced him when he was young and vulnerable. Jon remembered how debonair Gerald had seemed, cool, and wise, even spiritually advanced. *I didn't have a chance*, Jon thought. *I could never have resisted him and he knew it.*

I don't even find him attractive anymore, Jon thought. *He looks pasty and old especially in those ridiculous robes. He's just a pedophile dressed like a holy guy. I hate him!* Again he thought about killing Gerald but realized, not for the first time, that he would also have to kill himself. Miserable as he was, he wasn't sure he could actually pull it off.

He put the gun to his temple for a moment then set it down on the bed. *Little Skipper, loser, wimp, coward,* Jon thought, entering a familiar inner monologue. What could be worse than where he now found himself, surrounded by all these Zen hypocrites who think they are so much better than everyone else? Jon pictured the little old roshi woman and felt another intense burst of hatred. *She's as evil as he is. How can Gerald stand her! She beckons and he comes running. I should kill her too,* he thought.

A tumult of emotions burned in Jon's throat and belly and he began to cry. *I can't stand this*, he thought. *I should just kill myself right now. Then I won't have to feel this!* But Jon still felt squeamish about using a gun to kill himself. It seemed like it would be too painful. He would use pills. That's what he'd tried before, he just hadn't used the right procedures. But this time he'd done his research. He had 50 Ativan in his suitcase, a bottle of scotch and a tough plastic bag to pull over his head. He had a whole plan he'd been hatching since he discovered Gerald's treachery. Kill Gerald and maybe Melanie, then himself. But it would have to wait until tonight.

Jon felt a brief sense of relief as he contemplated his escape plan. Then his doubts returned. *What if I don't die? I'll never make it in prison.* Jon felt the rising of familiar urges. He went to his toiletry kit and pulled out a straight razor. *I have to clear my head*, he thought, *then I can carry out my plan.* Jon took one of his towels and spread it across his lap smoothing out the folds carefully. He rolled up his sleeves and made a cut on his left arm above the elbow, then one nearer his wrist. When he saw the blood flowing his mind cleared and he began to feel calm. The sensation was painful and satisfying. But he needed more.

Jon spread his second towel on the bed. He took down his trousers and made two similar cuts on each of his thighs which were already crisscrossed with scars. More blood flowed and at last he found the relief he was seeking. As his emotions subsided he took alcohol from his kit, cleaned his cuts and the razor and expertly applied bandages. Now he was ready to write his suicide note and then take a little nap. When he woke, he would go to Gerald's.

·

Ulysses and Ray stopped for lunch at Mateo's Restaurant in Taos before making the visit to Luis's mother. The dining room was empty because of the snowstorm, but the kitchen was open. A fire of piñon logs burned in the corner kiva fireplace. The little room with its latilla ceiling was warm and cozy and smelled of sopapillas.

Ulysses ordered a bowl of green-chile stew. "Is Casimira still living in that trailer in Rancho de Taos?"

"Yes, I believe so. I haven't seen her in years," Ray said. He was having the red and green chile enchiladas called 'Christmas.' "She doesn't come up to the dances or feast days anymore. I think she's become a recluse. Luis had been staying with her off and on since he got out of jail."

"She's got some rotten judgment, that woman. First, she keeps house for a priest who abused both her kids, then her daughter kills herself, and now this."

"It's not all bad judgment," Ray said, shaking his head. "She'd heard the rumors about Father Miller. Tribal members told her to watch out for him." He cut into his enchiladas and scooped out a bite, blowing on it to cool it. "She wouldn't believe us. She liked the job. She liked living in that big house."

"Well, now she's lost both her children, " Ulysses said. "Helluva price to pay. Though I remember she barely reacted when she heard Silvia was dead. Seemed like she didn't really like the girl." He took another bite of his stew and winced at the spicy green chile. "I've heard Randolph Miller, before the allegations against him were well-known, was thought of as a charismatic dude. Is that why no one ever tried to bring charges against him?"

"Maybe. But nobody would take on the Church in those days. They were just too powerful," Ray said.

"You know that the gun found at the site was registered to Miller, right? Do you think Luis had it or did he steal it from his mother?"

Ray took a moment to chew and took a sip of coffee. "I'm thinking Casimira kept it for a memento. She's a strange one." The waitress came by to refill their water.

"We know Miller was abusing in California too, before he ever came here. The bishops transferred him. Lots of people wanted revenge off that guy. My predecessor, though, could find no wrong in a member of the Catholic clergy."

"Trujillo?" Ray frowned at the name. "True enough, but there were other people on the case. That FBI guy from Albuquerque had a go at it and found nothing. Poindexter. He's retired now. He suspected someone murdered Miller but never had a suspect."

"And they never found any hard evidence about his disappearance either, right?"

"That's right," Ray said, wiping his mouth with his napkin. "He could still be alive."

"Was Luis in any trouble before the drugs?" Ulysses asked. "What was the story with the younger man who was killed, Luis's friend?"

"Elías Chacón, Luis's cousin. He fell off the rectory roof onto the driveway. Broke his neck."

"And Luis was at the rectory when it happened?"

"Yeah. They had a whole big crowd but no one saw it, apparently. Luis was questioned but it was ruled an accidental death."

Ulysses finished his stew, ate a sopapilla with honey, and asked for the check. "Let's get this over with." They paid and went out to the Expedition. Ulysses swept snow off the windshield. "How much accumulation do you think we're going to get?" he asked.

"I'll guess about a foot," Ray said. "Maybe more. Hey, Ulys, I'll go see Casimira. It's really my job."

"Do you mind if I come along? I want to look over the place. Might see something."

"All right." Ray was feeling stiff from the hike and was thinking about a nap. He was glad to have Ulysses help out with this situation at least until the FBI got involved. A homicide on Indian land would trigger an investigation, even if a perfunctory one, that was the law. Ray knew a lot of the liaison work of the FBI investigation would fall to him. The tribe's governor was getting treatment for prostate cancer and was delegating most of his duties. Ray, with his state pension and Social Security, could afford to take on many hours of largely unpaid work better than others on the tribal council. He and his wife Clarice lived simply and had no debts. Recently, though, the extra workload made Ray think about giving up his position as war chief.

Ulysses turned into the old Plaza at Rancho de Taos south of town with its much-photographed adobe church and surrounding square of small shops selling rosaries, Spanish retablos and tourist souvenirs. At the east end was the old rectory, a three-story building with a flat roof and large white-framed windows, now used for a parish hall and administrative offices. A rutted road led to a few tumbledown empty houses and a singlewide trailer that sat at the edge of an arroyo behind the old rectory. Smoke poured from a chimney that poked out from one of the front windows.

Ray said, "Let me go to the door first."

"I wonder if she already knows." Ulysses felt a moment of compassion for Mrs. Duràn who was about to find out her last remaining child was dead. He took off his hat and stood at the foot of the steps as a frail, wizened woman with long, loose, gray hair opened the door a crack. She held a cigarette in her right hand. "It's about Luis, right?" she asked.

"Yes, Mrs. Duràn," Ray said softly.

She took a draw on the cigarette and flicked it, still burning, across the snowy yard. She opened the door wider. "He can come too," she said, indicating Ulysses.

It was hot and smoky inside the trailer. A television was tuned to the weather channel. Crowded in the kitchen-living room were a big couch and two recliners. The men sat on the couch and Casimira sat at the kitchen table where she'd been working on a crossword puzzle. Ray introduced Ulysses. She gave no sign she recognized him.

"Is he dead?" Casimira asked Ray.

Ray nodded.

"Where did you find him?" she asked. Her long, thin mouth and deep brown eyes displayed no emotion.

"He fell off Pecu-una sometime last night," Ray answered.

"Fell or was pushed?" the old woman asked.

"We don't know yet. "

"Did he die quick?"

"Most likely. He fell about a hundred feet. I'm sorry."

Casimira nodded and looked out the milky window in silence. "He was a good boy," she said at last, "but he had his demons."

"Did he have any enemies that you know of?" Ray asked.

She shook her head. "There were people he hated. But I don't know of any hated him."

Ulysses spoke up. "Mrs. Duràn, I'd like to ask you some questions about the past—about Randolph Miller and Elías Chacón. Is it okay to do that now?" He watched to see if her expression changed at the mention of those names. It didn't.

"Okay. Do you want some coffee?"

"No, thank you," Ulysses responded, wondering if it was rude to refuse.

Ray spoke up. "I'll have a cup, thank you." The old woman went to the sink, filled a kettle and turned on the stove.

"Was Luis using drugs since his release from prison?" asked Ulysses.

"How would I know?"

"Was he dealing drugs?"

"I don't think so."

"You don't know for sure?" He watched her face. It remained impassive.

"He had him some money. I don't know where it came from. He was giving me rent and buying gas for his truck. He bought groceries." Her voice broke and Ulysses thought she might be about to cry. *She misses his money*, Ulysses thought. Ray stood up and offered her his handkerchief but she waved it away.

"When was the last time you saw him?" Ulysses asked.

"About ten days ago. He was fine at the time. Then he was gone. He probably relapsed." To Ray she said, "Get the creamer and sugar out the cabinet."

Ulysses rubbed his knees and took a deep breath. "So, Luis had money but you don't know where it was coming from?"

"No. It wasn't like when he was dealing. Nothing flashy was going on. He wasn't gone as much and no strangers were coming around. Prison changed him. I think he got smarter. Anyway, we made peace with each other." For the first time Casimira's face showed sadness.

"He forgave you for what happened with Father Miller?" Ulysses asked.

She didn't answer. The kettle boiled and she stood up and turned her back as she made the coffee. Ray put a log in the woodstove. When she turned back around her face had resumed its blank expression.

"When was the last time you saw Father Miller?"

"Like I told the police back then, I saw him on Pentecost that year. It was the fortieth anniversary of his ordination. We had a big crowd. I never saw him again."

"May, seven years ago?"

"Yes."

"When did Elías come to live with you? Your nephew?"

"Grandnephew. His mother, my niece, had died. He was only six but he was already in trouble. Father Miller agreed I should take him in."

"Did you know Miller was abusing him?"

"I had warned him about Father. He could be touchy-feely, you know. But if anyone was an abuser it was Elías. He was a thief. He stole from me, from Luis, even stole from Father."

Yeah, Ulysses thought, *an abuser who was a six year old orphan.*

"Elías died the same day you last saw Miller?"

"That's right. Elías fell off the roof of the rectory and broke his neck. Two weeks before his twenty-seventh birthday."

"Did you see him fall?"

"No," she said, shaking her head vigorously. "Like I told the sheriff we never knew why he was up there in the first place." She stirred her coffee and took a sip. "Probably shooting up." She glanced at her crossword puzzle, picked up her pencil then put it back down.

"When did you find out Miller had been abusing Silvia?" Ulysses asked. The old woman looked at him as if she finally recognized him.

Ray interrupted, "Mrs. Duràn, if this is too much we can come back later."

She waved him off. "Father didn't really favor the girls. Silvia hated him for other reasons."

"When did Luis get out of prison?" Ulysses asked. He already knew the answer.

"He got out at Easter that year. She died the week after."

"So, she killed herself just a week after he got out of prison?"

Casimira nodded. She was clutching her cup with both brown, bony hands and staring at Ulysses.

"Do you have any idea why she took her life?" Ray asked.

"No. She could have done anything she wanted. She was smart and pretty. But she was never satisfied, you know." She shifted in her chair and looked out the window again. "She was always angry."

"May I use the bathroom?" Ulysses asked. The old woman indicated the far end of the trailer and Ulysses made his way down the narrow hall. As he passed the first bedroom, he noticed that the bed was made and two piles of clothing were neatly folded on top. The bedside table was empty. Two pairs of shoes were placed neatly against the wall by the door. It looked as if no one had stayed in that room recently. In the small bathroom he saw a tray of prescriptions in Casimira Duràn's name—blood pressure medication, thyroid pills and an antidepressant. No signs of Luis there. He returned to the kitchen, where Ray and Casimira were sitting in silence.

Ray took a sip of coffee and cleared his throat. "Mrs. Duràn, you know that Randolph Miller's body has never been found. Do you have any reason to believe he is still alive?"

Casimira's eyes widened for an instant. "I assume he is still alive," she said. "In hiding. That's what I believe."

Ray continued in his soft tone. "Do you know if Luis believed he was alive?"

"We never talked about it. But he had nightmares of him."

"Did Luis know anything about his whereabouts?"

"No, no."

"Did Luis ever talk to you about Miller and Elías?"

"No. Luis hated Elías and Father, both. Father ignored Luis but was always kind to Elías. He gave him money and took him to Santa Fe to see Silvia and out to eat. Elías was a pretty boy, you know."

"Did Luis have a gun?" Ulysses asked.

"I never saw a gun."

"We found a gun near his body."

Casimira said nothing. She picked up her crossword.

"It was registered to Randolph Miller."

She didn't look up. "I don't know anything about that."

"Okay, Mrs. Duràn. Thank you for your time. Again, I am sorry for your loss." Ray stood up, and so did Ulysses, who felt awkward in the small space. Ray opened the door.

"When can I see his body?" Casimira looked at Ray and Ulysses saw real grief in her face for the first time.

"I will call you," Ray said. "We'll get to the bottom of this."

Ulysses followed Ray down the icy steps and got into the driver's seat. He started the engine, then got out to scrape the windshield again. It had amassed at least an inch of snow while they'd been inside. "This is getting bad," he said. "I better take you back to your truck before I go into the station."

"I may need to revise my prediction. Looks more like a foot and a half. Did you see anything on your trip to the bathroom?"

"It looked like Luis hadn't been there recently. His room was tidy. There were clothes folded on his bed and nothing of his in the bathroom."

"Did you notice Casimira's gun?" Ray asked.

"No, I didn't," Ulysses said, surprised.

"Up under the table was a shiny new 45, " Ray said. "I noticed it when I bent down to put wood in the stove."

"I guess she had to replace the one Luis took," Ulysses said.

Ulysses dropped off Ray in Taos. Snow was falling steadily. Ulysses wondered kind of accumulation there would be in the higher elevations. When he tried to call Rosemary, he couldn't get a signal.

Chapter III

After going over Roshi Melanie's to-do list, Jo went outside to help Tomàs shovel snow and spread salt on the walkways. New snow came down so fast that the work seemed almost futile.

"You're going to have fun getting back and forth to your cabin, no?" Tomàs said. They started shoveling the first set of steps on the walkway to the dormitory.

"I'll use my snowshoes," Jo said.

"I don't think Melanie wants me to go home. She said I should stay in her upstairs bedroom."

"I guess she feels more relaxed with you around."

"She's going to kill me with all this shoveling, Josie."

Jo liked that Tomàs was the only one she knew who called her by her childhood nickname. "Will things be okay at your house overnight?"

"As long as the mountain lion doesn't get my elk. Did the sheriff tell you anything about the man they were looking for?"

"No, nothing. But I've been thinking about some things I saw last night and also this morning. Things I didn't tell him about."

"Like what?"

"Last night I saw someone running down the trail to Lizard Head in the dark. I told him that but I didn't say I was pretty sure it was Gerald."

"And this morning?"

"I saw Gerald again, when I was giving the zendo a final going-over. He was up near my cabin."

"That doesn't sound like Gerald to hike out in the snow," Tomàs said. "Did you tell Melanie?"

"No. She has so much on her mind with this snowstorm and the retreat about to start."

"You should call the sheriff and tell him about Gerald. Why don't you call him before the silence starts?"

"Maybe I will," Jo said, feeling a sick sensation in her stomach.

"Hey, you know what," Tomàs said, setting aside his shovel, "I don't think this is helping. It's snowing too hard."

"I agree. I'll go check on the guests in the dormitory. They can come down Gerald's driveway instead of using the stairs."

Jo sprinkled the last of her salt on the stairs and walked to the dormitory, entering by the east door. It was quiet and warm inside and all the room doors were closed. When she came back outside Jo saw Roshi Melanie and Alan walking down the hill from Gerald's, so deep in conversation they didn't even acknowledge her. Jo wondered if she should talk to Roshi before she called Sheriff Walker and decided against it. She went into the little library off the dining hall, closed the door and found the sheriff's card in her pocket. *At least the phones are still working*, she thought as she called his number from the library landline.

"Is Sheriff Walker available?" she asked the woman who answered.

"Who may I say is calling?"

Jo heard the sheriff's voice. "I'll take it, Lorraine." Then, "Hello, this is Walker."

"Hi, this is Jo McAlister at Sleeping Tiger."

"Hello, Ms. McAlister."

Jo swallowed hard and said nothing.

"Did you remember something you wanted to tell me?" Ulysses prompted.

"Yes, two things, " Jo said, trying to steady her voice.

"Go ahead."

"I think the man I saw under the trees was Gerald Beatty. I'm not positive, but I'm pretty sure it was him."

"Who is Beatty?"

"Roshi Melanie Hirsh's sensei, my boss, actually. And then this morning I saw Gerald again down by my cabin which is near the trail. Before I saw the other trail runner."

"It would be unusual for your boss to be near your cabin?"

"Yes."

"Would you be willing to come to the station and give a statement?"

"I can't, Sheriff. We have the retreat. Plus, the roads—"

"Okay, I'll come to you," Ulysses said. "And thank you for the information."

Great, Jo thought, *now I've gone and done it.* She put the phone down and sat for a few minutes in the library. This would definitely impact the retreat and Gerald would not be happy with her. But a man was dead and the circumstances were clearly suspicious. *I had to do this. It's the right thing to do. Roshi will back me up.*

●

Heavy snow continued to fall. Tomàs figured that by now Highway 68 had been closed in the Rio Grande canyon, from Taos to Velardé and the high road to Taos was impassable. No one was going to make it in or out. He put chains on his pickup and drove home to check on things before staying the night at Melanie's. Tomàs drove down the Peñasco Road and turned onto the Forest Road, which lay deep in undisturbed snow. He parked in front of his house. The thermometer by the door read 23 degrees. More than two feet of snow had piled up on the flat roof, which worried him. He should climb up and shovel some off. Instead he went inside and opened the stove, which still held glowing embers, and stuffed it full of gambel oak and piñon. He opened the dampers to let it catch, turned on the faucets in the sinks in the kitchen and bathroom and plugged in his electric pipe heaters, then went back out to check on the chickens and the elk carcass. He would need to dress the elk tomorrow or risk losing it.

Tomàs loved everything about this little place he'd inherited from his mother, especially the field. With the acequia running just above its gentle slope to the Rio del Pueblo he could grow enough hay to sell some and keep enough for the horse he hoped to buy in the spring. He had in mind an Andalusian, a mare he could breed. He'd keep one of her daughters for a companion and for his grandchildren to ride. Andalusians were strong horses, with noble heads and a romantic past and big enough to carry a man his size.

Tomàs looked out over his hayfield to the draw where the river ran under ice. He relished the peace of this place for a few minutes. He found himself thinking of Jo and imagining her here. *I'd like to make her dinner,* he thought, *and share a bottle of red wine. Is she really too young for me,* he wondered. He figured she was about twelve years his junior. *I wonder if she'd want a baby?*

Tomàs went back into the house, closed down the stove, packed clean socks, underwear and his toothbrush, grabbed a flask of whiskey, locked up, and put the key on its ledge above the front door. It was only 4:00 pm but dusk was already settling in.

•

At 3:30 Ulysses drove through the Taos plaza. The little square, with its old hotel, galleries and shops, was empty. In fact, the whole town was more or less deserted as people holed up waiting for the storm to pass. Even the grocery stores had closed and sent their employees home.

He tried Rosemary again but couldn't get through. *I need to go check on them*, he thought and wished he'd had the presence of mind to pick up milk and bread while there was still any to be found. He was comforted to know that Rosemary, raised Mormon and always a stickler for supplies, had canned milk aplenty and had probably made bread. She had two years of wood, enough canned vegetables from her garden and dried beans to last them well into any apocalypse.

He parked in front of the sheriff's station. His secretary, Lorraine Baca, looked up when he came into the public area of offices where she presided. Of indeterminate age between sixty and eighty, Lorraine had been secretary at the sheriff's office since she was in her thirties, a job she'd inherited from her mother, Isobel. Short and ramrod straight with the copious wrinkles of a smoker lining her brown face, Lorraine was the institutional memory of law enforcement in the county and was reputed to be unerring in her assessment of character and possessed of overall good sense. But she'd been suspicious of Ulysses from the moment she met him. "You're too young to be sheriff," she'd said, and avoided his handshake. *And too Anglo,* Ulysses thought. Nonetheless Lorraine worked just as hard for him as she had for Sheriff Trujillo, to whom she remained loyal. Still, Ulysses hadn't been able to give her the performance evaluation she wanted. She had different priorities than his and her priorities ruled. That had to change.

"Your wife sent word not to worry. She and the children are fine."

"Sent word?"

"She got on a Carson Electric man's radio somehow."

"When?"

"About fifteen minutes ago."

There was Rosemary again, so adept at problem solving. She knew he'd be worried about her and found a way to communicate she was fine. He wished he could hire her as a deputy.

"Here comes our coroner," Lorraine said, looking out the window. She knew everyone's car.

Dr. Vigil, a man in his sixties with silver hair, a bolo tie and a formal manner, kissed Lorraine on the cheek and nodded to Ulysses. "Sheriff," he said with a slight bow, "I have my report on the body that came in earlier today."

"That was quick," Ulysses said, "I didn't expect you until the weather cleared."

"Lorraine knew I was in town visiting my daughter," Vigil said, patting Lorraine on her padded shoulder. "So I thought I might as well save a trip."

"What did you find?"

"Luis Duràn was killed by the fall, of course. Time of death between six and midnight."

"Can you determine if he was pushed?"

"Can't say. But he had a large bruise on his chest, as if he'd been punched or perhaps kicked, and one on his upper right arm. And, of course, wounds on the face and back of the head."

"Was the bruising new?"

"Consistent with the time of death."

"Anything about the head wounds seem like foul play?"

"Impossible to say. He could have hit his head before he fell or after."

"So he could have been struck on the head by someone?"

"It's possible."

"Anything else?"

"I'll let you know if the toxicology shows anything."

"Thanks, Doc."

Dr. Vigil nodded to Ulysses and helped himself to a cup of coffee from the pot Lorraine always kept fresh. The two of them started speaking in Spanish.

Ulysses went into his office and closed the door. He hadn't been there since nine o'clock that morning when the call came from Ray asking for help locating Luis Duràn. The stack of personnel folders had disappeared off his desk, no doubt refiled by Lorraine. In their place was a pile of phone call memos. Ulysses thumbed through them, then took off his boots and lay down for a nap on the couch. In a few minutes he was asleep. He'd always had the capacity to fall into a nap quickly and his staff knew better than to disturb him. They knew he had small children and frequently didn't get a full night of rest. In twenty minutes he'd be up and refreshed, but when awakened accidentally he'd be as grumpy as a bear.

Ulysses fell into another foreboding dream. He was standing on Lizard Head looking west. It was sunset. Below him, where Luis's body had been found, stood a priest in long, black robes carrying a crozier. Four acolytes dressed in white followed him in a procession into the dark.

When Ulysses awoke, he found Ray sitting next to him in his desk chair. "Hey, what are you doing here?"

"I have to make sure you're not sleeping on the job," Ray said.

Ulysses laughed. "Good one. "

He overheard Lorraine taking a call for him and opened his office door. "I'll take it, Lorraine," he said. It was Jo McAlister from Sleeping Tiger. When he got off the phone he said to Ray, "Want to go over to Sleeping Tiger? I have to interview someone."

They walked toward the Expedition in the early dusk. The wind had shifted to the north and a small circle of clear sky stood on the western horizon. The cold felt bitter.

"It's going to clear off. Supposed to go to 10 below tonight."

"Did you go back to the scene?"

"No, I went home and took a nap. But the boys who picked up Luis found this hanging on a juniper tree not twenty yards from the body. It's a scapular."

Ray held up a clear plastic evidence bag. Inside was an old-fashioned devotional necklace of a type worn by some religious Catholics. This one had a picture of an angel with a sword standing over a devil he had just slain. The plastic covered picture hung from a brown and green crocheted cotton lanyard.

Ulysses remembered his dream. Something to do with a priest and altar boys. Had Luis been an altar boy? What about the murderer?

"Any tracks around it?"

Ray shook his head. "Nope."

The men rode in silence for a while. "Who's that in the picture?" Ulysses asked. Ray, raised Catholic, knew far more about the religion than Ulysses, whose parents described themselves alternately as pagans or agnostics.

"Saint Michael the Archangel. He happens to be the patron saint of police officers. But he wasn't human like most saints."

"What?"

"He was an archangel. Not a human. There are a bunch of archangels who are also saints, St. Gabriel, St. Raphael…"

"Lucifer?" Ulysses asked.

"Yep. He was an archangel. But he turned into a devil."

"So someone left that thing there after we found the body?"

"Yeah, probably. The men said it was in plain view, so I think we'd have seen it."

"But who and for what reason?" Ulysses asked.

"Maybe the beginning of a descanso?"

"Who would build a little shrine in the middle of nowhere? Only the killer."

"He's sending us a message."

•

Jon Malvern woke up and for a moment he couldn't remember where he was. The room was dark. He'd slept much longer than he'd planned. The dread and agitation from earlier returned full force. The cuts on his thighs were throbbing. *I have to get this over with,* he thought, but a tiny doubt in the back of his mind continued to fester. What if he couldn't follow through? Maybe he should wait?

Jon got up and checked his gun, a new silver 9 mm he'd bought six weeks ago. When he took it to the shooting range to learn how to use it another patron had called it "the number one ladies' gun." But Jon was confident it would do the job if he could just bring himself to pull the trigger. He put the loaded gun in the pocket of his coat, put on his gloves and went out of his room. All the doors were closed as he walked down the hall but he could hear voices in one of the rooms. Jon went out into the cold toward Gerald's house.

He saw a flashlight beam in the second story, but it was quickly extinguished as he approached. Was Gerald watching him from an upstairs window? Jon went around to the back and onto the back porch. He peered through the back-door window and knocked several times. He tried the door but of course it was locked. He noticed that there was no dead bolt. He could easily break the single pane glass and unlock the door. He was looking around for a rock when someone come out of the dormitory and lit a cigarette, a heavy-set woman. She looked over her shoulder and noticed him standing there, then gave an uncertain little wave.

You loser, you fucking loser, Jon screamed inside himself, beginning his litany of self-loathing. His will to act evaporated. Crying in frustration, he went back to his room, took an Ativan and lay down on the bed. As the drug took effect he started to feel less distressed. *Well,* he reassured himself, *I've cased the place now. I'll go back after midnight, break in and kill him.*

•

Tomàs helped Carmen finish prepping the first night's dinner. She'd made her most popular meal, cheesy vegetarian green chile enchiladas, with calabacitas, a mixed green salad, and horchata and brownies for dessert. After dinner, the eight day retreat silence would begin. Usually the first night of a retreat was festive, but Tomàs noticed that tonight's mood was somber, perhaps because only half of the expected guests had made it. All the staff knew they'd had found a body in the vicinity but the attendees hadn't been told yet. Melanie was more distraught than Tomàs had ever seen her, worried about how the attendees would feel knowing that a suspicious death had taken place nearby. When Jo told her the sheriffs were coming back to ask questions, Melanie had sighed deeply but said nothing.

Tomàs knew Melanie had agonized about whether to cancel the retreat. She had considered offering transport to Taos for anyone who wanted to leave right away. But Tomàs had pointed out that getting there at night in the storm would be more dangerous than staying put in their warm, cozy quarters with the doors locked. "Okay, my friends," Melanie said to Tomàs, Jo and Carmen, "Let's make this sesshin worthy of the dharma." She went back to her house to rest before dinner.

Later, Melanie and Alan sat together in front of her kiva fireplace where Tomàs had built a small fire of piñon. The flickering light chased shadows around the darkening room while outside the wind blew snow against the western-facing windows. The sun had just set but the moon had not yet risen. Alan was already dressed in his retreat clothes, black yoga pants and a black silk sweater over a turtleneck. He was drinking scotch, his last for the next eight days. Melanie, in a chenille robe and slippers, nursed a glass of red wine.

"I don't know what to believe," she said softly. "And I don't know what to do."

"You have to tell the police, Melanie. He's stolen from you—from all of us. And now he's hiding."

"He's in his room, he just won't come to the door. His note said he thought he had the flu."

"Of course," Alan scoffed.

"Anyway, he's there. His car is still in the garage."

"How dare he refuse to speak with us? He knows silence starts after dinner. He's not going to get away with embezzlement by not coming out of the house."

"He's done this before. Once he stayed in for three days."

"If you don't tell the police, I will, as chairman of the board." Alan looked out the window toward Gerald's house. "I thought I saw a light earlier. It's pitch black now."

"Look, Alan, the sheriff will be here any minute. Please, please don't reveal anything to them about Gerald until we've spoken with him."

"We cannot afford to wait long, Melanie. You should know that."

"How bad *is* the money situation? Should we cancel the retreat?"

"My God, no. That is the last thing we should do," Alan said. "We need every penny right now. It's as simple as that. I'll know more when I've had time go over all the accounts."

"Poor Gerald. He's been so lost for so long," Melanie said, putting down her wine glass.

Alan poked the fire and added another small piece of wood. "I just want to make sure we don't get lost with him."

After she finished helping Carmen set up the buffet, Jo saw the sheriff's car pull up at the garage. She headed out to meet them.

"Come with me," Jo shouted over the wind. Ulysses and Ray followed her to Roshi Melanie's house. Jo rang the bell and Alan invited them into the warm, dimly-lit living room. Two plush sofas sat on either side of a central kiva fireplace. Melanie, already in her robes, sat in a leather chair closest to the fire. When the men sat down, Jo turned to leave.

"If you can stay, Ma'am, that would be good," Ulysses said.

Roshi nodded to Jo and she sat down next to Alan.

"I'm Melanie Hirsh," she said, introducing herself to the two lawmen. "I am the spiritual director here. This is Alan Wolfe, the chairman of the Sleeping Tiger board. Gentlemen, I hope this can be brief. We are about to start a retreat. Our attendees will be expecting us in about twenty minutes for supper."

Ulysses introduced himself and Ray and pulled off his gloves. "I'll be as quick as possible," he said. "As I informed Ms. McAlister, we had a suspicious death last night. A young Picuris man was found dead at the foot of Lizard Head." He looked at Jo. "Please tell us again what you heard and saw last night."

"At about six o'clock I went out on my front porch. I saw a man running down the trail from Lizard Head in the dark. I can't be sure but I thought it was Gerald."

Melanie's eyes darted toward Alan. Alan's lips were a tight line.

"Gerald Beatty?" Ulysses asked.

"Yes."

"What made you think it was Gerald?"

"He was definitely the right height and build. And there was something about the way he moved. It was dark and cloudy but with the full moon there was some light. I'm sure it was him."

"Then what did you see this morning?" Ulysses asked.

"I was in the zendo making preparations. Out the west window I saw Gerald, walking toward my cabin. About thirty minutes later I saw another man running up the trail that runs behind my cabin."

"What did the runner look like?" Ulysses asked.

"Medium height? I didn't get a good look at him but I think he was wearing a ski mask."

"Is it unusual for Gerald to be near your cabin or on the trail?" Ray asked.

"I've never seen him on any of the trails before last night. And he's never visited my cabin in the three years I've lived here."

"Never?" Melanie asked.

"Not that I'm aware of, Roshi."

"What made you suspicious about the man running on the trail?" Ulysses asked.

Jo thought a moment. "We do get the occasional hiker, but it's very infrequent. And with the storm coming it just felt odd."

"Okay, thank you, Ms. McAlister. I'll let you get back to your duties."

Jo got up to leave. "Go ahead with dinner when it's time," Melanie said, "Alan and I will come when we can."

Ulysses sensed something between the two people left in the room with him and Ray. The woman seemed sad and fearful and the man looked angry.

"Did Gerald Beatty know a Picuris man named Luis Durán?" Ray asked from the shadowy banco beside the fireplace.

"I don't know," Melanie said. "Several young men, workmen, came here from time to time to meet with Gerald. I thought they were from Taos, but I don't know any names."

"Luis was in his thirties, slightly built, dark-skinned with long hair. He sometimes wore an earring," Ray said.

"He could have been one of them, I don't know." Melanie set down her wine glass and looked at Alan. *She looks worried*, Ulysses thought.

"Gerald lives on site?" Ulysses asked. Melanie nodded. "Have you seen him this afternoon?"

Alan spoke up. "We were supposed to meet with him this afternoon but he didn't show up. We knocked on his door but he didn't answer. He'd left a note on his door that said he was sick."

"What was the meeting about?" Ulysses asked.

"Finances," Alan said.

"Any problems?"

"I'm not sure we should be discussing this," Melanie said softly.

Ulysses drew in a deep breath. "Ms. Hirsh, this is a man who was possibly seen near the crime site at the approximate time of death and who might have known the deceased. Anything is relevant at this point."

"We aren't sure about any irregularities yet, Sheriff. Alan is chair of our board and will be looking closely at the books after the retreat."

"Was Mr. Beatty stealing from you?" Ray asked.

Melanie stood up. "We have to get down to the dining hall now. Please excuse us."

"We will want to speak with Mr. Beatty," said Ulysses. "Does he have a car on the property?"

"Yes, a black Volvo. It's in the garage."

Ulysses and Ray stood. "Continue with your schedule," Ulysses said. "We'll check back with you. And be careful. It's going down to 10 below tonight." He handed his card to Melanie.

"Thank you, Sheriff Walker, Mr. Pando. I'll show you the walkway to Gerald's," she said as they went out into the windy night. "There aren't many lights up there."

Ray pointed at the sky, with the moon now showing through patchy clouds at the edge of the eastern mountains. "We can find our way."

Chapter IV

Ulysses and Ray slogged up the snowy driveway toward the dormitory. Lights were on in about half of the first-floor rooms but the rest of the building was dark. In the shadow of the building to the north stood Gerald's house, a narrow, wood-frame structure with two stories. From the front they could see no lights. Ulysses climbed to the icy front stoop and knocked on the front door.

He paused, then knocked again. "Mr. Beatty, please come to the door. This is the Sheriff," Ulysses said loudly. He shone his flashlight in the front windows but they saw no one.

Ray stood in the snow, his breath steaming in the cold air. "He's not coming."

"Mr. Beatty," Ulysses yelled, "I'm leaving my card in your door. Call me so we can talk. I need to ask you some questions."

They walked around to the back of the house which was nearest to the dormitory covered by a small porch. Ray shone his flashlight on the concrete back deck and looked at the tracks. "Looks like there's been some coming and going in the past few hours. But that would be expected. Nothing here to write home about."

Ulysses peered into the back-door window.

"See anything?" Ray asked.

"A refrigerator door standing open, light on. A few beers and a loaf of bread, not much else in there," Ulysses said. "Odd."

"I hope he doesn't try to escape tonight," Ray said, stamping his feet. "It's too damn cold. Let's get out of here."

•

The dining room was bright and noisy when Melanie and Alan came in through the kitchen. Jo, dressed in retreat black, stood behind the buffet with Carmen, greeting participants as they passed through the line. *Jo has a good poker face,* Melanie thought, as her student scooped out calabacitas and smiled and spoke to everyone by name. Carmen, serving portions of enchiladas, looked harried and distracted. Tomàs stood near the outside door watching the room. When she caught his eye, he smiled at her and his face lit up. Astrid Berg stood next to him, chatting animatedly, but Tomàs didn't seem to be listening.

Astrid rushed over and hugged Melanie. She was also wearing her roshi robes, which surprised Melanie since it was not customary. "You'll be tanto, right, Astrid?" Melanie hoped Astrid hadn't misunderstood her role.

"Yes, of course. But I can do dokusan too if you need a break, Melanie."

"It's kind of you to offer. But I think I can handle it. Did you get a good rest this afternoon?"

"Oh, yes. It's nice not to be in charge. And our retreats are so big compared to this one. This will be... intimate," Astrid said. She patted Melanie on the shoulder.

Melanie noticed irritation rising in her and deepened her breathing. She remembered the intention she'd made this morning, *give no offense, take no offense, never retaliate.* She smiled at the other woman as kindly as she could.

"Yes, I hope so," Melanie said. "It's good you are here. How long has it been?"

"Four years. I was looking so forward to seeing everyone! What a shame the storm kept so many old friends away."

"Well, you can't fight Mother Nature," Melanie said, scanning the room to distract herself from Astrid's odd, self-satisfied smile. She noticed Alan sitting with Gary and Lynne, who already seemed to be practicing silence. "Folks may still make it tomorrow," Melanie said, knowing how unlikely that was.

"You aren't going to cancel? I wouldn't blame you."

"No, I'm not planning to," Melanie said in a soft voice with all the steadiness she could muster. She brought to mind the equanimity and calm face and manner of Roshi Akira, her teacher, dead now twelve years, and the image settled her. "We'll start right on time tonight."

"Well, then, I better get something to eat." As Astrid walked toward the buffet, Anne Stein came up to Melanie and embraced her. "It is wonderful to see you," she said. "This feels like a homecoming."

Melanie held on to Anne's hug. "Oh, dear one, *it is* a homecoming. Where is Alexis?" Alexis was Anne's wife.

"She couldn't make it this year," Anne said, "but she sent you this little gift for you, Roshi." She handed Melanie a small package.

"How thoughtful of her," Melanie said, and slipped the package into the side pocket of her robe. "I bet I know what it is!" Melanie collected Zuni fetishes, and Alexis always brought one when she came to retreat.

"I heard Gerald is sick," Anne said.

"Yes. He won't be here tonight. Some kind of virus he doesn't want to pass around apparently. Jo will cover his duties."

"If there's anything else I can do, I'm willing," Anne said. "Of course, timing all the sits and leading kinhin will keep me pretty busy!"

"You'll have your hands full," Melanie said, smiling at her student, now a full professor and well-known researcher on mindfulness as a treatment for PTSD.

Jo came over and encouraged Melanie to go through the buffet with her. "Make me a plate, will you?" Melanie asked. "I want to say hello to everyone first." Jo made two plates and sat down at a table with Jon Malvern and Marci Kelly, while Tomàs and Carmen ate in the kitchen, as usual.

Marci, still excited at experiencing her first retreat, chatted energetically.

"The main thing is to use the rest breaks to really rest," Jo said as she watched Roshi Melanie make her way around the room. "Don't be tempted to get work done. Except your samu, of course!"

"What is that?" Jon asked.

"Your work assignment. We try to keep it simple but samu is part of every sesshin. If you haven't signed up yet, the sign-up sheet is in the zendo anteroom above the shoe shelf."

"Oh, okay, I didn't know about that," Jon said. Jo noticed he was fidgety and attributed it to being worried about the days of silence and meditation ahead. "This is all new for me," he said. "I have so much to learn!"

Melanie hugged and chatted with Gary and Lynne and then approached the table where Astrid, Thérèse Boisvert and Malcolm Downs were sitting.

"You've both attended a long retreat before?" Melanie asked Malcolm and Thérèse.

Malcolm nodded.

"This is my third sesshin but my first Rohatsu, Roshi," Thérèse said in her Islands accent. "My zendo is currently without a roshi so I decided to come here."

"Where are you from?" Astrid asked.

"Empty Sky in Scottsdale. Our roshi died last August. Don't you remember me? We met in October."

"Oh, yes, of course," Astrid said. "Roshi Patricia was a great friend of mine."

"Where are you living now?" Astrid asked Malcolm.

"Oh, you two know each other?" Melanie asked.

"Roshi Astrid and I met during one of her retreats a few years ago," Malcolm responded. To Astrid he said, "I live in Los Alamos now."

"That's close by," Astrid said. "You could come here for zazen, couldn't you?"

"My work keeps me too busy," Malcolm answered. "Taking time like this is a real indulgence." To Melanie he said, "I'm looking forward to your dharma talks, Roshi."

"I hope they are worth the anticipation." She nodded to them both and walked over to Jo's table to eat her dinner. Jon carried his plate to the kitchen window and left. Thérèse took her dessert and sat down at Marci's table. Left alone with Malcolm, Astrid began lecturing him about the importance of being part of a sangha loud enough that Melanie could hear every word. Malcolm chuckled but made no comment.

Alan brought his dessert and sat down next to Melanie. "You decided not to say anything about the storm or…Gerald?"

Melanie shook her head. "For everyone's practice, at this point the less said the better. It will just fill up the mind."

When Jo returned to the dining room, she noticed the lights of the sheriff's SUV as it was leaving the property. The silence would begin with the first sit in forty-five minutes. Jo looked around the empty room. Everyone had left to prepare for the evening sit. Carmen's cousins, Dorcas and Yolanda, were washing dishes. *So far, so good*, Jo thought, as she walked to the zendo to check the room—*no one has asked to leave, at least not yet*.

Jo entered the warm, quiet zendo. She could hear Lynne and Gary speaking to each other in Lynne's room. She picked up the samu roster and checked to make sure everyone had an assignment for their volunteer work as a part of Buddhist practice. The senior staff positions were already assigned to long-time students of Roshi Melanie's.

Jo heard voices coming from Roshi Astrid's room farther down the hall. One was Alan's voice, just above a whisper, the other voice was Astrid's. Jo walked down the carpeted hall to place the donations basket next to the sutra notebooks below the evening gong. As she neared the zendo the conversation was unmistakable. She heard Alan say, "She's just not competent. I had no idea it had gotten this bad!"

"It is time for a change," Roshi Astrid said in a low, emphatic voice, "past time. You need to make the call. You know I can cover for you."

Jo felt sick to her stomach. She ducked into the shadowy zendo just before Alan came out of Roshi Astrid's room and crossed the hall into his own.

Jo stared at the altar, trying to calm herself. *What on earth is going on?* she wondered, though her gut already knew. Alan and Astrid were going to challenge Roshi Melanie's leadership. Jo paced between the rows of cushions, noting who was seated where by the name cards people had placed in front of their zafus. She was wondering what to do but quickly realized there was nothing she could do. Usually at this time before a retreat Jo felt a sense of calm and spaciousness. Tonight she felt afraid and angry. The sesshin would start in thirty minutes. She needed to compose her mind.

Just then the lights went out all over Sleeping Tiger.

•

The wind blew steadily and as the sky cleared the temperature dropped. The moon was bright but the thick swath of Milky Way was still visible. Jo saw that Tomàs was setting up the generators to restore power to the campus—one for the dormitory and superintendent's house and another for the kitchen, dining room and zendo. Roshi Melanie had an airtight woodstove in her kitchen that, together with the fireplace, could keep her house warm enough. The noise of generators was far from ideal during a silent retreat but nothing could be done, since most of the buildings had no other source of heat. Jo was thankful Tomàs had thought to stockpile extra gas, probably enough to get them through the night. The electric co-op crews would be busy and maybe by morning the power would return.

When the generators started, the dining hall lit back up. To conserve power in the zendo Jo lit kerosene lamps and put out extra blankets for people to take into their sleeping rooms. She stepped outside as people came slowly down the driveway from the dormitory, lighting their way by flashlights.

Jo took a moment to make her intention for the retreat. She remembered a quote from Dōgen: "If you cannot find truth right where you are, where else do you expect to find it?" She checked her watch, stepped up to the bonsho and "invited" the bell to ring the first time by striking it firmly with a wooden mallet. Then for ten minutes she sounded the bell in a proscribed pattern, alerting everyone to the approaching time to gather in the zendo. The bell's sonorous tones blotted out the generator's noise.

The participants filed in silently, slipping off their shoes and placing them neatly on racks and hanging their jackets on assigned pegs. After they had used the bathrooms and gotten sips of water, they went to their cushions and stood in two rows facing each other, awaiting Roshi Melanie.

Once everyone had assembled Melanie came in with her notes and a flashlight. When she arrived at her chair, Anne used wooden clappers to signal everyone to bow.

"Be seated," Melanie said. Anne rang the bell to signal that Roshi would now give her "Cautions," the traditional orientation to the upcoming eight days.

Jo sat on her cushion in the middle of the back wall and looked around the room. Roshi Melanie sat in the front middle, her back to the altar, with Roshi Astrid beside her to the right. To Astrid's right began one row, with Anne and the bell placed at the front nearest the altar, followed by Alan, Gary and Lynne, and beside Lynne, Gerald's empty cushion. To Roshi Melanie's left was another row where Thérèse, Marci, Jon and Malcolm sat. Roshi Melanie and Lynne sat on chairs.

"It is traditional to give Cautions at the beginning of every sesshin, and now I will do so." She cleared her throat and began to speak without looking at her notes. "Rohatsu is when we celebrate the enlightenment of the Buddha. This retreat is time we set aside to devote to our mindfulness practice. We leave behind our daily concerns to transcend the mind's chatter and look into our true nature. Individually, we balance mind and body. Together, we balance the needs of the individual and those of the community. Thus, we realize a harmonious condition."

As Jo listened, she noticed her heart rate was still elevated. She began to pace her exhalations to be much longer than her inhalations, a technique she'd found helped to calm her. She glanced at Roshi Astrid, who sat in lotus position, with her eyes open but cast down. Alan was looking at Roshi, his face impassive. Jo noticed disgust rising in her toward them and began counting her breaths to release these thoughts.

"Please keep to the silence," Melanie continued. "If you have questions about your practice you may speak with me in dokusan. If you need a special dokusan with me or if you have an emergency you can speak with jisha, Gary. If you have a facility problem you can speak with doan, Jo. Otherwise remain silent even during meals, when working and in shared bedrooms. Do not study, read or write. Stay in your practice. Work during your samu time and rest during rest periods.

"You do not need to make eye contact with anyone. Eye contact, smiling, greeting one another, are distracting and unnecessary. There is enough intimacy in simply sitting together. These methods are tried and true ways to find harmony and community during sesshin. They will guide us toward the experience of essential nature."

Jo heard Carmen and Tomàs say goodnight on the walkway outside the zendo. Carmen's husband had come to take her and Dorcas home in his four-wheel-drive truck.

Roshi Melanie continued the Cautions but Jo's mind drifted away to thoughts about Gerald. *Would he really not show up to the retreat at all? That was so like him!* When her focus returned to the present Roshi was finishing her opening instructions.

Roshi Melanie smiled. "Remember, there is no particular virtue to being in pain. Try to find a comfortable way to sit and if you need to change do so at the breaks. And don't worry about remembering all these procedures. The procedures are meant to enhance your mindfulness, not the other way around." Anne rang the bell. Everyone stood and bowed. Anne then led a single file of participants around the rows of cushions in the very slow walking meditation called kinhin.

Jo joined the line, and as she walked, she focused on her koan, a particularly thorny one about how the elbow doesn't bend outward. She'd been struggling with this one for a month and had hoped she'd have a breakthrough during Rohatsu. Koan practice was supposed to lead to a state of enlightenment. For Jo the odd little riddles always befuddled her until suddenly revealing themselves in a surprising moment. But her mind was too busy tonight, she felt, to make much progress on her koan. Her thoughts jumped about from Alan and Astrid to the poor man who was killed on Lizard Head to the temperature in the dormitory and back to Gerald. The sound of the dining hall generator bothered her.

Anne used the wooden clappers to signal the return to place and clacked again for everyone to bow. They settled into their seated postures as she rang the bell three times. The first twenty-five-minute sit of the retreat was underway. Jo felt dread at all the sitting that lay ahead, a rare feeling for her. *This must be how Tim felt*, she thought. Her husband, always so active, such a problem-solver, chafed at all the time spent sitting and accepting. Jo felt a pang of grief, intense at first, then softening into a sadness more like loneliness. She was surprised to feel tears filling her eyes.

•

As Ulysses drove back to the station, he sifted through the details of the day. He felt sure that Gerald Beatty had been inside when they knocked on his door. But the empty refrigerator with its open door gave him pause. *Was he planning on fleeing?* Another detail that teased him was the scapular found near Luis's body. He knew that Sleeping Tiger had once housed a Benedictine monastery and then a re-education center for troubled priests, named after St. Michael. Some Picuris Indians were practicing Catholics. But who, other than the killer, had known about the location of the body?

Once he got back to his office Ulysses started making lists of what he needed to do or delegate, including obtaining a search warrant for Gerald Beatty's house for tomorrow. It was a long list. Then he considered the extraordinarily cold night that lay ahead. His full-time deputies, Angela Romero who had been with him for two years and Josh Montoya for one, were still pretty green. Ulysses wanted to talk with them to make sure they were oriented to all that could happen in the county on a night like this.

As usual Angela had thought of many of the tasks, such as checking all the usual places homeless people were bedding down and making sure they got to a shelter. She was even prepared to check on dogs chained up outside on the edges of town and at familiar spots on county roads. Josh hadn't thought much beyond responding to things that happened, like motor vehicle accidents. Ulysses gave him a checklist of potential risks he'd overlooked and asked him to check on each one. He talked with Meghan who was handling 911 dispatch, then called Rosemary to tell her he was heading home. She didn't even ask him to pick up anything for the house, just said that she'd be happy to see him and told him to be careful.

At about nine o'clock Ulysses drove his pickup north toward Arroyo Hondo. The snowplows were out clearing and salting the roads. Rosemary and the children would be asleep by now, most likely. At the turnoff he put the vehicle into four-wheel drive and felt the tires grab the snowy road. It was 2 miles to his little homestead of thirty acres. He passed the two other small holdings, one occupied by an older couple who'd come to the commune in the 1970s and the other one abandoned.

His parents built a rambling adobe forty-five years ago, and he and his sister Paloma had grown up there. Montgomery and Diana Walker had come to New Mexico from Oregon before he was born at Vedanta, a commune and eclectic spiritual community based loosely on the teachings of an American swami. The house sat at about 7,500 feet in the foothills of the Sangre de Cristo Mountains. When Ulysses was growing up the house was one story and had just one bathroom with a big cast-iron bathtub his father had hauled from Alamosa, Colorado. Ulysses and Paloma had shared a bedroom until she was twelve and he was eight, when his father added another bedroom.

The community had long since dispersed. His father, a master carpenter and Vietnam veteran, died ten years ago from Parkinson's, and his mother, a breast cancer survivor and retired teacher, had moved to Albuquerque to live with Paloma, an immigration attorney who was divorced and raising a teenage son. Ulysses and Rosemary had bought the homestead from his mother.

Ulysses built a two-story addition after he and his family had moved in, adding bedrooms and a shared bathroom for the children and new kitchen, built to commercial code, for Rosemary. She made jams, jellies, salsa and chutneys that sold well in Taos. They still used the old kitchen for every day cooking, and he and Rosemary slept in his parents' old bedroom, the room where he was born. It had a ponderosa pine beamed ceiling, kiva fireplace and three big windows he'd recently replaced that looked east, south and west. His next project was expanding the old bathroom, adding double sinks and a separate shower with a glass enclosure. He loved to fantasize about and plan for his next building project.

He crossed the cattle guard onto his property as the moon rose over the mountains and shone down on five acres of snowy pasture, garden and orchard. A small chicken house and the goat and sheep shed stood behind the garden fence. The animals were bedded down in thick straw, huddled together for warmth. Behind the house the land rose silent and dark, cloaked in piñon and ponderosa pine, spruce and fir. A little aspen grove fringed the pasture to the east. As a child he'd love to play in the grass and wildflowers that grew abundantly in their light shade.

The lamp was on in Paloma's former bedroom, which now held Rosemary's loom. The wind had died down and a thin plume of smoke from the big Ashley woodstove lifted straight from the chimney to the bright stars. Rosemary was a homemaker of extraordinary talent and a highly competent mother, gardener, cook, seamstress, electrician, plumber and auto mechanic. The woman could fix anything and she put up with the demands of Ulysses's work and the rigors of semi-isolation in Arroyo Hondo. He often wondered what he'd do without her.

Ulysses parked in the garage, grabbed the radio and walked toward the house, ready to climb into bed after a very long day. He opened the front door into the warm mudroom and took off his boots, hung up his coat and hat and removed his gun from its holster. He pulled the clip out and put it and the gun in the safe and locked it. In the kitchen there was a pot of herbal tea on the counter and two loaves of fresh sourdough bread cooling on racks.

Rosemary came in, brushing her long, curly hair. She put a finger to her lips. "I just got them down." She smelled of coconut moisturizer and honey. He kissed her.

"Been weaving?"

"I was reading my Bible."

"Seriously?"

"Yes, seriously. How was your day?"

"Long. Crazy. We had a suspicious death."

"Where?"

"Out on Picuris Pueblo land. Near the Buddhist retreat center."

"Who?"

"A young man, tribal member, lived in Taos with his mother. How was your day?"

"Fun. We made a snowman. Then Katie came by and took the kids sledding and I got a nap." Katie was a single woman in her fifties who lived with her elderly mother about a mile up the road. She helped Rosemary with the children and sometimes in the kitchen. Rosemary saw her as a godsend but Ulysses found her annoying. He thought she lacked common sense.

"Are you hungry? I made vegetable soup and the bread's still warm. Change your clothes and I'll dish it up for you."

When they sat together at the kitchen table, Rosemary with her tea and Ulysses with his late dinner, Rosemary asked, "Why is the death suspicious?"

"He fell off a cliff. Or was pushed. The wind made it so there weren't tracks up there. We have no real clues as yet."

"I wonder what he was doing there?"

"Meeting someone, probably, but we don't know just yet. He had a weapon but it hadn't been fired."

"Will FBI step in since it was on Picuris land?"

"Nominally, yes, but it's kind of small potatoes. Ray Pando and I are going to work it together until they do. Also, something might going on up at that retreat center, Sleeping Tiger, which is adjacent to where we found the body," Ulysses said. "That's probably all I should tell you."

"Who am I going to tell?" Rosemary said, clearing away his bowl and plate. She loved to be let in on the details of his work. Rosemary wasn't a gossip but she still liked to know what was going on.

Ulysses stood up and stretched. "Let's go to bed," Ulysses said, walking over to Rosemary at the sink. He wrapped his arms around her and kissed her neck.

•

After the final sitting, the participants filed out of the zendo and headed to their sleeping quarters. As Jo came out into the cold night she saw Tomàs refilling the gas in the generator near the dining hall.

He smiled and said, "Want to go with me to check on the boiler?"

Jo nodded, trying to keep to the silence. Tomàs rattled on about the cold (already down to 5 degrees), and the five-day forecast (clear tomorrow, another storm expected on Tuesday) while Jo listened. He was not a meditator but a lapsed Catholic who still occasionally went to church and even took communion while disavowing belief. They headed toward the dormitory, which was lit up on the south side first floor as participants got ready for bed. There were no lights on in Gerald's house.

"Did Gerald show up?" Tomàs asked.

Jo shook her head.

"I wonder where he is?"

Jo put her finger to her lips to quiet him as they approached the east door. She had a moment's urge to tell him what she'd overheard in the zendo from Roshi Astrid and Alan but thought better of it. They went inside. The dormitory felt warm, and the boiler, propane with electric ignition, was still running. "Now if the power can just come back on," she whispered.

"I just saw a repair truck," Tomàs said in a normal speaking voice.

Again, Jo put her finger to her lips and they both laughed.

"Let's go out the other door," Tomàs whispered. "I'll walk you to your cabin."

"You don't need to," Jo said.

"I don't mind, Josie," Tomàs said. "I'll feel better if you let me."

They walked down the silent hall and out the west door. With the wind calmer, the cold was less penetrating as they trudged down the slope to Jo's cabin. A thin spire of smoke from her chimney showed her fire still held. A great horned owl hooted its five-beat call twice. Jo and Tomàs walked in silence until they reached her front porch.

Jo stood on her top step, her head level with his. "Goodnight," he said, smiling and bowing slightly. Jo reached over and hugged him, surprising them both. He hugged her back, taking in the rose scent she wore. Then he turned and walked back to Roshi's second floor guest room. Thinking of Jo he fell into a deep sleep.

Gerald woke up in the dark with a start. Someone was pounding on the back door again. He successfully dodged someone earlier, a couple of sheriff's deputies. Gerald jumped up and threw on a robe. It was probably Malvern coming again to confront him. He considered trying to talk with him but realized how stupid that would be. A screaming fight now would only make it harder to escape. Gerald grabbed his car keys and slipped on his shoes. He didn't have time to get dressed. Luckily he had warm clothes and boots in his car, along with his passport, computer, phone and plenty of cash. He'd been planning this departure for weeks but now, suddenly, his plan seemed risky. Still, he had to try. Staying here meant consequences that were too dire. He could even face jail time. If he made it to Mexico he would hide out for a long time, until he figured out what to do.

Gerald crept down the stairs in the dark house. When he reached the bottom he sprinted across the living room to the front door, opened it as quietly as he could and slipped out. He ran down the hill toward the garage falling twice in the powdery snow, wetting his flimsy nightclothes. It was much colder than he expected. Just before he ducked into the garage he looked over his shoulder and noted that no one had followed him. Gerald chuckled at the ease with which he'd evaded his former lover.

He got into the Volvo and put his key in the ignition. He hoped his new snow tires would get him to Santa Fe on the back roads. *Dare I drive in my pajamas on a night this cold?* He decided he had no choice, started the car and turned on the lights. That was when he saw the shadow of someone standing behind the car. Before he knew it, that person had slipped into the front passenger seat.

Chapter V

Melanie was awake at 4:30 and reviewing her first talk over a cup of coffee and a buttered scone. The house was quiet and she assumed Tomàs was still asleep. The kerosene lamp provided a wan, yellowish light.

She'd hardly slept and felt apprehensive and queasy. She couldn't focus on her talk. Luckily it was an old one on the Heart Sutra she'd written when she was a sensei at the Wakeful Mind Monastery, under its first roshi, Akira Matsume. It almost didn't matter that Melanie couldn't focus because she had memorized the talk years ago, drawn as it was from her beloved teacher's talks. It was a favorite of her students and she had given it before as first teisho. *The dharma never changes*, Roshi Akira liked to say, *and it never decreases. It only increases!*

Roshi Akira was one of the first female Zen Roshis in the US. She had given transmission to Melanie in 2005 and also to Junsu Ito, who had been Astrid's teacher. She died shortly thereafter. What had followed Melanie hated to recall. It was dharma combat at a level Roshi Melanie had only heard about in old stories. Who would take over Wakeful Mind, with its reputation for integrity, purity and simplicity, developed through Roshi Akira's years of impeccable leadership? Who would inherit control over the large, diverse sangha, the elegant monastery with its zendo, gardens, bakery and famous kitchens that produced products sold in gourmet stores throughout southern California?

Roshi Melanie hardly knew how to compete with Junsu Ito, a distinguished-looking Korean man with an austere demeanor, a mind like a razor and the skills of a businessman. He was said to have lived in a monastery in Kamakura for many years before coming to Wakeful Mind in 1990. After Roshi Akira's death, Junsu Ito quickly gained the backing of the sangha's well-heeled elite on the board of directors—all except Alan Wolfe, new to the board at that time. Junsu Ito was drawing capacity crowds in hotel ballrooms in San Francisco and New York while Melanie, even though her students were fiercely loyal, could scarcely fill a conference room in Los Angeles.

Before long Melanie realized her best path would lead her away from Wakeful Mind Monastery. Eventually she founded Sleeping Tiger, accompanied by Alan, Gerald, Gary, Lynne and Anne. That was eleven years ago. Gerald had located the perfect property, which had been owned by the Archdiocese of Santa Fe. It was semi-abandoned and affordable given the buyout from Junsu Ito and donations from sympathetic students.

Melanie took another sip of coffee and looked at her watch: 5:15, nearly time to put on her robes and go to the zendo for the opening chant, readings and vows. The front door opened. Who was coming in at this hour without knocking? Alan, followed quickly by Tomàs, came into the kitchen looking alarmed.

"Gerald's car is gone," Alan said. "He must have left during the night."

Melanie's stomach lurched. "He can't have gotten too far," she said, "that car is not very good in the snow."

"Do you want me to look for him?" Tomàs asked. "It's 8 below. If his car broke down it wouldn't be good."

"Why don't you call the sheriff?" Alan asked Tomàs. "They can find him."

"Tomàs, I don't want you out there looking for him. Alan, go ahead and call the sheriff."

Just then the lights came back on. "Thank God," Melanie said. "At least one thing is going our way!"

•

Ulysses woke before dawn and climbed over Monty's warm little body to put his feet on the cold floor. Amelia and Monty both had crawled into his and Rosemary's bed in the middle of the night, waking him only briefly before settling back down. The room was chilly but the bed was dry and everyone was fast asleep. He turned on the coffee pot Rosemary had set up the night before, loaded more wood into the stove and sat down in the living room to meditate while the coffee brewed. He had just begun breathing deeply when he remembered his dream.

He was in the kitchen of Gerald Beatty's house. The refrigerator door stood open. When Ulysses went to close it, he saw a body inside, frozen beneath thick, transparent ice, its face contorted in fear. Ulysses continued trying to meditate, turning to his favorite mantra, "just this," on the inbreath, "moment" on the outbreath. Remembering the dream, Ulysses felt a wave of fear. *Fear*, Ulysses recalled his father saying, *False Evidence Appearing Real*. Ulysses had found that wasn't always true, of course. Sometimes evidence *was* real and worthy of feeling afraid, even if this dream was not such evidence. Ulysses sat a few more minutes, hearing the coffee pot gurgle as it finished its cycle. He got up before he felt the settled feeling he had come to expect from meditation.

Ulysses showered, poured himself a cup of coffee and checked his phone for messages. Angela had called to report she had picked up and transported one homeless man in El Prado, cited two people for dogs chained outside with inadequate shelter and that Josh had dealt with a DWI, a one-vehicle accident near the Taos Gorge Bridge, minor injuries. There was also a message from Alan Wolfe at the Sleeping Tiger saying that Gerald Beatty had fled during the night. They didn't know what time or where he might have gone. They said his car had front-wheel drive and snow tires. Ulysses checked the weather for the coming day—high in the teens, winds at 15 miles per hour and partly cloudy.

Ulysses spread peanut butter on a piece of toast and grabbed a couple of apples and a thermos of coffee. He strapped on his holster, took his gun out of the safe, put in the clip and checked the safety. He went back into the bedroom to kiss Rosemary goodbye. She was only dimly awake. "Be careful out there," she whispered. "See you tonight."

"Need anything?"

"How about a three-day weekend?"

The moon was setting and the wind had stilled. The road was as it had been last night, the snow dry and well packed. No one else had driven in or out. The main road had been plowed. *If the roads by Sleeping Tiger are this good it will make it easy for Beatty to get away,* he thought.

The drive let him shift from being Ulysses, husband, father and lover of simple pleasures, to Sheriff Ulysses, elected protector of Taos County, a role that felt especially heavy this morning.

He allowed his mind to wander over its questions. Why had Gerald Beatty absconded? Was it because he had killed Luis Duràn or because of his financial mismanagement? Was Beatty being blackmailed? Ulysses reflected on the connection between Luis Duràn and Randolph Miller, the priest in Taos who had disappeared. Was there any connection with Sleeping Tiger?

Ulysses pulled into the station and parked in his designated spot. Angela Romero was in the front room filling out paperwork from the night before, her feet propped up on the chair opposite her. She took her feet down as soon as Ulysses came in, stood up and said, "Good morning, Sheriff." Angela was a small, slender woman with glossy black hair in a tight bun and a large revolver on her hip. She lived alone with her cat, Mr. T, a cross-eyed Siamese whose photographs decorated her desk.

"How's it going, Deputy?" Ulysses asked.

"Good, sir. You got word about the guy, a Mr. Beatty, missing up at that retreat center?"

"Yep. Where's Deputy Montoya?" Ulysses poured himself a cup of coffee and checked the little refrigerator for milk. Lorraine had bought a quart of some flavored, sugary liquid for everyone else and a pint of regular half and half for him. That she'd remembered he didn't like holiday-themed coffee flavors was a good sign. After two years on the job he might be entering the realm of acceptable.

"He clocked out fifteen minutes ago. Zach is coming on," she checked her phone, "in ten minutes." Ulysses felt the annoyance he was starting to associate with Josh Montoya. Leaving early was minor infraction but it happened too often.

Ulysses went over the events of the night before with Angela and read through Josh's cursory report. Lorraine arrived, bringing a casserole dish of tamales carnitas. A delicious, spicy smell filled the office. Zach and Mark, part-time deputies arriving for the day shift, helped themselves as Angela signed off for the day. This was new, Lorraine bringing food. *I bet she did it when Trujillo was sheriff*, he thought.

"Tamale, Sheriff?" Lorraine had brought Christmas plates and served him two tamales steaming in their cornhusk wrappers. She made eye contact and smiled at him, both rare behaviors.

"Don't mind if I do." Ulysses smiled back at the older woman who had been so cold and dismissive of him since he started on the job. *She's clearly trying to improve*, he thought. "Did you make these?"

"Lord, no, Sheriff, I work too hard to have time to cook. My sister made them."

"I'll take them with me for lunch," he said, grabbing two more. "I'm going to see what I can find on the homicide and the missing guy from the retreat center."

Lorraine approached him with her "this is serious" look and handed him a printed invitation.

"Sheriff, the Democratic Party wants you to attend their big Christmas party on Thursday. They want you to speak, too. Consuelo's on the Plaza at twelve noon sharp. Lunch provided. I need to let them know. Will you go?"

"Thursday?" Ulysses said taking the invitation. He dimly remembered that his campaign manager had told him to go.

"Everyone will be there including Ernesto Ruiz. Say yes?" Ernie Ruiz, a protégé of Ràmon Trujillo, ran against Ulysses in the primary two years ago. In northern New Mexico whoever won the Democratic primary usually won the election.

"Okay," Ulysses said reluctantly, "tell them yes." He hated these things but showing up was necessary for re-election. "Find out what they want me to talk about."

Lorraine smiled. "Good, Sheriff," she said as if to a small child. "I will find out."

"Lorraine, do you know anything about the old Benedictine monastery near Peñasco? Why did the Diocese buy it?"

"Oh, Sheriff, it was like fifty years or more that the monks left! I believe that when Diocese bought it they made it into a place to send priests that weren't, you know, really right? They kept it kind of quiet. Sheriff Trujillo could tell you more about it. Archbishop Sullivan built a house for himself out there, planning to retire there, but he changed his mind I guess. He and Sheriff were good friends back then."

"Was it called something like "St. Michael's'?" Ulysses asked.

"Society of St. Michael was the name, I'm pretty sure."

Ulysses went into his office and closed the door. He ate one of the tamales and thought about what Lorraine had told him. Everyone now knew that these priests who "weren't right" had often been placed in poor parishes and reservations needing priests all over New Mexico, West Texas and Colorado. The Church hierarchy had to have known these men would not be cured of their perversity enough to work with children again. The whole situation made Ulysses angry.

The sun was coming up as Ulysses got into the Expedition. His cell phone rang.

"Want to come over to the Pueblo?" It was Ray Pando's gruff baritone. "I think we found Beatty."

"Alive?"

"No, not alive. Found in front of the church by the altar society lady about an hour ago."

"I'm on my way."

•

Gerald Beatty's stiffened body lay in a fetal position in the plaza of San Lorenzo, the historic adobe church at the center of Picuris Pueblo. Ulysses got out of the Expedition to meet Ray, who stood talking with EMTs just outside the crime-scene tape. No one else was around in the plaza, which smelled of wood smoke from the morning fires in nearby homes. The wind blew snow over Beatty's corpse. He was barefoot and wearing a wet robe and pajamas.

"Looks like he froze," Ray said. "Not sure how he got here. Deputies haven't found his car yet."

"What time was the body found?"

"About 5 am. By Billie Arguello who was going to unlock the church and turn on the heat so she could clean. She saw the body and called me."

"Strange he ended up here," Ulysses said.

"It's only five miles from Sleeping Tiger," Ray said. "Shorter if you go on the trail over the ridge."

Beatty's eyes were closed and his face looked peaceful. Ice had crystallized on his robe and hair, and his hands were frostbitten.

Ray said, "I used to see this in Albuquerque after a real cold night. Alcoholics mostly. Looks like he's been dead several hours."

"How did he get this far dressed like that?"

"Probably came in his car at least part of the way. His tracks lead to the road. He must have walked on the road for a piece."

"From those ice crystals it looks like he's been in water."

Just then Ray's radio squawked. A voice on the other end said, "Found a late model Volvo sedan stuck in a snowbank about a half a mile up the BLM Forest Road. It's unlocked with the keys inside."

"Any fresh tracks?" Ray asked.

"Nope, no tracks around the car. Somebody swept them."

"Go over toward the ridge trail—you know the one I mean?"

"No, Boss, what trail?"

"Never mind. Don't touch anything, just come on back." Ray looked disgusted. "These kids don't know the country," he said to Ulysses. "All they know is their goddamn phones. I have a hunch how this body got wet and where we might find some tracks."

Ray directed the EMTs to take Beatty's body to Taos and call Dr. Vigil, the coroner. He and Ulysses climbed into Ray's pickup and drove through the waking pueblo toward the main road, turning toward Sleeping Tiger. They hadn't gone even a mile when Ray pulled off on a plowed drive to the Picuris waste disposal lagoon, a square half-acre pond with high embankments full of brownish-green water and ice.

They got out. In the deeper snow just off the gravel were car tracks and footprints. "Looks like there was some kind of tussle near the edge," Ray said. "I think he got dunked here, poor bastard."

"Maybe he wasn't going to die fast enough."

"Maybe not." They went over to examine the tracks. "He was already shoeless," Ray said, pointing out the footprints. "Looks like the other guy was wiping his tracks. Not sure we can get a good impression. Let's go over to the ridge trail."

They drove up the snowy pueblo forest road. "There's the Volvo," said Ulysses. Ray led the way on foot up the road for about 300 yards to a small arroyo. The snow was deep, and someone had been walking there recently. On the floor of the driver's seat were a pair of loafers.

"So, what do you think happened?" Ray asked.

"I think the killer comes to Sleeping Tiger, kidnaps Beatty, forces him in his pajamas into his own car, and plans to leave him out in the cold along one of these roads to die. There's no traffic along here on a night like this. But somehow the killer thinks better of it—Beatty might get rescued before he dies. To reduce that possibility he dunks him in the septic field, then turns him loose, figuring he'll be dead in twenty minutes, tops. Then he heads back toward Sleeping Tiger on this trail and makes it to wherever he was going before daylight."

"Sounds reasonable," Ray said. "Beatty runs along the road, wet and freezing, makes it to the plaza, and collapses in front of the church as the killer heads over the ridge?"

"That's what I'm thinking," Ulysses said. "But I don't think we can get a serviceable print there. The guy was wearing snowshoes."

•

Ray and Ulysses pulled up at Sleeping Tiger just as the sun came up over the mountains and lit up the snowy grounds. They parked at the garage and walked toward the dining hall, where the retreat attendees were eating a silent breakfast after the dawn meditation block.

"Let's go in through the kitchen so we don't disturb the "Rosh" just yet," Ulysses said.

Carmen stood at the kitchen door watching them with an expression of worried curiosity. With the power back on, the kitchen was back to normal. Carmen offered a steaming basket of breakfast burritos and Ray took one. She told them to help themselves to coffee from one of the large carafes. While Ray ate his burrito Ulysses nursed a cup coffee, his third of the morning.

After they'd eaten, Tomàs led them to the adobe home where they'd met the night before.

"Did you find him?" Tomàs asked when they got inside.

"Yes," Ulysses said, "we found his body over at Picuris. It looks like he froze to death."

Tomàs whistled under his breath. He went upstairs to tell Melanie. While they waited, the lawmen sat at the kitchen table. Melanie Hirsh came in, ashen-faced.

"Did someone kill him?" she asked, waving away a cup of coffee offered by Carmen.

"We don't know," Ray answered, "but it looks suspicious."

Melanie took in a deep breath, pulled out a chair and sat down. "Tell me what you know," she said in a voice barely above a whisper. Tomàs stood in the doorway.

"Someone found his body this morning, very early, lying in front of the church at the pueblo," Ray said. "He was poorly dressed for the cold. It's likely he froze to death. We found his car about a mile away. There's a lot of stuff in the trunk. It looks like he was planning to flee."

"Oh my God," Melanie said and began to cry.

Tomàs shifted his weight and sighed. Everything about Beatty bugged him, including how his death caused Melanie so much pain.

"Can I see him?" Melanie asked.

"His body is at the morgue now," Ulysses said. "The procedure is for someone to confirm the identity and the coroner to determine cause of death. Then the body is made available to family for burial arrangements."

"I'll go identify him for you," Tomàs said to Melanie.

Melanie shook her head. "No, I should go. But can you drive me and come in with me?"

"Yes," Tomàs said, "but I don't see why you would want to go."

Melanie sobbed. "He was like family to me and he has no one else," she said.

Ulysses stood up. "Ms. Hirsh, Mr. Pando and I will need to conduct interviews with all the people staying here last night. We'd like to get started as soon as possible."

Melanie blew her nose and sat up in her chair. She seemed to realize for the first time that this would bring the retreat to an end. "I understand, Sheriff," she said. "At some point I will need to call everyone together and tell them Gerald is dead. Some of them will want to go home right away."

"No one should leave, Ma'am," Ulysses said, "until we have interviewed them and given them clearance."

"My God," Melanie said, stifling a sob. "Do you think someone here is—could be—involved?"

"The simple answer is yes; it could be someone here. Our interviews will help us gather more information," Ulysses said. "Can you set up a room we can use?"

"Shall I go get Jo?" Tomàs asked.

"Yes, go get her," Melanie said in a whisper. "She's so good in a crisis." Melanie went to the sink and splashed cold water on her face. She turned back to Tomàs. "But don't let anyone else know what is going on, okay? Not just yet. I'm not ready to face everyone."

The sesshin participants were on an hour break after breakfast for samu and rest. The dining room was empty except for Carmen and Dorcas, who were washing up from breakfast and speaking softly in Spanish.

"What is going on, Tomàs?" Carmen said when he came in.

"Have you seen Josie?"

"She was on her way to her cabin. Answer me, what is going on?"

"I can't say yet," said Tomàs, looking over at Dorcas scrubbing the big oatmeal pot. "But don't worry, you'll know soon enough."

Carmen clucked disapprovingly at being put off. "I think I know what," she said. "I am not blind."

"Please keep this to yourself, Tía," Tomàs whispered. Dorcas continued scrubbing the lightly burned pot as if not listening, banging it loudly against the stainless-steel sink.

"Tomàs, do you think I am a gossip?" Carmen said in Spanish as he walked out toward the zendo.

Tomàs found Jo walking on the snowy path toward her cabin and ran to catch up with her.

"Jo," he said, a little breathless as she turned toward him, her eyebrows furrowed and her face pink from the cold. "They found Gerald. He's dead."

Jo had to catch her breath. Her hazel eyes darkened as she took in the news. After a long pause she asked, "How did he die?"

"They think he froze. They found him in the plaza at Picuris." Tomàs put his arm around her shoulder. "They are calling it suspicious."

Jo leaned into Tomàs's chest. Another suspicious death. She shuddered. "I should go talk with Roshi. There is a lot for us to do before everyone is told. Though God knows what we'll say."

"The sheriff wants to talk with everyone. Melanie sent me to get you. She is really upset. I don't think she knows what to do. Maybe you can help her make a plan." As they made their way down the path Jo noticed how the snow glittered like tiny prisms in the morning light.

"Tomàs, I need to tell you something but you need to keep it in confidence," Jo said. "Can you promise me?"

Tomàs nodded gravely.

"Last night I overheard Alan and Roshi Astrid talking in Astrid's room. It sounded to me like they were planning to … I'm not sure exactly what … but maybe *remove* Roshi Melanie somehow. Like they were plotting some major change here." Jo looked at Tomàs as he took this in. "I don't think this has anything to do with Gerald's death but I do know Alan never liked Gerald."

Tomàs was silent for a few moments, his breath steaming in the cold air. Finally, he said, "Josie, you have to tell Melanie. It isn't safe for her not to know, especially now."

"What are we going to do about the sesshin?"

"The sheriffs plan to interview everyone here," Tomàs said. "They want a room set up for it. I can do that. You go help Melanie figure out what to tell everyone, and how and when."

Jo thought about the implications of all the attendees knowing not only about Gerald's death but also about the death of the Picuris man, Luis Duràn.

"Could these deaths be related? It's so weird that Gerald was found at Picuris Pueblo and the other man was Picuris and he was found here. Melanie never told anyone about the first suspicious death, and now here is another." Jo felt fear creep up her spine. "Plus, this thing with Roshi Astrid and Alan. This will be overwhelming for her."

The two began walking quickly toward the zendo. Jo looked at her watch. In thirty minutes she needed to ring bonsho for the first morning sit. "Listen, Tomàs, come with me first to Roshi's and let's get a plan. Then you can set up the interview room and I'll go back into the zendo so we can keep to the schedule while the interviews take place."

Jo looked closely at Tomàs, trying to keep calm. "We need to be very mindful about everything we do from now on," she said.

●

Ulysses had Beatty's car towed to the Taos Police garage where it could be checked for evidence, then called to make sure the body had arrived at the morgue so that Dr. Vigil could do the postmortem that afternoon. Ulysses and Ray headed over to Picuris to interview the tribal secretary who had found the body on her way the church that morning.

Mrs. Arguello lived near the church in a small adobe with turquoise-framed windows and doors and a TV antenna on the roof. A newer model red pick-up truck was parked in back. An old woman in a denim skirt and work jacket was leaning over the door of a glowing horno, loading loaves of bread and a sheet of bizcochitos in to bake. She stood up, placed the door board over the opening, and dusted her hands. Her black hair was coiled into a bun and she wore coral earrings on her long earlobes.

Ray greeted Mrs. Arguello in Tiwa and they conversed a bit before she turned to Ulysses and regarded him with her discerning black eyes. "Good morning, Sheriff Walker, would you like a cup of coffee?" She held open the door for him.

"Maybe just a glass of water, Mrs. Arguello," Ulysses said, removing his hat.

"Call me Billie," she said, "everyone does."

They followed her into the house, which was clean and sparsely furnished. On the old linoleum floor sat a table and two chairs, two recliners and a flat-screen TV tuned to the morning news from Albuquerque. A savory-smelling stew was simmering and the windows were steamed over. She poured herself and Ray coffee and got a glass of water for Ulysses. She sat at the table and the men sat side by side on a Spanish-style wooden bench near the woodstove.

Ulysses began. "How are you feeling after finding the dead man this morning?"

"Oh, fine," she said cheerfully. "I seen dead before. I worked as a nurse up at Taos many years."

"Tell us how you found him?"

"On Mondays I clean the church. It was especially early this morning because we had Mass here last Sunday so there is more to do. We only have Mass here twice a month. The rest of the time we go to Peñasco. I like to get the linens first and wash and iron them, then come back when that's done and sweep and vacuum. I had just been lying in bed waiting to get up. I don't sleep so well," she laughed and took a drink of coffee. "At five I walked over to the church. The moon was low but bright, you know. It was real cold. No wind. I saw him just as I got to the steps up to the front door. He was lying on his side all curled up like that. I knew right away he was dead."

"Did you approach him?"

"No, I wouldn't want to go near him. I called the rescue squad right away."

"How long before they got here?" Ulysses asked.

"About ten minutes. They came from Peñasco. Once they got here, I went closer to see if I knew him. I didn't."

"What did you do then?" Ray asked.

"I went in the house and made breakfast. I got the linens from the church to soak them and called my sister-in-law, Agnes."

"Anything else you remember, Mrs. —Billie?" Ulysses asked.

"No. That was it. But you might want to talk to Agnes," Billie said. "She told me that the old mama dog who had puppies on her porch was growling before daylight and woke her up. She looked out her front window and saw someone with a flashlight in the arroyo near her trailer."

"Okay, thank you, Billie, we'll visit your sister-in-law and see what she can tell us."

"Sure you don't want coffee?" Billie asked. "I got to get my cookies out of the horno. I'm getting all my cooking done before the next storm."

"No, that's okay, thanks," Ray said, standing up. "Would you like me to bring in any wood?"

"I sure would. If you'd fill up that wood box right there, I'd be most appreciative." While the men filled up her wood box, Billie put some warm cookies in a paper bag for them.

Agnes Duràn lived in a silver and turquoise trailer next to an arroyo and surrounded by piñon pines. A small garage to the west of the trailer held several cars and a tractor. A man was pulling out of the driveway in his truck as Ulysses and Ray pulled in.

"Billie must have told Agnes we were coming. Leroy doesn't care much for me," Ray chuckled as he waved at the man. "I arrested him once in Albuquerque."

Agnes shooed a dog off the built-on front porch as they came up the stairs. The dog growled, jumped from the steps, and skulked off into the chamisa brush. Agnes had dark circles under her tired, wary eyes and did not smile at the two men. She ushered them into her narrow living room where a television was tuned to an old sitcom and cleared some newspapers off the couch for them to sit down. She hadn't said a word. She sat opposite them and waited.

Ray began. "You know we had a dead man on the plaza this morning."

"Yes, I know it," Agnes said. "Think it has anything to do with Luis falling off Peca-una?" She grabbed the remote and turned off the television.

"We don't know, Mrs. Duràn," Ulysses said. "I am sorry for the loss of your nephew."

"Had you seen Luis recently?"

"No. We haven't seen much of him since he got out of prison. He came by to help Leroy with his automotive business once or twice. Not like before. He used to be here a lot." Agnes shifted in her chair and looked at the floor. "Leroy had seen Luis once or twice in Santa Fe. I've been sick with this fibro for nine years now and can't do anything. I never go anywhere, hardly even to Mass or feast days. Leroy does all the shopping, most of the cooking." The air was stale and smelled of pipe tobacco and cooking grease. She looked at Ray and nodded. "So I notice things, especially at night since I don't hardly sleep."

"Tell us what you saw last night, Mrs. Duràn," Ulysses said.

"The dog barking woke me up. I went to the front window to look out but didn't see anything. Then I came back in the bedroom and I saw a light in the arroyo. Like a flashlight. Couldn't see a person but the light was moving fast up the arroyo. Someone walking or running in there."

"What time was it?"

"I don't know. About 2:30, I guess. I woke up Leroy but he said he didn't see anything. He can't see worth a damn in the dark."

"What did you do then?"

"I went back to bed. Lay awake a long time hurting, then fell back asleep."

"Anything else?"

"You know that arroyo connects with the long trail up to Peca-una?"

"Yes," Ulysses said. "Why?"

"Nothing. I just wondered if whoever that was in the arroyo was headed over the ridge, back to the monastery. I think I know the man who was killed," Agnes said. "He lives over there at that place. He came around one time looking for Luis."

"When was that?" Ulysses asked.

"This fall, maybe late October. Right after the first big snow."

"Did he say why he wanted to find him?"

"Said he owed Luis some money."

"Did Luis work for the guy?" Ulysses asked.

"Not that I knew of. But they did know each other somehow. Don't think it was drug-related, though."

Ray spoke up. "Do you think Luis was using recently?"

"I don't know. I'm not supposed to tell you this, but Leroy got Luis into NA. They went to a meeting together on Thursdays over to Peñasco. Luis even had a sponsor. But he might have gone back to drugs. So many do."

"Do you have any idea why someone might have killed Luis?"

"No idea. He was a sweet boy, really. He was never right, though, after Silvia and Elías died. That was why he turned to drugs."

Chapter VI

After her emotional meeting with Roshi Melanie, Jo rushed to ring bonsho. She struck the bell precisely at nine-fifty to let anyone in earshot know that they had ten minutes to get to their places for the mid-morning block. As she rang the bell, she tried to calm her racing thoughts. Was Roshi thinking clearly? Could they really carry on with the sesshin now that Gerald was dead? When would she finally tell everyone?

Jo wasn't used to doubting her teacher's wisdom. Over the years as her student and later as her employee, Jo had found Melanie to possess common as well as ethical sense. She had never known her to put money over principles. Zen tradition included deep reverence for one's teacher and a willingness to follow their direction. This was the first time Jo had ever felt herself wavering.

In the past few hours Jo was starting to wonder if Roshi Melanie's judgment was impaired. The news about Gerald's death, followed by Alan and Roshi Astrid's plot and the death of the Picuris man was too much for her to take in with equanimity. Jo and Tomàs had wanted to call off the sesshin and send people home as soon as the sheriffs would allow. Roshi Melanie was adamant that the sesshin should go on, even as people would be called out one by one to be questioned. She said that the events, including Gerald's death, were just part of Mara's illusion, and they couldn't let it distract the meditators from their practice. Seriously, Roshi Melanie was invoking Mara now, the demon who tried to distract the Buddha from Enlightenment?

This was a departure from Roshi Melanie's usual level-headedness. She tended to stay away from religious-style beliefs like gods and demons. It seemed odd to Jo and crazy to Tomàs to continue with the sesshin under the circumstances, but they gave in to Roshi Melanie, because they didn't feel they could overrule her.

77

The participants were filing into the zendo for the morning sit. They wouldn't know anything until the sheriffs began to question everyone. Jo could imagine how betrayed some participants might feel by not being told the whole truth right away. Roshi Melanie's best intentions could lead to an ugly situation.

Alan approached Jo in the entryway and asked her to step outside. His long face wore a frown and his jaw was set. His hands were hidden in the pockets of his black jacket. "What is going on?" he asked in a harsh whisper.

"What do you mean?" Jo asked shivering. She'd left her coat inside.

"Where is Gerald? And why are the sheriffs hanging around?"

"I can't tell you anything right now," Jo said. "Let's go inside."

"Where is Melanie?" He looked over his shoulder toward her house.

"She's in the house finishing her morning talk. I need to go in." Jo went inside, slipped off her shoes and walked down the silent hall. All the participants except Alan were standing in front of their cushions waiting for Anne to start the sit. Gary had lit sandalwood incense and its curling smoke and pungent sweetness filled the chilly zendo. As she looked at the altar, Jo inadvertently made eye contact with Roshi Astrid, who was scowling. Alan came in and stood in front of his cushion just as Anne slapped together the wooden clackers. Everyone bowed deeply and sat down. Anne rang the first of three bells as people settled into their seated postures for the first twenty-five-minute meditation of the block.

Jo's mind was so active she began to count her breaths to settle down. She counted each full inhalation and exhalation up to ten and then started over at one. This practice was the first one she'd learned when she'd first come to Sleeping Tiger for retreats eight years ago. Gradually her mind settled from discursive thinking to isolated thoughts, images and awareness of her body.

Her mind offered her the image of Roshi Astrid's glare but she let it pass. Up came the image of Alan, looking suspicious and alarmed. She let go of that one as well. She felt a tickle on the side of her nose that she was sure would become an itch before long but stayed with her practice of keeping still and counting her breath. The sun lit up the bamboo floor as the morning canted toward midday. The next storm, expected to blow in tomorrow, offered itself as a topic for thought. *What do we need to be ready?* Again Jo let it go. There was nothing to do, nowhere to go, just this moment.

She heard Lynne Shumann begin to cough. Eventually Lynne arose from her chair and walked out to the entryway. This brief distraction made Jo want to move too, but she continued to work on stilling her mind and body. An image of Tomàs arose, surprising her with the sensations that accompanied it. *I really like him*, she thought. She dwelt for a moment on his steadiness with Melanie. He knew just what to do. She felt safer too, when he was around. She remembered he would be gone this afternoon for a few hours to cut up the elk he'd shot.

Jo pushed aside these thoughts finally and brought her mind back to the room. It was quiet in the cold, light-filled space. There wasn't much fidgeting or noise from this experienced group of meditators. Even beginners like Marci Kelly sat quietly. Jon Malvern looked to be dozing. Jo's mind suddenly brought forward the image of Roshi Melanie when Jo and Tomàs came in to speak with her. Her hair looked uncombed and she'd spilled toothpaste or something on her roshi robes. Her sobs seemed to have exhausted and addled her.

She reacted to the news about Alan and Roshi Astrid with confusion. Then she seemed to draw herself up and became resolute. "I will handle this. I will know what to do. Don't say a word. Just continue with the schedule." Roshi Melanie insisted that nothing, no betrayals by her students, not even a murder, would interfere with the sesshin. Jo had to admit that this was in character for her. When she valued something or someone it took precedence over other more practical matters.

•

The bell rang signaling that twenty-five minutes had passed. *Wow, that was fast*, thought Jo, *and I spent almost the whole time thinking*. She rose to her feet and stood by her pillows waiting for the signal to bow. Roshi Melanie came in, well-groomed and wearing a fresh robe. "Sit comfortably," she said and everyone sat down. "Dear Bodhisattvas," she began her talk, as she always did, and Jo felt herself relax. This at least felt normal.

Just then, Jo heard a car pulling up to the garage. *The sheriffs*, she thought. She bowed quickly and rushed out of the room. Alan followed her.

"I can handle this," Jo said.

"I am in charge here," Alan said.

Jo noticed Sheriff Walker approaching them with a determined set to his jaw. Ray Pando stood behind the vehicle gazing at the horizon. "Sheriffs, please come with me to Roshi's house," Jo said in a loud whisper. "You've met Alan Wolfe. He wants to come with us."

Ulysses replied, "I'm not ready to interview you just yet, Mr. Wolfe. You can go on back into the temple." He and Ray followed Jo toward Melanie Hirsh's house. Carmen and Dorcas stood at the window staring out at them.

"The zendo," Alan corrected, "Listen, Sheriff, I have some questions for you."

"They'll have to wait," Ulysses said in an even tone. "I'll answer them when I call you for your interview." They reached the door to Ms. Hirsh's house and Jo held it open for them to enter.

"What in the hell is going on?" Alan hissed. "I am the chairman of the board of this retreat center and I demand to know!"

"Mr. Wolfe, a man has died under suspicious circumstances. We are going to be questioning everyone here. In the meantime you can continue with your retreat, which is what Ms. Hirsh has requested."

"No, no, no," Alan said, jabbing his finger at Ulysses, "you cannot tell me what to do about this retreat."

"That is true. But you cannot leave or talk to one another during this process. So you might as well continue the retreat." *What an ass*, Ulysses thought.

"We'll see about this," Alan said under his breath. He glared at Ulysses and refused to look at Jo. *He's decided I am his adversary*, she thought. As Alan turned back toward the zendo, Jo wondered if he'd retaliate against her.

Jo led the men up the stairs and into the spare bedroom that faced the zendo where Tomàs had removed one of the twin beds and put out a card table and three chairs. Ulysses took out his recording equipment, notepads and pens, and checked his watch.

"That guy Wolfe seems like a real piece of work," Ray said. "Think it might be good to get him done early?"

Ulysses wished Ray hadn't spoken that way in earshot of Jo, who was also an interview subject. Ulysses never forgot that sheriff work differed from police work because sheriffs were accountable to the voters. He frowned at Ray and called Jo in.

"Ms. McAlister, I would like to start with you. Then I'll interview Ms. Hirsh, during her lunch break."

"That's good. I'll tell her."

"Have a seat," Ulysses said. He turned on his recorder. "Please state your name and your position." He regarded Jo with his calm, blue gaze, his expression mild and even friendly. Ray sat in a soft leather chair, which he had pulled into a little patch of sunlight.

"Josephine Claire McAlister, retreat manager."

"Where were you last night, Ms. McAlister?"

"After the evening sit, I went with Tomàs Ulibarri to check on the boiler in the dormitory, and then he walked me to my cabin, where I spent the rest of the night."

"Did anyone stay with you last night?"

"No, I was alone."

"How long have you been in your current position?"

"Three years last August."

"Were you acquainted with Luis Duràn?"

"No."

"What was your relationship with Gerald Beatty?"

"He was my supervisor here, but I had known him before that because I had come here for retreats."

"Were you two friendly?"

"No, not really. He was … a difficult person to connect with."

"How so?"

"He was prickly, uh, reactive—"

"Did you quarrel?"

"I tried to stay out of his way. I did my job and expected him to more or less leave me alone. We never argued but he was sometimes… quite abrupt with me."

"You have described seeing Gerald Beatty on the night Luis Duràn was killed. Was there anything unusual about what you saw?"

"It was odd to see him out on a cold night. Gerald hated the cold. He wasn't one to go out for a hike even on a warm day. Then I saw him the next day also, walking outdoors."

"What kind of relationship did Gerald have with other staff at Sleeping Tiger?"

Jo thought for a moment, looking out the window at the sun shining on glittering snow. "Carmen could be a little snippy with him but I never saw her actually confront him. Tomàs gets along with everyone, so far as I can tell. I think Gerald didn't like Tomàs, maybe was a little jealous of him. Anybody Roshi really likes he doesn't—didn't—like much. He was very possessive of her."

"How long have you known Melanie Hirsh?"

"I became her student seven years ago. I've known her about eight years."

"What do you know about her relationship with Gerald Beatty?"

"Roshi seemed to have a special fondness for him, though I've never understood why, exactly, beyond that they'd known each other a long time. She treated him like a son almost, but they aren't related. He relies—relied—on her. Without her I'm not sure how he would've taken care of himself. But sometimes he wasn't very nice to her. He complained a lot about all he had to do when actually he did very little beyond keeping the books and the shopping."

Jo was a little surprised at how her thoughts and feelings about Gerald sounded. She never allowed herself to talk about Gerald or anyone in this way. It did not constitute "right speech"—part of the eightfold path of Buddhism—and Jo's natural inclination had always been away from gossip and divisive speech. But now that Gerald had died under suspicious circumstances it felt right to be telling all this to the sheriff, with his pleasant but authoritative demeanor.

"Did he often leave the retreat center?"

"Gerald did all the grocery shopping, which took him away a lot and he usually picked up the mail in Peñasco two or three times a week. I think he went to Taos at least every week, but also to Santa Fe and even Albuquerque. Wednesdays and Fridays were his town days. The rest of us stay closer to home. Especially Roshi. She hardly ever leaves the property—it is a monastery to her."

"How about you? Do you often go into town?"

"Not very often," Jo said. "I haven't been to Santa Fe in about six months. If I need anything, which mostly I don't, I usually go to Taos." *This is kind of a monastery for me too*, she thought.

"Did people come here to see Gerald?"

Jo thought for a few moments. "Before Tomàs was hired Gerald had some workers come out to do things he and I couldn't take care of. Heavy work. Some of the people hired didn't work out so well. Roshi hired Tomàs on Carmen's recommendation and we haven't had to hire out any work since. Nobody else came here to see Gerald."

"How do you get along with Tomàs and Carmen?"

"Really well," Jo said. "They are hardworking and trustworthy. Technically I'm their supervisor but I never have to say anything to either of them." She looked over at Ray, who appeared to be dozing in his spot in the sun.

"What do you know about Alan Wolfe?" Ulysses continued.

"Alan was one of the founders here and also one of Roshi's biggest supporters after Roshi Akira died."

"Akira?"

"Roshi Akira Matsume. She was Melanie's teacher before Sleeping Tiger. She had also been the teacher of Gary, Lynne, Gerald, Anne and Alan. Alan either raised or contributed some of the original money to purchase the place. He lived here with the original crew but left after about a year. I'm not sure why. He went back to Santa Barbara and started a real-estate investment company. Since then he has made a great deal of money, on top of what I was told he inherited from his father. He's been chairman of the board since the founding, so I guess you could say he holds the purse strings."

Ulysses glanced at Ray, who still sat with his eyes closed. Ray liked to listen to an interviewee's voice without other sensory input. He said it gave him clues.

"Are he and Ms. Hirsh close?" Ulysses asked.

"I always thought so. But I don't really know Alan. He and I have never connected. Alan is Roshi's student but sometimes it seems like she is a little afraid of him. She wants to keep him happy. I don't have any proof of that. It's just an impression." Jo wondered if she'd been too judgmental about Alan. She was trying to stick with facts. She weighed whether to say anything about the conversation between Alan and Roshi Astrid last night.

Ray opened his eyes and sat up. "Do you have any other information about Alan Wolfe that you aren't telling us?" he asked, startling Jo. Jo took a deep breath. Ulysses sat with his elbows propped on the table and his chin resting on his hands looking at her intently. Ray wore a frown on his craggy, brown face. *Why did he ask that? Should I just say it? Could this cause harm?*

"Anything else?" Ulysses asked in a softer tone. He thought this woman was well-meaning but withholding for reasons probably related to her Buddhist beliefs.

"Last night I came into the lodging area of the zendo to check on things before the first sitting. I was standing outside Roshi Astrid's room and I overheard part of a conversation they were having. It sounded like they are not satisfied with Roshi Melanie's leadership here. I thought they were considering removing her somehow. It really surprised and upset me."

"Can you recall the details of this conversation, Ms. McAlister?" Ulysses asked. To the best of her ability Jo recounted what she overheard. "It was your impression that Berg and Wolfe had some kind of plan?"

"I don't know, but they had clearly talked about it before. They sounded like co-conspirators." *Now I've gone too far*, she thought. "They were whispering, I mean."

"What do you know about their relationship?"

"Hardly anything. She was a student of Melanie's at first but then switched to another teacher, Junsu Ito. She hasn't come to retreats here in some years, since she received transmission from him."

"Transmission?" Ray asked.

"That is when a teacher is preparing to die and passes his or her teaching mantle to a new teacher, usually a long-time student."

"So, Astrid Berg got transmission from a teacher other than Melanie Hirsh?" asked Ray.

"Yes. When Melanie left Wakeful Mind, Akira's sangha in Ojai, California, to come to New Mexico, Astrid stayed in California with Junsu Ito. She took over his community after he died, to continue his lineage." *Should I tell them about the scandal?* she wondered. *No, I don't need to go there.*

"Have you told Ms. Hirsh what you overheard?" Ulysses asked.

Jo nodded. "This morning."

"How did she take it?"

"Roshi Melanie was already very upset about Gerald when Tomàs and I arrived. She'd been crying," Jo said. "But she told us not to worry about it, that she would know what to do. That is typical for her. She never wants anyone to worry about anything."

"Okay, Ms. McAlister, that is all for now," Ulysses said, standing and stretching his long limbs. He looked at his watch and took a drink of water. "Would you mind sending Mr. Ulibarri to me right away, and then ask Ms. Hirsh to come at lunchtime?"

"Yes. What should I say to Alan?" Jo asked.

"Nothing yet. Just carry on with the retreat while you can."

•

Jo came downstairs. Someone, probably Tomàs, had closed the drapes in the living room and built up the fire in the kiva fireplace, where three upright piñon logs glowed red in the darkened room. She put on her coat and boots and found Tomàs getting into his truck.

"How'd it go?" he asked.

"Not too bad," Jo said. "Both sheriffs are nice enough. Alan Wolfe is angry he's not in control and is being difficult. Oh, and they want to see you next."

"Damn, I was headed home."

"They probably won't keep you long." They walked outside as a Taos deputy sheriff drove up. "Now what?" Jo asked.

"Maybe they have a warrant to search Gerald's house," Tomàs said.

Tomàs slipped inside and took off his boots, then knocked on the door of the interview room. "Sheriff Walker will be back in a little bit," Ray said and indicated a chair for Tomàs to sit and clicked on the tape recorder. "What is your name, job title and how long have you worked at Sleeping Tiger?" Tomàs wondered why this Picuris man was interviewing him instead of the sheriff. Jo had told him Ray was Picuris war chief and his cousin was the governor.

"Tomàs Ulibarri, maintenance, fourteen months."

"Where were you last night?"

"I spent the night in this house."

"What time did you go to bed?"

"I walked Jo McAlister's home, then came back here and read for about an hour. I guess I went to bed about 10:30."

"Did you hear or see anything suspicious during the night?"

"No."

"Would you hear a car starting up in the garage?"

"I would if I wasn't asleep. But I'm a pretty sound sleeper."

"Is this where you live?"

"No. I live about a mile from here toward Peñasco. I inherited my mother's property on the Rio del Pueblo. I was staying here to keep Melanie company after the first suspicious death."

"What is your relationship with Melanie Hirsh?"

"She is my employer."

"Nothing more?" Ray asked, raising his eyebrows.

"No. I am fond of her. Everyone is."

"Tell us about your relationship with Gerald Beatty."

"He was the boss of my boss, Jo McAlister. Jo is like a friend. Gerald was like a boss."

"Did you have any arguments or conflicts with him?"

"No. I try not to get into arguments if I can help it." Tomàs smiled. Ray did not. "I tried to do as I was told."

"What was he like to work with?"

Tomàs paused. "Well, mixed. He wasn't that in touch with what was going on around here so he left me alone a good bit. But then if he noticed something he didn't like he was all over me about it."

"He wasn't that in touch with what was going on?" Ray asked. The door downstairs opened and shut quietly and they heard someone coming upstairs.

"He was gone a lot, doing the shopping and whatnot. And when he was here, he was often holed up in his house working on the books. He didn't take a lot of interest in the plumbing or the vehicles, those kinds of things. Before I got here, he hired that stuff out."

The sheriff due to point of view came into the room sat down. He leaned back in the leather chair and folded his hands behind his head.

"Can you tell me about a time when he got upset with you?" Ray asked.

"Anything to do with repairs on his house was tricky. He was super private and very particular about me never going in there unless he was there. I did that once, early on, and he got furious with me and almost fired me."

"What were you doing?"

"Replacing parts on his downstairs toilet. I thought he'd be happy about it being fixed when he got back from town. I was wrong."

"When was this?"

"Right after I started here."

Tomàs shifted in his chair. The icicles on the roof were dripping in the late morning sun and the room was warm. He wondered what was for lunch.

"Did you know Luis Duràn?"

"Is he the man who fell off Lizard Head?"

"Fell or was pushed."

"I know some Duràns but not a Luis."

"Okay, Mr. Ulibarri, that should do it for now."

Ulysses asked, "Carmen is your aunt?"

"That's right."

"She's a great cook."

"She sure is," Tomàs said.

Ulysses and Ray stood up and shook hands with Tomàs and he went out and downstairs.

Ray said, "He didn't care for Beatty, that's for sure. He doesn't seem like a killer but he served in Afghanistan so he's learned how to kill."

"Killing in a war is different from cold-blooded killing."

"True. I'm just saying he would know how to do it."

"And he's someone who could have easily known both victims. Still, he doesn't strike me as a killer either. Should we let Ms. Hirsh eat before we interview her?"

"Good idea," Ray said. "I could use some lunch myself."

As if on cue, Jo and Dorcas came in with trays. Lunch was tortilla soup, green salad and tamales carnitas, a pot of coffee and flan for dessert. Ulysses remembered the tamales in the Expedition. *These will be better*, he thought. "This is very kind," he said. "You will have to let us pay."

"No, no," Jo said. "You're welcome to make a donation if you want. I'll get you a pitcher of water and some glasses from downstairs."

"Please tell Ms. Hirsh to eat before coming for her interview."

"I already told her. She's exhausted. It wouldn't be good for her to miss a meal."

The men ate in silence. Everything was fresh and delicious and there was plenty of it. The tamales were especially spicy thanks to Carmen's trademark red chile. As they were starting in on the flan Ray asked, "So what's the main takeaway from this morning?"

"That Beatty was an all-around unlikeable guy. And very touchy about his privacy. The guy was certainly hiding his financial shenanigans and probably more than that. I asked Angela to look into his background. I'll check with her after we talk with Ms. Hirsh."

"The piece about Alan Wolfe and Astrid Berg plotting against Ms. Hirsh was troublesome," Ulysses continued. "Wolfe was her student but also the chairman of her board? And Astrid was her former student and then "received transmission" from someone else? We should find out whatever we can about that Junsu Ito dude. Seems like having a former student made a roshi by someone else could create a few complications. What did you get?"

"Well," Ray said, "I've been thinking about who in this crowd is strong enough to get around in all this snow, especially in the middle of the night. Also, I was wondering if Tomàs is a little sweet on Jo. Tomàs may be a bit of a ladies' man, but Jo reminds me of a nun. A pretty nun, but a nun. And Alan Wolfe is going to be trouble."

Ray looked out the window. The sunny morning had clouded over and the wind was picking up. "Another front is coming in tonight, more snow," he said. "It'll probably be wetter snow."

Ulysses said, "Just when I thought we'd get a break."

Ray pushed back his chair and went outside for a smoke.

•

Roshi Melanie Hirsh silently composed herself in the interview chair. Her face was drawn and she looked small and frail in her black robes.

"Hello, Ms. Hirsh. I will try to be brief with my questions so you can get some rest."

"Thank you, Sheriff. I slept poorly last night."

"Please state your full name and your position here."

"Karen Melanie Hirsh, Spiritual Director, Sleeping Tiger."

"Where and when did you meet Gerald Beatty?"

"I met him in the 90's in California. He came to me for therapy. Before I became a roshi I was a psychotherapist."

"What brought him to therapy?"

"That's confidential, Sheriff."

"Mr. Beatty is dead."

"The dead still have confidentiality."

"Really?" Ulysses said, raising his eyebrows doubtfully. "How long was he in therapy?"

"About six years."

"That's a long time."

"But not unusual."

"When did he become your Zen student? "

"He showed up at Wakeful Mind when Roshi Akira was still alive and began his study. He took vows shortly before she died and then transferred to me after."

"Wouldn't that be a dual relationship? The kind that are frowned upon by mental health licensing boards?"

"We had completed therapy more than two years before, so there was no ethical violation," Ms. Hirsh answered, unruffled.

"Where were you last night?"

"I was here at the house."

"Who was with you?"

"Tomàs Ulibarri, my employee, stayed here in one of second-floor bedrooms. My bedroom is on the first floor."

"Did you hear or see anything suspicious last night?"

"No, nothing. I was awake off and on, but I didn't hear anything."

"Would you hear a car starting up in the garage?"

"No. My bedroom is on the northwest side, farthest from the garage. And my hearing isn't the best."

"You and Alan Wolfe had recently discovered that Gerald Beatty was mismanaging the finances, is that correct?"

"Yes, I discovered it quite by accident. I usually left the finances to Gerry. He did a good job; he was obsessive about it. But I went into the accounts about a week ago to prepare for a meeting with Alan. The annual board meeting was scheduled for right after Rohatsu. I was surprised at how low the operating account was. It was down $15,000 less than it was supposed to be. When I asked Gerry about it, he got very upset. He said he had borrowed the money but would pay it back very soon."

"Borrowed it for what?"

"He wouldn't say. He wouldn't answer any of my questions. He just said he would have the money back to me by ... today."

"Did you have any idea why he stole the money?"

"No. I believed he borrowed it for something very private and he would pay it back. Of course I told him that taking it in the first place was a violation of trust."

"What do you know about Mr. Beatty's habits that could cause him to take the money? Did he use drugs or gamble? Did he have debts he couldn't pay? Was he planning on starting another life somewhere?"

Ulysses studied Melanie Hirsh's face. She didn't make eye contact with him. She sat still and composed, and her voice was even and soft. She finally spoke up. "I don't know and I don't want to speculate. Not now. I just can't think about it because it is too painful."

"Do you know of any reason why someone would blackmail Mr. Beatty?"

"No, I don't," Ms. Hirsh said softly. She pulled a tissue out of her pocket and wiped her eyes. *Is she hiding something or still protecting "confidentiality,"* Ulysses wondered?

"Were there other accounts he handled for you?"

"Our investment accounts. We have an endowment, all of which is invested. Alan and I need to look into the accounts to make sure they are...," Hirsh paused, searching for the right word. "Untouched," she said, finally.

Ulysses and Ray exchanged glances. "So you don't yet know if he stole funds from the investment accounts?" Ray asked.

"No, not really—" Hirsh broke off. She made eye contact with Ulysses for the first time, her face ashen. "Sheriff, I know I trusted him more than I should have. This is a hard dharma for me." Her voice trailed off. She sat back in her chair and closed her eyes.

"What do you mean, hard dharma?" Ulysses asked, feeling irritation he hoped didn't show. He'd heard the word dharma for years but had no clear idea what it meant.

"It is a painful but valuable spiritual teaching," she said.

"Do you think Beatty was involved in other crimes?" Ray asked.

"I have no information that he was, " Hirsh said softly. "I really have nothing further to offer you."

"Okay, whatever," Ulysses said and looked at his watch. *This woman irritates me*, he thought. *She seems to be hiding behind grief.* The sky had darkened and it was looking like snow again.

"It's one o'clock. Why don't we take a break and you go get some rest? When everyone meets back up at two-thirty we can tell them the situation. You and I can talk more later."

"When can I see Gerald's body?"

"Possibly soon. I'll let you know."

Roshi Melanie Hirsh got up and left the room quietly. As he took the tapes out of the recorder, Ulysses heard her close her door downstairs. He stood up and stretched his arms and back, then went out to the Expedition, where Ray was talking on his radio. "Angela wants to talk with you," he said.

"What's up, Angela?"

"Lots, boss. Forensics is done with the victim's house. Found hardly anything. Beatty's phone and laptop are missing. He was burning paper in his woodstove recently, and there was something peculiar hanging from his bedroom door, a scapular of St. Michael the Archangel."

"Bingo," Ray said from the passenger seat.

Angela continued, "The trunk of his car was crammed with stuff including a lot of clothes, a passport and a big bag of cash. It looked like he was going on a trip. And Dr. Vigil has the postmortem report ready. He's ruling it a homicide. If you want, I can call the next of kin to come identify."

"Yes, please do. It's Melanie Hirsh. She is the boss here."

"Roger that. Also, I got the background on the victim. Looks pretty interesting—did you know he grew up in Santa Fe and was once a Christian Brother?" Angela took a deep breath. "Just two more things, Sheriff. An Agent Tallichet from Albuquerque FBI wants you to call her. And counsel says we can't keep people on site against their will under current circumstances."

"I expected as much. Text me Agent Tallichet's number. I'm going to get in cell range and make a few calls. Call Josh and get him to come back in. I'll call you back too."

Ulysses and Ray made a plan for Ray to interview Carmen and Dorcas while Ulysses was off site making phone calls. They also agreed Ray would be present to answer questions if Ulysses wasn't back at the end of the rest time when Melanie would break the news to everyone before the first afternoon sit.

The grounds were quiet and no one was out and about. Wet snowflakes swirled around in the variable wind, making the whole scene look like a shaken snow globe. As Ray headed into the kitchen to find Carmen, Ulysses drove to Peñasco, pulling up in front of The Double Rainbow, Peñasco's only restaurant. It was the lull between lunch and dinner and no cars were in the lot. Thinking he could make his calls in relative privacy, he went inside the empty café. Red leatherette booths lined three walls, and tables clustered around a central woodstove. A bar with stools occupied one wall in front of an old-fashioned soda fountain, and a shelf beneath the big mirror held four full cake stands. Ulysses helped himself to a cup of coffee and sat down in a booth by the front window. His phone was already buzzing. It was Rosemary.

"Did I get you at a bad time?"

"No, this is a good time. I'm at the Rainbow."

"Oh, good. Can you believe this weather?"

"How much accumulation are they expecting this time?"

"Another four to six inches."

"How are the kids?"

"Oh, they're fine, just a little cranky. The story hour at the library got cancelled. But they made another snowman, and now they're listening to music. How's the case going?"

"We've started the interviews. Not much yet. I got a call from Albuquerque."

"FBI?"

"Yep."

"Well, that's good, isn't it?"

"We'll see. I don't know this agent. She's new."

"Ah, a woman. That's good too, right?" Rosemary teased.

"We'll see. Look, I'm not sure when I'll make it home but I'll let you know."

"Ten-four."

"I love you."

"Me too."

Ulysses dialed the number that Angela had texted. "Tallichet," a woman's voice said.

"This is Sheriff Walker in Taos, returning your call."

"Okay. I was calling about the two homicides up your way."

"Are you guys getting in?"

"Very likely. Are the homicides related?"

"Looks like it but we don't have anything solid yet." The café proprietor, Ernest Charley, came over with a piece of carrot cake Ulysses hadn't asked for. *This job is going to make me fat,* he thought. He smiled at Ernie, seventy or so, with white hair and an imposing handlebar mustache, who disappeared back into the kitchen.

"I've got some background info," Tallichet said. "I'll be up there tonight. I'll call you."

"Good, " Ulysses said. "You've got my number. Cells don't work over at the retreat center, but they have a landline."

"I've got that number."

A few cars passed slowly on the road, churning up the wet snow. A man came in and picked up a to-go order. Ernie refilled Ulysses's coffee cup and returned to the kitchen.

Ulysses liked to come here whenever he was in town. Ernie and his wife Millie once lived at Vedanta and had been friendly with his parents. Millie used to babysit for him when he was a toddler, and Ulysses was close friends with their oldest son Jack, who ran a hunting lodge near Valle Vidal.

Against his better judgment Ulysses took a bite of the carrot cake, knowing he would now have to eat every last bite, it was so good. He called Angela next. "So tell me what you found out about Gerald Beatty."

"Born in California in 1970," Angela read from her notes, "adopted by Moses and Mary Bellows of Santa Fe and named David. Both parents are deceased and David was their only child. He graduated Santa Fe High School and attended College of Santa Fe, majoring in business. Entered the Christian Brothers in 1987."

"Slow down," Ulysses said. "He entered the Brothers at age 17?"

"Looks like it. It wasn't that uncommon back then." She continued reading. "Attended the College of Santa Fe, lived on campus at the college for two years, did not graduate, was sent to the Society of St. Michael Center in 1991." She paused to catch her breath. "Which is now Sleeping Tiger."

"Weird. He was sent to the rehab center for pedophile priests?"

"Not as an offender. He went there to work, evidently. He was there about two years. He turned up in the Los Angeles area in 1993. That's when he changed his name. And he's no longer connected with the Brothers."

"Any arrests?"

"Two, both in the early 2000's, both dismissed. Felony possession of methamphetamine and solicitation."

"Party and play?"

"Sounds like it."

"What did Vigil say about the cause of death?"

"Hypothermia. Traces of sewage on his hair and clothing. And we got the forensic report on the car. They didn't find any prints or DNA. It was wiped down pretty good."

"Jesus, whoever did this was being really careful. These are not crimes of passion. Thanks, Angela, I appreciate the info. Are you on tonight?"

"No, sir."

"Okay, I'm going to call Lorraine." Ulysses listened to his voicemails and finished his coffee. He placed a five-dollar bill under his coffee cup, then called Lorraine to review the roster for the evening shift and check on any important calls. There were none that couldn't wait. Ulysses stuck his head into the kitchen to say goodbye to Ernie. "Thanks for letting me use my 'Peñasco office.' "

"Anytime, Ulys. Give Rosemary and the kids my love."

"Will do. Where's Millie?"

"Upstairs taking a nap."

"I'd like one of those," Ulysses said as he headed into the cold. The snowplows were coming out from the DOT depot east of town. He waved to the driver and started back to Sleeping Tiger, reflecting on what he had learned.

Gerald Beatty had been a Christian Brother and had worked for the archdiocese at the Society of St. Michael before it became Sleeping Tiger. That explained how he found the "perfect property" for Melanie Hirsh and her small flock ten years ago—he had lived there. Ulysses wondered if the information might also provide a clue to Beatty's connection to Luis Duràn beyond the St. Michael scapular. How much did Melanie Hirsh know about Beatty's years as a Christian Brother? A lot, Ulysses guessed, given that she was his therapist for so long. But maybe not everything.

Angela was able to confirm what Ulysses had suspected after his interview with Melanie Hirsh: Beatty had been a drug user who engaged in risky sexual behaviors like picking up strangers. And then there was the matter of his name change. People in Taos changed their names all the time. Many of the old hippies Ulysses grew up among had adopted names. But changing your name when you moved out of state had a different connotation.

Ulysses wondered how much involvement the FBI would want from him. The relationship between FBI and law enforcement in northern New Mexico had never been particularly friendly. The FBI tended to consider the region "occupied territory" filled with suspicious Hispanics, unruly Indians and crazy Anglos living off the grid.

Before he headed back into a cell-phone dead zone, he called Lorraine and asked her to get Angela to look into Agent Tallichet's background.

The roads were getting slick as snow continued to fall. As Ulysses came around the curve before the driveway to the retreat center, he felt the vehicle's traction give way for a moment before grabbing the road again. He slowed down just as a man got out of a car parked on the verge.

Ulysses rolled down his window. "Want a ride up to the garage?" The man waved him on. *What is he doing out here?* Ulysses thought. He looked at his watch: 2:25. The first sitting of the afternoon block would be about to start. But when he pulled up, the retreat participants were gathered around the doors to the dining hall and slowly filing in. *I guess the word is out,* Ulysses thought.

Chapter VII

As Ulysses approached the dining hall, Jo McAlister came out to meet him. "Ray Pando came into the zendo with Alan and told us all to come with him to the dining hall. I guess he wants to make an announcement." Jo was out of breath and looked flustered. "I tried to make them wait for Roshi Melanie to get back but Alan insisted."

"Well, it's probably high time they knew," Ulysses said, going inside. The participants were sitting in twos and threes and whispering among themselves. Alan Wolfe stood next to Ray, who looked relieved to see Ulysses. A striking woman with short, spiky red hair and light blue eyes sat nearby, sipping a cup of tea. She looked Ulysses up and down and smiled at him. *Who is that*, he wondered. He walked over to Alan and Ray and asked Alan to step aside.

"Sheriff, we need to tell everyone what is going on," said Alan. "Right now."

"Mr. Wolfe, have a seat. Let me speak a moment with Mr. Pando." Alan, fuming, sat down next to the redhead, who looked bemused.

"What happened?" Ulysses asked Ray.

"You tell me. While you were in Peñasco I interviewed the two cooks, Carmen and Dorcas, and was taking some notes when Wolfe came over. He said he knew 'everything that was going on' and it was time to tell everybody. He insisted he would do it with me or without me, so I went with it. I don't think it is a bad idea, actually, Ulys."

Ulysses sighed. "How did he find out 'everything?' "

"Says the roshi told him."

"Why didn't he want to wait until she came back?"

"According to him it cannot wait a moment longer. He said 'liability issues.' My guess is he's trying to take charge with the roshi away."

"Let's get this over with," Ulysses said. "I'll handle it."

"Be my guest," Ray said.

Ulysses leaned against a column in the middle of the room. The man Ulysses had seen near the Forest Road verge came in and sat at a table near the door. *I need to learn who all these people are*, thought Ulysses, irritated that he was not yet up to speed on all the details.

Ulysses cleared his throat. All eyes turned to him. "Hello, my name is Ulysses Walker and I am the Sheriff of Taos County. This is Ray Pando from the tribal council of Picuris Pueblo. You have no doubt seen us coming and going the last day or so." He paused and looked around at the faces. No one was smiling and a few looked confused or alarmed. He continued. "We've had two suspicious deaths nearby that have now been ruled homicides. I am sad to inform you that one of those killed was Gerald Beatty."

There were murmurs of shock and distress. A young man spoke up in a startled voice. "Are you saying someone murdered Gerald?"

Ray answered, "Yes, that is what we believe. And you are—?"

"Jon Malvern," the young man said in a voice choked with emotion. "When was he killed?"

"Sometime very early this morning."

"What about the other death? Were they both killed here?" Malvern asked.

Alan Wolfe tried to take charge. "Neither man was killed here on the property. Listen, they don't even know if these deaths are related. They just want us—"

"Excuse me, Mr. Wolfe, let us handle this. If you would, please, be seated, " Ulysses said. Alan sat back down.

"Sheriff, why weren't we told? Are we safe here?" Gary Shumann asked.

"We are telling you now. We will do our best to keep everyone safe. We recommend—"

"What if we want to leave?" Gary asked, looking at his wife. Lynne was sitting with her hand over her brow and her eyes closed. "My wife is ill."

Alan said, "I demand we be driven to Santa Fe as soon as possible."

"Please remain calm, everyone," Ulysses said in his most authoritative voice. Then, in a gentler tone, he continued. "Right now, you cannot get to Santa Fe. The roads are very bad and getting worse. Highway 68 through the canyon will be closed soon if the snow continues as expected. Flights out of the nearest airports are likely to be grounded again at any time. And we would like to interview everyone before you go."

"I object, Sheriff," Jon Malvern said. "I don't think we should have to stay here." The other participants began to murmur in agreement.

Melanie and Tomàs came into the dining hall, their coats and hats dusted with snow and their faces flushed. Tomàs stood in the kitchen doorway and watched as Melanie scanned the room. She took a moment to grasp what was going on.

"Friends," she said. Everyone turned to look at her. "Let's not lose our purpose. We are here to experience the present moment in equanimity. Let's return to our retreat and let the sheriffs continue their work." For a few moments no one said anything. Roshi Astrid put down her tea mug and whispered to Alan.

"How long will these interviews take?" Alan asked.

"Not sure," Ulysses said. "But you should plan on being here tonight. "

Marci Kelly spoke up. "Why can't we stay at a hotel in Taos?"

"Once you are interviewed you can leave—if the roads allow," Ulysses said.

"Who goes first?" asked the man Ulysses had offered a ride to.

"Your name, sir?"

"Malcolm Downs."

"We'll take you one by one," Ulysses said, "and we'll try to make this quick."

Roshi Melanie spoke up loudly from the back of the room and everyone turned to look at her again. "My friends," she said more emphatically, "let's return to the zendo now. Remember, three things cannot long be hidden: the sun, the moon and the truth." She turned and left the dining hall, followed by Anne, Gary and most of the others.

Ulysses turned to Jo. "How many are staying here? We'll need a list with everyone's name."

"I made a list for you," she replied. "Ten, total. Three staff and seven guests."

"I also need the names of employees who come and go."

Jo went into the kitchen and spoke to Carmen. "Do me a favor? Can you give the list of maids and extra kitchen helpers to Sheriff Walker? I'd like to be in the zendo for the next sitting and Tomàs won't be back for at least two hours."

"I'll do it," Carmen said.

"Thanks." Jo walked out, noting that everyone had left except Roshi Astrid and Alan.

"Take me first," Alan said to Ulysses, "then Roshi Astrid."

"Sit tight," Ray said. "We'll come when we are ready for you."

Alan and Roshi Astrid exchanged a look and left the dining room. Ulysses nodded to Ray.

"Why don't you start with the woman who is sick? Lynne Shumann is her name, I think. I'm going to use the landline in Hirsh's kitchen to make some calls and then rest my eyes for a bit in the other upstairs bedroom."

Ulysses went into the library and closed the door. He called Angela. "What did you find out about Agent Tallichet?"

"She's brand new to the Albuquerque Bureau, thirty years old. Been in New Mexico about six weeks, four years total time in the FBI. Originally from Lubbock, graduated from Texas A&M, likes to ski, downhill and cross-country, fluent in Spanish, unmarried. When I suggested a meeting tomorrow morning she said she's coming up tonight."

"She should bring her cross-country skis," Ulysses said. "What's it like in town?"

"Very quiet. Everyone is hunkered down. Josh and Zach are out on patrol. A car turned over in the horseshoe curve south on 68, the driver was transported with minor injuries. Mark is coming in. Lorraine went home. Meghan is handling 911 now until Dakota comes in for the night shift."

"Thanks, Deputy." Ulysses hung up and dialed Agent Tallichet. "This is Sheriff Walker in Taos County. Got a minute?"

"Yes, I'm glad you called. What are the roads like up there?"

"Bad and getting worse. They closed the Rio Grande Canyon, but a badge can get through."

"Is that the way to come?"

"Definitely. The high road will be worse."

"I'd like to get up there tonight."

"Have you looked into anything on Luis Duràn?" *I can always ask*, he thought. Usually information traveled one way only—from local law enforcement to the FBI, not the other way.

"Why do you ask?"

"An agent out of your office—"

"John Poindexter?"

"Yeah, I know he's retired but I'd hoped to talk with him about some things, like Randolph Miller. Luis Duràn's mother kept house for him."

"Yeah, Pointdexter looked into all this before he retired but then it kind of went cold. I'll bring the files, but there's not much there."

"Is there anything that connects Beatty and Duràn? I figure if we can know more about what those two had in common it could lead us to the killer."

"Well, Beatty knew Miller before he was sent to Taos," Tallichet replied. "Miller had a parish in Santa Fe and Beatty's family, the Bellows, were members."

This was more than Ulysses usually got from the Feds. Maybe she was going to play nice.

"Where are you staying?"

"Sagebrush Inn, south of town."

"Call this number when you get in. I'll be here."

It was 3:00 p.m., naptime for Ulysses. He went up the stairs to the back bedroom, which was small and empty except for a double bed with a duvet and lots of pillows. Ulysses lay down and was asleep within a minute. He began to dream that he was flying over Taos. Below him were several angels with white-feathered wings and flowing robes. One of the angels looked up at him, revealing the twisted, hideous face of a gargoyle. It wielded a sword that shot flames into the houses and fields below. Several other angels were laughing demonically. Ulysses was falling from the sky when he woke up with a start, his heart pounding. *This was a genuine nightmare*, Ulysses realized. He wondered what it could mean. *Whatever it is*, he thought, *it isn't good. Now I've had three troubling dreams related to one case.* That had never happened before.

Ulysses tidied up the bed, then went into the bathroom to splash cold water on his face. When he came out, Lynne Shumann was exiting the interview room. She didn't speak or make eye contact but crept down the steps and slipped out the door. Ray was stretching when Ulysses came in.

"So what you got?" Ulysses asked.

"Lynne Shumann is one observant lady," Ray said. "She told me all about Wolfe and Berg going in and out of each other's rooms at all hours. She overheard some of their conversations, said she couldn't help it. Guess she hardly sleeps. She knew they were plotting to remove Hirsh. She's very loyal to Hirsh but thinks she gave Beatty too much leeway. Lynne Shumann knew about Beatty's history of drugs. She thought he had PTSD, maybe from something in his childhood. She also said she thought the red-haired woman, Astrid Berg, was up to 'her old ways,' seducing attractive men at retreats. Shumann thought she had her eyes on Malcolm Downs."

"I thought he had his eyes on her," Ulysses said. "I guess retreats make people amorous."

Ray looked out at the sky. "'Supposed to go below zero tonight, then clear off. But I don't think it will. Clear off, that is."

Ulysses said, "Didn't the old timers say it can get too cold to snow? Or is that a myth?"

"Usually it doesn't snow if the temperature is below 15 degrees."

"It's ten now and snowing like crazy."

"That's because there's so much moisture in the air," Ray said. "Should I get Alan Wolfe?"

"What did you find out from the two cooks when I was in Peñasco?"

"Carmen did not have kind words for Beatty. She said he hung out with the wrong kinds of people in Santa Fe—hard partiers, according to her Santa Fe cousin, whose son used to run with the same crowd. But her biggest complaint was that he was a terrible grocery shopper. Dorcas didn't have much information. But she also thought maybe Astrid and the guy from Los Alamos were getting pretty friendly. So, what's next?"

"Let's interview Gary Shumann. That way when he needs to leave with his wife, they'll be good to go."

•

The zendo was quiet and appeared tranquil for the first sit of the afternoon block. Jo noticed that everyone had returned after rest break except Alan and Roshi Astrid. Roshi Melanie led the participants walking in kinhin for almost ten minutes to settle their minds before zazen. When the first sitting was almost over, she went into her office to prepare for dokusan. During this first round of interviews everyone was supposed to present themselves to the teacher. *We each get two interviews today*, Jo thought grimly—one with Roshi Melanie and one with the sheriffs.

Jo heard Roshi Melanie ring the bell to signal she was ready. Gary, as jisha, got up and tapped Jo, Jon and Malcolm. They followed him into the hall. Jon and Malcolm sat in the two chairs placed there and Jo went into Melanie's office. She bowed deeply and sat in the chair across from her teacher. Roshi Melanie, who hated the cold, was wrapped in a wool blanket. She smiled at Jo and nodded, indicating she was ready to receive Jo's koan presentation.

Jo didn't know what to say. This didn't seem like the time to work on a koan. Everything felt upside down. "I'm very worried about what is going on," she whispered.

"Show me this *I* who is worried," Roshi Melanie replied. Her expression was stern.

Jo noticed feeling very irritated. How could Roshi Melanie remain in her role now, with everything going on? But had it ever been otherwise? Maybe if she nailed her koan she could get her to talk about something else.

"My elbow cannot bend backwards," Jo said. "Knowing this limitation, I am free."

"Yes, that's it," Roshi Melanie said. "We are free when we accept reality. Well done. Now go on to the next koan." She prepared to ring her bell.

"Wait, Roshi, we have to talk." Usually the words 'go on to the next koan' would have delighted Jo. It meant that she had "passed" the koan. But Jo wanted Roshi Melanie to talk about what was going on in the "real" world"— the breakdown of the sesshin and the threat of a killer on the loose.

Jo took a deep breath. "I am worried and I think you should be too. I don't believe we are safe here."

"Worries take you out of present moment" replied Roshi Melanie. "Nowhere is truly safe, or truly dangerous." She rang the bell to dismiss Jo.

Jo left the dokusan room feeling angry. Jon Malvern went in after her. Malcolm Downs moved closer to the door and Thérèse Boisvert filled the empty chair.

What in the hell am I going to do? Jo wondered. *I need to talk with Tomàs.* Just then Gary came up and whispered, "Can you take over as jisha? I just got called to be questioned." Without waiting for her answer he left. As she took her seat by the door Jo noticed that Roshi Astrid and Alan had come in and were sitting in meditation. *At least they are behaving themselves outwardly*, Jo thought. She tried to calm her mind but found her anger impossible to ignore. How could Roshi Melanie be so obstinate?

Jo dreaded the coming night: snow still falling, temperatures dropping and unknown threats lurking. From her EMT background Jo had the unshakeable conviction that safety always came first, and Roshi Melanie's insistence on staying in the sesshin felt downright crazy. She had never before doubted her teacher's grasp of the wisdom of the dharma, but now she found herself questioning everything. Who were these people who sat immobile with their eyes downcast when a killer was at large? And how could they call themselves Buddhists when they were ready to pounce on one another at the least provocation? *Wow, girl, you are getting carried away*, she thought. But she couldn't deny that the still, chilly room in which she sat no longer felt like a safe haven.

From her seat near the door Jo saw Jon Malvern come out of dokusan looking shaken and Malcolm Downs go in. Jo tapped Anne, the bell ringer, to take the seat in the dokusan line behind Thérèse. Anne passed the bell to Lynne. Jo returned to her cushion and had just started to settle when Lynne rang the bell signaling the end of the sit. Everyone stood, bowed, and began to walk slowly in the clockwise circle of kinhin. *I'm not sure I can stand this*, Jo thought. *As soon as Gary comes back, I'll go look for Tomàs.*

•

Ulysses settled in for an afternoon of interviews. Someone had cranked up the furnace and the room was overly warm. He hoped to send Ray home in a few hours. He knew that Ray would not object. In the meantime, Ray was downstairs interviewing Marci Kelly at the kitchen table. From time-to-time Ulysses could hear Marci's raised, emotional voice.

Gary Shumann came in quietly and sat down. He was a big man and fit for his age. He seemed at ease, relaxed even.

"Do you have any questions for me before we start?" Ulysses asked.

"No, not really," Gary said, wiping his glasses with a handkerchief and putting them on. "I am concerned about my wife and want to get her out of here. She doesn't take too well to stress these days."

"Name and occupation?"

"Gary Michael Shumann, retired."

"What did you do for work?"

"I was a high school physics teacher."

"Where were you last night?"

"In the dormitory asleep from about ten p.m. until five a.m."

"Can anyone vouch for your whereabouts?"

"I was in the bathroom twice during the night. Prostate, you know. I saw the guy from Los Alamos early—Malcolm—and the younger guy later. I think his name is Jon."

Ulysses made a note. "What time?"

"Not sure, maybe around 2:00 and then again around 4:00?"

"Did you see anything unusual during those times?"

"No. When I get up at night I try to enter my meditation practice. It makes it easier to get back to sleep."

"How long have you been associated with Melanie Hirsh?"

"Since the late eighties, when she came to Wakeful Mind for the first time," Gary replied. "We were all students of Roshi Akira together. Lynne and I met Akira in Japan in the seventies and helped her come to the US to spread the dharma."

"You've been Zen students for a long time?"

"Yes, since my early twenties. My wife even longer. We were both born in Japan. My parents were Christian missionaries. Her father was a rear admiral who was stationed there. We met at university."

"What did you know about Gerald Beatty?"

"Gerald came to Wakeful Mind in 1998. He was a favorite of Roshi Akira's and also of Melanie's. He was kind of troubled."

"What do you mean 'troubled'?"

"He seemed traumatized. He was anxious and irritable. As my wife says, he didn't read social cues very well. We were both teachers, so I guess we tend to make social diagnoses." He shifted in his chair and looked at his watch.

"Did you ever see any evidence of criminal behavior?"

"No. But people suspected him of using drugs and ... uh ... other things."

"What kind of other things?"

Gary's eyes flickered away from Ulysses's. For the first time he looked uncomfortable. "I have no first-hand experience of this, but he was suspected of seeking out underage sex partners."

"Where did you hear this?"

"Again, it was rumors. In Zen we try not to repeat rumors. But I will if you think it is necessary."

"You've said they were rumors. Go ahead," Ulysses said.

The older man took a deep breath and rubbed his forehead. "Roshi Akira's student Junsu Ito first came to Wakeful Mind around 1990. Junsu Ito was a very gifted man, intelligent, persuasive and, I think, ambitious. Roshi Akira respected his intellect and speaking talent. She gave him transmission before she died. Some people suspected Junsu Ito of misbehavior but it was never proven."

"What does this have to do with Gerald?" Ulysses asked.

"When Gerald arrived at Wakeful Mind, he and Junsu became friends. The rumor was that they frequented sex clubs together down in LA where there were underage prostitutes, boys and girls both." Gary cleared his throat and his ruddy face became redder.

"No one reported this?" Ulysses asked. He was feeling disgusted with this crew.

"No. So far as I know no one took it upon themselves to investigate and no, no one reported anything. Gossiping is discouraged as divisive speech. I think Melanie knew about the rumors but she didn't believe them. Melanie's mind just didn't go there."

"What do you mean?"

"Roshi Akira used to say 'true nature is Buddha nature' and Roshi Melanie, more than anyone I've ever known except Akira, tries to see Buddha nature in everyone. Not me. I've seen too much. Sometimes all I see is Mara, the adversary. I guess that's why Roshi Melanie is enlightened and I am not," Gary said, with a little laugh.

"Let me get this straight. There were rumors that both Gerald and Junsu Ito were engaged in sexual abuse of minors but no one said anything because they were trying to see the Buddha nature of the perpetrators?"

"I'm not sure Melanie knew about it."

"You said she didn't believe it."

"Isn't that the same thing?"

"It's one thing not to know and another thing to be in denial," Ulysses said. Gary said nothing. Ulysses took a drink of water and checked his temper. "You said it was never proved about Junsu Ito. Can you elaborate?"

"Before Roshi Akira died, she gave transmission to Junsu and to Roshi Melanie, including control over Wakeful Mind, which had become very successful financially. Typically only one person inherits that role so the battle was on for who would take over the retreat center. Roshi Melanie lost. The donors went with Junsu, but of course he was eventually disgraced. Which is why I don't call him 'Roshi.' Didn't Melanie tell you about it?"

Ulysses didn't answer, "Go on," he said.

"Well, Junsu was a better speaker, more dynamic, had the whole mystique going on," Gary continued. "Melanie couldn't compete. She just was not slick enough, too Brooklyn, and not business-minded. Anyway, a group of us split off from Wakeful Mind and came here. About five years ago Junsu got arrested with a fifteen-year-old girl. The scandal ruined him. He gave transmission to Roshi Astrid and then killed himself." Gary cleared his throat and looked out the window. "It almost destroyed Wakeful Mind. But they've gotten back on track in recent years, I think."

"How did Gerald do here?"

"At first he seemed to be doing better. But after about a year, Lynne and I suspected he was using again."

"Using what?"

"Cocaine, methamphetamine, alcohol."

"What made you suspect that?"

"Sometimes he was out all night. Then he'd come home and sleep all day, missing meditation. Lynne smelled alcohol on him, that kind of thing."

"Why did you leave Sleeping Tiger and go back to California?"

"This place couldn't support as many of us as we had originally hoped. Melanie's retreats never drew big crowds. It was too cold here for Lynne and the job market was terrible. We went back to get teaching jobs."

"Did you ever go back to Wakeful Mind?"

"God, no. This is the only place we do zazen. We love Melanie. But at home we've joined the Unitarians." Gary took a drink of water and relaxed in his chair.

Ulysses looked at his watch. It was three-thirty. "Thank you, Mr. Shumann, you can go back to the zendo now." Ulysses followed him down the stairs and went into the kitchen where Ray was writing notes at the table.

"Anything interesting from the woman you interviewed?" Ulysses asked.

"Marci Kelly. Yes, a couple of interesting things. Yesterday on the way to the dining hall she saw Jon Malvern peering into the kitchen window of Beatty's house. Then later that night she said she heard weird sounds in the attic."

"What kinds of sounds?" Ulysses asked.

"Knocking and bumping, that kind of thing. She's scared out of her mind and can't wait to get out of here. What did you get from Gary Shumann?"

Ulysses told Ray what he'd learned from Gary about Wakeful Mind, Junsu Ito and Gerald. "What is with these people?" Ulysses asked. "It seems like the more religious they are the worse they are."

Ray chuckled, "You just figuring that out, Bro? Seriously, abuse of kids is everywhere. Religious, nonreligious, every culture, all classes—you know this, Ulys."

Ulysses swallowed and shook his head. "Evidently, this Junsu dude was charged for sex with an underage girl. It had been going on for years, and nobody said boo. After he got caught, he passed his holy stuff to Astrid Berg and killed himself."

Ray whistled. "What did Shumann think about it all?"

"I'd say the guy has had a crisis of faith," Ulysses said. "He seems less a true believer than his wife, from what you said about her."

"I thought Zen didn't have beliefs," Ray said.

"I think that's a pose. All spiritual paths have beliefs. But still, don't you think it's interesting that Lynne said nothing about the underage kids and her husband spilled the beans? Usually it's the woman who tells the story."

"Maybe she didn't think it was relevant, Ulys."

"Not relevant? Christ, it may be the most relevant piece of all."

Ulysses thought about his nightmare. He was not a believer in dreams. But since he started paying attention to them, Ulysses had to admit that sometimes they gave him clues. The creatures that looked like angels were actually demons. *The unconscious is a powerful oracle,* Rosemary liked to say.

"What about the sounds in the attic of the dormitory?"

"Good question," Ray said. "Could be squirrels. They can make a terrific racket if there are enough of them. Listen, I'm going out for a smoke. Want me to get somebody for you?"

"How about Alan Wolfe?"

"Finally. But wait until I get back."

"No, let's do this now. You are smoking too much anyway. I'm going to tell Clarice on you."

Ray laughed. "You know how to scare me," he said. "Okay, I'll get him now."

When Alan Wolfe came in, Ulysses immediately noted the man was as tense and irritable as Gary Shumann had been calm and self-possessed. Wolfe glared. "I want you to know I will hold you accountable if something happens to any of these attendees."

"Noted," Ulysses said. He disliked this officious man with his superior manner. "Please take a seat. Tell me your full name and your role with Sleeping Tiger."

"Alan Wolfe, Jr. I am the chairman of the board. I am also the CFO of Sterling Real Estate Partners in Santa Barbara, California."

"Where were you last night?"

"I was in my room in the zendo from about 9:15 until just after 5:00 a.m."

"Was anyone with you?"

"No, I was alone all night."

That's a lie, Ulysses thought. "What was your relationship with Gerald Beatty?"

"We were both students of Roshi Melanie Hirsh." Ulysses also noted the past tense, Was Alan still a student of Melanie Hirsh?

"Did you know Beatty well?"

"Obviously not. And I have no idea who might have killed him."

"Other than being her Zen student, what is your relationship with Melanie Hirsh? Can you give me more details?"

"She is a long-time colleague and friend," he answered, looking out the window, where snow continued to fall steadily.

"Do you trust her?"

"I'm not sure what you mean by trust." Wolfe made eye contact with Ulysses for a moment, then shifted in his chair and looked away again.

"Do you think she is an honest person?"

"Yes, insofar as I know. I think she was very tolerant of some of Gerald's bad behavior. And I don't think she has a head for money."

"Have you and Astrid Berg been talking about replacing her as roshi?"

"That is none of your business."

"Are you refusing to answer this question?"

"Yes. It is not germane to your inquiry."

Ulysses made mental note to come back to this question. What did Wolfe have to hide?

"Have you looked into how much Gerald might have embezzled?"

"No. But I do know that money is missing from the operating account. I plan to look into the investment accounts very soon." Ulysses would bet that Wolfe had been all over the accounts by now. Why wouldn't he say so?

"What did you know about Gerald's relationship with Junsu Ito?"

"Nothing. I stay away from gossip."

"You had heard the gossip?"

"Yes, I had heard it. But I don't want to comment on it."

"Do you know anything about Gerald's past before he came to Wakeful Mind?"

"No. I never developed a personal relationship with him and no one ever spoke to me about his past." Wolfe took a deep breath and let out a loud sigh.

"What is your relationship with Astrid Berg?"

"She is an acquaintance." Wolfe looked down quickly and to the right. He had done that several times, and Ulysses thought it was a tell.

"How long have you been acquainted?"

"I met her when she first came to Wakeful Mind. Since she left, I have seen her only rarely… until recently." He looked down to the right again.

"Under what circumstances have you interacted with her recently?"

"We met in L.A. about a month ago."

"For what purpose?"

"I would rather not say."

"Was it to discuss replacing Hirsh as roshi?"

"How is this relevant?" Wolfe retorted.

Ray spoke up for the first time, surprising Wolfe. "Do you know any of the other participants at the retreat?"

"Almost everyone. It would be easier to ask who I don't know."

"Who don't you know?"

"That young man, Jon, I never met him. I have not met Malcolm Downs but I have heard his name. I keep track of who goes to sesshins in the region. I only recently met Thérèse and Marci when I visited Empty Sky, an old established Zen community in Scottsdale. Their roshi died suddenly earlier this year of an aneurysm."

"Are you aware of a relationship between Malcolm Downs and Astrid Berg?" Ray asked.

"No." Again, the look down and to the right, almost imperceptible.

"Okay, Mr. Wolfe, you can go back to the zendo."

"Sheriff, once the roads are cleared, I expect us to be allowed to leave. Please keep me informed about your progress with the interviews."

"Thank you. You can go now," Ulysses said, looking at his watch. It was nearly 4 p.m., time for several more interviews before dinner.

Ray watched Wolfe leave. "He obviously didn't want to talk about Astrid Berg. Or much else, for that matter."

"He's not only tightlipped, I think he's lying."

"About what?"

"I think he knew about Gerald's past and probably all about the business with Junsu Ito. And I wonder why he was at Empty Sky in Tucson? Do you think these Zen people recruit followers?"

"Not that I've ever heard." Ray laughed. "They seem like a pretty inwardly focused bunch."

"Yeah, but think about it. A big operation like Wakeful Mind or even a smaller one like Sleeping Tiger—doesn't it need to generate income by getting more members? It's a business. And doesn't every religion want more recruits?"

"No, Ulys, not everyone. We don't. We don't even tell anyone what we believe."

"Yeah, but you do let people come to your dances. Isn't the next one is coming up soon?"

"Day after tomorrow. The Deer Dance. Come by the house. Clarice is cooking."

"Are you dancing?"

"Hell, no. I'm too busy. But my son and granddaughter are. You come."

"See, you are recruiting."

Ray laughed. "No way, man. I don't think those Zen people do either."

"I think they do. When a roshi dies, there's a group of followers looking for a leader, maybe a new home. Whoever scores that bunch has more years in business to look forward to." Ulysses took a deep breath and let it out slowly. "Who's next?"

"How about the red-haired lady?" said Ray.

"Okay, Astrid Berg. I'll go get her. I need to stretch my legs."

•

When Gary came back to the zendo, Jo took the opportunity to leave. Her mind was a turmoil of doubt and confusion. She put on her coat, hat and gloves and headed out into the cold. The sun had just set behind the thick cloud cover, giving the landscape a gunmetal-gray gloom. Snow fell, slow and steady, but the wind had died down. Growing up in the Sierra Nevadas, Jo had seen snows like this go on for days. But this was unusual for sunny New Mexico.

Jo pictured herself in her parents' earth-berm house, hunkered down by the pellet stove with a book while her brother played Nintendo. Her parents were in the kitchen arguing. They never raised their voices, but the house was so small Jo could hear almost every word. She remembered they were arguing about Ananda Das, the spiritual leader of their community, a charismatic Indian man. Jo's mother was Ananda Das's secretary and her father had come to believe they were having an affair. Remembering, Jo felt the scared, sick feeling she had felt listening to her father revile the man she'd been taught to revere. That was the feeling she had in the dokusan room. Disillusionment.

Tomàs drove up the drive and parked his truck. He came out onto the walkway and found Jo standing there looking miserable.

"I need to talk with you," Jo said.

"Let's go to the library," Tomàs said. He closed the door. "What's wrong?"

Jo told Tomàs about her interview with Roshi Melanie and the feeling she had that something was terribly awry. "She's not herself, Tomàs. She's in complete denial about what is going on here."

"You think she doesn't want to face something?"

"I'm sure of it. She didn't want to face how thoroughly Gerald was not a good guy and now she doesn't want to face that we might have a murderer in our midst."

"Josie, I agree. She's distracted. She's grieving Gerald's death, his murder. Much as we couldn't stand the man, he was like a son to her."

"I guess," said Jo. She realized she had sounded panicky. Tomàs's voice was reassuring.

"Besides, Gerald was found over at Picuris. Why do you think the murderer is here?" Tomàs did not look afraid. He looked relaxed and calm. He put a hand on her arm. "Don't get me wrong, I don't think this is a safe situation either. There could be a murderer on the loose. I just prefer to think about how to keep the perimeter safe."

"Okay, then, how *do* we keep the perimeter safe?"

"Well, for starters, you aren't staying out there in the cabin. You should sleep in Melanie's other upstairs bedroom."

"I had already thought of that."

"And all of the guest rooms have windows and doors that lock."

"But most people have to go out of their rooms to use the bathroom. Should we see if we can get police protection?"

"Yes. Someone to watch the dormitory and the zendo."

"Should we tell Roshi Melanie?" asked Jo.

"What if she says no? I say we just go ahead and do it."

"It could permanently damage our relationship with her if we go over her head."

"And if we don't, someone's *life* could get permanently damaged."

Tomàs remembered reporting a problem with the wiring in one of the barracks where his men were housed at Bagram in Afghanistan. He feared someone would get electrocuted, but he couldn't get the captain to take him seriously. Nearly everyone in his unit had been shocked at least once in that bathroom, and everyone stopped taking showers there. Eventually a new arrival who hadn't been warned was so badly shocked he had to be medically discharged. Tomàs wouldn't let any boss override his safety concerns ever again.

"We have to be proactive. We should talk with the sheriff," Tomàs said.

"Okay, I'll do it the first chance I get." Jo turned to go. "I am dreading going back to the zendo. The hardest part is feeling I can't trust Roshi Melanie. I've always trusted her."

"Listen, Josie, no one is perfect. Melanie is kind and she's wise. But the person you most have to trust is yourself. If you don't trust yourself you will regret it."

"Of course, that's true. I just hate to be disillusioned."

"Would you rather be in the illusion or see reality as it is?"

"What are you, enlightened?" Jo asked. Tomàs laughed and put his arm around her shoulders. She wanted to go into the warm, bright kitchen with him and visit Carmen. Instead she knew she had to go back to the zendo. It was her duty, or so she thought. On the walkway she passed Sheriff Walker leading Roshi Astrid toward her interview.

Roshi Melanie was still conducting dokusan. Anne had gone in with Melanie, and Lynne sat in the other chair waiting for her turn. The rest of the participants were circling the room in kinhin. On the surface it was like any other long sesshin afternoon. Jo joined the line behind Thérèse Boisvert. She now had no koan to work on because she hadn't had time to look in her book for the next one. She began following her breath, her eyes focused on the bamboo floor and Thérèse's feet ahead of her and tried to get her mind to settle. *Probably I am overreacting*, she thought. What self-respecting murderer would be here at a Zen sesshin walking in a circle in a darkening room or sitting in a line waiting to talk nonsense?

Jo heard Melanie ring her bell and the door open for the next interviewee. Gary, covering for Anne, clacked the wooden sticks and everyone returned to their places. Kinhin was over. The participants stood with palms together, and at Anne's signal they bowed and took their seats. Jo listened to the sound of the ringing bowl dying away and felt relief at last in the silence.

•

Astrid Berg sat down across from Ulysses in the interview room. Ray sat in his chair by the darkening window. "How can I help, Sheriff?" She smiled, showing perfect teeth.

"State your name and relationship to Sleeping Tiger."

"Kathryn Astrid Berg. I am a friend of Sleeping Tiger and Roshi of Wakeful Mind Zen Center in Ojai, California."

"I just have a few questions for you." Ulysses took notes to avoid eye contact with Berg, who he sensed might be a pretty good reader of people.

"Certainly."

"Where were you last night?"

"In my room in the zendo from about 9:30 until about 6:00 a.m."

"Were you alone?"

"Yes."

"Did you come out of your room for any reason?"

"No."

"What was your relationship with Gerald Beatty?"

"He was an acquaintance from the past when we were both students at Wakeful Mind. Before I was elevated to roshi."

"Did you have any reason to dislike, distrust or fear him?"

"No." Berg's face was relaxed but Ulysses noticed she was gripping her hands tightly. *You are lying*, Ulysses thought. *Gerald knew all about Junsu Ito's behavior and maybe also about your arrangement to keep his secrets.*

"What is your relationship with Melanie Hirsh?"

"I am fond of Melanie." Astrid smiled. "We are peers." *You* would *emphasize your place in the hierarchy*, Ulysses thought.

"Were you her student at one time?"

"Yes, briefly."

"And how does she feel about you?"

"She is fond of me, I think." She gave an insincere-looking smile.

"Are you and Alan Wolfe discussing removing Ms. Hirsh from her position at Sleeping Tiger?" Ulysses watched to see if his question surprised her. It didn't seem to.

"Certainly not. Why would we do that?"

"Because of financial mismanagement?"

Berg lifted her long, reddish eyebrows and widened her light eyes. "I'm not aware of any mismanagement."

This is going nowhere, Ulysses thought. He wasn't willing to reveal what he heard from Jo McAlister. It was enough to know that this woman thought it was just fine to lie to a law enforcement officer during a murder investigation. He changed course.

"What did you know about Junsu Ito's illegal activities with underage girls?"

This question did not seem to surprise her either. She frowned. "I knew nothing about these allegations until they were made. They were never proven."

"Is it true that you kept his activities secret in return for being his successor?" Ray asked from the shadows.

Astrid looked over at him as if seeing him for the first time. "How dare you!" she said, sitting up in her chair and turning to glare at him. "Am I a suspect?"

"No, Ms. Berg," Ulysses said. "But we can't rule anything out."

She stood up. Ulysses noticed she was quite tall, over six feet, with broad shoulders and large hands.

"Please sit back down. I have a few more questions."

Berg sat down and took a deep breath. She looked far less composed now.

Ulysses searched his mind. What else did he want to ask her?

Ray again spoke up. "How do you know Malcolm Downs?"

"I met him at Wakeful Mind," she said impatiently. "At one of my sesshins."

"Who else do you know here?"

"Melanie, of course, and I had met her assistant, Jen, right?"

"Jo."

"Yes, Jo. And I know Alan, Gary, Lynne and Anne. I've met the Black woman; I can't remember her name. That's it."

"Do you know any reason why someone would want to kill Gerald Beatty?"

"No, I don't," Berg answered. "May I go now?"

"Yes, thank you, Ms. Berg."

She left in a huff. Ulysses felt he had probably gotten as much from her as he could in one interview. He couldn't rule her out as a suspect.

Chapter VIII

Jon Malvern came into the interview room and sat down with a sullen expression. "Can I leave after this?" he asked.

"We'll see," Ray said. Jon looked around at the older man as if he hadn't noticed him before.

"Tell us your name, age and where you are from."

"Jonathan Scott Malvern, 36, San Diego."

"What do you do for a living, Mr. Malvern?"

"I manage my family's properties," he said. "We own some apartment complexes and rental houses." He cleared his throat. Ulysses noticed that the skin around his eyes was swollen and puffy.

"How long have you been in this kind of work?"

"Since I graduated from college."

"Where were you last night?"

"In my dormitory room."

"All night?"

"I went to the bathroom in the middle of the night."

"What time?"

"I don't know. Well after midnight."

"You were seen on Gerald Beatty's front porch peering into his windows," Ray said. Malvern flushed. He turned to look at Ray with irritation and fear, Ulysses thought.

"When was I seen?" Malvern asked.

"Before the dinner meal."

At this answer Malvern appeared to relax. "I knocked on his door but he didn't respond."

"You knew Gerald Beatty?" Ulysses asked.

"I knew him years ago in L.A."

Ulysses looked up from his notes. This was interesting.

Jon continued. "We were ... lovers for about three years. Before he got involved with Wakeful Mind." He met Ulysses's steady gaze, then looked away. Ulysses noted that Jon's face was sweaty.

"Have you been in touch since?"

"Yes, mostly email. Sometimes we talked by phone. But I hadn't seen him in probably six months."

"Have you seen him since you've been here?"

"Just briefly in the dining hall, yesterday."

"Do you know anything about his death?"

"No. It's a ... shock." Malvern swallowed hard. For a moment he looked like he might cry, then he quickly recovered.

"Did he know you were coming to this retreat?"

"I didn't tell him but he must have seen my name on the list. He'd stopped answering my email. He never picked up when I called. I decided I'd just come ahead and surprise him. Then he was sick that first night and now ... he's dead." Jon's eyes filled with tears.

"How did you meet?"

"At church."

"A Catholic church?"

"No, Episcopalian. St. Bede's in Ojai."

"Were you both members?"

"My parents were. Gerald was going to the AA meetings there and then he started coming to services."

"How old were you when you met?"

"Fourteen."

"Was this your first sexual experience?"

"Yes."

"Did anyone know about this?"

"I think his therapist knew. But no one else." *Melanie Hirsh*, Ulysses thought.

"Were you angry with Gerald for molesting you when you were a minor?"

"It was consensual," Jon said. "I know I was underage, but I have never believed he molested me. When he broke up with me, I was devastated."

"Why did he break up with you?"

"He said his therapist was going to report us."

"Who was his therapist?" Ulysses asked. He kept his face and voice steady.

"He would never tell me," Jon said angrily. "We could still be together if not for her."

Jon was quietly crying. He tugged at the sleeves of his shirt. Ulysses noticed what looked like cuts on his left wrist.

"Have you also been in therapy?" Ulysses asked.

"What business is that of yours?"

"Just answer the question, please."

"Yes. I've been in therapy all my life, since before Gerald."

"Have you ever harmed yourself?"

"Can I go now? I feel sick to my stomach."

Ulysses spoke slowly. "Mr. Malvern, we would like you to stay in the vicinity until we can interview you further."

"You have no right to keep me here."

"We can talk again in the morning."

"Why? Am I a suspect?"

"I'm not charging you. But we need you to answer more questions."

Malvern stood up. "This is not right," he said angrily. "I'm going to call my attorney."

"That is your prerogative," Ulysses said. "You can go back to the zendo now if you like."

"I'm not going back in there. This place is a joke." Jon stood up abruptly, knocking over his chair. He glared at the two lawmen, then darted from the room and stomped down the stairs. He left the house slamming the door behind him.

●

"That guy clearly has a motive." Ray said after Jon had gone out the door.

"Yeah, for Beatty. But what about the Duràn murder?"

"We don't know for sure the same guy killed them both," Ray said.

"The scapulars?"

"Oh, yeah. But that doesn't really prove anything. Maybe Beatty killed Luis and someone else killed Beatty but they all three knew each other."

"And all of them liked St. Michael the Archangel?"

"Not all that far-fetched, Ulys."

"Granted. But, do you believe Malvern doesn't know that Melanie Hirsh was Gerald's therapist?"

"He knows," Ray answered. "Do you think that puts her in danger?"

"It makes me uneasy," Ulysses said. The two men went silent, wondering. "I don't think that guy is stable. Did you see his wrists? He's been cutting himself."

As the afternoon moved toward evening, snow was still coming down. Ray had said this was what winter used to be like years ago before warmer winters had become the norm. To Ulysses the weather just felt *wrong*. The question of keeping these people safe overnight loomed.

"I think we have time for one more," Ulysses said. "Who should it be?"

"What about that guy from Los Alamos?" Ray said. "He's the last male, right?"

"What are you, some kind of sexist?" Ulysses laughed.

"Look, man, where I come from it's the men who do the killing."

"Yeah, mostly," Ulysses said. "But there is at least one woman here who could qualify."

Jo McAlister approached Ulysses on the walkway to the zendo. "Sheriff," she said in a whisper, "can I have a word?"

"Of course," Ulysses said. They went into the library off the dining hall.

"I'm worried about the safety of our participants," Jo said. "With the weather I don't think anyone will be able to get to Taos. It'll be dark soon and the roads are icy. I think we need police protection tonight."

Ulysses took a deep breath. She was right and he knew it. How was he going to pull this off?

"I'll look into it, Ms. McAlister," he said.

"I can't take maybe for an answer, Sheriff," Jo said. "I believe we are at risk. We need someone on site periodically checking the zendo and the dormitory. There is a murderer at large."

"Listen, I don't want you to get, uh, overly worried." *Rosemary wouldn't like my choice of words*, Ulysses thought. *Damn.*

"I am *not* overly worried. I want to protect vulnerable guests on our property."

Ulysses had to admire Jo's comeback. "I need to consult with my staff and see who is available," he said. "But I'll do my best to have a deputy here checking on things during the night." Who could he spare? His only choice was Angela, and she was expecting the night off. On the other hand, she was the one he thought most capable.

"Thank you, Sheriff. That would be reassuring. I can make a station for him … or her, in here."

He paused. "Have you spoken with Melanie Hirsh about this?"

Jo frowned and shook her head. "I haven't. Roshi Melanie is not herself since Gerald's death. I am not sure she recognizes the true risks of a killer at large here. But I am quite worried and so are other staff, including Tomàs Ulibarri. We would feel a lot safer if you could have someone on site to help us … be on the lookout." Jo sensed that Ulysses was also concerned. This made her feel both reassured and more afraid.

•

Malcolm Downs followed Ulysses into the interview room and sat across from Ray, who was taking the lead. Downs nodded to both men and appeared unperturbed. Ulysses observed him from his chair by the window, noting the long blonde hair, large hands, no rings, short nails and a small Celtic cross tattoo on his right wrist.

"What is your name and age?" Ray asked.

"Malcolm Downs, 35."

"What do you do for a living, Mr. Downs?" Ray asked.

"I work at the Los Alamos National Laboratory."

"What do you do there?"

"What I do is classified. I can give you my supervisor's name and contact number if you need more information."

"Where do you live?"

"1201 Aspen Glen, in Los Alamos."

"Did you know Gerald Beatty?"

"No."

"Where were you last night?"

"I was in my room in the dormitory."

"All night?"

"Yes."

"Someone saw you in the bathroom at about 2:00 a.m."

"I had to go to the toilet."

"Did you leave the building?"

"No."

"What brings you to this retreat?"

"I've been interested in the practice of Zen Buddhism for a number of years."

"Do you know anyone here?"

"Only Astrid Berg. I met her at Wakeful Mind about four years ago."

"What is the nature of your relationship?"

"I'd say we are acquaintances."

"Nothing more?" Ray leaned in.

"Uh—well, we had a one-night stand during a retreat."

"Is that unusual?" Ray asked.

"Apparently not," Malcolm answered, smiling—*smugly*, Ulysses thought.

"Is that what brought you here, to reconnect with her?" Ray continued.

"No. I have no interest in her, neither sexually nor as a teacher."

"But you did have sex with her during a retreat she led?"

"Yes. She was seductive. And I was ... vulnerable. We had sex one time. I think she enjoyed it." Malcolm smiled again. His brown eyes were alert and intelligent.

"You were vulnerable?" Ray asked.

"Between girlfriends. Astrid is attractive. She seduced me and I succumbed."

"Do you know any of the other participants?"

"You asked me that. No, I do not."

"Did you know Luis Duràn?"

"No."

"Did you ever know a Father Randolph Miller?" Ulysses asked.

"The name is vaguely familiar. Didn't he disappear a few years ago? It might have been in the news? No, I don't know him."

"Have you heard of the Society of Saint Michael?" Ulysses watched for his reaction. None was apparent.

"Yes, I have heard of it but I don't know anything about it. Does it still exist?" Downs asked.

"No, I don't think so," Ulysses asked. He wasn't getting much of a reading on Downs beyond cheeky self-confidence.

"Where did you live before coming to Los Alamos, Mr. Downs?" Ray asked.

"I was at Cal Tech for several years in graduate school."

"Where were you born?"

"In Santa Fe."

"Did you grow up there?"

"My parents worked for the Lab. We lived in Santa Fe part of my childhood and part in Los Alamos."

"Okay. Thank you. You can go get your dinner," Ray said.

"Thank you, gentlemen." Downs nodded to them and left the room. Once he heard the outer door close, Ulysses said, "He is one cool customer. But with a secret security clearance he is used to answering questions. Did you notice the tattoo? It was a Celtic cross."

"Does that mean he's a Christian?" Ray asked.

"Who knows?" Ulysses said. "Maybe. And what about his remarks about Astrid Berg?"

"He's no gentleman," Ray said. "Are you going to get some dinner?"

"No, I got to go back to Taos. I'll get some there. You?"

"Clarice will have something at home. Matt is coming to pick me up at six."

"Jo McAlister asked to have law enforcement stay here tonight. I'm going to ask Angela to do it."

"She's good but don't you want one of the guys?"

"You got anybody you could spare?"

"Ulys, the war council guys all have duties for the dance. I got nobody I can send."

"Okay, then it's Angela."

"I'll see you in the morning, then" Ray said.

"See you then, my friend, if not before," Ulysses replied.

Now that he was alone, Ulysses realized there were still two more retreat participants to interview, Anne Stein and Thérèse Boisvert. He decided to start with the younger woman first and went down to the zendo to fetch her.

Once in the interview room, Thérèse sat down, still bundled in her purple parka and wearing a blue mohair beret. The expression in her dark eyes was wary and she looked sad and exhausted.

"What is your name, age and relationship to this Center?"

"Marie Thérèse Boisvert, 49. I am a retreat participant; I have no other relationship to Sleeping Tiger."

"What do you do for a living, Ms. Boisvert?"

"I am a clinical social worker, working mainly with children."

"Did you know either Gerald Beatty or Luis Duràn?"

"No."

"Where were you last night?"

"I was in my room in the dormitory all night."

"Did you hear or see anything unusual?"

"No."

"Were you familiar with any of the retreat participants before coming here?"

"I know Marci Kelly from my sangha, Empty Sky, in Scottsdale. Alan Wolfe and Astrid Berg, I have met. They came to Empty Sky in October."

"Why were they there?"

"Our roshi died a year ago in July, quite suddenly. We were devastated. We had a search committee for a new roshi, and Wolfe and Berg expressed interest in helping us."

"Was Berg looking to relocate?"

"No, they wanted to 'acquire' our facility, run lots of expensive retreats and have Berg be the titular roshi. I don't think she was planning to live at Empty Sky, just visit from time to time. We weren't interested." Boisvert paused and frowned.

"Go on," Ulysses said, feeling she had more to say.

"Roshi Patricia was kind. Everyone loved her—great speaker, good administrator, a role model. Our sangha was not similarly impressed with Roshi Astrid. Had I known she'd be here I don't think I would have come to this retreat." She paused.

"Go on, Ms. Boisvert," Ulysses said. "Is there anything else you'd like to tell me?"

"Yes," she said after a moment. "I've been thinking about this, Sheriff. A long time ago I met Roshi Melanie at a social work conference in San Francisco. She went by Karen Hirsh then. She spoke on a panel discussion about maternal grief and loss. The topic was trauma to mothers from surrendering babies at birth."

"You mean trauma from putting babies up for adoption?"

"Yes, it was a new idea then but now it is widely accepted that women giving babies up for adoption frequently have traumatic grief reactions."

"Was this an area of expertise for Ms. Hirsh?"

"No, she spoke from her personal experience."

"Do you mean she talked of giving up a child for adoption?"

"Yes, the panel was mainly focused on new research but Melanie spoke about her own loss."

"What did she say about it?"

"She said she'd always regretted giving up her son. Evidently she searched for her child for decades before finding him. By then he wanted nothing to do with her."

"Have you been in touch with her since the conference?"

"No, and I didn't realize who she was until today. It suddenly dawned on me during meditation that I had met her before and who she was."

"Thank you, Ms. Boisvert. When you go back into the meditation would you please send in Dr. Stein?"

Ulysses stood up and stretched. He reflected on what he had just learned about Hirsh. Could Gerald be her long-lost son? If so, why would they keep that a secret?

It was nearly five o'clock and starting to get dark.

Anne Stein came up the stairs and into the room quietly. She offered Ulysses her hand to shake—a small, strong hand.

"What is your name, age and profession?" Ulysses asked. The woman before him looked calm but wary. Inquisitive eyes set off her weathered face.

"Anne Stein, 60, professor of clinical psychology, UCLA."

"What is your relationship to Sleeping Tiger Retreat Center?"

"I am a founding member."

"Did you know Gerald Beatty?"

"Yes, fairly well."

"Where were you last night?"

"In my room in the dormitory all night."

"Did you hear or see anything unusual?"

"I didn't see anything but I thought heard sounds in the ceiling or in the upstairs of the dormitory."

"What did it sound like?"

"It sounded like something or someone moving around up there."

Ulysses made mental note to check the attic first chance he got. "Was it steady or intermittent sound?"

"Intermittent. It wasn't loud. I wondered if it could have been an animal."

"Tell me about Gerald Beatty and his relationship with Melanie Hirsh."

Anne sat for a few moments looking to the side, then met Ulysses's gaze. "Gerald was kind of a lost soul. He had a very difficult childhood, I believe. He felt his adoptive parents didn't love him or accept who he was. He struggled with his sexual orientation. He joined the Christian Brothers very young which just made everything worse for him. Roshi tried so hard to help him but he wouldn't really accept her help."

"He was born in California?" Ulysses asked. He wanted to know what this woman, who knew both Beatty and Hirsh, believed.

"I'm not sure where he was born. But he grew up in New Mexico. When he was in his twenties he went looking for his birth parents and came to California. He found his father and ended up taking his name, although later he said he was a hateful man. But he never found his mother. He was told she was dead. At any rate, Melanie was more of a mother to him than anyone, but he seemed to resent her no matter what she did for him. We have a saying in my field, 'Dependency breeds hostility.' "

"Is it possible that Ms. Hirsh *was* his mother?" Ulysses asked.

Anne looked surprised. "No, I don't think so. I guess it is possible. Melanie was about twenty years older than Gerald. But I don't see why she would have kept that a secret." Anne sighed and looked at her watch, then out the window.

"Did you know anything about Gerald and underage boys?"

"I heard the rumors but I never saw anything with my own eyes, no."

"Why do you think someone would want to kill Gerald?"

"I've wondered. He was always secretive. He had a hidden life that involved drugs and risky sex years ago, before he came to Wakeful Mind. Maybe he fell in with the wrong crowd again here."

"Or sought out that crowd?"

"Yes, that would probably be more accurate."

"Did you know anything about his financial mismanagement?"

"No. That never came up during the time I lived here nor since I've been on the board. Managing the money was his main job and he was good at it as far as I knew. But I try to keep my mind focused on the practice and leave people's craziness aside, frankly. I have a stressful work life at the university and come to retreat to get away from all that. Usually I am able to. This time, not so much. It's pretty hard to stay focused with a murderer on the loose."

"What do you know about Alan Wolfe?"

"I've known Alan Wolfe many years. As my wife would say, 'He means well, bless his heart.' He's a difficult personality but is not a bad man. He used to be quite devoted to Roshi Melanie. Now I'm not so sure."

"What was his relationship with Gerald?"

"He tried to honor his vows and not hate Gerald," Anne said dryly, "but I think he mostly failed. Alan believed Gerald was a bad influence on Melanie and bad for Sleeping Tiger. Alan had invested a lot in this place, both financially and emotionally."

"Did you ever see them argue?"

"Several times. Alan has a bad temper and Gerald could be very provocative."

"Did they ever become violent?"

"No, no—at least I never saw it. But it's not that hard to imagine."

"What do you think of Astrid Berg? Do you know her well?"

Anne sighed and shifted in her chair. "I've known Astrid about fifteen years, since when she first came to retreats at Wakeful Mind. She kind of attached herself to me at the beginning. She was bright and attractive and she got noticed by Roshi Akira and Junsu Ito, among others. Still, to me Astrid seemed to have an emptiness at her core that Zen didn't touch. She once told me that as a child she'd been obese and other children bullied her. When she was in junior high she started to run track and became an elite athlete but it didn't really help her make friends. She could never overcome the feeling that to be accepted you have to be the best, the center of attention, all that. It makes her exhausting to be around. When I heard she was coming to this retreat I almost bowed out. But I didn't want to leave Melanie to handle it without full support. Melanie is a good person.

Good, and kind. Maybe a little naïve at times but a wonderful teacher." Anne's eyes filled with tears. "I hate that this is happening to her. It feels like her whole world is coming unraveled."

They sat in silence for a few moments. Anne wiped her eyes and took a drink of water.

"Thank you, Dr. Stein. You've been very helpful."

"Sheriff, are you going to have deputies present tonight? I don't think we are safe here without somebody."

"Yes, ma'am, we will. But everyone should lock themselves in their rooms as well."

"I usually have to go to the bathroom at least once a night," Anne said. "What should I do about that?"

"Maybe the women can go together in pairs to the bathroom," Ulysses said. "Unless there are any chamber pots around."

"I doubt if there are, but I'm going to look for one."

•

Ulysses drove slowly through the high-road villages and down to the main Taos road. The snow-packed road was all but empty of cars. Many houses had their Christmas decorations up, evergreen trees ringed in colored lights, lit-up wooden Santas with sleds and reindeer, even a few early farolitos. Ulysses thought over the afternoon's interviews.

What was the connection between the two murders? *Was* there a connection? What did the Saint Michael scapulars signify? Who among the people he interviewed had a potential motive and were physically strong enough to kill Beatty?

Among the men, there was Jon Malvern, the lover spurned. Alan Wolfe hated Beatty and was looking into the books he kept—possible embezzlement—but would that be motive enough for Wolfe to kill? Maybe there was more bad blood between them that hadn't surfaced. Wolfe and Berg both said they did not like Beatty, but then so did many others.

Astrid Berg was strong and physically fit. Gerald had known about the sexual abuse by Junsu Ito. Was it possible that she wanted to silence Beatty? Junsu Ito's suicide was well known to have been connected to his abuse of minors—no secret there. She may have been carrying other secrets, though, and maybe Gerald knew something damning about her?

She was known to engage in sexual escapades of her own, but presumably they were with consenting adults.

Gary Shumann had no apparent motive and seemed unlikely to be a killer, but Ulysses had learned to be skeptical of that sense *seemed*. Shumann was strong and fit and he knew the place well. Could he have had some hidden hatred for Gerald from their time together founding Sleeping Tiger? Then there was Malcolm Downs. Ulysses wondered why a scientist with a top secret security clearance would be attending a Zen sesshin. Was he just wanting to reconnect with Astrid? He seemed to have no established connection with Beatty.

At this point it seemed like any of these five could have killed Beatty. But why would any of them kill Luis? Ulysses hoped Agent Tallichet had some information that could shed light on a connection between Beatty and Luis. Ulysses mused on the possible familial connection between Melanie and Gerald. Did that matter at all to this murder investigation? He doubted it but it did seem to explain the protective mantle she continued to cast over him.

As he came into the outskirts of Taos, Ulysses realized how much he was enjoying working this case. Being out in the field felt like a welcome break from dealing with employees, budgets and office politics. Unlike those activities, Ulysses felt confidence about his abilities investigating a crime. But he knew such work was likely to be only a small part of this job over the long term since the crime rate was low in Taos County. *Enjoy it while it lasts*, he said to himself.

Ulysses arrived at the office just as Lorraine was getting ready to head home. She'd put up lights and a Christmas tree in the main room and set a crèche on her desk that Ulysses thought might break some law against religious displays in public offices. "Hi, Sheriff," she said, slipping on her coat. "Did you get any dinner?"

"No, not yet. What's been happening?"

She picked up her notes. "It's been mostly quiet all afternoon. Everything is closed except Albertson's. Fire and rescue have been busy though. There was a kitchen fire at the Garlic Lover Restaurant, no injuries, not much damage. Two men from El Prado got in a fight at Allsup's in Questa, but no one got hurt. Josh went out on a two-car collision south of town about an hour ago but I haven't heard back. Dr. Vigil said the toxicology report came in on Luis Duràn. He said he tested positive for methamphetamine, alcohol, cocaine and codeine." She grabbed her handbag and started out the door.

"Oh," she said, turning back, "the FBI lady has checked into the Sagebrush Inn. She wants you to call her. And Rosemary called. Said not to worry, everything is good."

"Okay, thanks, Lorraine. When did Angela leave?"

"About 3:00. Zack is coming in fifteen minutes."

"Who's on the phones tonight?"

"Dakota. She's in the back room right now."

"Okay, and thank you. You've done a great job these past few days."

"Thank you, Sheriff," Lorraine said, looking pleased as she headed out the door.

Ulysses called Angela and left a message asking her to call him as soon as possible. He was going to ask her to stay the night at Sleeping Tiger. Then he called the Sagebrush Inn and arranged to meet Agent Tallichet for dinner. It looked like the Wildflower Café was still open when he drove south of town to the hotel, a good place for comfort food.

Agent Tallichet stood under the front canopy of the Sagebrush Inn when Ulysses pulled up. She walked toward the Expedition, all of five feet tall, slender, wearing a black wool tam, jeans and a blue parka the color of her eyes. She put out her hand. "Sheriff Walker."

"Call me Ulys," he said, shaking her hand.

"LizBeth. Where're we going to eat?" She had a Texan accent.

"A little place called the Wildflower Café is open. I'll drive."

She picked up a bulging shoulder bag. "I've got some background notes for us." *This is different*, Ulysses thought.

LizBeth slid into a booth across from Ulysses. She pulled off her tam and ran her hands over her short blonde hair. The diner was empty and they ordered right away, a cobb salad for LizBeth and fajitas for Ulysses, coffee for both. Ulysses updated her while she took notes on a small laptop. She asked few questions as he detailed what was known about each murder and the background on Sleeping Tiger, Picuris Pueblo and the interviews completed thus far.

The waitress served them and set the check on the table. "We're closing at seven, due to the weather," she said. "Here's a carafe of fresh coffee if you want any, no charge." Then she retired to the kitchen.

"So what've you got for me?" Ulysses asked.

"Not a lot but what I do have is interesting," LizBeth said. "I got it from John Poindexter. I spoke with him this morning. Remember, he was the agent investigating Randolph Miller's disappearance." She pulled a stack of files from her bag and began paging through them.

"Miller had been pastor of a church in Santa Fe from 1975 to 1990, where he was accused of abusing both boys and girls, though it was hushed up and no charges were ever brought. Gerald Beatty's family attended that church in Santa Fe, Santo Niño, so they knew Miller."

Ulysses sat silent, eating his chicken fajitas.

Liz Beth continued. "Turns out Miller had friends in high places. They sent him to Taos, to be pastor of Saint Anthony's in Rancho de Taos. Casimira Duràn was his housekeeper. Poindexter thought he likely abused Silvia, Luis, and maybe a cousin, Elías. It appears also that Sheriff Trujillo was buddies with Miller. As was the archbishop, Sullivan, can't remember his first name."

"John," Ulysses said. "He's still the Archbishop. Must be over eighty. I know all this."

LizBeth looked up. "Okay, that's good," she said not taking offense. "Poindexter said Miller was a frequent guest of Sullivan out at the Society of Saint Michael, so he had to know Gerald there. And every year between '91 and 2000 Miller ran a two-week retreat for boys up in the Jemez Mountains. Literally hundreds of boys attended these things over that time period. Poindexter planned to interview one of Miller's assistants, but didn't get around to it. He said I should make sure and talk to him."

She dug in her bag for another file. "The assistant was a former Christian Brother, name of Eduardo Santos. He lives in Velarde. I checked and I think he's still at the same address. From the transcript it seems like Santos knew of both Luis Duràn and his cousin Elías Chacón. I'm going to interview him. My guess is he knows a lot and may establish a connection between Gerald Beatty and Luis Duràn."

Ulysses polished off the fajitas and poured himself and LizBeth cups of coffee. LizBeth had hardly touched her salad she was so busy talking. "Miller disappeared in 2012 on a Sunday afternoon in early May," she continued. "It was a busy day—big Mass for Pentecost Sunday, then a lunch at the rectory to honor Miller's anniversary of ordination. Then somehow Elías Chacón falls off the roof and dies. Poindexter originally thought it was a suicide, but he became convinced that Luis Duràn pushed him. He could never prove it. Miller wasn't implicated in the death because he was in his kitchen with some of the church ladies when Elías fell."

LizBeth took a drink of water. "Luis denied being on the roof and no one could be certain they saw him up there. At any rate, Sheriff Trujillo was called and Elías was pronounced dead at 2:30 p.m. Miller was not seen again after about 5:00 p.m. that day. His car was found parked near the Taos Junction Bridge the next day. It was wiped of prints, and empty except for a religious article."

"What religious article?"

"This," Liz Beth said, holding up a photograph of a scapular. "It was hanging from the rearview mirror."

"That's three for three."

Liz Beth looked puzzled. "You know what this is?"

"It's a scapular, something worn by religious Catholics, especially in the old days. St. Michael scapulars were found near the bodies of Luis Duràn and Beatty," Ulysses explained. "Whoever killed them must have also killed Miller. St. Michael is an avenging angel who wreaks havoc on devils."

"That's what I read too. Sounds like our killer is a fan." LizBeth tucked the photograph into her bag, put away her files and began eating her salad.

Ulysses's phone rang. It was Angela. She was coming down with a cold and sounded terrible. "I'm going to be unavailable for at least twenty-four hours while I try to beat this," she said. "I don't feel like having it hang on until Christmas."

"Go home and cuddle up with Mr. T," Ulysses said. "We've got this." He didn't feel anywhere near as confident as he sounded. Who else could do this? Once he hung up he texted Josh, Zach and Mark asking them to text him their whereabouts.

"I'm not feeling so cheerful about having an avenging archangel loose at this retreat," Ulysses said as they got into his car. "I was going to send my best deputy but she's sick. We're short-staffed right now."

"I'd like to go out there, but I don't want to stay the night," LizBeth said, looking at her watch. "It's seven o'clock. Can we go now?"

"I need to go home and check on my family," Ulysses said. "Why don't I meet you back at the Sagebrush at nine? Take a nap—we might be there awhile."

"Who's going to cover the rest of the night?" LizBeth asked.

"Whichever deputy gets back to me first." As if on cue, Ulysses's phone dinged with a text. "Looks like it's going to be Josh."

Chapter IX

Carmen had been cooking all afternoon while events, snow and worry swirled around in her mind. She was serving "make your own frito pies" with homemade corn chips, hot red chile, pinto beans, carnitas, cojita, salsa and guacamole. There was also tortilla soup and brownies for dessert. This meal was usually a crowd pleaser, but tonight the participants didn't look pleased. Tomàs came up behind Carmen and gave her a hug.

"Smells divine, Tìa," he whispered.

"Then why is no one eating it?" she whispered back. Dinner was half over but most of the food remained.

"Maybe you should serve beer with it," he said, laughing. Melanie looked over her shoulder and put her finger to her lips.

Tomàs thought the crowd looked thin. He counted heads, something he had always done on patrol and now was second nature. Four people were missing: Astrid Berg, Alan Wolfe, Jon Malvern and Malcolm Downs.

Once the slowest eaters had finished, Anne signaled and they all stood and bowed. Melanie spoke. "My friends, I know today has been stressful for you. I am also feeling the presence of Mara interfering with my peace. But isn't life like this? Don't give in! We will begin our evening zazen practice at 7:30. In the meantime, stay in your practice."

Jo went into the kitchen to speak with Tomàs. "Will you go with me to Roshi's to tell her I asked for police protection?"

"Of course," Tomàs said. "Did you notice four people missing from dinner?"

"Four? I only counted two."

"Berg, Wolfe, Malvern and Downs."

"Downs came early and carried his food out. Roshi Astrid said she had a bad headache and didn't want dinner."

"Okay, that leaves two unaccounted for."

They walked toward Roshi Melanie's. The snow had finally stopped. The sky was overcast, the wind was still and the temperature was in the teens. Jo knocked on the outer door and went in. The living room was dark but a light was on in the kitchen. Roshi Melanie came out of her bedroom. She'd been crying.

"I'm so glad I have the two of you," she said, trying to smile. "This is so hard. I wish it could all go away. But I know I have to face it."

"It is terrible to lose someone you love like this," Jo began.

Roshi Melanie interrupted. "Oh, Jo, I have to be honest. It isn't *just* Gerald, though God knows that's... horrible. It's Astrid and Alan, and the finances, it's everything." She wiped her eyes and invited them to sit. "I guess I'm feeling sorry for myself." Melanie adjusted her robes and cleared her throat to compose herself. "What did you want to talk with me about?"

Jo and Tomàs looked at each other. Tomàs said, "We spoke with Sheriff Walker. He thought we needed someone here overnight and said he would send one of his deputies."

Roshi Melanie looked skeptical, but Jo continued. "I made a space in the library the deputy can use. I'll feel better knowing someone is checking ... the perimeter." Tomàs winked at her.

Roshi Melanie sighed. "I know the sheriff is right," she said. "Whoever killed Gerry could be here in our midst and could kill again. I feel terrible that I've put all these people at risk."

"It isn't you who've put people at risk, ma'am," Tomàs said. "This isn't your fault—"

"Tomàs, some of this *is* my fault. I just..."

"We need to talk to the participants about sticking together and locking their doors and windows," Jo said, interrupting. "People should go in pairs to the bathrooms. I suggested to Gary this afternoon that he sleep in Lynne's room tonight. Astrid and Alan have ensuite rooms too."

"We can tell them a deputy will be here through the night," Melanie said. "I hope that will ease their minds. I'm going to end the retreat in the morning and get everyone out of here as soon as the sheriffs give me the go-ahead."

"The roads should be plowed and passable by mid-morning unless we get more snow. I know most people will want to leave early," Jo said. "I'm so sorry that your celebration turned out so terribly."

"We'll get through this somehow," Roshi Melanie said softly. She gave a rueful smile, stood up and returned to her bedroom. Tomàs and Jo went out and stood on the portal. With the moon two days into its waning phase the early evening was dark. Jo was surprised to feel Tomàs's arm around her shoulder. She leaned into his chest and he turned to kiss her. Jo kissed him back, surprised at herself. She pulled away at last feeling sheepish and confused.

"Do you need to get anything from your cabin?" Tomàs asked.

"I should get my pajamas and toothbrush. But I don't have time now. I need to ring the bell in ten minutes. What are you going to do?"

"Be on the lookout for the deputy, walk him around the place, check the generators. Those sorts of things."

Jo smiled and Tomàs started to kiss her again. Suddenly Roshi Melanie opened the door, wrapped in her coat and scarves. She looked at them a long moment. "I'll be in my study," she said, and headed toward the zendo.

●

The evening segment's first sit began at 7:30. Jo noticed that Alan, Jon and Astrid were missing. *Astrid must have turned in early*, she thought, *but where are Alan and Jon?* The schedule called for more dokusan tonight, but no participants had put out cards indicating they wanted an interview with Roshi, which meant that Melanie meditated with them at the head of the room, looking still and serene. Many of the other participants, Jo included, were fidgety. A few were dozing. Jo was glad Astrid wasn't there with the kyosaku. She would have had a field day tapping shoulders.

As she practiced zazen, Jo focused on the center of her body, away from her anxious mind and aching legs. She inhaled deeply and then exhaled for even longer, trying to settle into the present moment. She noticed sensations similar to how she'd felt when she had her interview with Roshi this afternoon. She acknowledged how full of doubt she was. What was testing her faith now? she wondered, then let that thought go.

A memory arose of the morning her mother left the family. It was in the early spring, a windy, raw day, and the fire in the woodstove had gone out overnight, leaving the kitchen ice cold. It was a school day, but no one had come to wake her or her brother. When she came downstairs, her father stood at the sink crying. He didn't notice she was standing there listening. She'd never forget the sound.

I'd better not let this feeling run away with me, she thought. She'd never really recovered from her mother abandoning them and going off with Ananda Das, the guru of their community. She'd lost her mother and her entire belief system in one fell swoop only a week after her twelfth birthday.

Jo put out her card requesting dokusan. Gary tapped her shoulder and led her to the waiting chair just as the bell rang for the end of the sit. As kinhin started Roshi came down the hall and went into her study. After a few moments she rang her bell and Jo went in. The two bowed to each other and Jo sat down.

"I need to tell you how I was feeling when we last spoke," Jo said.

Her teacher nodded, listening.

"I was very angry when you wouldn't take my fears seriously."

Roshi Melanie nodded again.

"It started to make me doubt you."

"Go on," Roshi Melanie said, looking calm and focused.

"I have had losses that make it hard for me to trust." Jo had never told Melanie about her mother. She'd told very few people, because remembering it made her re-experience everything.

"Sometimes it isn't wise to trust individuals. Trust the dharma."

Jo took a deep breath. "I want to trust you. I really do. But I'm afraid."

"There is no *me*, no *you*! Separation is a disease of the mind," Melanie said. "There is no separation between me and you, between me, you and the person who killed Gerry. Trust that."

Jo said nothing. Her mind was reeling.

"It's like Sengstan said," continued Roshi. "'Make the smallest distinction and heaven and earth are set infinitely apart.' What good is it to be a Buddhist only when all is calm and to lose your equanimity the moment things get chaotic?"

"I know," Jo said, "I am trying to remain focused. But why are there so many unscrupulous people on this path?"

"What 'unscrupulous people' are you speaking of?"

"You know who I mean," Jo said, trying not to show her impatience. "The killer, Astrid, Junsu Ito. Gerald!"

"'In choosing to accept some and reject others, you become blind to the true nature of things,'" Roshi Melanie said.

"Stop quoting scripture at me," Jo said quietly.

"I suggest you let go of both doubt and belief," Melanie said. "Recognizing that all things are essentially empty, you can live in your heart, without fear. Only then will you see your way clearly. That is what you must do, dear one. I also must practice this." Roshi Melanie rang the bell to dismiss her. Jo stood, bowed and went back to her mat, in more turmoil than ever. Malcolm went in to dokusan as she came out.

The evening was torture for Jo. She struggled to stay in her practice. Her face itched, her back hurt, her legs ached and she felt like crying. Her mind wandered over the past: her mother, Tim's last days, but finally it came to rest on Tomàs's kiss. She liked the way he smelled. She liked the way he kissed. But it was ridiculous to think it could go on. It was completely inappropriate. She was his boss!

The sit dragged on. Twenty-five minutes felt like an eternity, but at last Anne rang the bell. As Jo got up, she noted that her feet were as numb as stones. During kinhin people were coming and going from the bathroom. Therèse went for dokusan and Marci Kelly was sitting in the waiting chair. *At this point,* Jo thought, *you go into dokusan just to escape the cushion.* Jo peeked at her watch: 8:30, only thirty minutes to go. She noticed car lights coming up the drive. A few minutes later she heard voices, Tomàs and another man, the deputy probably. She went out, glad to have a task to perform and to escape her swirling thoughts.

•

Ulysses arrived home before Rosemary had put Amelia and Monty to bed. He took off his boots and coat, locked up his gun and came into the kitchen just as they came out of their bath, flushed pink from the hot water and ready for pajamas.

"Daddy, Daddy!" Amelia said. "What do you call a herd of buffalo taking a poop?"

"I don't know," Ulysses said. "Smelly?"

"A turd of buffalo," Amelia said, cackling. Rosemary came up and kissed Ulysses. "Welcome to my world," she said. Ulysses followed the children upstairs and got them into their pajamas. Monty informed him that it was his night to pick out the story. He had his favorite, "The Gorilla Did It," which Amelia hated.

"It has no words!" Amelia said. She was teaching herself to read and dismissed mere picture books as beneath her.

"It *does* have words," Monty said. "Daddy tells the words." He handed Ulysses the book. For once Amelia gave in and the two children snuggled next to their father on Monty's twin bed while Ulysses narrated the picture story of a little boy who kept doing naughty things and blaming it on an imaginary gorilla. It was a short story, so when he finished, he was cajoled to "read" it again, and even a third time. Then he tucked Monty into bed first, then Amelia, kissed them both goodnight and turned off the lights.

He found Rosemary in the kitchen. She'd made a pot of herbal tea. "You have time for a cup?" she asked, sensing that he was going back out.

"Sounds good. How was your day?" he asked, stroking her hair.

"I'm getting cabin fever." She poured him a cup of Roast Aroma. "But I'm okay. We're fine."

"I have to meet Agent Tallichet in about an hour," he said.

"I can always tell when you don't get into your skivvies that you are headed back out. What's she like?"

"Very young," Ulysses said. "But nice. I like her." He sipped his tea.

"Should I be worried?" Rosemary was the jealous type, in a reasonable sort of way.

"I think she's gay."

"You're going back to Sleeping Tiger?"

"Yeah. I'll show her around and we can make sure things are as secure as possible. I sent Josh over there too but it could be more than he can cover by himself. Not sure when I'll be home." Ulysses put several logs in the woodstove.

Rosemary sighed. "You must be so tired. I don't know how you do it."

"You must be tired too, with those little monkeys."

"I took a nap today when they went down for one. How's the investigation going?"

"It's a strange one," Ulysses said. "Do you remember about seven years ago when that priest disappeared from the church at Rancho de Taos? Randolph Miller?"

"Vaguely."

"Seems like his disappearance and these two murders are connected."

"How do you know?"

"I can't say. But it seems likely we are dealing with a repeat killer."

"No wonder you don't want to leave those people out there unprotected."

They drank in silence for a few moments. Rosemary took his hand and squeezed it. He squeezed hers back.

"I got a nap today, too, but I had a nightmare," he said. "It was a flying dream. I was flying over Taos, which was on fire. And below me were a bunch of flying angels who looked like gargoyles. Then I started falling and woke up. Whew!"

"Sounds lovely," Rosemary said. "What do you make of it?"

"I don't know except this thing is all bound up in religion. And you know how I feel about religion."

"Are you having more dreams lately?"

"Definitely. And they are getting darker."

"Ulys, listen to me. This is why I want you to delegate more crime fighting to your deputies. I don't think you've ever gotten over killing that man at Fiestas. It changed you. I don't want you to go through that all over again."

"It goes with the territory, Rosemary. You know that," Ulysses said.

•

Jo was determined to settle her mind during the evening's last sitting. No matter what, while on the cushion her practice had to take priority. Roshi Melanie had come back into the room to join the sangha for the sit, bringing her sutra notebook for the evening reading. Jo made a point of not checking who was there and who was missing, keeping her eyes focused on the floor in front of her mat. *This will be the last sit of this terrible sesshin*, she thought, then pushed that thought aside.

A fox shrieked causing her to break out in goose bumps. She thought of the old song her dad used to sing, "The Fox Went Out on a Chilly Night." As a child she'd been troubled by the lyrics about a fox killing penned-up ducks and geese: "He didn't mind the quack, quack, quack and the legs all dangling down-o." Her father used to laugh at her distress and remind her how in the end it all turned out okay because "the little ones chewed on the bones-o." She knew the little foxes had to eat but that never relieved her concern for the poor ducks.

Jo returned to her practice and thought she might be overreacting now, just as she had as a child. She dismissed that thought, and the next thought, and the next. Then the thought arose that she should check on Astrid, Alan and Jon. She remembered hearing that Roshi Patricia at Empty Sky had not shown up for an early sit and was found dead in her bathroom later that morning. She'd had an aneurysm burst and she died in the shower while everyone was sitting in zazen. *I have no desire to go checking on Astrid*, she thought, *which is probably precisely why I should do it.* Jo was brought back from these thoughts by the final bell of the evening. She felt dismay that focused practice, usually relatively easy for her, had seemed to elude her entirely.

As the sound of the ringing bell pulsed through the room, the participants sat, awaiting Roshi Melanie's evening message. She opened her sutra book and read from the Abhaya Sutra, one Jo had never heard her read. It was a discourse on the fear of death and how those who have abandoned passions and illusions no longer feared death. *Interesting choice*, Jo thought, looking around the shadowy room.

Roshi Melanie put down her book and spoke to the group. "This is the last sit of our sesshin. We must end early. In the morning you will be able to leave for Santa Fe or Albuquerque to return to your homes, weather permitting. Tonight keep to the silence and stay in your practice. Do not walk outside alone. Go in small groups to your rooms and lock yourselves in. Make sure your windows are locked. Do not go to the bathroom alone. Law enforcement personnel will be on site patrolling for your safety. The silence will end at dawn. Breakfast will be served at 7:00."

Anne rang the bell and everyone stood, bowed and began to file out of the zendo. Jo felt tension underneath the silence. Gary followed Lynne into her room and closed the door.

Jo knocked softly on Roshi Astrid's door. There was no answer. Maybe she was asleep? Jo also knocked on Alan's door. No answer there either. She put on her wraps and went outside. Tomàs was waiting for her near the door to the dining hall.

"Want to get your stuff from the cabin now?" he asked.

"Yes, I do, thank you," Jo said, and they started trudging across the snowy field toward Jo's cabin at the edge of the woods. Jo told Tomàs that neither Roshi Astrid nor Alan had answered a knock on their doors.

"Alan is at Gerald's house going through the finances. I saw the light on up there and went over to check."

"Isn't that off-limits?" Jo asked, alarmed.

"He said Melanie gave him permission."

"Maybe Astrid is there, too?"

"Could be. I didn't go in."

"I saw Gary and Lynne go into Lynne's room and lock the door."

"We should check all the doors in the dormitory. And also the boiler."

"Okay, let's get my stuff first and then go back that way."

Tomàs stomped the snow off his boots while Jo unlocked the door. The cabin was freezing, since the stove had long since gone out.

"Do you want me to build you a fire?" Tomàs asked.

"No," Jo said, "I'll just be a minute." She collected her nightgown and slippers and toiletries and put them in a small backpack. She felt nervous being alone with Tomàs. What if he tried to kiss her again? *I have to say something*, she thought. Tomàs was sitting in the rocker when she came back in. "I'm ready," Jo said, not looking at him. She opened the door.

"It seems like you are feeling uncomfortable," Tomàs said.

Jo turned to face him. "Oh, Tomàs, I can't … Yes, I am uncomfortable. We can't have that kind of relationship. I'm sorry."

"I understand, Jo," Tomàs said. "We are very different people."

"It isn't that, Tomàs. I am your boss. It is unethical."

Tomàs laughed. "Then I'll quit." He stood up. "No, say no more. We can be friends. Good friends, no?"

"Yes, we can be friends." She smiled at him and they shook hands.

"Let's get back," Tomàs said. "You must be tired."

"It has been a very long day." Jo felt relieved that she'd told him her feelings. They would put the kisses behind them.

Jo locked the cabin door and they headed up the hill toward the dormitory. They checked on the participants in the dormitory and reminded them of the safety precautions. Everyone was in their rooms with their doors locked. The boiler was functioning without problems and the building was warm. Jo was concerned about the tumbling noise it was making but Tomàs assured her that he had heard that many times before. He thought it was related to the hard water. As they walked out Jo said, "We should ask Alan if he's seen Roshi Astrid."

"Why don't you go ahead to bed," Tomàs said. "I'll go check on her before I turn in."

Jo yawned, exhausted, and readily agreed.

•

About an hour after the evening sitting finished and everyone had left the zendo, Astrid Berg stepped out of the shower and toweled herself dry. She examined her body, pleased with the tautness of her arms and legs (that new, very sexy trainer) and frowning at the dimpling in her fleshy bum. Her breasts, small, upturned with pink nipples, continued to look young, an advantage of never having borne children. She brushed her teeth and smoothed expensive face cream onto her well-preserved skin paying especial attention to her neck where she'd started to notice the slightest sagging. She put on cologne, slipped on a silk dressing gown and got into bed.

Astrid was glad she'd taken the night off. She hadn't really had a headache. She needed time to absorb what it meant for her now that Gerald was dead. Finally, there was no one to question her transmission ever again! At least no one with first-hand knowledge. Astrid felt pleased with her achievements. She'd been a roshi now for five years. Wakeful Mind, her center in Ojai, had fully recovered from its slump and the accounts were at an all-time high. She was even attracting a couple of Hollywood A listers. Her bid for Empty Sky in Phoenix had been unsuccessful, but now Alan wanted her to take over here. Of course she'd never be tempted to live here even part time, but if she could limit it to being "in residence" a few weeks a year she would consider the possibility. Being head roshi at a number of centers would be good for her brand. She could easily hire someone to cover for her while she was away. *Someone like that girl, Jo, maybe. She seems to have a good head on her shoulders. Or just let Melanie stay on as an assistant, that might work too.*

Astrid had nothing against Melanie. She was unsure of what people saw in her. The woman was pious but naïve and mediocre. And a terrible manager. Alan had every right to be displeased since it was mostly his money she was wasting. Melanie really hadn't deserved Roshi Akira's transmission. She was too weak. Junsu Ito, of course, had all the right traits to take over Wakeful Mind, smart, a good speaker, a good business head. Too bad he had that underage girl problem. Astrid smiled to herself remembering how skillfully she'd parlayed her knowledge of Junsu Ito's secrets to convince him to transmit to her. Remembering Junsu's fall she felt a twinge of guilt which she quickly put aside. *Why should I feel guilty about his sins? If I'd spoken up it wouldn't have saved those girls. They were already damaged. Far better that I could use what I knew to get Junsu to appoint me roshi. It was so convenient that he then killed himself! And now with Gerald also dead, no one will ever really know the whole story. All that's left is rumors and rumors fade over time. Meanwhile, I am advancing the dharma from a position of strength!*

Astrid snuggled down in the bed and began touching herself. An image of Malcolm Downs came to mind surprising her with its lusty intensity. Malcolm wasn't handsome, really, his eyes were a tad too close together. But he had the kind of body Astrid favored. She remembered when she'd been with him at a retreat, what was it, four years ago? He'd been muscled but lean like a wrestler then, with very little body hair. Since then he'd put on a few pounds but he would still be as well-endowed. Sex with him had been unsatisfying before because he lacked technique but he had plenty of staying power. Perhaps she could educate him about how to please her. There was undoubtedly something very sexy about Malcolm. Astrid couldn't decide what it was. Was it the long blonde hair or was it a hint of something kinky about him? She hoped to discover more tonight.

Before dinner she'd invited Malcolm to come by after the last sit and told him she'd unlock the door that led from the walking garden into the zendo. That way he could slip into her room without having to go by Lynne Shumann's room where she might hear him. But now Gary snoring away in the room providing additional sound cover. Alan was still up at Gerald's rummaging around.

Astrid heard a soft knock and jumped out of bed. She opened the door, grabbed Downs by the arm, pulled him into her room and locked the door.

∙

Ulysses set his canteen and the snack Rosemary had packed for him on the front seat of the Expedition. Although he felt restored by the brief visit home, he dreaded the night ahead. He responded to a text from Josh, who was now at Sleeping Tiger and wouldn't likely get it, to say he was on his way.

He ran a plan through his mind. If they could just get through tonight, he could send most people home in the morning. He would interview Shumann one more time very early and would ask Wolfe, Berg, Downs and Malvern to stay in Taos for further questioning. Agent Tallichet could have a go at them. He would also check in with her about backgrounds on those she planned to interview who were outside his jurisdiction, like Eduardo Santos.

And as soon as Angela felt better, he'd have her doing background checks. There were the two seemingly related murders of Duràn and Beatty, the presumed death of Miller, who knew Beatty and two other deaths, Elías and Silvia. *I'll figure this out*, he assured himself, although he couldn't think how. It was the most complicated case he'd ever handled.

LizBeth was out front of the Sagebrush Inn at nine o'clock when Ulysses pulled in. She got in the front seat and slung her backpack into the back seat. When she unzipped her parka Ulysses could see her shoulder holster and gun, which looked all the larger due to her small frame.

"Did you get some rest?" Ulysses asked.

"No," she said with a chuckle, "I was on the phone and wrapping up some paperwork. Did you?"

"No, but I got to put my kids to bed and see my wife."

"Did your deputy get out there?"

"Yeah, he texted me from Peñasco."

"So once we get there will anyone be awake?"

"Most people will have turned in. We can go to the main house and check in and you can meet the head lady. Then I'll walk you around the buildings and you can get the lay of the land. It's going to be really cold, not to mention dark, so we won't see the whole property."

"I'm glad your deputy will stay overnight."

"Josh isn't the brightest bulb. But if we can get the place buttoned down we can go home and get some rest, then come back in the morning. And if Josh needs backup during the night, he can call me."

LizBeth was quiet. She knew how different Taos County was from most other places she'd ever been. Not knowing its culture, terrain and history put her at a disadvantage.

The road was snowy and icy in places and its surface shone in the moonlight. In Peñasco, Ulysses's cell rang and was picked up by the bluetooth in the car.

"Hi, Ray," Ulysses said. "I've got you on speaker. Agent Tallichet is in the car with me."

"I just thought I'd say goodnight. Where are you?"

"I'm on the way to Sleeping Tiger to orient her. Josh should be there by now."

"Call me if you need me. Matt will come with me. He's on the war council now."

"He's just a baby."

"He's your age, Ulys. The council doesn't have to be old guys."

"Well, get some rest, Ray. Let's hope it's a quiet night."

"Sorry I didn't introduce you," Ulysses said when Ray hung up. "That was Ray Pando from Picuris. He retired from the Albuquerque police a few years back. Worked as a homicide detective for twenty-years and since the murders took place on or near Picuris land we are working together. He's also a friend."

"Tell me about the Picuris," LizBeth said.

"They are a small tribe, related to the Taos tribe, same language group. Been on their land about 1500 years. They used to be much bigger before the Pueblo Revolt in 1680. They were persecuted because they helped drive out the Spanish."

As they came onto the property Ulysses noticed that the driveway needed plowing. The snow was up to the Expedition's axles. They pulled up to the garage and saw that lights were on in the dormitory and in the main house. All the other lights, including those in the zendo, were out. Ulysses looked again. Lights were on in Gerald Beatty's house, just behind and to the west of the dormitory. "Who in the hell is in there?" Ulysses said angrily. "That's a taped crime scene."

Chapter X

When Jo came into Roshi Melanie's house, the lights were out in the kitchen and living room. Assuming Melanie had gone to her room, Jo crept up the stairs to the interview room, slipped out of her retreat clothes and put on her white flannel nightgown. Someone had stacked clean sheets and towels at the foot of the room's single bed, and Jo quickly made the bed and went to take a shower. As she was waiting for the water to get hot, she heard someone unlock the front door, come in the house, lock it again and come upstairs.

"It's me," Tomàs said to reassure her, when he heard the water running in the bathroom.

Jo got into the shower and allowed the steamy water to flow over and soothe her exhausted body. She wondered how the events of the past two days would affect her future. She felt profoundly uncertain about the survival of Sleeping Tiger, given Alan and Astrid's scheming. What would happen to Roshi Melanie? Would Jo be able to remain, and would she continue as Melanie's student? For the first time since coming to New Mexico Jo wondered if her decision to leave everything behind in California had been the right one. If she left now, where would she go?

Jo hoped the long hot shower would help her sleep. She toweled dry her hair, put moisturizer on her face, brushed her teeth and left the bathroom, turning out the light. The house was silent. Tomàs must have gone to bed. She assumed he had found Astrid or he would have told her. Jo went into her room, locked her door and got into bed. Before long she was deeply asleep. She didn't hear Ulysses and LizBeth knocking on the front door an hour later.

Tomàs, with Melanie behind him, let Ulysses and LizBeth in. Alan Wolfe and Deputy Josh Montoya came in with them. Tomàs built up the fire in the kiva fireplace and Melanie turned on the lamps on either side of the couch. Ulysses introduced everyone to Agent Tallichet.

"Would you like some tea?" Melanie offered.

"No thanks, we don't mean to stay," LizBeth said. "Sheriff Ulysses has shown me around. The FBI is taking over operations." She placed her card on the coffee table. "You can reach me at this number." LizBeth paused and dropped her smile. "Ma'am, we found Mr. Wolfe here in Gerald Beatty's office going through his papers. He said he had your permission, is that right?"

"Yes," Melanie said.

"Well, he doesn't have ours," LizBeth said. "No one is to go into that house or disturb its contents. It's a crime scene, do you understand? Anyone going in there will be cited and charged."

"Of course, Agent Tallichet," Melanie said. She looked at Alan, who nodded to her but said nothing. Josh remained standing, hat in hand. His eyes were fixed on LizBeth. The wood in the fireplace popped.

"Tomàs came to find us, concerned about the whereabouts of Ms. Astrid Berg. Everyone else is accounted for and in their rooms. Deputy Montoya checked," LizBeth continued. "Has anyone seen Berg this evening?"

"She came to the house to meet with me before dinner," Alan said. "We had arranged to meet at that time. After a short while, she said she was getting a migraine headache and went back to her room to take medication and try to get some sleep." Alan paused. "She takes Dilaudid for the really bad ones. And she uses earplugs. There's no doubt why she didn't answer her door. She's probably out cold."

"Who else wasn't at dinner?" Ulysses asked.

"Jon Malvern didn't come," Tomàs said. "Malcolm Downs came early and left with his food."

"Well, they are both accounted for," LizBeth said, looking at Ulysses. "We are going to leave you in Deputy Montoya's hands for the night. He will be based in the library off the dining hall. He has a set of keys and will walk through each of the buildings several times during the night. In the meantime, please stay inside and keep the doors locked. I'll be back in the morning around 8:00 a.m. No one is to leave until I give the go-ahead, hear?"

Alan started to pipe up and then seemed to think better of it. Melanie said, "We told people they could leave first thing."

"Well, you told 'em wrong so we'll have to correct that," said LizBeth

"Will you be coming back, Sheriff Walker?" Tomàs asked.

"Josh can reach me if I'm needed," Ulysses said. He stood up and warmed his hands by the fire. He was surprised by LizBeth's authoritative tone. Josh also seemed to get the message that this small woman was not to be trifled with.

Outside the dining hall door Ulysses took Josh aside to repeat his orders. The young man looked sleepy but he had a thermos of strong coffee to help him stay awake. Ulysses gave him the meal Rosemary had packed: homemade bison meatloaf on whole wheat bread with sundried tomatoes and onions and an oatmeal raisin cookie, all of which was no doubt tastier than the baloney sandwich Josh had packed for himself.

Ulysses and LizBeth headed back to Taos. The sky was clearing and the waning moon was midway up the sky. Ulysses dropped LizBeth off at the Sagebrush and checked in at the station. Dakota was on the phones in the front room and Mark was on patrol. So far it was a quiet Tuesday night in Taos County. Home and bed were starting to feel very enticing.

•

Tomàs woke with a start. He sat up, confused for a moment about where he was and why he was awake. He leaned over to switch on the light but it didn't come on. He got out of bed and tried the overhead light. The power appeared to be out again, which meant he needed to get the generators going and check on the boiler in the dormitory. He cursed softly as he got out of bed and dressed in the dark.

The gas-powered boiler, connected to a radiant heat system, was old and cranky and had a pilot light. Power outages raised fears for Tomàs about carbon monoxide even though the system supposedly had failsafe mechanisms and there was an alarm fitted. Tomàs dressed quickly and headed out into the night of clear, starry skies. From the position of the moon he figured it was between 2:00 and 3:00 a.m.

Tomàs went to his truck and got out a flashlight and tools. It was bitter cold but at least it was not windy. As he made his way up the snowy hill, he felt the knot of dread in his belly he used to feel on night patrols in Afghanistan. The big stone dormitory loomed ahead. For a moment he thought he saw a light flicker in one of the upstairs windows. Tomàs watched as he walked closer but he saw nothing else. *I'll tell Josh about it when I finish with the boiler*, he told himself. *He can check it out.*

When he entered the east door Tomàs wondered how long the boiler had been out. The dormitory was already getting chilly. The building was too big and had too little insulation to stay warm for long. He flicked on his flashlight. No one was in the hall and all the doors were closed. As he passed the staircase leading to the upstairs, he shone his light up at the door. Closed, as always.

He went into the boiler room and unpacked his tools, squatting by the big silent machine.

Tomàs began the process of troubleshooting. The pilot light was out, which could cause problems when the power came back on. Tomàs was looking for his lighter to relight the pilot when he felt something cold against the back of his neck. It was the barrel of a gun. A voice whispered, "Turn off your flashlight, stand up slowly and don't make a sound."

Tomàs did as he was told. "Back out with your hands up. Close the door behind you." Tomàs felt intense fear, a flood of adrenaline and a collapsing sensation in his guts. His heart was pounding and he broke into a rank sweat. He remembered this feeling from combat and steadied himself with a deep breath. Images of his family and his farm arose in his mind. He saw an image of Jo right before he'd kissed her.

I can do this, he said to himself as he backed out of the boiler room. He resolved to kill whoever was threatening him, with his bare hands if necessary.

Even in the dark Tomàs sensed the identity of his abductor from his body mass—Malcolm Downs, he thought, younger, maybe fitter but smaller than me. As Tomàs led the way toward the east door with Downs behind him, his mind was racing. Maybe he only had a few moments to act. What should he do?

The gun pushed deeper into the back of his neck. He heard Downs muttering to himself in Latin. Tomàs vaguely recognized the words, the Dies Irae, a prayer from the Mass for the Dead.

"Hail Mary, full of Grace, the Lord is with you," Tomàs said softly, hoping to distract his attacker.

"Shut up," Downs growled.

"Please don't kill me, Brother," Tomàs said. "Let's pray together."

Downs continued mumbling.

They crept down the icy driveway Tomàs in front and Downs right behind with his gun pressed into Tomàs' back. No one was stirring and all the buildings were black. The moon was directly overhead, illuminating the expanse of snow and the dark woods surrounding Sleeping Tiger. Tomàs caught his breath to try again. "Let's pray, Brother. Our Father—"

Downs cut him off. "If you make another sound, I will kill you."

Tomàs knew Downs meant what he said. In fact, it was just a matter of time before he would *have* to kill him because of what Tomàs now knew. They walked past the path to Roshi's house and then past the dining hall and the zendo. As they came to the garage area, Tomàs remembered Downs's car parked at the end of the driveway on a pullout of the Forest Road. He wants to take me offsite and kill me, he thought.

Downs's car had been dug out from the snow and the windshields wiped clean of snow and ice. Tomàs noticed that he had chains on all four tires. *This guy was prepared before I came along. Wonder where he was going and why?*

As they neared the car, a dim sketch of a plan developed in Tomàs's mind. Downs would no doubt try to put him in the trunk. When he was fiddling with opening it, Tomàs would make his move. He would try to tackle him and get his gun or run for his truck where he had a loaded .45 in the glove box. It would be risky but not riskier than getting in that trunk. Tomàs imagined with deep satisfaction blowing the guy's head off. They neared the car, a heavy Audi sedan. Downs went to open the trunk. As if divining Tomàs's plan, Downs swung around and pushed his gun into Tomàs's face.

"Back up," Downs said. When Tomàs was more than an arm's length away, Downs grabbed his key fob and popped open the trunk. "Get in," he said. Tomàs slowly approached the empty trunk, with Downs behind him. He faked lowering himself toward the it, pivoting instead to thrust his elbow into Downs's throat as hard as he could. Downs fell back choking. As he fell, his gun fired inflicting a close-range graze to the side of Tomàs's head. Then Down's gun and key fob fell from his hands into the snow while he coughed and gasped.

His head exploding with pain and bleeding profusely, Tomàs could not tell the extent of his wound. Blood streamed into his eyes. Tomàs figured the bullet had grazed him or he'd be dead. As if in a dream he saw Downs rise from the snow and lunge toward him. Before Tomàs could react, Downs head-butted him in the chest and knocked him to the ground. Winded, Tomàs saw the Audi's key fob in the snow beside him. He grabbed it and tossed it as far as he could toward the roadside snow bank. Then he saw the gun, just behind the rear wheel, near enough to reach. Tomàs grabbed it and managed to fire off a wild round, completely missing Downs who began rummaging in the backseat.

Tomàs's head was pounding. He felt disoriented and numb like he was about to pass out. He tried to shoot at Downs again but he couldn't hold up his right hand. He lay back in the snow. "St. Michael, protect us in battle," he said. "Servant of the Holy Ghost, pray for us." It was an old prayer he'd learned as a child. Downs stood over him holding an AR-15. That was the last thing Tomàs remembered.

●

Jo was awakened by a loud sound. She flicked the light switch—nothing. The power was out. She quickly got dressed and knocked on Tomàs's door. When there was no answer, she opened the door. The bed had been slept in but the room was empty. She heard Melanie moving around and hurried downstairs. Melanie was lighting a kerosene lamp in the kitchen.

"Where is Tomàs?" Jo asked. "He's not in his room!"

"I don't know," Melanie said. "Did you hear that sound? Was that a gunshot?"

"I heard something," Jo said. "Where is the deputy?"

Jo started to put on her coat to go look for the deputy but another round of gunfire stopped her. "That sounds like an assault weapon," she said.

Melanie looked terrified. "What on earth is happening?" whispered.

Jo blew out the kerosene lamp. "Stay back from the windows," she said. Her hand shook as she picked up the phone. No dial tone. "Somebody must have cut our power and phones," she said. Then there was a loud pounding on their door. "It's Deputy Montoya," a voice said. "Let me in!"

Jo peered out the window, saw Josh standing there alone and opened the door. The deputy rushed in, speaking on his radio. His hand was wrapped in a rag soaked with blood. "I've been hit in the hand," he said as he locked the door behind him. "A man is down, out near the road."

Jo ran to get a clean cloth for his wound. She heard the voice on the radio ask the condition of the man down.

"I don't know. I couldn't get near him," Josh said into the radio. "Send backup now."

"Let me look at your hand," Jo said. She felt calm and clear-headed as she tended to Josh, who was trembling and seemed like he might go into shock. She couldn't tell the extent of the wound but it was definitely not minor. She wrapped his hand tightly in a towel and had him lie down on the floor with his arm elevated. "Who is the man out by the road?" she asked.

"I'm not sure. A big guy."

Melanie and Jo looked at each other. *Tomás*, they both thought.

"Who is the gunman?" Jo asked.

"Not sure. There was too much going on."

Melanie brought him a blanket and pillow and a glass of water. "How long will it take for them to get here?" she asked. Josh lay on the rug breathing in short choppy breaths.

"About fifteen minutes."

Jo made a tourniquet for Josh's arm as Melanie held his other hand. Applying the tourniquet kept Jo from thinking that whoever was out there with an assault rifle might be coming to the house to murder them all.

•

Ulysses was in a deep sleep when his cell phone woke him. He rolled over and picked it up off the bedside table.

"Sheriff," Dakota said, "there is an active shooter at the retreat center. Automatic weapon."

"Where is Josh?"

"He's been hit in the hand. He's in the main house. A lady there is a paramedic. A man is down near the road, condition unknown. Mark and Zach are on the way."

"I'm on my way," Ulysses said. "Radio Mark and Zach and tell them to call everybody in, even Angela. We need her if she can stand up. Call Agent Tallichet at the Sagebrush and Ray Pando at Picuris. Get him to bring Matt, his son."

Rosemary had made coffee before Ulysses finished dressing. She poured him a thermos and made one for LizBeth.. He put on his shoulder holster and his warmest parka. "Them devils must be a-flyin'," Rosemary said, recalling her husband's dream.

"I hope there is only one of them."

"There's always more than one," Rosemary said. "Be careful, Ulys."

"You know me," he said, "the very soul of careful."

"Listen to me," Rosemary said. "I have a very bad feeling about this one. I have since the beginning. Please, please, don't take undue risks, Ulys, Promise me."

He hugged and kissed her. "I'll be good," he said, "I promise."

Ulysses headed straight to Sleeping Tiger. He was driving through Taos when Zach got him on the radio. "We're here, Sheriff, no sign of the shooter. There's a man in the snow in need of medical attention. Shot. Looks like a head wound. He's out. Josh is none too good either. Can we call Peñasco Rescue?"

"No active gunfire?"

"Not since we got here, about ten minutes ago. Looks like there was a struggle. We found a set of car keys. He must have set off on foot."

"Can you cover the man who's down?"

"We've got a space blanket on him."

"Okay, call Peñasco but tell them the situation. Tape the site and stand by the man down. I'll be there in about twenty-five minutes." He put on his flashers and sped up. He flipped on his siren and increased his speed as much as he could on the icy road.

By the time Ulysses arrived at Sleeping Tiger, Peñasco Fire and Rescue had already loaded Tomàs Ulibarri onto a gurney and a tech was putting in an IV. Tomàs was semi-conscious, shivering and covered in blankets.

LizBeth Tallichet stood at the back of the van debriefing Josh, who lay on the other gurney looking shaken and in pain. He was getting fluids too. Before long the van was closed up and headed to Holy Cross Hospital, lights flashing, no siren. Ray and Matt Pando had arrived in Ray's truck earlier and had started down the Forest Road on foot, following the tracks. Mark and Zach drove down to Picuris, where the Forest Road intersected with State Road 75.

Ulysses looked at the tracks around the back of the Audi and examined the key fob Mark and Zach had found. He did a quick survey of the inside of the clean, late-model car and verified that it belonged to Malcolm Downs. Ulysses saw a missal in Latin, a gun case and a metal box full of what looked like plastic explosives and detonators. Agent Tallichet came over to the car.

"Good morning, Sheriff," she said. Ulysses handed her the thermos of coffee Rosemary had made for her. "Wow, thank you," she said.

"Thank my wife," Ulysses said. He showed her what he had found. She flipped through the missal, which was stuffed with holy cards.

"Looks like our guy is religious," she said, "and had access to high-quality explosives. I called in the ATF."

Ulysses looked inside the unlocked gun case and noted a Beretta M9, a Glock, a silencer for the Beretta and a place where a gun was missing. There was also a plastic crate full of extra rounds for an AR-15. All of it had been neatly hidden under a soft cashmere blanket, black, like the car's leather interior.

"Hiding in plain sight," LizBeth said.

"Yep," Ulysses said. "I didn't look into this car. Should have."

"This guy Downs is kind of a unicorn. Not what we see every day. Not what we expect." LizBeth was being kind, Ulysses thought. Unusual in an FBI agent.

"Still. I should've looked."

"Was Downs your prime suspect?" She took a sip of coffee. "Mmm, my favorite, French roast!" She smiled her winning smile. *She's very pretty*, Ulysses thought, quickly remembering it was inappropriate to notice the attractiveness of a female colleague.

"I didn't have one. But he was on the list. He is the most obscure to me. I know next to nothing about him."

"Well, that is all going to change in about two hours," LizBeth said. "The guy has a security clearance, which means we can have all the data we want on him. And it's likely these explosives are stolen from the LANL." She pulled a plastic bag out of her jacket pocket. In it was a black balaclava. "I found this in under the front seat," she said, "it might come in handy later."

Ulysses noticed Ray and Matt coming back up the Forest Road empty handed. "Hello, gentlemen," he said. "What did you find?"

"Hey, Ulys," Ray said, a little out of breath from trudging through the snow. "The guy has gone to ground somewhere. Wiped his tracks like a fucking pro. Excuse me, ma'am."

"No worries," LizBeth said.

Matt, taller and slimmer than his father but with the same hooded eyes, high forehead and long hair bound in a bun, shook hands with Ulysses and LizBeth. "We followed him for less than a mile. Then he went off the road and started obscuring his trail. We lost him in the dark. The guy is skilled. But we'll find him. We know this place better than he does."

"Could be he's headed for Picuris," Ulysses said. "You guys should go home and keep your village safe."

Ray and Matt conferred in Tiwa. Ray said, "Matt will go back and watch over the pueblo. I'll stay here for now."

"Thanks," Ulysses said. "We can use your help."

LizBeth checked her weapon and looked at her watch. "Let's get these folks out. I've got the dormitory; you guys take the church or whatever it is. I think the dining hall is the safest place right now. The killer could be anywhere at this point."

Ray was wearing his side arm. Ulysses grabbed his semi-automatic rifle and ammunition out of the Expedition and they walked toward the zendo.

Ulysses banged on the locked external zendo door. "Sheriff, open up," he shouted. After a few moments Gary Shumann came to the door and opened it a crack.

"Is the shooter still out there?" he asked. Ulysses could see Alan Wolfe behind him with a drawn gun.

"Put the gun down, Mr. Wolfe." Ray said. Wolfe complied and Ulysses and Ray came swiftly into the cold zendo, locking the door behind them. "Yes, the shooter is still at large. We want to get everyone into the dining hall where we can keep you safe."

"Who is it?" Alan asked. "Who has done this?"

"Not able to say at this time," Ulysses said.

"I'll go get Lynne," Gary said. "Give us a minute to get dressed."

Ulysses went inside the dark hall. Alan was banging on Astrid Berg's door and yelling for her to get up, but there was no response.

"Did you see her earlier?" Ulysses asked.

"No, none of us saw her," Alan said. "The deputy woke us up after midnight when he came in to check on us. He walked around the building and shone a light into her window. She wasn't in her bed but the lights were on in her bathroom and he heard the shower running."

"It's still running," Ulysses said. He backed up and rammed his body against her room door, which broke open easily. He shone his flashlight around the room but it was empty, as was the small bathroom. He turned off the shower, which was running ice cold. Ulysses felt sick to his stomach. Berg was gone, *God knows where*, and Ulysses felt responsible, angry and, for the first time, afraid. Alan Wolfe was at his back. "Where could she be?" he said. "Do you think she's been kidnapped?"

Ulysses didn't answer. His mind was racing through details of what could have happened. What kind of killer was this man? What was his motivation? Ulysses had a sinking feeling that he was dealing with a systematic killer, possibly a psychopath. The scapulars made it appear likely he'd killed at least three men: Luis, Gerald and Randolph Miller. And what about Astrid Berg? Was she a hostage? This was the man now loose and desperate in Taos County on his watch. Ulysses knew he had to act fast, but how?

He thought about the C-4 they found in Downs's car and what Downs might have booby trapped. The dormitory or the zendo? Probably not the dining hall because it would be hard to access and had no attic or other hiding places. LizBeth made the right call to get everyone there now but people needed to be taken off site as soon as possible. "Let's move, everyone." Ulysses and Ray hustled Gary, Lynne and Alan out of the zendo.

Melanie was already in the kitchen lighting kerosene lamps and candles. She'd lit the gas range and had a pot of water on the stove for coffee. "Do we know where Astrid is?" she asked Ulysses.

"No, we don't at this point," Ulysses said.

"Where is Jo?" Melanie asked.

"She asked to go with Agent Tallichet to evacuate the dormitory," Ulysses said. "They are going to bring everyone down here."

"Do you think you could get the generator going?" Melanie asked Gary.

"Is it safe to go out there?" Gary asked.

"Not much is safe at this point," Ray said.

"I'll go out with you and cover you," Alan said.

"Okay, I'll give it a try." Gary and Alan went outside.

Ulysses turned to Ray. "Can you stay here to watch over the people until we can send them to Taos? As soon as you can get everyone rounded up it would be good to get them out of here."

"Sure, I can do that. But where are you going?"

"I'm going after Downs," Ulysses said. "He's got a head start but he may have a hostage, which will slow him down."

"By yourself? I don't know if that's a good idea, Ulys."

"I can move faster and quieter alone. I have a chance of surprising him and maybe saving her. I've got to do this. Oh, and tell Tallichet to check the dorm attic for explosives."

"Okay, man, it's your call. But you'd better go now before she gets back and pulls rank on you."

•

Jo walked with her flashlight behind Agent Tallichet, who had a semi-automatic weapon over her shoulder and a pistol in her hand as they moved carefully up the icy driveway. While she had seen many crime scenes and accidents, Jo had never been in a situation like this, nor had she ever wanted to be. She only hoped to help the frightened guests trapped in the dormitory for whom this armed FBI agent was a stranger.

Her mind kept returning to Tomàs and his current condition, about which she knew next to nothing. She'd heard he'd sustained a head injury but did not know how serious. *Any head injury is serious*, she thought.

"Unlock the door," Tallichet whispered to her. Jo found the right key and did as she was told. The generator down by the dining hall started up and startled her. Tallichet swung open the heavy door and they entered the frigid building. What if the perpetrator was inside? Tallichet was already checking the bathrooms.

Jo knocked on the first door. "Thérèse, please wake up. We have to evacuate the building." Thérèse opened the door fully dressed. "What's going on?" she asked in a whisper.

"We are going down to the dining hall, where it is warmer and we have light."

"Are we in danger?"

"We'll keep you safe, ma'am," Agent Tallichet said. "Don't worry."

They went down the hall knocking loudly on every door. Everyone was already awake.

At the staircase to the second floor, Jo shone her flashlight up to the locked door at the top. She saw that the hasp was not in its usual position and the padlock was missing. Downstairs the door to the boiler room stood open. Jo saw Tomàs's toolbox right inside the door. "I think someone might have been in the attic," Jo said. "And maybe that person surprised Tomàs at the boiler."

"Let's get everyone out, now," Agent Tallichet said, continuing to knock on doors. "I can come back later and check the attic." The C-4 in Downs's trunk loomed in her mind.

The participants emerged from their rooms, dressed but confused and frightened. Jo counted heads. One was missing: Malcolm Downs. Agent Tallichet knocked loudly on his door and opened his door, gun drawn. The room was empty and the bed was made as if no one had slept there.

Tallichet shone her flashlight quickly around the room. "Let's get going," she said. Jo heard the urgency in her tone and shepherded everyone down the icy driveway. Her watch read 5:30. It wouldn't be light for another hour.

Inside the dining hall the overhead lights were on and Roshi Melanie had made coffee and set out bread, butter, a bowl of apples and a tin of oatmeal cookies. People began helping themselves and whispering to each other in small groups. Everyone seemed calm except Jon Malvern, who sat by himself looking morose and agitated. He glared at Melanie when she offered him a cup of coffee but said nothing.

What's with him, Jo wondered. *Is he in on this?* She felt wary of Malvern.

Agent Tallichet and Ray Pando were having an intense conversation in low voices. Jo wondered where Sheriff Walker was. She went to pour herself a cup of coffee. Roshi Melanie stood at the buffet drinking her second cup.

"Have you heard anything from the hospital?" Jo asked.

"Nothing," Melanie said. "They are being very tight lipped."

"Where is Astrid?" Jo asked.

"Missing. They broke down her door. She wasn't in there."

"Malcolm Downs?"

"Also missing. He wasn't in his room and all his stuff is gone."

"Could they have left together? I think they were involved."

"It is best not to contemplate the karma of others," Roshi Melanie said, paraphrasing a scripture. She placed her hand on Jo's arm and gave a little squeeze. Jo covered Melanie's hand with her own and the two stood in stunned silence watching the lights of two vehicles pulling up the driveway.

Agent Tallichet peered out the window. "It's the ATF crew," she said to Ray, "and the FBI hostage team. Thank the Lord." Looking greatly relieved she went out to greet them.

Chapter XI

Ulysses returned to Astrid Berg's room to search for any sign of what might have become of her. Her bed was unmade and rumpled. A red silk robe lay across a chair and a coat and boots were in her closet. Who had left a shower running and locked the door? Ulysses began to wonder if Astrid had ever come back from her meeting with Alan. Had Downs captured her up there? Or had she willingly gone to his room? Ulysses thought the best way to find her was to find Downs.

Ulysses remembered what the Picuris woman, Agnes Duràn, had said about someone going up the trail near her house the night Gerald Beatty was killed. In Picuris, that trail climbed to meet a spur off the dirt Forest Road onto public land managed by the Bureau of Land Management. Once on the Forest Road, the Peñasco Road and Sleeping Tiger driveway were not far, maybe three miles. Ulysses thought he could make a short cut from Sleeping Tiger by going up Lizard Head and picking up the trail to Picuris there. It wasn't graded, and now it was snow-covered, but it was shorter than the Forest Road which was too deep in snow to be passable in the Expedition.

At the bottom of the cliffs the trail ran straight across a basin for about a mile before climbing to another hogback. Over that ridge was Picuris. Ray and Matt thought that Downs had run down the Forest Road and maybe cut off on the spur. They thought he was traveling alone, but couldn't be sure. He definitely had snowshoes. Ulysses thought Downs had at least an hour head start. The shortcut over Lizard Head might buy Ulysses fifteen minutes or more if he really moved.

At his vehicle Ulysses put on snowshoes and took out his emergency backpack. He checked his weapon and his ammo and made sure his canteen was full. He chewed on some bison jerky and took a long drink of cold water.

He felt confident, almost exhilarated.

The night was still and windless. The big misshapen moon gave a fair amount of light. Ulysses crossed the meadow in front of Jo's cabin and picked up the trail to Lizard Head. He thought the spur he was looking for came into this trail below the cliffs but he wasn't sure if he had to cross the Rio del Pueblo before he found it. He wondered how frozen the river would be. He reminded himself it was very shallow up here and picked up his speed on the switchbacks. After about twenty minutes he was at the top of Lizard Head, breathing hard and sweating. *Where would Downs go to ground*, he wondered.

He paused to get his breath and then peered out from under the trees to look at the vista below, which encompassed twenty thousand acres of public land and another thirty thousand of Picuris land. At the foot of the cliffs, near where Luis's body had been found was an open patch dotted with big ponderosa pines. To his right was a sloping area that led to piñon and juniper groves, and above that, more woods and another high hogback crowned with blocky basalt rim rock. Surrounding it were forests of pine, spruce and fir in the upper elevations. On the other side of the hogback was the village of Picuris, where Downs might be headed. Or did Downs have a hideout somewhere? There was no point in trying to track him in the dark but in a half an hour it would be light enough. Ulysses decided to head toward Picuris.

The pueblo was only about two-and-a-half miles as the crow flies, but in deep snow over hills it meant an arduous slog. Ulysses sat on a rock to take off and stow his snowshoes and put some yak-tracks over his boots. He began a careful descent on the steep, slippery trail. What sounded like a thousand coyotes started their pre-dawn, demented yelping. Ulysses hoped he'd have time to cross the open ground before the sun rose.

As he was descending Ulysses considered what he knew about the man he was pursuing. Downs was younger but Ulysses had a good three inches on him. Downs was heavier. He worked at Los Alamos and had a security clearance, which indicated a good level of intelligence and technical abilities. It also explained his knowledge of and access to explosives like C-4. Ulysses was glad LizBeth had backup from the feds.

As he picked his way carefully down the steep path, Ulysses thought again about what might have happened to Astrid Berg. He figured Berg had run into Downs on her way back from her meeting with Alan Wolfe. He remembered how Downs had talked about her in his interview, with so much disdain. Was he, like so many killers, a hater of women? Did he rape her? Kill her and stash her body in the woods? Or was she with him now?

Ulysses upbraided himself for not seeing signs in Downs' personality before. He'd never felt this much pressure as a police officer. He was just part of a team that did a job. Now as sheriff he felt responsible for everything that happened in the whole damn county.

Ulysses slipped on some scree and fell on his side just as a deafening explosion lit up the sky to the east of Lizard Head. For a moment Ulysses panicked. *What the hell was that?* The C-4. Ulysses's heart began to pound and his mind raced. Did the killer booby trap something at the retreat center? Ulysses broke into a cold, prickly sweat. Ray and LizBeth were there but he would be needed until other agents or state police arrived. Ulysses started back up the exposed path which was treacherously steep.

The pop of gunfire startled him. Bullets pinged off the rocks in front of him. Ulysses, visible in the moonlight, raced for a large rock outcrop down the trail to take cover. *No going back now,* he thought, not with that exposed climb.

The bastard must have waited to see his bomb go off, Ulysses thought. *Otherwise he'd be nearly to Picuris by now.* Ulysses hunkered down behind a group of boulders about half way down the cliffs and caught his breath. He thought for a moment about Rosemary and the children, but quickly put them out of his mind. Thinking about them would only make him emotional and he needed all his wits. His mind ricocheted off what he knew like the bullets coming at him. He tried to imagine what Downs would do next. This guy had killed one man by pushing him off a cliff. He'd killed another by dunking him in a sewage pond and causing him to freeze to death. Ulysses thought guns were not Downs's preferred method of murder. He had only injured Tomàs and Josh with his guns. *But he is shooting at me now,* Ulysses thought.

He saw another sheltering boulder pile about twenty-five yards away. He could run from there through the sliver of shadow made by a stand of spruce near the bottom. He took a deep breath and ran toward the boulders. No shots rang out. *Either he didn't see me run or he is sneaking up on me,* Ulysses thought.

As he picked his way across the snowy slope in the shadows, sweat was running down the back of his neck. He realized he was in a battle with a masterful predator. His two years as sheriff and the previous seven years as a police detective had not prepared him for someone so skilled and determined. Ulysses tried again to push aside his thoughts. He realized he needed to get on his game or he could die. Once again he felt exhilarated but his confidence had diminished. He picked his way down the last of the slope as the moon was setting behind the western hogback.

He was just past the covering shadow of a big spruce when something jumped on his back like a cougar, knocking him hard to the ground on his right shoulder. The man rolled over him and down the steep hill. Ulysses grabbed his rifle and got to his knees, but his adversary was already pointing an automatic weapon at him. Downs stood over him mumbling something under his breath. He gazed at Ulysses for a long moment. Then, still mumbling, he raised the AR-15 over his head and thrust the butt down on Ulysses's head. Ulysses, in a blaze of pain, lost consciousness.

•

It was still dark but the dining hall had warmed up considerably. Carmen had arrived and made more coffee but Ray had stopped her from making a hot breakfast. There was already too much going on, he said, and it would delay evacuation.

LizBeth and the federal agents had grabbed some food and were suiting up to go outside. They all checked their weapons and radios. Jo went around the room pouring coffee and trying to reassure the participants, even though she felt sick with anxiety and dread. Lynne, ashen-faced and wrapped in a down comforter, sat with her eyes closed, her hands wrapped around a coffee mug. Marci and Thérèse talked together in worried voices about Astrid and Malcolm Downs. Where were they and were they all right? Was Downs a suspect? Anne, Alan and Gary began comparing notes about when they had last seen either one. Jon Malvern loudly announced that he had seen the two together outside the zendo during dinner.

Ray had just sat down across from Malvern intending to question him when an earsplitting explosion shook the dining hall, shattering the glass in the one west window. Flames lit up the sky and debris fell on the roof. LizBeth and the other agents ran out the back door, weapons drawn. It took a few moments for everyone else to realize what had happened. The dormitory and Gerald's house were ablaze. The comfort of the dining hall was destroyed by the strange flickering light of the inferno on the hill. The participants huddled on the east wall. Marci was crying and Thérèse was comforting her. Ray turned to Melanie, who was standing with Anne Stein. The generator took that moment to run out of gas and the room went dark.

"Do you have your car keys?" Ray asked Melanie, shining his big flashlight in her direction.

"They're hidden in the garage," she said.

"The van keys too?"

She nodded.

"Take Carmen and the Shumanns and get out of here," Ray said. "Go to Taos and stay there until further notice. Right now." He turned to Anne Stein, "Can you drive a van in snow?" he asked.

She nodded. "Yes. I used to live here."

"Get the keys, load up everyone else except her," he said, indicating Jo. "Are you willing to stay and help?" Jo nodded, feeling she had no choice. Ray had Anne and Melanie put their numbers in his cell phone. "Now, go to Taos," Ray said. "Don't worry about your stuff, just go."

"I need to get my laptop," Alan Wolfe said.

"No," Ray said. "Did you hear that explosion? Do you see that fire? Now get out of here!"

Melanie and Anne led their small groups out to the garage and in a few minutes Melanie's car's taillights were receding down the driveway. Shortly after that the van followed.

"What do you want me to do, Ray?" Jo asked.

"Go refill that generator," he said, "then come back here. The state police are sending a search team in a helicopter as soon as it gets light. This is probably the safest place for now."

Ray's radio crackled. It was Matt asking about the explosion, which he'd heard from Picuris. While Ray conversed with his son, Jo realized that even though the killer had fled he could have circled back to pick them off one by one. The thought sent chills down her spine, but she went outside to refill the generator anyway.

There was one full gas can left. *That should take us into mid-morning with some to spare*, she thought. As she filled the tank, she thought about how Tomàs made sure they never ran out of supplies. She pictured him in a hospital bed, bandaged and with an IV attached to his arm. It wasn't an easy image for her. She wished he had never gone out to check that damn boiler. It occurred to her that his little homestead was near the area where the murderer had fled. So much for feeding his chickens, she thought.

It wasn't hard for Jo to accept that Malcolm Downs had to be the killer. She'd felt uneasy around him all along, a sense she'd attributed to his smug, somewhat arrogant manner on the first evening. Those kinds of immediate reactions to people, like distrusting someone because of a feeling, were things she actively worked to reject, as part of her effort to be nonjudgmental. *Was that wise*, she wondered. Maybe a little distrust wasn't such a bad thing. *It's just this situation*, she thought, reassuring herself. *It could make anyone a little paranoid. We've had two murders in three days and now an explosion and fire.*

Actually, Jo thought as she finished pouring the gasoline and screwed on the cap, *maybe we've had three murders*. She pictured Astrid Berg as she last saw her and felt a nauseating sense that the woman was dead. Malcolm Downs had killed her and hidden her body, maybe in the dormitory. But why? None of this made any sense. Did some people just enjoy killing?

Jo finished her task and with one hand on the door to the dining hall she paused and looked east. Dawn light already dusted the horizon a soft yellow. The morning star shone in the indigo above, like the diamond earring of a goddess against blue-black hair. "I am awakened together with the whole earth and all its beings," she whispered, recalling the words the Buddha was said to have spoken on the occasion of his enlightenment. He had gazed at the morning star and become fully himself, "*which is what enlightenment is*," she remembered Roshi saying. Jo realized that today was Bodhi Day, the anniversary of Buddha's enlightenment. For a moment she let go of her fear and felt a flicker of joy. "I can have faith in my breath if nothing else," she said, feeling reassured by this touchstone.

Then she heard the loud sirens of fire trucks headed their way. That sound always roused her blood and made her feel better. She remembered how she'd felt racing down the road in a vehicle that was making those urgent, authoritative sounds. *We're coming to help*, the sirens said, *hold on!*

She waited at the garage for the trucks to pull into the driveway. She would show them how to cut around behind Roshi's house on the gravel road and pick up the pavement on the other side, which would take them closer to the dormitory.

·

Tomàs was awake and partially upright in his hospital bed. Morning light fell on the empty bed beside him. His face and the side of his head were still numb from the local they gave him to stitch him up. If that bullet had entered his head rather than grazing it, he'd be dead. *Maybe I should go to confession*, he thought.

Tomàs knew he wouldn't be able to sleep in this bright, noisy place, so he was waiting on breakfast and thinking about his brush with death. He tried to piece together as many details as he could remember. After he and Jo parted, he'd gone to check on Astrid. When she didn't respond to his knocks he spoke with the deputy and asked him to check on her again in about an hour. Then he went to bed and slept deeply for several hours. Why had he awakened in the first place? That was a mystery. He hadn't been aware of any sounds, but suddenly he was wide-awake and trying to turn on the light, realizing the power was out. Then on the way up to the dormitory there was that flicker of light he thought he saw in the upstairs of the dormitory.

He had talked himself out of concerning himself with that, but why? Clearly, Downs might have been up there doing mischief. He was too focused on the boiler. Tomàs had shone his flashlight up the stairs and the door had been closed but was it also locked? Why didn't he go up there to check? He thought about how his mother had always said, "Don't go looking for trouble." That motto didn't work for Tomàs. He tended to get involved. In Afghanistan on patrol, he had to look into anything that wasn't as it was supposed to be. And it didn't work last night either. Too bad he hadn't brought his gun.

Then there was the fact that Downs completely got the jump on him. Tomàs prided himself on his acute senses but he had not heard a thing. And why didn't Downs kill him when he was standing over him with the AR-15? Remembering that image Tomàs felt the kind of chills that made his mother say, "someone just walked over my grave."

I am really lucky, Tomàs thought again. He felt he needed to give this event some thought with regard to the rest of his life. He'd been on autopilot. He needed to change some things. An image of Jo popped into his mind. *I'm not giving up on her*, he thought. All of a sudden he felt very tired. He was dozing when Agent LizBeth Tallichet knocked on his door. She was holding a tray with two cups of coffee.

"How're we doing?" she asked. Tomàs noticed her taking in his IV and head bandage.

"I've been better," he said, laughing. "But I feel pretty damn lucky. I think I got religion out there, if you know what I mean."

"Do you feel like talking?" Tallichet sat in a chair beside his bed and unzipped her coat.

"I can talk. But first tell me, is everyone okay?"

Tallichet pulled off her wool hat and ruffled her hair. "Josh Montoya is in surgery as we speak. He is expected to recover but his hand will need reconstructive work. Sheriff Walker took off after the perpetrator and has not yet checked in. Everyone else is well and accounted for except Astrid Berg. She's missing." Tallichet put her cardboard tray on the bedside table.

"That's not good," Tomàs said.

"No, it's not. Hey, I brought you a cup of coffee."

"Thank you," he said, taking a cup. He was relieved that Jo and Melanie were okay but worried and a little guilty about Astrid.

"How's your head?"

"Could be worse." He patted the bandage around his head and another on his face. "The bullet grazed my skull and tore into my cheek. Plus, I had hypothermia from lying in the snow for about thirty minutes. But if I'm okay today they will discharge me tomorrow." He took a sip of coffee. "I'm going to have one hell of a scar."

"Do you hurt?" Tallichet asked.

"The meds help." Tomàs finished his coffee and wished for a second cup just as a woman came in with a breakfast tray, poured him another cup and left the pot.

Tallichet helped herself to a second cup. "So what happened last night?"

"I woke up sometime between two and three, not sure why. When I realized the power was out, I went up to the dormitory to check the boiler. Sure enough, the pilot was out. I had just relit it when Malcolm Downs put a gun to my head" – Tomàs touched the back of his bandaged neck – "right here."

"Did he say anything?"

"He told me to stand up and be quiet. He was kind of praying under his breath."

"What sort of prayer?"

"It was in Latin. I've heard it before, back when I was an altar boy. It was something from the Mass for the Dead."

"What did you do?"

"I started praying too!" Tomàs said, laughing. He took a bite of eggs and ate a piece of sausage. "Wow, this is terrible," he said, continuing to eat. "I started saying the Hail Mary. Honestly, I don't know why, but I thought maybe I could get on his good side."

"Then what happened?"

"Oh, I forgot something," Tomàs said. "Before I got to the dormitory, I thought for a moment I saw a light upstairs. Like a flashlight." He buttered another piece of toast.

"But you aren't sure?" Tallichet asked.

"No, not sure." Tomàs poured his third cup of coffee. "These are very small cups," he said. "But you guys should look up there if you haven't already."

Tallichet cleared her throat. She remembered her promise to Jo to go back and check on the upstairs. She'd eaten breakfast instead. *Goddamn,* she thought, *I should have gone to check.* Then it occurred to her that had she gone back she might be dead right now. "The dormitory blew up about an hour ago. It is pretty much destroyed. The bomb squad is checking it out now."

"Was anybody in there?" Tomàs swallowed the hard, dry toast and took a drink of water.

"We don't know yet," Tallichet said, shaking her head. "I hope not. Did you see any of Downs's weapons or explosives?"

"No. I saw the trunk of his car but only briefly. I think it was empty. He was planning to put somebody in it, like me. We had a little struggle. I elbowed him in the throat and his gun went off, which is when I got hit. He dropped his keys and his gun, both of which I grabbed."

"Did you get a shot at him?"

"Yeah, but I missed. He went and got his rifle out of the car."

"Why didn't he kill you, I wonder?"

"I have no earthly idea. I was praying for real then. He was standing over me with an AR. My guardian angel saved me I guess." Tomàs lay back against his pillows feeling drained. He'd forgotten that last part. Had he prayed aloud? He flashed on the strange sense of acceptance he'd felt. Tomàs's head began to throb.

"Do you need anything?" Tallichet said. "Do you want someone to call family?"

"I'll call my daughter later. No, I'm good. I hope you find Ms. Berg."

"Thanks for the info." LizBeth turned to leave. "Get some rest."

•

Once everyone was gone, the ATF swept the kitchen and dining room and Ray and Jo sat together waiting for word from Ulysses. The Peñasco and Dixon fire department volunteers were busy keeping the nearby woods and buildings from catching fire while the superintendent's house burned out of control. The main structure of the dormitory was stone, but what was left of its interior had burned to ashes. Two state fire marshals had arrived and, together with the ATF, they waited for the volunteers to spray down the site until it was cool enough to enter. When they were ready, Ray and Jo went outside to watch the agents and marshals in their protective gear methodically search through the debris. The whole property stank of smoke, burnt materials and chemicals.

She looked out over her former refuge and sanctuary, now charred and smoking, the air around it filled with the noise of engines and crackling radios. She felt a profound sense of loss. How would this little world of peaceful retreat ever recover its safety and beauty? What would happen to Roshi Melanie, Tomàs and Carmen, and to her, after all this violence?

Jo brought to mind the Buddhist principle of impermanence. *No matter how much I try*, she thought, *I cannot preserve things as they are.* She remembered Melanie's words on this: "*The only constant is change. All that you cling to from attraction and all that you push away from aversion will pass away. Therefore, do not cling and be in peace.*" Jo felt cold comfort in this teaching. She realized she had confused the external peace of Sleeping Tiger with the peace residing within her. But the realization only made her feel sad.

Jo heard the approach of a helicopter.

"It's the staties," Ray said. "They're looking for Ulys. I hope they find him. He's been gone a good little while." The noise of the chopper was familiar to Jo from the many life flights of her past, but now it filled her with dread instead of hope. Ray radioed his son and talked in Tiwa for a few minutes. Jo listened to the sound of the ancient language shared in the back and forth on the radio. She felt exhausted and realized she was hungry.

"Matt has the war council watching the roads and trails into our pueblo and no one has seen Ulysses, or anyone else this morning. Everybody's real busy getting ready for the Deer Dance. "

"When is that?" Jo asked.

"Tomorrow. Starts at dawn. It's going to be warmer tomorrow, which is good."

"Shouldn't it be postponed?" Jo asked. "Isn't it too dangerous?"

"Not much chance it will be postponed," Ray said. "It's been going on for at least five hundred years." He paused and looked at Jo who was shivering. "You should get inside," he said. "We'll catch this guy today, don't you worry."

Ray, however, looked worried to Jo. Ulysses had not made radio contact even once since he left five hours ago. A noisy radio would be a disadvantage when hunting a perpetrator. Ulysses had probably turned it off. And cell service was almost nonexistent in the area. But still, why hadn't he at least checked in?

Jo stood by while the FBI agents on the hostage team took apart the sleeping rooms in the zendo and busied themselves entering some of the contents into evidence. By eleven o'clock, the power and phone lines, which had indeed been manually disabled, were restored. Jo cleaned up from breakfast and started to make sandwiches for anyone who needed lunch. Then the phone in the library rang.

It was Lorraine Baca, Sheriff Walker's secretary. She told Jo that Josh Montoya was out of surgery and stable. At least the injury was to his left hand and he was right-handed. They expected that with specialized surgery in Albuquerque he would recover at least partial functionality. She said the other man, a Mr. Ulibarri, was doing well and hadn't needed surgery, just a lot of stitches. Jo breathed out a deep sigh of relief. She planned to call Tomàs as soon as she could.

Lorraine also said that Rosemary Walker had called in the mid-morning, quite worried about her husband. "Actually this is completely unlike her," Lorraine said. "She is usually a real trooper. Give her a call, will you? You can tell her the latest of what you know. I've got my hands full with all the calls I'm getting here." Jo wrote down Rosemary's number and called it. Rosemary answered on the first ring.

"This is Jo McAlister from Sleeping Tiger Retreat Center. Is this Mrs. Walker?" Jo could hear kids yelling in the background.

"Rosemary, yes. Thank you so much for calling. Have you seen or heard from my husband?"

"I saw him this morning just before daylight," Jo said, feeling that had been a very long time ago. She looked at her watch. It was eleven thirty.

"Where did he go?" Rosemary asked. Her voice sounded anxious.

"He is tracking a suspect. He went up a trail toward Picuris before sunrise."

Rosemary told her children in a firm voice to "pipe down." She took a deep breath. "Was the killer armed?"

"Yes, he was armed," Jo said. She sensed again the danger that Sheriff Walker might be in at the moment. "A state helicopter is looking for them now," she added.

"There's no cell service out there, is there?"

"No. But the FBI search team is there, too. They'll report in soon, we hope."

"Will you call me as soon as you hear anything?"

"Of course," Jo said. She reflected on all that was at stake for Rosemary.

Jo returned to the kitchen and continued making sandwiches. She heated up leftover tortilla soup, cut up some apples and made two pots of coffee.

Ray was the first to come in. He poured some coffee and put a sandwich on a plate.

"They'll be down in a few minutes, " he said. "Nice of you to make some food." Jo knew from his tone of voice that something had been found.

"How's it going up there?"

"They found what looks like bone fragments. And three teeth." Ray pushed his sandwich aside and took a drink of black coffee. "They'll take it to their forensics lab in Albuquerque. We won't know for a while who or what it was. "

Jo sat down on a kitchen stool. "How horrible," she said. *It must be Astrid*, she thought with a shudder.

"Has Ulys checked in?"

Jo shook her head no. "I spoke with Rosemary. She hadn't talked to him either. She's really worried about him."

"I guess so," Ray said. "I'm getting a little worried myself. The FBI search crew hasn't found anything. They've got three guys on the ground but the deep snow is slowing them down."

The ATF and state fire marshal came and placed their evidence bags on a back table. Then the two agents, who had searched the dining hall and Roshi's house and had been cataloging the zendo since dawn, put several additional evidence bags on the same table. The men were joking among themselves as they washed up in the big auxiliary kitchen sink and then sat down to eat. They seemed unperturbed by what they had found and felt no need to observe the kinds of proprieties they might have maintained in front of the public. As they joked about one man's upcoming wedding and started sharing Christmas plans, Jo remembered what it was like to work with men like these. They all had to deal with random violence, cruelty and stupidity every day at each accident or crime scene. This is just one more such scene, maybe a little more dramatic than most. Feeling more like a victim than a first responder, Jo went around the room and poured everyone coffee. Ray, sitting apart from the others, had eaten only half his sandwich.

Jo decided to call Tomàs from the library. As she approached the evidence table along the way, she slowed down to look at the bags. She saw a knitted necklace with a picture of an angel, a clear case with bone and tooth fragments, and a letter. She leaned in for a closer look. It was the letter she'd seen on Roshi's desk the first morning of the retreat – the letter to Gerald, in Melanie's handwriting.

•

Ulysses returned to consciousness and found himself strapped down on some kind of travois with his hands and feet bound, tape over his mouth and eyes and a throbbing pain in his head. He was disoriented and panicky and tried to figure out where he was and what was happening to him. The last thing he remembered was picking his way down the Lizard

Head trail and being attacked from behind. He wondered how long he'd been unconscious.

Ulysses surmised from his available senses that he was lying in a snow bank under an evergreen tree. He was blindfolded and his arms and feet were tightly bound. He could feel a bit of sun on his face and heard a creek gurgling nearby. He listened more closely and thought he could make out the sound of soft snoring.

Ulysses thought he heard a helicopter. A minute later he was sure of it. Were they looking for him? It was probably the state police, searching the surrounding tens of thousands of uninhabited acres, much of it deeply forested and with few roads. As the helicopter passed, sounding not far away, the snoring stopped. Ulysses heard the man get up and rummage through a bag. He sensed the man was standing over him, watching him and listening to his breathing. Ulysses felt his stomach lurch in fear. He was completely helpless before this killer.

"You're awake," the man said. He pulled the tape off Ulysses's mouth and held something to his lips. A canteen. As Ulysses raised his head to drink he nearly passed out from the pain in his head. He got several gulps before the man removed the canteen and offered him a nutritional bar, the kind Rosemary sometimes put in his lunches. Tears welled up in his eyes as he thought of his daughter who called them "Daddy bars." He took a bite and began to chew. *Why is he feeding me?* Ulysses wondered as he continued to eat slowly. The man was eating too. The helicopter passed overhead, giving Ulysses a flicker of hope, but it didn't come as close as the last time.

Ulysses wondered if anyone would be able to track them. He thought about the travois he was lying on and realized it might be a very good tool for obscuring the tracks of feet. Ulysses listened for the helicopter but it didn't come close again. Eventually he fell back into semi-consciousness.

He awoke to Downs dragging him over the snow. The smooth movement made Ulysses realize he was probably on a graded trail of some kind. He searched his mind and remembered the little used cross-country ski and overnight yurt trails somebody had built in the 1990s. He'd never seen them but had heard they still existed. Downs was now dragging him across the creek on a wooden bridge, a much rougher ride. Then they were back on the snow. *We couldn't be more than a few miles from Lizard Head. If trackers make it over this way, I have a chance,* he thought.

Downs continued to pull Ulysses over the snow and deeper into the forest. Downs took frequent rest breaks and gave Ulysses more water. He thought he heard the helicopter one more time from a distance.

The forest was quiet and the day grew warmer. Ulysses thought the temperature might be above freezing. Occasionally he heard the soft plop of snow falling from the low-hanging evergreen boughs and the cries of crows and ravens.

Toward midday Downs stopped pulling the travois. It sounded to Ulysses like he was going up stairs and unlocking a door. He went up and down the stairs a few more times as if carrying things into whatever building they were near. At last he came near Ulysses. "I am going to untie you. If you try to escape, I'll kill you. "

Downs freed Ulysses's hands and feet and helped him stand. Ulysses was stiff and ached all over but felt good to be able to move his limbs. Downs led him up some steps and into a space that smelled like canvas. *This must be one of those yurts.* Once inside Downs made Ulysses sit on the floor and retied his hands. He took the tape off Ulysses's eyes. Downs sat across from him on the wooden platform floor looking relaxed and bemused.

"Now I will conduct an interview with *you*," Downs said, pulling off his cap and beginning to brush his long hair with careful strokes. "To determine if you are a servant of Lucifer and therefore must die, or if you are innocent of these doings and may be vouchsafed to live." He chuckled. His blonde locks shone in the bit of sunlight coming through the windows of the yurt.

Chapter XII

After she left the Holy Cross Hospital that morning LizBeth called into the Albuquerque office to get updates on the FBI bomb and search and rescue teams. She felt relieved that in addition to her four agents doing search and rescue there were two local fire crews, the fire marshals and a state police search helicopter. As she drove, she conversed with her research officer, Ben Ruiz, who gave her some basic information on Malcolm Downs.

"He was born in Los Alamos. His parents both worked at the Los Alamos National Lab—Cyril and Evelyn Downs, both naturalized Americans born in England. The subject was raised Catholic, baptized at Santo Niño Church in Santa Fe. He went to Los Alamos public schools. In 1996 he graduated from the New Mexico Institute of Mining and Technology. He went for further study at Cal Tech but dropped out before getting his Ph.D. and returned to Los Alamos. He is currently working on the plutonium pit project as an engineer. He never married and has no children. His parents are retired and live in Scottsdale."

"Any priors?"

"A domestic dispute with a girlfriend in Santa Fe in 2012. He was referred to the anger management class at Esperanza. His security clearance was removed for about six months. That's about it."

"Okay, thanks, Ben. Find out everything you can on a woman named Astrid Berg. She runs an outfit called Wakeful Mind in California. Zen Buddhist."

"You got it," Ben said.

"I'm going to Los Alamos to talk with the security clearance folks. Call them and let them know I'm coming, okay? Also going to see a Mr. Eduardo Santos if you can text me a physical address on him. All I have is a post office box in Velardé."

"Will do. Be careful out there!"

LizBeth stopped at the Taos Plaza and picked up a breakfast burrito and a cup of coffee and drove south on Highway 68. The two-lane road crossed the high mesa to the east of the Rio Grande Gorge and offered panoramic vistas of the dramatic gorge and the mesas and mountains to the west. The sky was a cloudless, deep blue and the snow sparkled.

LizBeth thought about Dawa, the woman she loved and hoped to marry, a neurology resident at UT in Austin. Dawa loved New Mexico because it reminded her of Tibet, the country her parents had fled as children in the early 60's, a place of endless sky, snow-capped mountains and high plateaus. *I'll bring her to New Mexico for a long weekend around Christmas*, LizBeth thought, *and maybe we'll go skiing.* She hated being apart from her lover and best friend but LizBeth had to take this job when it came along or pass up the promotion that came with it.

The road, which had wended through a number of deep curves as it descended, ran right along the blue-green Rio Grande for miles through a narrow canyon. South of the canyon she turned toward Los Alamos National Laboratory, built into the Jemez mountains to house the Manhattan Project in World War II and still partly responsible for the country's nuclear arsenal. LizBeth had been warned that LANL, or the Lab as it was locally known, was notorious for circling the wagons whenever there was any kind of security breach or scandal. *Just like the Catholic Church*, she thought.

At the security post that marked the entrance to the Lab, LizBeth showed her badge and asked for directions to building #38, where she was to meet with Specialist Alicia Holt, administrator for the security clearance group. She drove through woods and fields to a collection of unremarkable one-story buildings and fenced areas before finally arriving at a low-slung structure that looked almost like an elementary school. The only sign she saw was the number 38 on a fence post as she drove up. She parked in front where the lot had been scraped clear of snow.

Ms. Holt's office door was open when LizBeth arrived. LizBeth showed her credentials to the thin grey-haired woman in a pink twinset and tweed skirt. She was invited to sit in a chair across from her desk. "I'm sure my assistant Ben explained why this investigation is urgent?" LizBeth began, looking around for the files she hoped to be viewing.

"Yes, I did receive a call, " Holt said calmly, riffling through the papers on her desk and not making eye contact. "We have not had time to put together a full report, of course. But I can give you a brief summary." She pulled out some handwritten notes.

The older woman cleared her throat, preparing to read her notes. LizBeth interrupted her. "How long until we can get the full report, ma'am?"

"I can't tell you, Ms. Tallichet," the woman said, mispronouncing her name. "We are very busy here in this office."

"That's 'Tal-li-chay'," LizBeth corrected, smiling. "It's a Cajun name. French." Usually this routine relaxed people.

Holt nodded but showed no sign of softening. She reached for her reading glasses.

"Ms. Holt, you realize that we are investigating a number of homicides and aggravated arson, right? How difficult is it to locate the information we have requested?"

Holt blew her nose into a handkerchief and patted her gold and diamond cross necklace. She again opened her desk drawer and pulled out a sheet of paper and a stick of gum which she unwrapped and popped into her mouth. She handed LizBeth a photocopied sheet that read, "Procedures Required to Access Secret Clearance Data: Steps for Law Enforcement."

"I am familiar with these procedures, Ms. Holt, but they do not apply in this case, as I'm sure you realize." LizBeth pulled a yellow highlighter out of the jar of pens on the woman's desk, "May I?" She highlighted a sentence and gave it back to Holt. "You can see right there that the FBI is exempt in a capital murder case."

Holt glared at LizBeth, chewed her gum and looked out the window. "We do not have the records in this office. Do you want the summary or not?"

LizBeth wondered if someone had coached Holt to stonewall like this. Had the records been misplaced? Was this a cover-up or incompetence? She looked at her watch, startled to see it was nearly eleven o'clock. "Give me the summary," she said at last. "However, I want you to know we will need the entire report by close of business today."

Holt put on her glasses and read from her notes. "Malcolm Downs has worked here since 2006. His work record has been "fully satisfactory." He had one infraction, an arrest in Santa Fe for stalking, which resulted in a six-month revocation of his clearance. The police record was later expunged. Both of Downs's parents were Lab employees. His mother retired in 2002 and his father in 2007."

"What kind of work does he do?"

"He works as an engineer in our plutonium pit program. He's an explosives expert."

"Has any C-4 gone missing at the site?"

"Not that I am aware of, Ms. Tallichet."

"C-4 was found in Downs's car and it was used to detonate a large blast this morning near Peñasco." Holt said nothing but to LizBeth it appeared she knew about the explosion. "The arrest in 2012, you said it was for stalking. Was there domestic abuse?"

Holt looked at her notes. "It wasn't domestic abuse and it really wasn't stalking. He violated an order of protection."

"What was the victim's name?"

"Silvia Duràn. She was a student at the College of Santa Fe."

"Were there any other issues regarding Downs's security clearance over the years?"

Holt again looked her prepared notes.

"Downs was in therapy for depression off and on for several years. He was hospitalized after the incident with Ms. Duràn for several weeks. This summer he was hospitalized overnight after an altercation with some people in his support group."

"What kind of support group?" LizBeth asked.

"A group of conservative Catholics who meet for Latin Mass twice a week. All of them exemplary employees." Holt folded her notes and placed them on her desk.

"I need the name and contact information for Downs's therapist," LizBeth said. "And can you give me a contact for the religious group?"

"Dr. Lionel Case is the psychiatrist," Holt said, "He has an office in Pojoàque." Holt gave her a phone number that LizBeth put into her phone. "I'll have to get back to you with the other name." Holt stood up as if dismissing LizBeth.

"I expect to be able to pick up the files this afternoon. How late are you here?"

"I am here until 3:30 today. I cannot guarantee I will have them by then."

"Do your best, Ms. Holt. We need the information to save lives."

She walked out to her car surprised at how angry she felt. LizBeth was not entirely surprised at the veiled hostility of Alicia Holt. She wondered if she should attribute her attitude to the reflexive secrecy of the Lab's culture. Or maybe Holt didn't like her because she was an FBI agent and looked gay.

As LizBeth drove down the mountain from the Lab, the beauty of the Española valley and the Sangre de Cristo Mountains to the east lifted her spirits again. The temperature felt positively balmy, even though it was only about 35 degrees. She mused on her conversation with Alicia Holt.

First was the information that Downs had stalked Silvia Duràn in 2012. LizBeth did not know how that fit exactly beyond the fact that Silvia was Luis's sister. Then, *did the Lab not know it was missing C-4?* They certainly knew. And what was this "support group" who attended a Latin Mass twice a week at work? LizBeth would have bet good money that Holt herself was a member of Downs's religious group. But the most important piece of information was Downs's history of psychiatric hospitalization. LizBeth thought about how best to interview his psychiatrist. Psychiatrists were typically adamant about protecting confidentiality even with a character like Downs, but now that lives were at risk...

•

LizBeth pulled into a gas station to call Dr. Lionel Case. She got his receptionist, identified herself and her mission and asked to speak with the doctor.

"He is in session," the receptionist said. "I will give him this message before his next patient and ask him to call you back." Ben had texted her a location for Eduardo Santos that was about ten miles away. She filled up her gas tank and headed north on 68 to the small town of Velarde, along the Rio Grande. From the high road she looked down into the pretty agricultural village with its houses and large fenced pastures to a small central plaza with a spired church. LizBeth drove past the minimart, the fire department and the senior center, which occupied the higher part of town. She turned onto a county road next to a large fruit stand, closed for the season. As she drove toward the river, she waved at a couple of locals who waved back. Passing an apple-packing barn, a large vineyard and a shrine to Santo Niño, she pulled into a driveway next to a neat one-story adobe house surrounded by a low wall.

LizBeth parked and got out. The air smelled clean and moist and the sun felt warm. She opened a white wooden gate and went up to the front door and knocked. As she waited, she noticed a statue of the Virgin Mary in a concrete grotto, two apple trees and Christmas lights around the front door. She rang the bell and in a moment the door opened. A Hispanic man in his seventies looked out at her, then opened the storm door a crack. He leaned on a cane.

"Hello?"

"Hello, are you Mr. Eduardo Santos?"

The man frowned. "Who are you?" He was a small man dressed in corduroy pants, a flannel shirt and bedroom slippers and had a napkin tucked into his shirt. A woman about the same age came out of the kitchen, wiping her hands on her apron.

LizBeth showed her agent card. "Agent LizBeth Tallichet, sir, FBI. Have I interrupted your lunch?" LizBeth asked. "I can come back in half an hour."

"No, no," said the older gentleman, holding the door wider. "Come in, we were finished. All except dessert."

"Oh, you done it now, Eduardo," the woman said, laughing. "We always knew you were a criminal!" She was tall with a long neck and grey hair tucked into a tidy bun.

"Hush now, Lucretia, don't go telling on me!" To LizBeth he said, "You don't look old enough to be FBI! What is this about?"

LizBeth followed them to the kitchen, which smelled of red chile. Lucretia pulled out a chair and indicated LizBeth should sit. The remains of a meal of carne adovada were on the table as well as apple empanadas dusted with confectioners' sugar and a pitcher of Tang. Lucretia was already serving LizBeth a plate. "You don't have to feed me," LizBeth said unconvincingly.

"You are hungry, no?" Lucretia said putting the plate in front of her. "It's lunch time. You won't get better."

"Well, thank you kindly," LizBeth said and took a bite. The pork was tender and the chile was mild but flavorful. "This is delicious." She ate for a while in silence while the older couple had dessert.

"My sister has been cooking all morning," Eduardo said. "I can't eat enough to please her. So what brings you to our little casa?" He refused a second empanada and put his hands, brown and gnarled, on the oilcloth. He had thick grey hair and a well-trimmed mustache over a full mouth. His dark brown eyes were large and expressive.

"I am investigating some events connected to the disappearance of Father Randolph Miller."

Lucretia clucked disapprovingly and spoke to her brother in Spanish. LizBeth heard her say "that pervert."

Eduardo sighed. "I already told the old sheriff everything I knew."

Lucretia said, "Why are you looking into that again? Don't you have anything better to do?" Eduardo poured LizBeth some Tang and put an apple empanada on a plate for her.

"We think it is connected to several recent murders. Would you be willing to answer some questions?"

"Of course. I'd love you to get that man," said Eduardo. "He did a great deal of harm to many." He looked out the window and then back at her and shook his head sadly. "He was a devil."

"How long were you a Christian Brother?"

Eduardo laughed and looked at his sister. "I still am a Christian Brother so far as I know. I joined in 1960 when I was 16 years old. They educated me, no? At the College of Santa Fe. Then they had me teach shop at St. Michael's High School for twenty-five years. I never was ordained. I remained a brother only. But I loved teaching the children, and the faculty was close knit. Those were happy years. But they ended in 1990."

Lucretia started clearing the table. LizBeth made a gesture to help but the older woman shook her head. "No," she said, "you do your work, I'll do mine."

"What happened in 1990?" LizBeth asked.

"I was transferred to the Society of St. Michael – you know, the place for the bad priests. They wanted me to run the physical plant. It was a big property and everything was always breaking down."

"Why do you think you were transferred?"

"I guess somebody had to do it. We had a new principal and a new archbishop, so it was time for changes. I wasn't on anyone's bad side that I know of. But they sent me there that fall, 1990. It was a terrible place."

"What makes you say that?"

"It was lonely. I missed my community. The residents, all of them, had been in some kind of bad trouble. They hid out in their rooms, they drank, they behaved like lost souls. One of them, an old priest from Arizona, hung himself in the chapel. I blame the administration, really. There was no spiritual life beyond daily Mass, no real rehab. After a few months there the residents would get shipped off to somewhere out of state that needed a priest and we'd get a new one. In those days that is what they did, just moved the bad ones around."

Lucretia brought Eduardo a glass of water and some pills. He swallowed the pills and looked at LizBeth. "And all of it was hidden, kept secret."

"What was the administration like?"

"Father Alphonso Griego was the superintendent. He had a drinking problem. He's dead now. Archbishop Sullivan was new to the state at the time, came from Chicago. He lived in Santa Fe but they built him a nice house out there for weekends. He loved to have dinner parties and the like. Randolph Miller visited frequently. Sometimes other big wigs like Sheriff Trujillo were there. But it was a closed group. I never attended." Eduardo's shook his head and clucked his tongue.

"Did you know David Bellows?" LizBeth asked, using Gerald Beatty's former name.

"Yes, I knew him. A young brother in my Order. He came to that place about a year after me. He was a favorite of Miller's. Miller was starting his retreats for boys then, at a camp near Jemez Springs, and he brought David on to help him, you know."

"Were you also involved in the retreats?"

Eduardo sighed deeply. Lucretia set a cup of coffee in front of him. She looked at LizBeth with a frown. "Lalo, it is time for your rest," she said pointedly.

Eduardo gently waved her away. "Yes, once. I was sent to help out but when I saw what was going on that was when I left."

"What did you see?"

Eduardo's eyes filled up. "Miller and Bellows were abusing those boys. They found the ones who were vulnerable, maybe poor, away from home for the first time. I found Miller in the boys' shower watching them and sometimes that other one, Bellows, he would bring a boy to Miller's cabin at night, an older boy for himself and a little one for Miller." Eduardo was gazing out the window.

"Do you remember any of the boys' names?"

"No. But there were lots of boys from parishes all over el Norte. Boys from Santa Fe, Los Alamos and all the pueblos. I told the archbishop but he wouldn't listen to me. He threatened to transfer me to St. Louis. I told him if he tried, I would go to the police."

"Did you go to the police?"

"I went to Sheriff Trujillo."

Eduardo cleared his throat and stood up. He looked at his sister for a moment as if confused about how to proceed. Lucretia stood also and glared at LizBeth. "This is too much for him," she said. "He has a bad heart. It is his siesta now."

"No, no," Eduardo said, waving her away again and walking to the back door. "I need to get outside, get some fresh air," he said. "Come, girl, you can talk to me outside." He picked up his cane and put on a jacket and boots. "I want to check on the bees."

LizBeth followed the old man out the back door and watched as he descended the steps carefully, holding tight to the handrail. The backyard held a clothesline, a grape arbor and four beehives on cinderblocks. Snow had melted around the hives.

"Lucretia can't stand to see me upset. Makes her upset too! But I want to tell you what I know. You see, I had always thought that the archbishop was hiding what was going on in order to protect the reputation of the Church. Our Church is very powerful here in New Mexico, for good and not so good."

The old man crept to the first hive and stood still listening. He took the rock off the top and slipped off the lid. Inside hundreds of bees were humming in their frames. Eduardo seemed satisfied with what he found.

"Ah," he said, "this hive has made it so far!" He quickly put the lid back on and replaced the rock. "These little creatures are like our family members," he said, smiling at LizBeth. "Lucretia and I are twins. Neither of us ever married. Our parents and our little brother are dead. Lorenzo died in Vietnam. So, it is just us. We take care of each other. And we love the bees. Have you ever had mead? I make it. I'll give you some to taste." He checked all the hives and found them all surviving.

LizBeth asked, "What made you think the archbishop knew about and hid the abuse?"

"When I was asked to help with Miller's summer camps, I didn't want to do it. The archbishop said it was my duty and that I was to protect the boys. I didn't know what he meant at the time. I thought he meant keep them from getting into trouble with each other. I knew what kinds of things go on with boys in camps, seminaries, boarding schools. I myself had seen it." He gazed to the horizon. "But I didn't know the danger would be coming from the priests. I was naïve that way. That had not happened to me. I had never seen it either."

"Did you think that Archbishop Sullivan was aware of what Miller was doing?"

"Not at the time, no. But later, when I came to tell him about it, I realized that he did know. He knew but was turning a blind eye."

"Why would he do that? Was he molesting also?" LizBeth asked.

"He had an image to protect, I believe. Miller gave these popular retreats all over. Very well attended and respected. Grant money was raised, you know? And the archbishop didn't want to upset the apple cart."

"What did you say to the archbishop when you told him about it?" LizBeth asked.

"I told him the truth. I told him that Father Randolph Miller was abusing the boys in the camp and it needed to stop. I quoted St. Matthew to him, 'Whomsoever offends a child who believes in me, it is better they have a millstone hung around their neck and be thrown into the sea.'"

"And what did Sullivan say?" LizBeth asked.

"He instructed me to be humble, quiet and obedient. He reminded me that my superiors would guide me and watch out for me and not to engage in any idle talk about all of this 'rubbish.' That was the word he used. Then he sent me back to work."

"What did you do?" LizBeth asked.

Santos was quiet for a few moments. "I did the only thing I could do to save my faith in God. I left." LizBeth touched his arm in sympathy and Eduardo nodded but continued to look at the sky.

"Even after I told the archbishop everything no one was removed, and the retreats kept happening. I took all my things and moved in here and have been here ever since." Santos looked at LizBeth and sighed. "For years

I got a monthly stipend from the Order. About seven years ago I started mailing them back. We don't need them. Lucretia has a good state pension."

"Did you ever hear anything further from Randolph Miller or David Bellows?"

"No. Trujillo sent a deputy to interview me when Miller disappeared, but I didn't have anything new to tell him. Then the investigation seemed to be dropped altogether. I imagine the archbishop was relieved."

"Does an archbishop have the power to influence investigations?"

"He did when Trujillo was sheriff."

"Did you ever hear anything about any of the boys who were abused at the retreats? Like maybe two Picuris boys, Luis Duràn and Elías Chacón?"

"No. I do remember a little Picuris child of maybe nine, cute as can be, up at the retreat. He was with his older cousin, I believe. I believe they were both abused—I know the little one was. But I don't remember their names."

"Do you remember any Anglo boys from Los Alamos?"

"No. There were boys from Los Alamos I believe but I don't have a clear memory of them."

The old man was watching a honeybee that had landed on his hand. He walked over to the first hive and gently maneuvered the bee onto the sill. "One time a few years ago an Anglo man came to see me about this. It was after Miller disappeared. I remember Lucretia took an immediate dislike to him. Didn't want him in the house. She can be like that. But I thought he was nice enough. He'd been at the Jemez retreats, he said, the year I was there. He wanted me to tell him why they stopped having them."

"What did you tell him?"

"I told him the truth. I told him what I had seen and what I had done."

"Did he ask about anything else?"

Eduardo paused. "He asked if I was still getting money from the archbishop."

"What did you tell him?"

"I never took money from the archbishop or from the archdiocese. Just my severance from the Order, which I eventually sent back. I told him that."

"Then what happened?"

Eduardo headed toward the kitchen door. He looked exhausted.

"He seemed relieved to get the information and he left."

"What did he look like?"

"I don't know, Anglo, young. Blonde hair."

"Was his name Malcolm Downs?"

"I don't know. I don't remember names as well as I used to."

•

Dr. Case had called back while LizBeth was in Velarde. He'd left a voicemail offering to meet with her if she could come by his office and gave directions. LizBeth drove to Pojoàque, a pueblo town about twenty minutes away.

Dr. Lionel Case saw patients in a territorial style house at the end of a cul de sac. Case's receptionist greeted LizBeth at the door and locked it behind them. She showed LizBeth into a conference room. Red germaniums were blooming in a south facing window. Dr. Case, a lanky, bearded African-American man in a tweed jacket and blue jeans, came in carrying several files and a clipboard which he placed on the conference table. "When I heard from you I cleared my afternoon," he said, shaking LizBeth's hand and inviting her to sit down. "Anything that combines the FBI and Malcolm Downs has to be serious."

"Yes, that is why I am requesting that you limit his doctor patient confidentiality. It literally is a case of life and death at this point."

"I understand. In fact, I plan to close my office after this meeting and not reopen until Downs is apprehended."

"You think he could be a threat to you?"

"I do." He put on reading glasses and opened one of the charts on the table.

"So, what can you tell me about his psychiatric history?" LizBeth asked.

"I'll just read a bit from my initial assessment." He spoke in a soft Southern accent. "Let's see, I'll hit the high points. Born August 3, 1980, only child, no significant medical problems, single, no children, lives alone. You no doubt know all this?"

LizBeth nodded. "Go ahead though, Dr. Case. We can make sure we have the same facts."

"All righty, then," Dr. Case said and moved quickly through other details from the first meeting. "Top-secret security clearance. Trained as an electrical engineer and explosives technician. Recently discharged from St. Joseph Hospital after two-week stay following suicidal threats made to his parents. Discharge medications: Fluoxitine, 90 mg, Seroquel, 400 mg, Clonazepam, .5 mg. Previous therapy: treated as a child for selective mutism, resolved. Presenting problem: psychotic depression related to recent arrest for assault, loss of relationship with "family friend" he assaulted and temporary loss of security clearance. Also reports conflict with other attendees at mandated anger-management classes at local domestic violence shelter. Reports history of interpersonal problems at work. Denies history of trauma or abuse. Initial diagnosis: major depression with psychotic features. Rule out narcissistic personality disorder."

"Did your assessment of him change over time?" LizBeth asked.

Case took off his glasses and closed the file. "Yes. When I first met him, he looked quite competent. I thought he was a depressed narcissist. Once he began to feel better he came only sporadically. He was mainly interested in getting his security clearance back. Even then I had no idea how disordered he was, but I knew his personality disorder included more than narcissism. I added borderline and sociopathic traits to his diagnosis. I began to suspect even more serious problems."

"Like psychosis?"

"Yes. I began to suspect he was delusional."

"What did you talk about when you met?" LizBeth asked.

"Mainly about his relationship with Silvia Duràn, from whom he was estranged. She had an order of protection against him. Downs was overly involved with her, had been for years. He was paying her school tuition and desperately wanted to reconcile with her. But I couldn't tell if she was more like a little sister or if the relationship was romantic."

"Why was he paying her school tuition?" Ulysses asked.

"I'm not sure," Case said, "He never gave me a convincing answer. Several times we talked about his parents. He came from a puritanical family," Case said. "His mother was a brilliant scientist and was often away from home at conferences, leaving Downs at his father's mercy most of the time. His father was punishing and cruel, and Downs had extreme shame about sex."

"Do you think he himself was molested?" LizBeth asked.

"Undoubtedly, but he was never willing to talk about it. It represented being a victim to him and that went against his belief in his uber-masculinity. He hated gay people and hated and feared women." Case set aside the first file, opened the second one and started leafing through the pages.

"Except little girls?" LizBeth asked.

"In the case of Silvia, that would be correct," the psychiatrist replied. "I always had a hunch his obsession with her was sexual in nature but I have no real evidence."

"When did you last see him in your office?"

"I haven't seen him in about six months. Not since his last hospitalization, I believe. Let's see," Dr. Case consulted another chart. "Yes, that's right, it was late last spring."

"Do you have any idea why Downs might have become homicidal?"

"Nothing certain." He paused. "But Mr. Downs had a hidden complex delusional structure, deep-seated. It only revealed itself when he became floridly psychotic."

"What is a delusional structure?"

"A fixed belief system that is not based in reality, like believing you are God, or Elvis's secret wife, something like that," Case said, chuckling and then stopping himself. In a more serious voice he continued, "For the most part Downs kept his delusions secret. But under a great deal of stress the mask could slip."

"When did you first see this?"

"After Silvia Duràn took her life. He decompensated after her death, terribly—not eating, not sleeping, not even bathing. It was the only time I ever saw him in recognizable anguish. He blamed himself for her death but denied killing her. I'm not sure he knew whether he had killed her or not. In one session around that time he said he was supposedly being trained to bring devils to justice. I asked if he was hearing voices and he admitted that he was. Downs believed the Church had gone astray and it was his job to help restore discipline. He said he'd tried to recruit Silvia to join the angelic force but he wasn't having much luck. He told me the "other side" was also recruiting her. According to him everyone was on one side or the other. I often wondered what side he thought I was on."

"So just what does the angelic force do exactly, in his delusion?"

"They are engaged in an eternal battle against Satanic forces, was what he said. Malcolm saw himself as a kind of assistant angel of death."

"What kind of devils?" LizBeth asked. "People or imaginary devils?"

"People. Pedophiles most especially, and their enablers. He had a special hatred for authority figures like clergy." *And law enforcement, LizBeth wondered?*

"Is he a psychopath?" LizBeth asked.

"I suspect so," Dr. Case said.

"Were you able to help him at all?" LizBeth asked.

Dr. Case sighed and shook his head. "No, sadly, Downs was impervious to anything I tried. I knew from experience that nothing dislodges a delusion like his, no amount of talk and no medications either. When I questioned his beliefs he either assured me he never intended to hurt anyone or he became belligerent. Then he stopped coming all together."

"Did you ever think to report him to someone? Like his employer?"

"Ms. Tallichet, I'm not sure you understand my position. Since he had never threatened anyone in particular there was no one to warn. And beyond that he had doctor-patient confidentiality. As scary as he was, I was his doctor first."

"Does Downs know where you live?"

"I think he might," Lionel Case said, closing his charts. "That's why my wife and I are going to her sister's cabin in Pecos for a week. I hope you catch him by then."

LizBeth left Dr. Case's office and drove back north toward Sleeping Tiger. On the way through the canyon she'd missed two calls from Ben. She called him back on the road from Dixon to Peñasco and got him on the first try.

"They haven't found Sheriff Walker," Ben reported. "The helicopter got called back to Albuquerque an hour ago. We've got our guys on the ground and a couple of guys from the nearby pueblo are out looking too."

LizBeth felt fear thinking how long the sheriff had been incommunicado. The man shouldn't have gone out there alone. If he was dead there would be hell to pay. *It'll somehow get blamed on me,* she thought, *even though he's the one that ran off half-cocked.* She felt a deep, familiar resentment. *I'm starting to develop a little attitude problem with these sheriffs, she reflected. Walker's not a bad guy. In fact, he's one of the better ones.* She adjusted her rearview mirror. "Anything yet on the evidence gathered this morning?"

"Berg is the only one not accounted for. Forensics has the remains they found in the building that burned. They are just fragments, really, and our guy says there's not probably not much DNA there. We won't hear anything definitive for a while. The boys picked up a strange letter from Melanie Hirsh to Gerald Beatty. Could be incriminating. I'll email you a scan. I didn't find much on Astrid Berg herself beyond stuff on her track-star days. Did you know she was on the Olympic track team in Barcelona?"

"What about since she's been a guru or whatever she is?" LizBeth asked. She cracked open her window.

"There was a lot about Wakeful Mind, the outfit in Cali she's connected with. The head guy there, Junsu Ito, got busted for involvement with an underage girl a number of years ago. Evidently, not his first, but the first time he got caught. A lot of people didn't like the way the whole thing unfolded. Junsu Ito ended up killing himself and that was the end of it. Senior people covered it up and Berg took over. She's been in her position ever since, four or five years at least."

"Nothing recent on Berg?"

"No, nothing since she took over as head honcho."

"Okay, hey, I got to get on the road, I'll check you later."

LizBeth reflected that if the remains from the dormitory were Astrid Berg's it was too late to do anything about it. But Downs represented a clear and present danger to the region. LizBeth wondered about his relationship with Picuris Pueblo. How well did he know the BLM land where he was probably now holed up? Maybe a good bit better than they had thought. She looked at her watch. It was 3:00 and would be dusk in ninety minutes. At the fork in the road leading off toward Sleeping Tiger, LizBeth turned instead toward Picuris.

•

After feeding the men, Jo tidied up the library from Josh's brief stay there, picking up a scarf, a notepad and some catalogues. One catalogue was open to a pony-themed pink bedspread and curtains. It looked like Josh had been Christmas shopping for children. *He seems too young to have his own children*, Jo thought, but maybe he has a niece. Josh was probably out of surgery by now. He was lucky he hadn't been hurt worse.

Jo sat in one of the leather armchairs near the window and tried to catch up with her feelings. She was deeply shaken by the events of the past few days. She'd had many losses in her life – first her parents' divorce and her mother leaving California for Florida, then, when Jo was seventeen, her mother's death in a boating accident. The most recent, of course, was Tim's illness and death, from which she knew she had not fully recovered.

Jo had seen her share of violent death working as an EMT. But the murder of Gerald and disappearance of Astrid felt altogether different. She was so angry at the murderer, an anger that challenged her commitment to equanimity. Even though Roshi repeatedly reminded her that the only refuge was in the dharma, Jo thought she'd found a perfect refuge at Sleeping Tiger. Maybe all she'd found was a place to hide. In that way she wasn't that different from her parents. As soon as this realization hit, she wanted to reject it.

But it was true. Her parents had escaped the chaotic San Francisco hippie scene in the seventies and settled in the Sierras at an ashram to chant, meditate and grow vegetables. Anandaville, the communal village where she grew up, was now a tumbledown collection of houses full of old-timers like her father who remained long after the community's spiritual leader had abandoned them. It was hard to visit Anandaville, but she missed her father's gentle presence terribly sometimes.

If she'd had access to a car Jo would have driven to Taos to check on Tomàs. Instead she had to satisfy herself with a phone call. Tomàs sounded sleepy and bored when she called him shortly after lunch. She apologized that she wouldn't be able to feed his chickens and explained why. He laughed and said they were tough old birds and would survive.

"Have they found Astrid?" he asked.

"No," Jo said. "But she might have been in the building when it blew up. They found some teeth and bone fragments."

"My God, that is gruesome. I worry about that sheriff," Tomàs said. "You haven't heard anything?"

"Nothing. His wife called two hours ago pretty concerned. I think Ray Pando and his son have gone out there to search. The FBI guys are still out there."

"I wish I could help," Tomàs said.

"Try to get some rest," Jo said. "When will you be discharged?"

"I'd like to go right now but they won't release me yet."

Jo wanted to say *"I wish you were here"* but knew that wouldn't be wise.

"Hey, are you safe there?" Tomàs asked. Jo realized she hadn't thought about her own safety for a while.

"I think so."

"Don't stay there alone," Tomàs said.

"Don't worry, I won't." When she hung up the phone, Jo realized that the volunteer firefighters, state police search-and-rescue team and the state fire marshals had already left the scene. Ray and the FBI agents had gone off into the woods. She stepped outside and looked up at the smoking hull that used to be the dormitory, relieved to see two ATF agents still picking through the ruins.

Jo saw Roshi Melanie's car coming slowly up the driveway.

"I'm so glad you're here!" Melanie said, getting out to hug her. "I didn't know what to expect, but I just had to get home." Melanie had dark circles under her eyes, and her clothes looked as if she'd slept in them.

Jo and Melanie began walking toward the site of the explosion. As soon as she could see the dormitory and Gerald's house, she drew in a sharp breath. "Oh, my God," she said, softly. "I can't believe it—the dormitory, the superintendent's house—gone!" She sighed deeply and closed her eyes for a few moments. "You know what, so be it! Those two buildings, they always seemed like they belonged to an asylum…or a prison." She looked at Jo with an expression Jo associated with Roshi Melanie having found a "teaching moment."

"It is not impermanence that makes us suffer," Melanie said, quoting a favorite line from Vietnamese Buddhist monk, Thich Nat Hahn, "it is wanting things to be permanent that are not." Roshi Melanie looked at Jo and smiled. Jo put her arm around her teacher and pulled her into an embrace. Jo wanted to tell her about Astrid but didn't know how to begin.

"Roshi, the ATF agents found human remains in the dormitory debris. It could be Astrid." Melanie stiffened and pulled back, beginning to cry.

"Oh, my God," Roshi Melanie said. "Will it never end?" They walked slowly to her house.

Once inside Melanie went into her bedroom and Jo heard the shower come on in her bathroom. Jo made them a pot of tea and turkey sandwiches. When Melanie came out in her bathrobe they ate in silence. Then they went to their separate rooms to lie down for much needed rest.

When Jo woke, she could hear Roshi Melanie on the kitchen phone telling Carmen not to worry about coming in. She said she'd put most of the attendees on a shuttle to the Albuquerque airport just before lunch. The others were staying in Taos to fly out of Santa Fe in the morning.

Jo looked out the upstairs window and saw that the ATF car was gone. She and Melanie were alone at Sleeping Tiger. She thought of Tomàs's caution: "Don't stay there alone." The phone rang and Jo picked it up in the bedroom that had been used as the interview room. It was Rosemary Walker.

"Have you heard anything?" Rosemary asked. Her tone was more subdued than a few hours earlier but Jo could feel her anxiety.

"Nothing yet," Jo said. "The helicopter was recalled to Albuquerque, but our agents plus Ray and Matt Pando are out searching now."

"That's good," Rosemary said, as if trying to encourage herself. "If anyone can find him it would be Ray. Who else is with you?" Rosemary was talking softly and Jo wondered if the children were napping nearby.

"Actually, I think Roshi Melanie and I are alone. Everyone else seems to have finished up and gone."

"You should *not* be alone there," Rosemary said, suddenly stern. "Come stay with me. I can put the kids in one room and give you and Melanie the other. Seriously, you should get out of there right away!"

Jo felt uncertain. "I'll see if I can convince Melanie to come."

"Don't try to convince her. Insist. That killer is still loose and you two are sitting ducks. I'm going to call Ulys's office and get the deputies to come for you."

"No, no, we have her car." Jo said. "I'll make her come."

"Promise?" Rosemary asked.

"Yes, I promise." She wrote Rosemary's phone number and address on a notepad. "I'll call you when we're about to leave." When Jo hung up, she heard the front door open and someone come in. Jo's stomach turned over in fear. She hadn't locked the door!

"Hello?" Roshi Melanie called from the kitchen. "Who's there?"

"I have some business to settle with you," a man's voice said from the living room. Jo froze. She felt as if she had entered a tunnel, where everything was far away and unreal. Whoever it was had gone into the kitchen. Jo crept down the stairs, unseen.

"Put the gun down, Jon. Let's talk." Melanie's voice was firm and calm.

Gun! thought Jo, her throat closing in fear. She slid along the living room wall, hoping she was out of sight from the kitchen.

"You ruined me," Jon Malvern said walking toward where Melanie sat at the kitchen table. "You made Gerald reject me."

"What do you mean?" Roshi Melanie asked, her voice quavering. Then realizing who he might be she whispered, "Are you Skip?"

"Remember how you made him break up with me?"

"I was trying to protect you. You were a child then. "

"Yeah, but I'm not a child anymore. Gerald and I have been lovers off and on for years. We were finally going to live together. But he said you'd found out about our plans and would report him as a child molester if he got together with me."

"Jon, Gerald wasn't telling you the truth. Please put the gun down. "You're very angry. Killing me won't bring Gerald back." She drew in a sharp breath. "Did you kill Gerald, Jon?" she asked.

"No! I wanted to kill him. That's why I came here. But somebody took care of that for me, didn't they? So now I only have to kill you and then myself."

Jo reached the fireplace where a heavy iron poker stood against some split logs and kindling. She grasped the poker and moved toward the kitchen door. The man had his back to her and held a gun leveled at Roshi Melanie.

"He borrowed money from me for a down payment on a house in Santa Fe. We were going to open a gallery together. Then I found out he had someone else, another boy. You knew all about this!" It sounded like Jon was crying.

"I didn't know all of it…Jon, I'm so sorry. Please don't hurt me…or anyone! Let's talk this through…"

Jo moved toward the open door with the poker in her right hand. *What am I doing?* she wondered. *Am I really going to hit him with this iron bar?* An adrenaline surge told her she was.

Jo stepped from behind the door and swung the poker at Jon's head, striking him in side of his face as he turned toward her. His gun discharged, the bullet hitting the living room wall behind her. Jo stood still, feeling oddly calm. Jon fell onto Melanie and then slid to the ground. The gun dropped from his hand and Jo picked it up. Blood was pouring from Jon's ear and his face clouded with pain and confusion. As Melanie and Jo looked on he lapsed into unconsciousness.

Jo called 911. She was connected with the sheriff's dispatcher, who said Rosemary Walker had already called in a wellness check and a deputy on his way. Jo reported the injured man and the need for an ambulance. She checked Malvern's pulse. It was elevated. She stood over him, holding the gun. It felt cold and heavy in her hand. The anger washing over her turned to sadness and she began to cry. Roshi Melanie took the gun from her hand and embraced her.

Chapter XIII

"What is it you want to know about me?" Ulysses asked. Seated on the plywood floor of the yurt with his bound legs stretched in front of him and his hands cuffed in front of him, Ulysses looked around him. The canvas yurt was about twelve feet in diameter and held a bed pallet, a table and two chairs. There was no electricity or running water, just two kerosene lamps, a potbellied stove, a composting toilet and a sink with a standpipe. The canvas looked old and was patched in places.

Downs's stuff was neatly stacked: a plastic tub of freeze-dried food, a small pile of kindling, a hatchet, ammunition, detonators, a water purifier and a pile of books. Downs was sitting on the pallet covered by an expedition-weight down sleeping bag. Beside him were a hand-crank radio, a flashlight and a rosary. *Perfect hideout for a murderer/survivalist,* Ulysses thought.

"Are you a religious man?" Downs asked.

Ulysses hesitated. "No, not really. I mean... no, the answer is no."

"Why are you stumbling over my very first question?" Downs asked, looking amused.

"I believe in God but I don't practice religion. My parents were sort of spiritual."

"What is your relationship with the Catholic Church?"

Ulysses wondered where the hell this was going. Downs held up a handgun and checked the loaded chamber, then placed it beside his hairbrush.

"I have no relationship with the Catholic Church. None whatsoever."

"Do you know Archbishop Sullivan?"

"Not personally, no."

"What is your relationship with Sheriff Trujillo?"

"*Former* Sheriff Trujillo of Taos County?"

"Answer the question."

"When he decided not to run for re-election two years ago, I ran against and defeated his anointed successor, for which I have earned his dislike. I have only a professional relationship with him and it isn't cordial."

"Did you know Randolph Miller?"

"No. I knew who he was, of course, and I have read about his disappearance, which happened before my time as sheriff."

"Did you know Silvia Duràn?"

Ulysses hesitated. Downs noticed his hesitation.

"I investigated the circumstances around her suicide when I worked as a police detective in Santa Fe."

"What did you find?"

"She died from strangulation, hanging from a viga in her dormitory. She did not leave a note, but her friends reported she'd been depressed for months so it was ruled a suicide and the case was closed." Ulysses sensed an opportunity to ask his own question. "Did you know Silvia?"

"Yes, I knew her," Downs said. "She took the wrong path in life."

Rejected lover, Ulysses thought. "She was too young to die that way," he said instead. "She had so much promise. She wanted to be a doctor, I'd heard."

Downs narrowed his eyes. "She thought a lot of herself," he said. "She could be very cruel." He stood and spat into the sink.

"Some thought she was murdered," Ulysses said. Downs seemed preoccupied with his own thoughts and didn't reply. He sat for a few moments with his eyes closed.

"Suicide is the only sin which cannot be forgiven," Downs said at last, opening his eyes and looking at Ulysses.

"I don't believe that," Ulysses said. "It takes a long time to die from hanging. Maybe she asked for forgiveness before she died."

"Enough about her," Downs said. "Did you know her brother?"

"Luis Duràn, no, but we are investigating his murder."

"I'll save you the trouble," Downs said. "I killed him. In my role as avenging angel."

Ulysses held back a snort of laughter. "Avenging angel?" he managed to say. "What is that?"

"Since you are not a religious man you won't believe me," Downs said, "but there are angels and devils that walk the earth disguised as ordinary people." He met Ulysses's gaze, smiling. "I am one of them."

"Are you an angel or a devil?" Ulysses asked. "You kill people, right? That sounds devilish to me." *I better watch myself here,* he thought.

Instead of taking offense, Downs chuckled. "What do you know about this kind of thing?"

"I'm educated," Ulysses said. "I studied religion in college. I've read the Bible."

"Look, it's a war. Angels against devils. Right now the devils are ascendant. Haven't you heard?" He seemed to enjoy the topic.

Are you going to kill me now after you've explained all this? Ulysses wondered, feeling a chill in his belly. Just keep him talking. "How do you know whom to kill? Are you told by someone?" Downs didn't flinch with Ulysses's switch from the hypothetical to the personal.

"Yes, we are. For example, I got my first assignment about ten years ago. Which I accomplished perfectly, I might add."

"Randolph Miller?"

Downs nodded and smiled acknowledging Ulysses's intuition. "That's right! I led him away in his car by promising him something he had always wanted from me but never gotten. I took him onto the Comanche Mesa just as I was told. I tied him there for a few days, and when nature took its course I buried him so well he has never been found."

"When nature took its course?"

"Thirst did the work for me."

Ulysses contemplated a man bound and left exposed on a rocky mesa to die of thirst. And a man who would carry out such a plan. "So you left him there and later went back and buried the body?"

"What was left of it. He'd fed a whole lot of vultures. He was mainly bones."

Downs lay back on his sleeping bag and put his hands behind his head. Ulysses continued his questioning. "And you also killed Luis Duràn?"

Downs stroked the light stubble on his upper lip and chin. "That was easy. I pushed him from a high place, just as he had done with Elías Chacón seven years before. A perfect balancing stroke of justice!" Downs looked at Ulysses and smiled. "It was very pleasurable for me when he fell."

"Why did Luis push Elías off the roof?" Ulysses asked.

"Elías knew Luis's secrets."

"Did Luis procure for Miller?"

Downs didn't answer. Ulysses wondered if Downs had lost interest in the conversation and was instead deciding how to kill him. They sat for a few minutes in silence.

"Were you abused, Malcolm?"

Downs chuckled. "That's what you all think. That I was abused. Listen, I am no victim. I am a victor," he said. "I have almost completed my retribution."

"So what gives you permission to exact retribution? Isn't that a role for law enforcement?"

"We are the ultimate law enforcement. I get my orders from the highest authority." He paused for a moment as if listening to something outside, then said, "You also kill, right? In the line of duty? Do you think you are innocent?"

Ulysses flashed on Johnny Catron's face the moment before his death. Did Downs know about the Catron incident? A beam of late afternoon sun illuminated the dust motes swirling in the yurt's shadowy interior. Ulysses changed topics.

"Do you ever find your job unpleasant?" Ulysses asked.

"Never," he said. "My worry is that I like it too much. You can understand that, right?" Downs' laugh was mirthless. He stood up and walked to the window.

Ulysses's fear returned full force. This man had nothing left to lose. What would happen as it got dark? Ulysses shifted position. "I need to pee," he said.

Downs pulled him to a standing position and helped him hobble to the composting toilet. As he shuffled across the plywood floor Ulysses took note of items that might be useful: a hatchet and a lighter near the woodstove, and a can of cookstove fuel and a knife on the counter in the makeshift kitchen. He felt relieved that he could move about relatively well. He figured he had a concussion but maybe not a skull fracture. When Ulysses finished using the toilet, Downs untied his hands and cuffed them with flex cuffs behind his back.

"You are a family man, am I right?" Downs asked.

"I have a family, yes," Ulysses said, warily. Leading him away from Rosemary and the children he continued, "My father has passed but my mother and sister live in Albuquerque." Ulysses swallowed and ventured, "Do you have a family?"

"No," Downs said, scratching his stubbly jaw. "My work is my life. I try not to get distracted." Downs lay back down and stared at the ceiling as if contemplating his next step.

Ulysses felt like Scheherazade. He had to keep this conversation going. "When did you get the mission to kill Beatty?" he asked.

"I'd been watching both Beatty and Duràn for months. I knew about their little meetings. I began following Luis first and he led me to Gerald. The retreat provided a perfect opportunity to catch Gerald."

"You had been to Zen retreats before?" Ulysses asked, remembering that Downs had met Astrid at a Wakeful Mind sesshin.

"Oh, yes. I am drawn to them. I am naturally very mindful."

"Were you having sex with Astrid Berg at this one, too?"

Downs did not reply. He began putting on his boots.

"Did you kill her?"

"Why don't you just shut up?"

"Is there is a right time and a wrong time to take a life?"

"Yes, there most definitely is," Downs said angrily, lacing his boots. He lifted the flap over the door and looked out.

"What was Gerald's sin?" Ulysses asked. He sensed Downs' irritation but felt compelled to keep him talking just to buy time.

Downs sneered at Ulysses. "You don't know?"

"How did you kill him?" This topic seemed to interest Downs.

"I prefer to find a natural way. The use of guns," he said, sliding the loaded pistol into his shoulder holster, "is frowned upon. Too traceable." He strapped on the holster and took his coat from its hook by the door. "It was a perfect night for hypothermia, kind of like tonight. Clear and very cold. Dunking Gerald in sewage first made it fast and especially apropos for his filthy ways. My supervisors like these kinds of touches."

Ulysses took in a deep breath and let it out slowly. So that was Downs' plan for him; death from hypothermia. "How did you know about Gerald's sinfulness?"

"I knew about him for many years," Downs answered. He filled his canteen from the standpipe and opened a pack of buffalo jerky. He took out a piece and put the rest in his backpack along with more energy bars. He began chewing on a piece as he spoke, his back to Ulysses. "When about twelve years old, I attended a summer camp for boys near Jemez Springs led by Miller, whom my supervisors called Moloch. Moloch was there, assisted by two Christian Brothers, Gerald and another man, a much older man who was without sin so far as I could tell. Gerald brought boys to Moloch to be fondled, maybe sodomized. Pretty children as young as eight, such as little Elías Chacón and older boys like Luis. His mother, Casimira, worked for Moloch. Her time is coming." He took a drink of water and bit off another piece of jerky. Downs was rambling and his face was sweaty. Ulysses wondered if he was psychotic.

"Who was Moloch?" Ulysses asked.

"Moloch was a god who demanded the human sacrifice of children. He was just a small time devil, really. We are more powerful."

Downs continued his preparations to leave the yurt. Ulysses felt didn't have much time but he didn't know what to do. He breathed deeply and tried to push down his desperation.

"You knew the whole Duràn family then?" Ulysses asked.

"Yes. I knew them before Casimira moved with the children to Taos. My parents used to take me to dances at the pueblo and we would go to their house on feast days. And I tried to look out for little Silvia. But I was not able to protect her. She turned too willful."

"Protect her from what?"

"None of your business," Downs said. "Hey, man, this isn't your inquisition. Why don't you tell me your sins? I can't give you absolution, of course." A look of pity crossed his face.

Ulysses took a deep breath and let it out slowly. "I'm not a particularly sinful guy."

"That's not what I've heard."

Ulysses's heart raced. "What have you heard?" he asked.

Downs threw back his head and laughed. "I'm teasing you. You look like you just shit yourself!" He found his hat and gloves and swung his backpack over his shoulder. "I've always enjoyed the effect I have on people when they know who I truly am, which is probably a failing on my part. Sheriff, I do know you are sinful. Right now, though, you are just in my way. But I am allowed a little collateral damage."

"Like with Astrid Berg?" As soon as he said it, Ulysses regretted it. Why did he want to antagonize this man?

"Precisely. Our interview is over." Downs put on his wool hat, grabbed a rosary from the floor and stuffed it in his pocket. Then he pulled off two pieces of duct tape and quickly taped Ulysses's eyes and mouth.

"It's almost dark," he said gleefully, as he went out the door.

•

Two deputies pulled up and parked beside what Angela noted was a strange car, *likely a rental*. She and Zack jumped out of the squad car, drew their weapons and ran toward the main house. As they came around the dining hall they saw the devastation of the dormitory and superintendent's house for the first time.

"This was all done by the guy the boss is tracking?" Zach asked and whistled under his breath.

Angela shook her head grimly. "I hope Sheriff's guardian angel is looking out for him." They neared the house and Angela drew her gun. Zack opened the front door.

A man lay on the kitchen floor, unconscious, his hands tied. A young woman, Angela guessed it was Jo McAlister, held an ice pack to his head. The poker lay on the floor beside him and his gun was on the kitchen table.

An older woman sat at the table, in a bathrobe. Both women looked shaken.

"Ms. Hirsh, are you okay?" Angela asked. Melanie nodded.

"I hit him pretty hard," Jo McAlister said. "I didn't know what else to do."

"Yes," Angela said, "and it's a good thing or he might have overpowered you." She picked up the gun with a cloth and put it in an evidence bag. "Zach, take this out and let the paramedics in. I'll need to get statements from both of you but that can wait until they get him out of here."

Two paramedics lifted Jon Malvern onto a stretcher and lifted him to a gurney. Zach handcuffed Malvern to the gurney and walked with them to the ambulance.

"Tell me exactly what happened, Ms. McAlister," Angela said.

"Melanie and I had a late lunch and then we both took naps. When I woke up I got a call from Rosemary Walker. Right after I hung up, I heard the front door open." Jo paused a moment and swallowed hard. "Neither one of us had thought to lock the front door. Then I heard this man here, John Malvern, downstairs threatening Melanie. I snuck down the steps and picked up the poker from beside the fireplace. He was pointing the gun at her and also threatened to kill himself. I didn't even think about it. I just hit him as hard as I could. His gun discharged and the bullet just missed her."

Melanie put her hand on Jo's shoulder. "You saved my life," she said. Jo said nothing. She felt numb.

Angela turned to Melanie. "Why would Malvern want to harm you, Ms. Hirsh?"

"It's a long story," Melanie said haltingly. "He felt I interfered with his relationship with Gerald Beatty."

"Interfered how?"

"It was a long time ago in California. Malvern was underage and I threatened to report Gerald if he didn't break off their relationship. I was Gerald's therapist at the time."

"Did he say anything about Beatty's death?"

"He said he had come here to kill Gerald but someone beat him to it," Melanie said.

"Were they still in touch after all these years?" Angela asked.

"I think they became reconnected a few years ago. Jon said Gerald borrowed money from him. Jon thought it was to buy a house in Santa Fe where they were going to live together."

"Why was Malvern going to kill him then?" Angela asked.

"Gerald had met someone else, evidently, and Jon had gotten wind of it." Melanie flushed and looked down. Jo was watching her intently. Was that a guilty look?

"Do you know who that person was?"

"I don't know his name. A young man. I think Gerald met him at the community college. He was taking classes toward high school graduation."

Jo felt her stomach turn. Was Melanie covering for Gerald going after a high school boy?

"Is there anything you would like to say, Miss?" Angela asked Jo.

"No, nothing," Jo said. All she could think about was the sensation in her hands of the poker smashing Jon Malvern's head. Jo ran to the sink and vomited. Melanie got her a cold washcloth and a glass of water and rinsed out the sink. "We've had a terrible twenty-four hours, Deputy," Melanie said. "I think we should get somewhere safe now and rest."

"Okay," Angela said, giving Melanie her card. "If you remember anything, like that boy in Santa Fe's name, give me a call at this number. We'll stay outside until you leave."

Melanie stood up when Angela left. "Why don't you pack and we can go to Rosemary's until things settle down?"

"I need a chance to clear my mind," Jo said. "Would you drop me at a motel in Taos?"

"Would you like me to stay with you?"

"No, I need to be alone for a while," Jo said. "I'm exhausted. Besides, Rosemary could probably use your support." They locked Melanie's house and got into her car. Both women were aware of a new cautiousness in their relationship. As the sun set they drove the snow-covered roads to Taos and Melanie dropped Jo off at an old budget hotel on the outskirts of town. Jo went into the dingy room, lay on one of the saggy beds and sobbed.

•

Ulysses sat, blind and mute and feeling cold, afraid and enraged. At first he could hear Downs moving around outside but then all he heard was silence. Ulysses figured Downs was eliminating any signs of their presence from the exterior of the yurt and then covering any tracks from where Downs had dragged him.

Ulysses considered his predicament. It was impossible to know whether Downs intended to kill him or not. Ulysses knew better than to trust the scruples of a psychopath. Downs could easily find a "natural death" for Ulysses by stripping him of his clothes and putting him outside for the night. If there was a way to get free, now was the time. It was already dark and Downs could be back any minute.

The plastic handcuffs cut into his wrists and his shoulders were sore from the position of his hands tight behind his back. Fortunately, Downs had applied the tape to his eyes carelessly and one edge was loose. Ulysses rubbed his face against the Velcro on his coat collar until the tape came free over one eye. Then he fell forward and edged on his side toward the center of the yurt looking for the hatchet he'd seen earlier. He located it beside the potbellied stove. He grabbed it in his teeth and sat up, his mind racing about how to make use of it to free his hands.

He struggled first to maneuver the hatchet behind his back which took much longer than he wanted and was intensely frustrating. A dozen times the hatchet fell out of place and had to be repositioned. Finally, he was able to place the hatchet between his wrists and pin it against his back. Precious moments passed as he feverishly moved his wrists to bring the blade against the handcuffs. Luckily, Ulysses knew this kind of handcuffs. They used them in the county with low level offenders. They weren't the strongest ones available, thank God, and relatively easy to break. And the hatchet was sharp. After minutes of frantic effort at last the plastic popped and his hands were free. Ulysses wiped his sweating palms and went to work on his feet.

Too soon he heard Downs outside the yurt. While his feet weren't free, Ulysses had created more room to maneuver. He stood and shuffled toward the door. Downs was coming up the stairs. Ulysses held the hatchet in one hand. As the door opened outward he leapt toward Downs and swung the hatchet at his head.

The hatchet made glancing contact, nicking Downs' ear, but he grabbed Ulysses's wrist and knocked him off balance. Ulysses jerked his arm free and swung again at Downs, hitting him in the shoulder with the sharp blade and knocking him through the open door and down the steps. Downs lay sprawled on his back in the snow, the breath knocked out of him.

Ulysses leapt from the top step onto the smaller man and the two struggled prone in the snow. Ulysses rose to his knees. The lust to kill Downs burned in his throat. He swung the hatchet again, hitting him hard on the shoulder and slicing into his coat. Downs grabbed Ulysses' arm, more firmly this time, and wrenched his shoulder hard, knocking him on his back. In the twilight the psychopath loomed over him, praying aloud in Latin with a hideous grimace on his bloody face. He fumbled at the shoulder holster for his gun.

I will not let him kill me, Ulysses thought with a surge of adrenaline. Ulysses head-butted his adversary in his gut, knocking Downs off him. Ulysses tried to stand. The pain in his head was overwhelming, and he fell back to the ground just as flashlights were shining up through the trees.

"Gun," Ulysses yelled. "He's got a gun!" Downs struck him with the pistol hard in the face, and Ulysses lost consciousness.

•

It had been about an hour since the FBI search team had headed back to Sleeping Tiger, parting ways with Ray and Matt, who continued to look for Ulysses. The men from Albuquerque weren't dressed warmly enough for the terrain. They weren't used to deep snow and their feet had been wet for hours.

Ray had seen nothing suspicious before they crossed the Rio Pueblo, but the light was fading and it was hard to be sure. Most of the snow on the bridge had melted, but on the other side Matt whispered, "Dad, look at this." In the bit of mud showing through they saw a print of a man's hiking boot.

"That's recent," Ray said. They continued on the trail, eyes now alert for patches of bare ground. They didn't see another track, but now that they'd seen one, they were more willing to believe that the smoothed patches on the trail were covered tracks.

"I think this trail may be connected to that snowshoe yurt trail that used to be out here," Matt said. "I wonder if he could be holed up in one of those yurts."

"It's going to be dark soon," Ray said. "Let's move."

They walked in silence through the darkening woods. Ray's mind drifted back to a time hunting for elk in the part of the woods with his uncle and cousins. There had been snow on the ground and the sun had just set when they came into a clearing and saw an old bull looking toward the west where the evening star glimmered. They were downwind and he hadn't seen or heard them. Without a thought Ray had aimed his shotgun and fired. The big bull had looked over his shoulder, as if surprised, then fell to his knees and rolled to his side. He had died quickly, blood pouring from the wound in his neck. The meat was tough but there was a lot of it. He had had a beautiful head with a long wooly neck and prodigious horns. Ray remembered how they had preserved his head for the Deer Dance. It was the year he and Clarice had gotten married, now thirty-eight years ago.

Matt had just switched on his flashlight when they heard a man yelling something about a gun. Immediately Matt turned off the light and took cover behind a big spruce. Ray came up behind him, gun drawn, as someone began shooting in their direction. They could see the muzzle flash, but Ray whispered, "Hold your fire. That was Ulys's voice." The shooting stopped and the two men waited for a few minutes. At Ray's signal they crept forward along the trail until they could see the conical shape of a yurt roof just ahead.

They heard Ulysses moaning and could make out his body lying in the snow. Matt circled the yurt looking for the gunman but he was nowhere in sight. Trails led off in several directions. Ray leaned over Ulysses. "Hey, buddy, we're here," Ray said, and squatted down. "Can you sit up?"

Matt and Ray pulled Ulysses to a seated position. Blood was pouring from his nose and lip, and he was barely conscious. While Ray tended to Ulysses, Matt looked at the tracks around the yurt. He couldn't tell which were the most recent. "Looks like the guy's gone," he said.

"That fucker rang my bell twice today," Ulysses said.

"Can you stand up?"

"I've got flex cuffs on my ankles," Ulysses said, wiping his bloody nose.

Ray took out his knife and cut Ulysses free. "Let's get you home," he said.

"Goddamn, that was some good timing," Ulysses said, rising unsteadily to his knees.

•

LizBeth drove up a winding canyon and crossed the cattle gate and partially frozen Rio Pueblo that marked the boundary of Picuris. The road took her past the sewage leach field and a fenced pasture where the tribe's herd of bison stood in small groups pawing at the snow. She estimated that the village consisted of about forty households scattered over open land, surrounded by trees up to the boundary with BLM land at the ridge crest.

At the center of the village stood an ancient adobe church with a bell tower, San Lorenzo's, presiding over an otherwise bare plaza. Behind the church stood a community center that housed tribal offices and a gym. To the west and north were the snow-draped peaks of the Sangre de Cristo Mountains, now gleaming in the last daylight.

LizBeth parked at the community center which was strung with blinking Christmas lights. The village was quiet but she could faintly hear voices coming from another plaza, where the pueblo had its sacred kiva. She checked her watch. It was four o'clock.

LizBeth had done some homework about the Picuris tribe. She discovered that they had occupied this beautiful valley since at least 1250 and were a federally recognized tribe of the Eight Northern Pueblos of New Mexico. Now a small tribe with only about 70 members, they had once been large and prosperous. When the Spanish returned after the Pueblo Revolt of 1680, the Picuris were persecuted. They never regained their former prominence.

Sitting in her car, LizBeth placed a quick call to her assistant Ben and left a message on his voicemail. "I'm at Picuris Pueblo. My cell phone is about to run out of charge. Get me wilderness search support, including canines, here, stat. If they can't reach me when they arrive, call a Mr. Ray Pando, Picuris War Chief." She left Ray's phone number while rummaging in her backpack for her phone charger. She saw a stout woman in a striped blanket-coat coming out of the tribal offices and locking the door. LizBeth got out of the car and said, "Excuse me, Ma'am."

The Picuris woman looked at LizBeth as if wondering what she might possibly want. "Hello?"

"Hello, Ma'am," LizBeth said showing her badge. "I'm Agent LizBeth Tallichet from the FBI. I'm sorry to bother you right now—"

"I'm actually glad to see you," Billie Arguello said, unlocking the door she'd just locked. "Come on in, it's warmer in here than it will be at home. She flicked on the lights and led LizBeth into her office. The sign on her door read "Tribal Secretary."

LizBeth sat down while Billie pulled her chair next to an antique rolltop desk and switched on a green-shaded desk lamp. From the large window behind the desk LizBeth could see the ceremonial dance ground. A tall ladder leading to the underground kiva poked out of the bare ground on one side. Men were sorting what looked like freshly cut spruce bows into piles while others stood around in small groups talking quietly.

"What is going on with you people, Agent Tallichet?" Billie asked, getting right to the point.

"I'm not sure what you mean, Ms. Arguello," LizBeth said.

"Call me Billie," she said. "Tell me what you doing. Things are getting out of hand around here."

"Okay. What exactly do you want to know about?"

"Listen, we've had two murders on our land. The first was a tribal member, Luis Duràn, my sister's nephew. The other happened right in front of our church. Now, my daughter's son-in-law, Matt Pando, and his father, our war chief are out looking for the murderer and it's about to get dark. What are you doing?" Billie's silver earrings caught the dying light.

"I'm sorry your peace has been disturbed by these events," LizBeth began.

Billie shook her head. "It certainly has," she said.

"As you know, there have been two murders," LizBeth said, "and an explosive arson up at Sleeping Tiger Retreat Center. Taos Sheriff Ulysses Walker has been seeking the suspect over BLM land since before dawn. Our agents and a state police helicopter have been combing BLM land between the retreat center and here much of the day. I have just authorized a more aggressive search with dogs tonight. We will find the perpetrator, Billie."

"I hope so," Billie said. "Who is your suspect?"

"We are seeking a white male in his thirties, a man by the name of Malcolm Downs. Do you know him?"

Billie was silent for a few moments. She let out a deep sigh. "Yes, I know him," she said, looking troubled. "I've been acquainted with him since he was a child."

"How do you know him?"

"His parents worked in Los Alamos with my late husband. They often visited at dances and feast days and brought him with them when he was a child. We always invited them to come by the house for food and they often came."

"Did you know them well?"

"Cyril was my husband's immediate supervisor. Evelyn was higher up and in a different department. They were odd people." She shook her head in dismay.

"And Malcolm?"

"He was about nine or ten when they started coming. He was a quiet boy but very smart. He could work a Rubik's cube in a minute. He used to play with my nephews, Luis and Benjamin Duràn. Benjamin is my sister Agnes's son. They were all about the same age."

"Did you and your husband have children, Billie?"

"Yes, a daughter, Felicia. She lives in Denver with her husband."

"What did Felicia think of Malcolm?"

"Not much. She kept away from him. But she never liked her cousins, either. She was always a very ambitious girl. She and her husband are both lawyers in Denver."

"Did you know Silvia Duràn?"

"Of course. She was a special girl. My sister's niece on her husband's side." Billie looked out the window at the gathering dusk for a moment. "What a tragedy," she said softly. LizBeth sat patiently waiting for her to resume her story.

"Luis was often taking care of his sister Silvia when he was here. Silvia was just a little thing in those days. Her mother had moved away to keep house for that bad priest in Rancho de Taos."

"Father Miller?"

"Yeah, that one. He had Luis and Benjie go to his sick little summer camp. I think they were both molested there."

"What about Silvia, did she go to that camp?"

"No, it was only for boys. But I will tell you this—my husband, his name was Amòs, caught Benjamin and Malcolm playing sexy stuff with Silvia when she was about five or six."

"How old were they?"

"Old enough to know better. Maybe seventeen."

"What happened to them?"

"Nothing. Agnes said it was just a game and no use to get all upset about. I knew it was wrong because those boys were too old for that kind of game. But I stayed out of it. And then, look what happened."

"What do you mean look what happened?"

"Well, Silvia, for one."

"I know she killed herself. Do you blame what happened with Benjamin and Malcolm for Silvia's death?"

"Partially. And Silvia might have been molested by that priest, for all I know. I guess I really blame her mother, Casimira. It's her fault what happened to her family. If I had it to do over I would have called the authorities on those boys. Maybe they could have gotten some help."

"What about Downs' parents, Cyril and Evelyn? What did they say about it?"

"They said it never happened. Out and out called Amòs a liar. And Malcolm denied he had touched Silvia. Said he was trying to protect her.

But Silvia told us they both touched her. Anyway, Malcolm got sent off to Socorro to school after that. I haven't seen him since. Benjie told me that Malcolm was paying some of Silvia's expenses at college when she died."

LizBeth paused, trying to think of what else to ask. On the dance ground it appeared that the evergreen boughs had been distributed and the men had formed a line to climb down into the kiva. Their shadows flickered on the adobe buildings as the sun went behind the mountains.

"It's getting dark," Billie said, "Where's the cavalry?"

"It will take them a little time to get here. In the meantime, the little I know about Ray Pando, I know he won't give up his search until it's pitch dark."

"Maybe you'd better come to my house then. I can warm us up some of the casserole I made for tomorrow."

"That would be really kind of you." LizBeth was hungry.

After being quiet all day the wind picked up as the sun went down, causing temperatures to plummet. The two women walked together toward Billie's home right off the plaza.

"Why wouldn't Ray have recognized Malcolm Downs when he met him at Sleeping Tiger?"

"Ray was gone from here for almost twenty years. Clarice is Isleta and they lived with her people. He worked with Albuquerque Police long enough to have a good pension. Anyway he only came back here about seven years ago when his mother died and he inherited her house. It's that one directly across the Plaza, just to the right of the community center." Billie pointed to a one-story adobe house with two chimneys and a deep front porch. Lights were on in the front rooms.

"How well does Downs know tribal land?" LizBeth asked as they went into Billie's house. The fire in her woodstove had died down and the room was chilly. Both women kept on their coats as Billie turned on lights in the kitchen and sitting room.

"Sit down," Billie said, indicating the kitchen table. "I'll warm up the food. Do you want coffee?"

"Just hot water would be great," LizBeth said.

Billie turned on an electric stove and put water in the teakettle. She reloaded the woodstove, then washed her hands in the sink before taking tin foil off a meaty-looking casserole on the counter. She scooped two large portions into a cast-iron skillet and placed it on a burner. By now the room was warm enough for them to take off their coats, which Billie hung on a peg by the door.

LizBeth repeated her question. "How well do you think Downs knows Picuris land?"

"I was thinking about that," Billie said. "I would say pretty well. Amòs and Leroy took all the boys hunting and to gather firewood lots of times. He was a smart boy and found his way around good. Malcolm was a natural hunter." She looked at LizBeth as she stirred the casserole. "He might be hard to find."

LizBeth wrapped her hands around the mug of hot water Billie handed her but said nothing. Clearly, Downs *was* hard to find.

"But if anyone can find him it would be Ray and Matt," Billie said.

LizBeth was thinking about the two Duràns, Luis and Silvia, both dead, and their cousin Elías, also dead. "Where is Benjamin these days?"

"Ah, Benjamin." Billie shook her head and sucked air through her teeth. "It's never easy with that one. That was the other thing that happened."

"What's the problem with him?"

"He got into more trouble a few years back. Sexual contact with a minor. His wife's daughter from a previous marriage. He's on parole as a registered sex offender."

"Do you ever see him?"

"He might be here tomorrow for the dance. He sometimes comes. Gets him out of the halfway house."

LizBeth let this sink in. Benjamin, the boy who Malcolm says molested Silvia, was likely nearby. He was sure to be on Malcolm's bad side.

"Would Benjamin stay at his mother's?" LizBeth asked, taking the plate of food Billie handed her. She saw by Billie's face that the same thought occurred to the older woman.

"Oh, God," she said. "He might be there right now." She picked up the phone to call her sister.

"Agnes," Billie said, "Is Benjie there?" She held her hand over the receiver and whispered to LizBeth, "He's there. He and Leroy are in the garage."

"Tell her to get them inside the house. Tell her we are coming right over."

Billie covered their food and the two women headed out the front door. It was now fully dark.

Chapter XIV

Ray, Matt and Ulysses arrived at Ray's house after slogging down the snowy trail for over an hour in the dark. Ulysses was weak but able to walk with support. Clarice met them at the door and immediately installed Ulysses in the back bedroom. It was warm, having its own gas stove, and had an old wooden bedstead with a freshly made-up bed, a leather armchair and a night table with a pink blown-glass lamp. Ulysses took off his coat, boots and pants and got into bed. Clarice brought him a big glass of water, a ham sandwich, a bowl of tomato soup and some Oreos.

Ulysses was ravenous and ate in silence. As the events of the day rushed over him he felt relief and horror. He could hear Ray in the other room calling the Peñasco EMTs. Matt headed out the front door for the kiva. He was still planning to dance tomorrow. Ray called LizBeth but her phone went directly to voicemail.

The Peñasco EMTs arrived with their stretcher to take Ulysses to the hospital but Ulysses convinced them to let him stay where he was. They checked his vitals and looked at his minor external wounds and the bruising on his face and neck. No broken bones, but he did have a low-grade fever. They pressed him to drink a lot of water, as he appeared dehydrated. Undoubtedly he'd had a bad concussion. He was advised to stay awake for two hours and then get a lot of rest.

They recommended he see his doctor the next morning, to make sure there was nothing more serious. The doctor would likely recommend rest for about six weeks. Ulysses heard all this with a vague sense of improbability. How was he going to rest for six weeks?

After the EMT's left Ulysses called Rosemary.

"I'm coming as soon as Katie gets here to watch the children," Rosemary said when she heard Ulysses's voice.

"You don't need to come, honey," he said. "I'm going to be fine. I'll be home first thing in the morning."

"I don't believe one bit of that," Rosemary said. "You'll be out looking for that man before daylight. I know you."

"Rosemary, I'm so sorry I've worried you—"

"I spent the past fifteen hours not knowing if you were dead or alive."

"I know, I'm sorry. Honey—"

Rosemary interrupted in a low, firm tone intended to convey maximum will without being overheard by Monty and Amelia. "Don't tell me this goes with the job. You didn't have to go out there by yourself. Ulys. Do you remember we have this agreement about unnecessary risks?"

Ulysses was silent. He knew better than to argue with her about the choice he made to follow Downs by himself. And she was right; he would be out after him again as soon as his head stopped pounding if only he could get past Ray and Clarice.

"Rosemary, this man is the most dangerous criminal we've had in Taos County in years. I have to do my job. If I don't, more people will die." Now it was Rosemary's turn to be silent. Ulysses could hear her steady breath and Amelia reading to Monty in the background. She was quiet for a long time.

"Let me speak with Ray," she said at last.

"Why do you want to speak with Ray?"

"You are on Picuris land now and he's in charge, right?"

"Well, technically, that would be Agent Tallichet of the FBI."

"Put Ray on the phone, please." She took a deep breath. "I love you, Ulysses."

"Okay, Rosemary. I love you too." He handed the phone to Ray, who had approached at the sound of his name.

Ray took the phone into the other room so Ulysses couldn't hear the conversation. He stayed on the phone a long time, and when he came back in the room, he looked stern.

"Your wife has some strong opinions about you staying put tonight."

"I know," Ulysses said.

"I'm going to allow that she is right," Ray said. "You need to rest up before going out again. And Tallichet would agree. You aren't going anywhere before at least noon."

"Come on, Ray, don't pull that on me."

"You are under my jurisdiction and I say to stay put," Ray said.

Ulysses had to admit it was reasonable. He could hear bathwater running in the next room. The thought of a warm bath and sleep almost brought tears to his eyes. Clarice came in, drying her hands on a towel. "Why don't you take a bath before you turn in? You look like you could use one," she said.

Ulysses laughed. "Glad to oblige." To Ray he said, "What are you going to do?"

"I'm going on patrol," Ray said. "I don't know where the hell Tallichet is. She's not answering her phone."

•

After she'd had a good cry, Jo got up from the sagging motel bed, washed her face and looked at herself in the mirror under the harsh bathroom lights. Her eyes had dark circles and there was a bruise on her chin she didn't know how she'd gotten. Jo started to regret her decision to spend the night in this dismal place given how she was feeling. But without a car she had no way to get anywhere else, unless she wanted to walk across the highway to Denny's. That option seemed even worse than staying in the dingy room, but she was starting to feel hungry.

Jo decided to call Tomàs at the hospital. It would distract her and cheer her up to talk with him, she thought. But when she was connected with the main switchboard, she found that he had left late in the afternoon and gotten a ride home from a relative. Jo looked in the phone directory in the room and was surprised to find Tomàs Ulibarri listed. Jo called the number and Tomàs answered.

"Hi, it's me," Jo said. "How are you?"

"I'm fine. Good actually. Glad to be home. Where are you?"

"I'm at the Chamisa Inn in Taos." Jo sounded pitiful even to herself.

"What are you doing there?"

Jo told him the whole story about Jon Malvern's attack on Melanie and how she and Melanie left Sleeping Tiger. Tomàs whistled under his breath. "That's crazy," he said, "Crazy! You must feel terrible, pobrecita!"

"I do. I'm just sick about everything."

"Let me come pick you up from there. A dumpy motel is no place to be when you feel like that. I can make you some dinner and make up my spare room for you."

Jo felt a stern voice warning her, *"You can't spend the night with your supervisee,"* but she pushed it aside.

"Are you well enough to do this?"

"I'll be there in twenty minutes."

Tomàs had stitches on his face and a bandage on his head but when Jo got in the front seat of his pickup he was smiling broadly. "Do you mind if we stop at Smith's? I'm out of coffee."

"No, indeed," Jo said, smiling and feeling much better. "Can't be without coffee."

During the grocery shopping, which included much more than coffee, Jo and Tomàs shared gallows humor about what they'd been through.

"How many times I cursed that damn boiler," Tomàs said. "I never thought one day it would blow the whole place up."

"Well, that isn't exactly what happened. But I know what you mean. If someone had told me I'd be whacking a guy in the head during a retreat I never would have believed them either," Jo said, laughing ruefully.

At the register a young girl started scanning their groceries. Instinctively both went silent until they were pushing the cart to Tomàs's pickup.

"I always knew you were ferocious," Tomàs said. "But what about Roshi? How was she when you left her?"

"You know Melanie," Jo said. "She always finds a teaching moment."

Tomàs put the bags in the back of his truck. "You aren't feeling so good about her, are you?"

Jo got into the cab without answering. "You should see the place. The dorm is a shell and Gerald's house burned to the ground. The fire trucks tore up the ground all around the place. It looks like a war zone."

"Won't there be a big insurance claim?" Tomàs said.

"Who knows? I'm not counting on us reopening."

"I guess there goes my job," Tomàs said.

"Oh, I'm so sorry, Tomàs," Jo replied. "Mine too."

"Maybe we could turn the place into one of those ghost tours for Halloween, like the one they have at the old state pen." He looked at Jo to see if he'd gone too far. She looked stunned at first, then had a fit of laughing.

"Oh, God, this is wild," she said, trying to recover.

"We've been through a lot."

"What would you like for dinner?" he asked, changing the subject.

"What do you have?"

"I bought a bag of meat balls. How about spaghetti? And I can make a salad."

"Sounds good. And I saw you picked up some Chianti."

"I did. We can have a glass while I make dinner."

Jo thought of how she and Tim liked to cook together on their days off, listening to a favorite radio show called "Back Porch Music" and drinking wine. She looked at Tomàs and wondered what it would be like to spend an evening with him, cooking and drinking wine and then getting ready for bed.

They drove for some time in companionable silence. At last, Tomàs turned onto the BLM Forest Road near Sleeping Tiger. It had not been plowed and there were only the one set of Tomàs's tire tracks since the snowfall. She looked at Tomàs driving, noticing his big hands and the ropy veins on his arms, how his head reached the top of the cab. Tim had been her height and slightly built. Tomàs saw her looking at him and smiled broadly. He touched her knee. "Warm enough?" he asked. She nodded.

Tomàs turned into the long drive that led to his little farm, a fragment of an old Spanish land grant that once encompassed the entire area but had slowly been stolen by US government and development interests. The farm was now surrounded by BLM land. Tomàs shifted into four-wheel drive and they slid down the drive guided by the headlight beams. There was a light on in the house and smoke coming out of the chimney. "It should be warm in there," he said. "I got home about 4:00 and was able to load up the stove. Those chickens sure were hungry and thirsty."

Tomàs parked in front of the house and unlocked the door. Jo stood awkwardly in the small living room with its warm woodstove and comfy armchairs while Tomàs unloaded the groceries and brought them into the kitchen. The house was cozy with its thick adobe walls, low ceilings and broad plank floors. The walls were mostly bare except for some Spanish retablos and tinwork. There were framed family pictures on the mantelpiece.

"Come into the kitchen, mi amiga," Tomàs said. He had set the grocery bags on the porcelain drain board and uncorked the Chianti. He poured a glass for each of them.

"It doesn't feel quite right to toast," Tomàs said, "but Salud!"

"Salud!" Jo said and they both drank. "I think it is fine to toast to health."

"Thank you for coming to my house for dinner," Tomàs said.

"Thank you for having me." Jo took another drink and felt the wine warming and relaxing her. She sat at Tomàs' kitchen table and poured herself and him another glass. He began to prepare a simple dinner and wouldn't let Jo help. She watched him move about the cheerful kitchen with its red curtains and cluster of houseplants on the deep windowsill, chatting about his farm, his mother, his aunt, his daughter and grandson. He peeled and minced garlic and chopped onions, sautéed them and added them to a jar of homemade sauce from his garden and then added the meatballs. The kitchen filled with a savory aroma. He made a salad and cooked the spaghetti. "Damn," he said, "I forgot parmesan. But here, I can grate this." He pulled a piece of cheese from the refrigerator. "Manchego will work."

Jo poured herself a third glass. She was beginning to feel very hungry but also sleepy. At last Tomàs put the spaghetti onto two yellow Fiestaware plates, served the salad and refilled his own glass.

"Buon appetito," he said and kissed her lightly but fully on the lips.

"Yes," Jo said, her body responding to his kiss. She kissed him back.

"Let's eat!" Tomàs said and sat down across from her.

Dinner conversation consisted of Jo telling Tomàs about Anandaville and Tim, and Tomàs giving her a brief history of his tours in Afghanistan and his divorce. *We have almost nothing in common*, Jo thought, as she also noticed her attraction to him deepening.

She's really fragile, Tomàs thought.

After dinner Jo washed the dishes while Tomàs went to make up the single bed in his spare room. She finished the dishes and left them on the dish rack, hung up the dishtowel and went to see where she would sleep. The spare room was actually more of an alcove. It had no door, was two steps up from the living room, across from the only bathroom and right next to Tomàs bedroom. Tomàs's room, its door being open, revealed a large unmade bed of white sheets, a down comforter and lots of pillows. Jo felt her anxiety rise. She wasn't ready for this.

"I'll let you use the bathroom first," Tomàs said, turning on the nightlight above the sink and squeezing past her in the small hallway. "I'm going to check the birds, bring in wood and lock up. Hold the toilet handle down until it flushes all the way, okay? There's a fresh washcloth and towel on a hook on the back of the door."

Jo took her overnight case into the bathroom and undressed. She washed her face again, put on night cream and brushed her teeth, slipped into her nightgown and was out of the bathroom and in bed before Tomàs came back in the house.

"Already turning in?" he asked from the living room as he loaded the woodstove for the night.

"It's been a really long day," Jo said from under her blankets. "You should get to bed too. You just got out of the hospital!"

"I just have a couple of things to do first," he said.

Jo watched him load a rifle and a handgun. He placed the rifle across the arms of the leather chair near the door and put the pistol on his bedside table. "Just in case," he said.

Then he locked the front door and the kitchen door and turned out the lights. He stood over Jo's bed. "Are you feeling okay?" he asked her.

"Yes," Jo said reaching out her hand, which he took in his. "Thank you for taking me in!"

Tomàs bent down and kissed her on the forehead. "Rest well," he said. Then he went into his room and closed the door.

•

LizBeth and Billie crossed Agnes's snowy yard in the frigid wind. The moon had not yet risen, allowing the clear skies to reveal the dense, clotted Milky Way. Billie knocked on the front door. Leroy answered and invited them into the warm living room. He and his son Benjamin were watching a basketball game on television. Agnes came from the sink where she'd been cleaning up from dinner and greeted her sister.

LizBeth introduced herself. Leroy, in his seventies, wore a flannel shirt and blue jeans. He glanced at the women and nodded. Benjamin wore a Harley Davidson t-shirt which barely covered his large belly. His hair was pulled back in a ponytail and he sported a gold eyetooth. He raised his hand in greeting, then turned back to the television. LizBeth noticed that his dark eyes had a look of desperation similar to his mother's.

"We have reason to believe that Malcolm Downs is in the vicinity," she began. Neither man looked at her. LizBeth picked up the remote and turned down the audio. "He is armed and considered very dangerous. He is the prime suspect in two recent murders." Both men's eyes left the television monitor for the first time.

"My God," Leroy said. "Malcolm Downs?"

"Yes. He is suspected of killing Luis. I am concerned Benjamin here might be a target."

No one said anything for a few moments. Then Billie spoke up. "He had a grudge against Luis, apparently. And we know he has a grudge against you, Benjie."

"He's a crazy son of a bitch," Leroy said. "Always was. But what can we do about it?" Agnes sat down suddenly on a chair. Billie put her arm around her sister.

"I want you to stay inside with the doors locked and the blinds pulled," said LizBeth.

Benjamin said, "Maybe I should go back to Santa Fe?"

"Benjamin, who knows you are here?" LizBeth asked.

"My parole officer and the staff at the halfway house. My therapist. Maybe a few other people."

"How did you get here?"

"I picked him up from the blue bus," Leroy said, indicating the regional transit bus.

"I want you to stay put until I tell you further. We'll see that someone is stationed outside to watch over the house."

"But tomorrow is the dance," Agnes said.

"I know. Are any of you planning to dance?"

"No, but we always go. At dawn. We always go." Agnes sounded fearful and confused.

"Maybe not tomorrow," LizBeth said. "It could be dangerous for all of you, especially Benjamin. Please stay inside and wait for further instructions."

There was a knock on the door. Billie flicked on the porch light and saw Ray Pando standing there. "Good evening," Ray said to Billie as she let him inside. To LizBeth he said, "Your phone has been going straight to voicemail for over an hour."

"Sorry about that," LizBeth said, putting on her coat. "It ran out of charge. Did you find Sheriff Walker?"

"Yes. Ulys is okay. He has a bad concussion but no broken bones. He's is at my house under the care of my wife."

"Thank God," LizBeth. "Where is Downs?"

"He got away," Ray said.

"Okay, we need to make a plan," LizBeth said.

In the other room Benjamin had turned up the volume on the game and the family was talking in low tones so as not to be overheard. Leroy got up and took a rifle out of the coat closet near the front door.

"Who is going to watch this house tonight?" Billie asked as Ray and LizBeth prepared to leave.

"We will have someone over here soon," Ray said. "Count on it."

•

Once they arrived at Ray's house, LizBeth followed Ray into the bedroom where Ulysses sat propped up in bed with a bowl of ice cream. He introduced the pretty woman in the chair next to him as his wife, Rosemary. Rosemary started to shake LizBeth's hand but ended up hugging her. "I'm here to make sure he rests," Rosemary said.

"Good idea," LizBeth said. Ulysses finished his ice cream and put down the bowl. He looked sheepish and said nothing. Rosemary left the room and Ray sat at the foot of the bed. LizBeth took the armchair. She was about to chastise Ulysses about going off like the Lone Ranger but decided against it.

"This guy is the real deal psychopath," Ulysses said wiping his mouth. "If it weren't for Ray and Matt I'd be dead."

"We'll do a complete debrief later," LizBeth said. "Remember, you are under orders to rest. But first, you injured him in the shoulder, is that correct?"

"I landed two blows on him with a hatchet. One grazed the side of his face and the other sliced into his shoulder. I would imagine he has lost some blood."

"Matt thought his tracks led east," Ray said. "Maybe toward that cutoff trail."

"Back toward Sleeping Tiger?" LizBeth asked.

"Yeah, but he could double back anytime, like the fox he is," Ray said.

LizBeth told them about her concerns for Benjamin Duràn and the possibility that Downs would come to the Deer Dance to wreak havoc.

"Could happen," Ulysses said, "but how would he know Benjamin was here?"

"Benjamin said he told lots of people," LizBeth said. "I didn't ask when he told them. Downs has been kind of isolated for the past four days so it's hard to imagine how he would know."

"Word travels fast up here in el Norte," Ulysses said. "You'd be surprised."

"We have to consider who his next victim might be. Before I heard about Benjamin, I was thinking Downs would go after Archbishop Sullivan," LizBeth said. "Miller was tight with Sullivan, wasn't he? Or Casimira Duràn."

"Downs told me 'her time was nigh' or some such crap," Ulysses said.

"Casimira is a very likely target." Ray agreed.

"Downs had years to go after Sullivan and never did. Sullivan is not in good health and doesn't get out much," Ulysses said. "Although I heard he was going to be at a luncheon for Trujillo one day this week." Ulysses sighed and rubbed his head. "Actually, the lunch is tomorrow. In Taos. I am supposed to go."

"You are in no shape to—" Ray started.

Ulysses interrupted. "I know, don't worry, I won't fight you on that one. I hate those things."

"Look, I still think Benjamin is the most likely target. He's nearby, and fresh out of jail. And he is an actual child molester, not just an enabler," LizBeth said.

"Bottom line we just can't predict what this guy is going to do," Ulysses said. "But we know this is likely to be a fight to the death. He must know we're closing in on him and he has nothing to lose at this point."

"I have to focus on keeping Picuris safe," said Ray. "The whole community is involved with the Deer Dance. If the weather holds, we'll have dozens of visitors arriving beginning at dawn. I've called up the war council to make sure we have the manpower we need to protect everyone."

"Aren't some of them dancing?" LizBeth asked.

"Most of them but not all."

"I've asked for a search-and-rescue team with canines to hunt for Downs," LizBeth said, stretching her legs and arms. She looked at her watch. "They should be here by now."

"I can keep watch tomorrow from right here. Gives me something to do," Ulysses said.

"You are off duty." LizBeth said.

"At least bring me a gun," Ulysses said. "There's a good view of the plaza from here. Something might go down."

"You're supposed to be resting, as in eyes closed," Ray said.

"That's right," Rosemary said, coming back into the room to shoo everyone out. "You've sat up your two hours. Why don't you snuggle down and go to sleep? I'll come join you after I check in with the babysitter."

Ulysses obediently slid down into bed and pulled up the wool blanket and quilt. Rosemary closed the curtains, kissed him goodnight like a child and turned off the light. He felt disoriented and queasy and his head throbbed.

In the living room Ray and LizBeth looked over a map of pueblo and BLM lands to help her direct the canine team. Then Ray left to continue his house-to-house check in the pueblo, and Clarice went into her bedroom. Rosemary sat down in an armchair by the woodstove and took out the novel she'd been trying to read for almost a year, *Home* by Marilynne Robinson. LizBeth stood at the window watching the snow swirling in the light of a lone sodium vapor lamp near the church. Her phone rang.

"Tallichet," she answered.

"This is Buddy Roque from Federal Police, BIA."

"Yeah? Where's my canine team?"

"The team in your region has two men out sick so my team got assigned. But we're in Grants. It'll take us about three hours to get there. Still want us?"

"Jesus, man, yes, I want you," LizBeth said, not caring if her disgust at the delay showed.

"It's snowing right smart over here," Buddy said. "Are you sure?"

"Hell, yes, I am sure," LizBeth said. "Hurry yourself."

"Okay, ma'am. Take it easy, we'll be there."

Rosemary looked up from her book. "Little delay?"

"Yeah, a big delay. Three hours."

"Why don't you just stretch out on the couch and get some rest?" Rosemary picked up an afghan and some throw pillows from a chair for LizBeth. She nodded wearily, took off her boots and stretched out. Rosemary covered her with the afghan. In a few minutes LizBeth was sound asleep. Rosemary turned off her reading light and went to get in bed with her husband.

●

Jo suddenly woke from a deep sleep. She lay still and listened, all her senses alert, her heart pounding. The wind howled around the house, causing something on the roof to bang intermittently. *That's probably what woke me up*, she thought and snuggled back down in her warm bed. A log settled in the stove and she could hear Tomàs softly snoring. She was almost asleep when something woke her again. A slow step, a creaking board on the front porch. Her fear rocketed to panic. She jumped out of bed.

"Tomàs," she whispered frantically, opening his door. "Someone is on the front porch." Tomàs threw off the covers. He wore nothing except a pair of camouflage boxers and wool socks. He grabbed the pistol and cocked it just as the front door opened.

A man wearing night-vision goggles crept in. Tomàs glimpsed an automatic rifle. He grabbed Jo by the arm and pulled her into his room. He put his finger to his lips and closed the door.

"I know you're in there," Downs said in a calm, steady voice. "I don't want to hurt you. But I will if you disobey me."

Tomàs said nothing. He pushed Jo to the floor on the far side of his bed and crouched down near the closet, holding his gun steady in both hands.

"Come on out with your hands up," Downs said in a mocking tone. "I have enough firepower here to blow that door down in one short burst. You don't want that, do you?"

"What do you want with me, Brother?" Tomàs said. "What can I do for you?"

"Come on out, Amigo, or I'll unleash hell."

Tomàs looked across the bed at Jo pressed flat to the ground. He handed her his gun and gave her a reassuring nod. Would Downs know there were two people in this house?

"Okay, Brother," Tomàs said. "I'll come out. I'm coming out now. Be prepared, I'm half naked." Jo was amazed at Tomàs's calm, almost jovial tone.

He opened the door, and light from the living room poured into the small bedroom. Tomàs walked down the two steps into the living room with his hands in the air. Jo breathed deeply, trying to calm her racing heart. She dried her sweaty hands on the sheets and took a good look at the gun she was holding. It was a Smith and Wesson 45 and it was old. It didn't appear to have a safety. She made mental note to hold it away from her body and be ready for a powerful kick when she fired it.

"Sit down," she heard Downs say. "I see you had made some preparations for my visit. Unload that shotgun, please." Jo could hear the shells dropping to the floor. "Now, pick them up and give them to me," Downs said.

"What's wrong with your shoulder, my friend?" Tomàs asked.

"None of your business. Nice little place you have here. Did you inherit it?"

"Yes, I did, from my mother," Tomàs said.

"I like Spanish people," Downs said. "Good Catholics, hard working."

"Can I get you something to eat?" Tomàs asked.

"That won't be necessary," Downs said. "Who was sleeping in that other bed?" he asked.

Jo felt sick in her belly and couldn't control her trembling.

"My daughter was here yesterday," Tomàs said.

"Oh, okay. Who is here today?"

"You and me, Brother," Tomàs said. "How did you get in here?"

Downs chuckled. "You are one of the good people, Amigo. Good people do simple, stupid things that put them at risk from people like me. Like putting their keys in obvious places. I got in by taking the key off the lintel where you 'hide' it and unlocking the door." He chuckled again. "You made it easy."

"What can I do for you, Mr. Downs?" Tomàs asked again. Hatred for Downs coursed in him but his demeanor remained polite.

"Very simple. I will be needing your truck. If you just give me your keys I will be on my way. And as long as you don't come after, you'll be free from me."

Tomàs felt relief flooding over him. Would it really be so simple?

"I'll get you the keys, but they are in my pants pocket in the bedroom."

"I'll come in there with you."

Jo was in a panic. The bed was so low she couldn't hide under it. If Downs turned on the light, he'd see her right away. She looked at the open closet door and wondered if she could make it in time. It was too risky. She held tight to the gun, her finger on the trigger.

Tomàs entered the bedroom with Downs right behind him. He pulled his trousers off the floor and reached in his pocket for the truck keys. He had just handed them over and was backing out of the room when Downs flicked on the overhead light.

"Ah-ha, you lied to me," he snarled. "You were bedding down with Ms. McAlister here. Now I can't trust you! I'll have to take her—"

Jo fired the pistol, a wild shot that just missed Tomàs but disoriented Downs.

Tomàs threw himself at Downs and fell on top of him. He pounded Downs's wounded shoulder, causing his automatic weapon to spray bullets into the living room ceiling before it flew from his grasp. Downs grabbed a knife from his belt and slashed at Tomàs, cutting him across his bare belly just below the navel. Jo rose to her feet, the gun in her hand, and moved toward the door as if in a daze. She leveled the gun at Downs and shouted, "Drop the knife. Drop it. Now!"

Downs held his hands in the air. "Or what, you'll shoot me? Look how your hands are shaking! You little slut."

Jo fired the gun at Downs' feet and he dropped the knife. He looked at Jo, as if assessing whether she was likely to shoot at him again. Then he scooped up the keys from where they'd fallen on the floor and backed toward the door. "Good night," he said, with a little bow, and dashed out the door to the truck. He was tearing down the driveway before Jo could react. She felt outside of herself and as if everything, including her, was unreal.

Jo slammed the front door and turned to Tomàs, who lay on the floor gripping his abdomen, where a four-inch long gash was bleeding profusely. Blood had run over his boxer shorts and legs and onto the floor. Jo ran to the kitchen to call 911 but the landline was dead. "Do you have a cell phone? The landline isn't working," she called from the kitchen.

"No," Tomàs said in a strained voice. "Cell phones don't work out here."

"Do you have a first-aid kit?"

"In the bathroom under the sink," Tomàs said.

She found his well-stocked first-aid kit in a small duffle bag. Jo pulled the sheet off her bed and arranged some towels to protect the couch from the blood. Tomàs was in a lot of pain but he was quiet and co-operative.

She helped him lie down and then inspected the wound. It was a clean swipe about a quarter-inch deep, but had a mean hook at the end where the knife had exited. Jo washed and disinfected the wound then applied two large butterfly bandages, which significantly reduced the bleeding. She cleaned up most of the blood with a washcloth before covering him with a blanket.

"Josie, there's some Vicodin in there from the last time I went to the dentist. Can you get me a couple?"

Jo found the medication and gave him a glass of water.

"Thanks for taking care of me," he said.

Jo was starting to come back to herself. *Funny how work clears your head*, she thought. She took the key out of the front door, locked it then sat back on the couch next to Tomàs.

"In the morning we'll need to get you to the hospital. You are definitely going to need stitches."

"I'm giving them a lot of business lately," Tomàs said.

"I'm going to need to call the sheriff and let them know we've seen Downs and he has your truck."

Tomàs raised up on his elbows and looked at Jo. "How are you going to do that?" He shook his head slowly. "You cannot go out there alone," he said.

"You certainly can't go anywhere right now," Jo said. "Somebody has to go. It's information they need. It could save somebody's life."

"Listen to me," Tomàs said. "You can't go out of this house. That man is a stone-cold killer and he could be out there right now waiting for you to 'disobey' him so he can shoot you! He has night vision! Trust me, the life you need to save is your own."

Jo let out a long breath. "You're right. Dammit. I know you are … but someone should let them know he's got your truck."

"Jo, the FBI has got this tonight. When it's light, when we can see around us, I'll go over to Sleeping Tiger with you and we can call Ray." He stroked Jo's hair.

"You aren't in any shape to walk a mile in the snow, Tomàs."

"Okay, true enough. But come on, let's get some sleep."

"Do you think he'll come back?" Jo said, looking at the door he'd come through only a few minutes before.

"Why would he? He's not after us. He's got another agenda. Hey, help me up."

Jo supported Tomàs to a seated position and he held onto her hand. "Do you want to sleep in my bed and I'll take the small bed? That way I'm between you and the door."

Jo picked up the shotgun shells from the floor and held them in her hand. "I think I'll feel safest if we are in the bed together," she said.

Tomàs whistled under his breath. He picked up the shotgun and took the shells from Jo.

"That doesn't mean you need to do anything," Jo added.

"That's good," Tomàs said, as Jo helped him up the few stairs, "because I couldn't, much as I might want to."

•

Everyone in the house was soundly asleep when Buddy Roque arrived with two BIA officers and pounded on Ray's front door. LizBeth awoke and let them in just as Ray came from his bedroom fully dressed, having slept in his clothes.

LizBeth looked at her watch. "Did you get lost, or what?"

"It took me awhile to round up the troops," Buddy said. "I prefer the beagles but the shepherds were nearby so that's what I got. And yes, I got lost. I'm new to this territory."

Buddy was a short Texan in his fifties with a ruddy face, a mustache and a receding chin. He was accompanied by two officers, Taos Indians, men who looked to be in their twenties. They all introduced themselves.

"All righty then," LizBeth said as she took them to the map. "Let's get you guys oriented." She pointed to a trail on the big topo map on Ray's living room wall. "Go past this trailer home," she said, pointing to Agnes and Leroy's residence, "and take the mesa trail right past it, here. When you pick up a scent, follow it until you find him, then call for back up." She pulled the black balaclava she'd taken from Downs' car out of its plastic bag. "Let the dogs sniff this. I'll be here with my radio on. And be careful out there."

Buddy pulled aside his coat to show his side arm. "We got long guns too," he said, "in the car with the dogs."

Buddy radioed LizBeth shortly before dawn to tell her they had tracked Downs from the ski yurts to Tomàs Ulibarri's house where he had broken in and stolen Ulibarri's truck, injuring him in the process. Once again, Downs had escaped. Buddy gave LizBeth the description of Tomàs's truck and its license number. "He's been gone about ninety minutes," Roque said. "So it's all yours. One of our crew is picking up the van at your place and coming to get us. Sorry we couldn't have caught him for you." LizBeth called an APB on Downs in Tomàs' truck, told Ray where she was headed then she put on her boots and was out the door before anyone else in the house was awake.

When LizBeth arrived at Tomàs's house the BIA crew were sitting in the living room waiting on their van, drinking coffee with the dogs curled up near the woodstove.

"How did Downs know how to find you?" LizBeth asked Tomàs as Jo handed her a cup of coffee.

"I'm not sure he did," Tomàs said. "He might have come wandering up by the yurts and seen the house through the trees. Jo woke up first. She was sleeping in the alcove. He found my 'hidden key' above the door and let himself in."

"How bad are you cut?" LizBeth asked. "Do you want me to call it in?"

"I've got two butterflies on it and I'm watching it," Jo said. "But yes, do call it in. It's the only way we can get to the ER."

Tomàs and Jo told their story for LizBeth. Jo was muted in her recounting, as if still struggling with what she'd witnessed. Tomàs seemed less fazed. He was embarrassed about having his key out for a psychopath and angry about losing his truck.

"But that's twice the guy has stopped short of killing me," he said. "God knows why."

The BIA van arrived as dawn was lighting up the horizon. The crew was needed on an urgent call to find some lost cross-country skiers south near the Puyé Cliffs. LizBeth radioed Peñasco fire-and-rescue to come for Tomàs and said goodbye to him and Jo.

LizBeth drove to Peñasco where the Double Rainbow was just opening for the day. She took a booth by the door. The diner was empty except for her and the proprietor, an older gentleman with a white handlebar mustache and red muttonchops who was reading the *Taos News*. He brought her a cup of hot coffee and a menu. An FBI agent named Randi whom she'd never met was tasked out of Santa Fe and would meet her at Picuris in about an hour. The sun was just peeking above the horizon. LizBeth checked her messages and listened to a voicemail from Lionel Case, as he'd promised but she had not expected.

"Ms. Tallichet, this is Dr. Lionel Case calling you back. I've had a chance to look at my notes since our conversation earlier today. There are others you might want to warn about Downs, people at Los Alamos National Lab. Call me if you want their names. As I indicated I am closing my office now and will be unavailable until he is apprehended. But after you catch him, I am happy to help however I can. Good-bye."

Great, thought LizBeth, *even more places he could be going to kill.* The proprietor came by and refilled her coffee cup. "Long night?" he asked. "Would you like a piece of pie? The bourbon pecan is a favorite."

Chapter XV

In the predawn hours Ulysses lay dreaming he was flying over the pueblo during some kind of ceremony. A crowd of spectators encircled some Picuris men who drummed and chanted. Rosemary, Monty and Amelia stood among the spectators crowded toward the front. Suddenly, an explosion engulfed the church in flames and everyone started running in a panic. From the air Ulysses could see his family caught in the stampede of people trying to escape.

Ulysses woke up, gasping from the nightmare. His hands and feet were numb and he felt lightheaded. For a moment he didn't know where he was. Then, as he realized his whereabouts, he recalled that the Deer Dance began today.

Rosemary's place in bed was empty. Ulysses couldn't remember her getting into or out of bed, which was unusual as he was usually a light sleeper. The room was chilly and it was still dark outside. Ulysses felt the lumps on his cheekbone and the back of his head and the many cuts and bruises on his body. He noticed how stiff and painful his neck was from how he'd slept and began to roll his neck in an effort the loosen its tightness.

Ulysses could hear Clarice and Rosemary in the kitchen talking. He could smell coffee. *Must be about six thirty*, he thought. He switched on the bedside lamp and stood up, looking for his pants. They were not on the chair where he'd left them. He felt dizzy and sat back down.

Rosemary came in with two cups of coffee. "Get back in bed, Ulys," she said gently. She handed him a large pottery mug of coffee. He leaned forward as she placed another pillow at his back and covered him up.

"Where's Ray?" Ulysses asked. He took a sip of the hot coffee.

Rosemary sat in the chair by the bed. "He went on patrol about twenty minutes ago. The men have gone into the kiva. How'd you sleep?"

"Like a log," Ulysses said. "Dead to the world." He decided not to tell her about his dream.

"We aren't used to having an uninterrupted night," Rosemary said. "I've got to get those monkeys to stop getting in bed with us every night."

"This is the first time we've ever both been away from them all night."

"And it's probably the first time we've slept the entire night through since they were born."

"I slept with my parents until I was seven," Ulysses said.

Rosemary rolled her eyes. "I know, I know," she said. "And I slept in my own crib from the day I was born." She smiled. "How are you feeling?"

"Not that frisky. Where are LizBeth and her crew?"

"LizBeth left to meet the BIA canine crew at about 5:30." She touched his forehead. "I don't think you have a fever."

"What time is it? Has she checked in?" Ulysses asked, setting down his coffee cup and throwing off the covers.

"Hold up, there, Ulys. You aren't going anywhere, remember?"

"Did the canine crew have any luck?"

Rosemary sighed. "They tracked him but he got away again. "

"So he's still out there?"

"Look, Agent Tallichet has it covered." Rosemary sounded exasperated. "Get back in bed, please."

Ulysses obeyed and looked at his wife. He could tell she was holding back anger. "I'm sorry I broke my promise," he said.

"Let's get through this then we can talk about that," Rosemary replied. "But thanks for the apology."

Clarice knocked on the door and said, "Want some bacon and eggs? How about toast?"

"That sounds good, Clarice. I'd love some," Ulysses said. Never one to turn down breakfast, Ulysses wasn't sure he could eat it. "What time do things get going for the dance?"

"Oh, you know how it is, Ulys, it's impossible to say for sure – probably in about an hour," Clarice answered.

"When are you going to the dancing ground?" Ulysses asked.

"After I finish with breakfast and get dressed. You want to come, Rosemary?"

"Yes, after I call and check in with the children," Rosemary said.

"Clarice, did Ray leave a weapon for me?" Ulysses asked.

"Yes, he did," Clarice said, pulling open the drawer in the bedside table. "He said it was loaded and the safety is on."

"Just the one clip?"

"Just the one. I guess he wants you to be able to defend yourself from the bed but not much more."

"And not to get out of it, except to go to the bathroom," Rosemary said.

Rosemary called home and Ulysses got to speak with his children for the first time in two days. They'd just had breakfast and were watching cartoons in their pajamas.

"Daddy, did you catch the bad guy?" Amelia asked.

"Not yet, Bean, but I will," Ulysses said.

"Then will you come home?"

"Yes, I will. I can't wait."

"Me either, Daddy." She handed the phone to her brother.

"Daddy, did you shoot your gun yet?" Monty asked.

"No, son, I didn't have to. It wasn't called for." Ulysses had never shot his gun in the line of service as sheriff, and this had become a concern for his younger child who hardly knew of his police work in Santa Fe.

"I think you should shoot your gun today," Monty said, then set the phone down and walked away. Ulysses could hear Katie, the babysitter, telling him to get dressed.

"I think he forgot about the phone," Ulysses said and handed the phone back to Rosemary. "He wants me to shoot my gun today."

"Well, I don't," Rosemary said.

•

The morning dawned clear, bright and cold. Ulysses watched as Rosemary and Clarice walked across the snow-covered plaza. He looked around the plaza but saw no one stirring. He noticed that in addition to the traditional wooden ladder always propped against the church, there was an additional one on the same side, maybe left behind by the workers who'd recently repaired the stucco.

Not long after everyone left, Ulysses got out of bed, found his clothes hanging in the closet and slowly dressed. It took more effort than he had expected. His boots were still wet so he placed them near the gas stove.

He pulled the chair over to the window and put Ray's Glock and shoulder holster underneath it. The Picuris men had begun to drum and sing.

People were arriving, bundled up against the cold. Families with children, elders leaning on walkers, young tribal members from Albuquerque or Santa Fe dressed in colorful blankets, the women in deerskin moccasin boots, Hispanic and Anglo neighbors and friends who attended dances regularly and stayed after to eat with their tribal hosts—all were heading across the plaza to watch the dancers from the edges of the open space.

Ulysses had gone to dances his entire life, first with his parents and sister, then by himself. The family often spent Christmas Eve and Christmas Day at Taos Pueblo for the bonfires and the Deer, Buffalo or Matachine dances. Ulysses had acknowledged to Rosemary that what he experienced at the dances was as close as he got to a spiritual experience, even though he couldn't articulate what any of it really meant. For him, the dances inspired awe, and an ancient sense of oneness with all creation and all time.

When the men came out of the kiva to begin the dancing it never failed to send shivers up his spine and bring tears to his eyes. There would be a rifle shot and then the men, bare to the waist, draped with spruce boughs, their heads hidden within real animal heads of deer, elk, even bear and cougar, would file down to the dance grounds. They would be followed by the women, defying the cold in ceremonial clothing that left their midriffs or shoulders bare and holding rattles or corn in their uplifted hands. Then they would all begin to dance in the ancient, prescribed way, sometimes moving for hours to the steady drumbeat and chant. Ulysses felt in his bones that something primal and eternal found its expression in these dances.

Ulysses thought briefly about disobeying everyone's orders and mingling with the crowd at the dance ground. *But it will likely be an hour before the dancers come out of the kiva*, he realized. *At least from here I can see the people coming and going.* He sat down and put his feet on the windowsill. In a few minutes he was asleep.

•

Gunfire woke Ulysses with a start, but he immediately realized it was the traditional shots fired by Picuris men at the beginning of the dance. He'd been out for almost an hour. Ulysses stood up and stretched, stiff from sleeping in the chair. Cars and trucks filled the parking area near the plaza and lined both sides of the road as far as he could see, but few people were milling around. They had mostly gathered at the dance grounds, where the dancers were now moving in long lines in rhythm with the drumming. The women and girls in their colorful outfits weaved in and out of the men's lines, and many dancers wore eagle feathers in their hair. Ulysses remembered how the dances at Taos Pueblo had seemed interminable when he was a child. Sometimes he wandered off from his parents to sit against a sunny wall and listen, sometimes dozing. His main interest back then was the abundant and delicious pies and cakes Mrs. Martinez always served in her crowded home after the dances.

Ulysses tried to shake off the fogginess of his mind. He was about to lie down on the bed when he noticed a group of tribal members crossing the plaza heading toward the dancers: an older man in blue jeans, a flannel shirt and a fringed leather jacket, a woman wrapped in a colorful blanket who walked with a slight limp, and a younger adult man, probably their son, bow-legged with a big belly, wearing coveralls. A tall, strongly built man, who Ulysses recognized as a cousin of Ray's, followed them. He had a holstered gun on his belt and a watchful demeanor. *He's probably on the war council*, Ulysses thought. Was the younger unarmed man Benjamin Duràn, who LizBeth said might be on Downs's hit list? Why in the hell were they allowing him to go into that crowd?

He watched the group take their places in the front of the western side of the circle, where the sun struck an old adobe building. Ulysses resumed his chair by the window. He scanned the scene for Rosemary and Clarice but couldn't pick them out from the crowd. The last blue shadows from roofs and portals began to fade in the morning sun. The snow on the south-facing slopes glistened, as if starting to melt.

Ulysses was irritated to be sidelined like this. *Why do I always have to push beyond my limits*, he asked himself for maybe the thousandth time. *Is it just being the "big alpha dog in charge" as Rosemary says? Is it the whole re-election thing? No*, Ulysses thought, *the crux of my problem is the damn adrenaline rush. That's what drove me to run off after Downs alone. And that's what got me this head injury.*

Ulysses reflected that even though he was careful and almost methodical in much of his life, when it came to this part of his work, he was way too impulsive. Rosemary was right. This trait wasn't a good fit with being a family man. But what else could he do? This work felt like his only true calling.

Ulysses first had this flaw pointed out to him when he was working in uniform in Santa Fe. It was a hot evening in mid-September during Santa Fe's Fiestas. The plaza was packed with local families and tourists enjoying the music and craft booths while awaiting the Entrada, a reenactment of the return of the Spanish twenty years after the Pueblo Revolt of 1680. Ulysses spotted a known gang member, Johnny "The Nub" Catron, standing between the bandstand and the façade of the Palace of the Governors holding a pistol by his side. The man's white face was sweaty and he looked scared. He was scanning the crowd as if searching for someone. Ulysses was moving through the crowd, his hand on his gun, his eyes on Catron. In the moment when the gang banger spotted his target and raised his gun, Ulysses tackled him and the two men wrestled on the ground. Johnny got free and aimed his gun at Ulysses. Catron's eyes darted around as the crowd as if seeking help. He hesitated a moment as people backed away murmuring, giving Ulysses time to retrieve his gun. Then Catron turned back to Ulysses as if resolved to kill him. Ulysses shouted to the man to drop his gun or he would shoot. Catron looked around and then back at Ulysses, holding his gun steady, a sneer on his young face. Without hesitation Ulysses shot him in the chest. Within moments the man was dead. Ulysses remembered the painful remorse that flooded him.

First, Ulysses was investigated for wrongful death, then cleared of the charge, then commended by the mayor and the press for saving Fiestas. In the end, though, his chief had written him up for "nearly getting himself and others killed." The powerful Catron family still held enough power to get him censured. His boss said he should have radioed another uniform who was closer by for backup.

The trancelike singing and drumming continued. The crowd was watching quietly and the rest of the pueblo was virtually deserted. Ulysses tried to remain vigilant but found himself dozing off frequently. He was about to give up and go back to bed when he noticed LizBeth and the other agent, a woman, walk across the plaza toward the crowd. LizBeth and her companion both looked warily above, behind and to both sides as they approached the dancers.

Ulysses put on his socks and damp boots, picked up the handset to Ray's landline together with the gun and holster and walked out on the front porch. He dialed his work number and Lorraine answered.

"Good morning, Lorraine," Ulysses said, "Is Angela around?"

"Sheriff, I thought you were in the hospital!"

"No, I'm here at Picuris. Where's Angela?"

"But wait a minute, we heard you were injured. Should you be on duty?"

"Lorraine, let me speak to Angela." Lorraine sighed and clicked off and Angela picked up.

"Sheriff," Angela said, "I'm glad you called. There's a lot going on here."

"Yeah, like what?"

"Early this morning Downs stole a truck up near Sleeping Tiger. We found out about dawn but he hasn't been seen since. We just got word to warn some people that they might be in danger. Several people aren't answering their phones so I'm going out to check on them."

"Who's not answering the phone?"

"Archbishop Sullivan for one."

"My God, do go check on him. Also Casimira Duràn, Eduardo Santos and the former Sheriff Trujillo. Benjamin Duràn knows and he's got people watching him."

"Okay, thanks I'll take care of it. Where are you?"

"I'm sitting on Ray Pando's front porch. I can see the dance from here and also a lot of the parked cars. What kind of truck did he steal?"

"A green Toyota with dual rear tires," Angela said. She gave him the license number.

Ulysses scanned the parking lot and the sides of the road he could see from where he sat. "I don't see a truck by that description from here. Does Ray know?"

"Oh, yeah, and the FBI, too. He won't get far in that truck."

"Well, you better go check on Sullivan and Trujillo," Ulysses said. "Call me with any updates."

Ulysses wondered if he could manage to walk down to the road to look for the stolen truck. It wasn't far, just across the plaza and down a few steps to where he would be able to see all the cars and trucks parked nearby. But he knew it was a foolish idea given how weak and lightheaded he felt.

That kind of behavior could get him killed. And if Downs didn't kill him, Rosemary would.

Ulysses tried to change the channel in his mind away from his regretful, self-critical thoughts. He started imagining the bathroom remodel he was planning and felt the soothing effect of considering a glass shower with the rainfall showerhead Rosemary wanted and a low-flow toilet to save on well water.

Suddenly, Ulysses sat bolt upright. Across the plaza and in the back of the crowd Ulysses saw Rosemary. With her were Amelia and Monty. Ulysses felt rage and fear. Had the babysitter brought his children here? Why on earth would she do such a thing? He stood up, felt dizzy and sat back down.

At that moment the chanting and drumming stopped. The dancers were going back into the kiva, signaling a break in the dance. The crowd began to disperse—there was no telling how long the break would last. Ulysses momentarily lost sight of his family among the throng of people milling about, talking in small groups and going in and out of buildings.

He recalled his dream. The dream had predicted Amelia and Monty would be present. Ulysses turned to look at San Lorenzo's church, which had been on fire in the dream. Just behind the front parapet he saw the black top of someone's head. His adrenaline spiked. Was that a tribal member? Or was it Downs? The head disappeared. Ulysses crouched down in front of his chair and placed the phone on the floor, his eyes trained on the edge of the front parapet. For a long few minutes he saw nothing move on the roof. Then, for an instant, he saw sunlight glance off the scope of a rifle.

Ulysses's mind became focused and clear. Downs was up there. He had to be brought down. He posed a risk to everyone, including Ulysses's own family. Ulysses put on his holster and picked up Ray's gun which felt unfamiliar to his hand and scooted back into the shadows along the house wall. How long had Downs been up there? Had Downs seen him? Not yet, or he'd be dead. Ulysses cursed the ladders that had been left propped against the wall, giving Downs immediate access to the highest ground in the pueblo. He remembered something about a ladder from a dream but couldn't remember what it was.

For a few moments his vision swam from the effort to remain still and crouched. He lifted the gun and looked down the sights. His instincts told him he was too far away for a decent shot. And if he missed, Downs would round on him and shoot him where he stood. Ulysses waited.

A rifle shot signified that the Deer Dancers were coming out of the kiva for the second part of the dance. The spectators returned to the dance grounds. Picuris men, bare chested and wearing deer antlers and spruce boughs and women and girls holding boughs and rattles began dancing to the drumming in intersecting lines.

Ulysses was aware that this was the moment Downs was probably waiting for. He crept along the porch as if in a dream. He felt no fear, only a laser focus and an intense drive to stop Downs. But he was aware that he was significantly weakened. His limbs felt like jelly and his head throbbed. At the end of Ray's porch was a small open space brightly lit by the sun and visible from the church roof. If he could get across that space without Downs seeing him, he could go behind the house next door and maybe get a decent shot. Even if he didn't kill him the fire would draw the attention of the Picuris armed security who might help bring him down.

Ulysses crept on his belly to the end of the porch and waited behind the low retaining wall at its end. He remembered he had only one round of ammunition. He lifted himself once, ready to slip over the wall and onto the ground, but at that moment he saw that Downs was now fully visible, scanning the crowd which was focused on the dance. Ulysses paused, watching Downs' head in its black cap, the rifle in his right hand. The sun reflected off the sparkling mica-flecked surface of the church and hurt Ulysses's eyes.

When Downs crouched down again, Ulysses swung his legs over the wall and jumped and rolled across the exposed space until his back was up against the next building. He paused, taking deep breaths, dizzy and sweating. Now at least if Downs turned toward Ulysses, he wouldn't see him. The drumming and chanting continued and the reverent crowd was quiet.

Suddenly, Downs began shooting, firing single shots into the crowd of people who screamed and ran in all directions trying to escape the bullets, some even running toward the church. *Just like in my dream*, Ulysses thought.

Adrenaline surged, filling him with an intense rush of fearless energy. He stood up and ran as fast as he could, behind the house nearest the church where Downs, high above him on the roof, had his back to Ulysses. The firing had paused for a few moments and Ulysses could hear people screaming. Downs fired several more deliberate targeted shots. As Ulysses came around the house to the exposed area just below the church roof, he again checked his sights. Close enough, though at a steep angle. *Now or never*, Ulysses thought, just as Downs, as if sensing his presence, turned toward him. He pulled off his hat and flung it away from him, his blonde hair falling around his shoulders.

Ulysses, trembling, aimed and fired a shot, missing Downs. Downs was smiling now and speaking but Ulysses couldn't understand what he was saying. As Ulysses took aim again, Downs slowly raised both his arms as if giving a blessing, the sun creating an aura around his head.

Ulysses shot twice, hitting Downs and knocking him backward. Now he was hidden from view below the parapet. Ulysses put his gun in the holster and began to climb the ladder. When he looked up he saw Downs looming over him, injured with a wound to his torso, a pistol in his hand aimed at Ulysses's head. As he raised it toward Ulysses, shots from behind Downs knocked him forward. He fell from the roof to the ground. Ulysses saw Ray come running from the other side of the church toward Downs, Matt and another man close behind.

Ulysses and Ray, guns drawn, approached Downs, who lay on the snowy ground of the plaza sprawled on his back. He was dead. He had multiple bullet wounds in his chest. He wore a St. Michael scapular that was now soaked with blood. Ulysses fell to his knees looked into his adversary's open eyes, feeling a primitive, momentary triumph. Then waves of relief hit, followed by a strange and penetrating sadness. He knew this feeling. It came from taking a human life. Ray crouched beside him and put an arm around his shoulder.

A crowd began to gather.

"Please move away for your own safety," Ray said, standing up, the gun in his right hand. The crowd was slow to move, but Matt and others began to direct people toward their homes or cars.

"You nailed him, Sheriff," LizBeth said, smiling. "Good job." The other agent stood scanning the roofs in every direction.

"*We* nailed him," Ulysses said, indicating Ray who had already moved to assist the injured. Ulysses sat in the snow, his head spinning. "Let's get you back in the house," LizBeth said and she and Randi helped him stand.

•

After Ulysses was led back to bed, Rosemary and the children rushed into the room. Monty let go of his mother's hand and ran in crowing, "Daddy, Daddy, you shot your gun!" Amelia came behind, quietly twirling her sweater into a knot. She stood beside her father and put her hand on his shoulder. "Daddy," she whispered. Ulysses drew her to him and kissed her, then hugged Monty.

"I've missed you guys," he said. "I'm so glad you're safe and sound."

"I saw that man get shot in the leg," Monty said, laughing. "He was right across from me."

Rosemary took Monty by the arm and said, "Monty, it's not funny. That man was hurt bad. His name is Benjamin. He's going to the hospital."

"Will he die?" Amelia asked, catching her breath.

"No, I don't think so." Rosemary picked Monty up and placed him on her hip. He put his arms around her neck.

"The bad guy was dead, dead, dead," Monty said.

"Shhh…" Rosemary whispered, stroking her son's gold curls. "We'll talk all about it later."

"I want to go home," Monty said, sighing deeply.

"Yes, let's go home now," Rosemary said. "Are you guys hungry?"

"Starving," Monty said. Amelia was silent.

"Shall we go to Peñasco and get something to eat?"

"Yay!" Monty said.

"Can I have a piece of carrot cake?" Amelia asked perking up a little.

"Yes, you can. Now run to the toilet and we'll go right to Peñasco." Clarice, who'd been standing in the doorway, directed the children to the bathroom.

"How on earth did the children get here?" Ulysses asked Rosemary when they had gone out.

"Katie didn't realize she'd be putting anyone in danger," Rosemary said. "Her mother fell and she needed to go help her. She couldn't reach me so she just brought the children to me, just before all hell broke loose." Rosemary leaned over and kissed her husband.

"It scared me to death to see them there," Ulysses said.

"I know, Honey. I'm so sorry. Listen, we're going home. Get someone to drive you as soon as you can."

"Really? You're not going to give me grief?"

"Like I said earlier, Ulys, we have to talk."

LizBeth came by after lunch to interview him. She took off her coat and hat and sat in the chair by Ulysses's bed, looking exhausted. "How're you doing?" she asked.

"Better," Ulysses said unconvincingly. He took a sip of water. "I'm still pretty puny." He lay on the bed propped up on pillows. "Ray's going to run me home this afternoon. He's still wrapping up from the shooting. I heard Benjamin Duràn is in surgery now. We're lucky no one else was hit."

"Yeah, Duràn lost a lot of blood. I hope he makes it." LizBeth ran her hand through her hair. "Hey, I've got some bad news." LizBeth looked at the floor. "We've had another fatality. Archbishop Sullivan. Your deputy Angela Romero found him hanging from a balcony at his house. It was made to look like a suicide but we're pretty sure it was Downs. We found Tomàs Ulibarri's truck in a ditch south of the rectory and Sullivan's Mercedes is parked here. So we know for sure Downs was there."

"Shit," Ulysses said, "excuse me. Well that was predicted. Too bad we didn't stop it. Do we know a time of death?"

"Here's what it looks like. Downs broke into Tomàs Ulibarri's house sometime after 3 a.m. and stole his truck. Ulibarri was injured but not seriously. Jo McAlister was there also and she is unhurt. We believe Downs drove right to the archbishop's house and killed Sullivan about 5 a.m. Then he came here and climbed up on the roof before dawn. We found some tracks around the back of the house next door. He hid himself carefully. It was all thought through, except of course for you being here. A brutally efficient killer, that one."

"Sullivan found hanging – sounds like Downs's m. o. He said he liked to make his kills look natural," Ulysses said. "Makes you wonder about Silvia Durán, doesn't it? "

"The death of an archbishop is going to be investigated up the wazoo," LizBeth said. "Not like a young Picuris college student. But Silvia's death might get re-examined in the process." LizBeth touched his shoulder. "Hey, man, you were a hero today."

"Thanks, LizBeth. I feel lucky to have been in the right place for once. Still, there will be people who want my head because I didn't protect the archbishop."

"Probably. But more are going to want to see a parade in your honor. Ray's too."

"You know my wife and children were in that crowd."

"I know, I saw them. Too bad they had to witness such a thing."

"It makes me furious. They are way too young to see something like that." He lay back against the pillows, tears filling his eyes.

"Hey, I should let you sleep." LizBeth rose to go.

"When do you expect the DNA results from Sleeping Tiger?"

"Sometime next month," LizBeth answered, "if we're lucky with the holidays coming up. Listen, you rest up, okay? We'll debrief this horror show later."

"Before Christmas?"

"Unlikely. But soon after."

Chapter XVI

Ulysses took two weeks of sick leave some personal leave before Christmas, planning to return to work the beginning of the second week of January. During his time off he rested, read a book on Zen and sourced materials for their bathroom remodel, including some discounted apricot colored travertine for the shower surround and floor.

Ulysses and Rosemary had a long talk about his broken promise and how to resolve the conflict between work and their family life. While nothing was resolved, Ulysses felt relief when Rosemary finally forgave him. She said, "I knew when I married you that you could be reckless. I realized your job involved risk. It is just very hard to accept because it means that one day I might lose you."

"I can try to change," Ulysses said, knowing how silly it sounded. "I did learn from my experience." *I wish I could change*, he thought. *She deserves better.*

"Just what did you learn?" Rosemary asked looking skeptical but squeezing his hand.

"I learned that nothing is more important to me than you and the children. Nothing."

"Well, keep that in mind the next time a wild psychopath is on the loose in your county, will you?"

Both Ulysses and Rosemary worried about signs that Monty and Amelia had experienced trauma during the Deer Dance. Amelia became aware of the reality of death and talked about her fears especially at bedtime. Monty started biting his sister, something he'd never done before.

Rosemary found a therapist in Taos who came highly recommended for her competence in dealing with children who'd been exposed to traumatic events. After meeting with her on her own, Rosemary made appointments for both children.

The family spent a quiet Christmas mostly alone. They decorated a small tree and exchanged homemade presents. The children were immensely proud of the presents they'd made with help from Rosemary. It was the first year that one or other extended family didn't descend for the holiday, and Ulysses and Rosemary relished the pleasures of bright days and long quiet nights, the woodstove keeping them warm and Rosemary supplying treats like homemade trifle, a gingerbread house, and eggnog. For Ulysses she made a blackberry cordial, heavy on brandy and infused with healing herbs. Ulysses and Rosemary found themselves having more sex than usual, especially on afternoons when the children attended a play group.

They welcomed a few visitors. Ray, Matt and Clarice brought them a box of homemade spicy bison jerky a week before Christmas, and Angela, Lorraine and Zach brought tamales, biscochitos and piñon nuts on Christmas Eve. Lorraine told Ulysses that while Josh was making a good recovery he probably wouldn't return to work. His family wanted him to go back to UNM to finish his degree. From Ray, Ulysses learned that Benjie Duràn was recuperating at his parents' home and was expected to make a full recovery and return to his halfway house. The pueblo had removed the ladders from the church and improved security plans for the dances. They were already preparing for the Buffalo Dance on New Year's Day. After Christmas the days were sunny and warm enough that most of the snow at their elevation melted, except in the northern exposures and under the evergreens, where three feet of snow could last for months.

From Lorraine, Ulysses learned that Governor Montaño had appointed a special inquiry into the death of Archbishop Sullivan to make sure all appropriate steps had been taken to protect him. A local group protesting abuse by clergy was also demanding an inquiry into allegations that Sullivan was fully cognizant of Randolph Miller's predatory behavior toward children, including at his summer camps. Brother Eduardo Santos of Velardé was quoted as a corroborating witness to their allegations.

On New Year's Day, LizBeth showed up with her girlfriend Dawa, a willowy Asian woman with horn-rimmed glasses and long black hair in a ponytail. Dawa brought a casserole of black-eyed peas and collards, said to bring good luck in the New Year in North Carolina, where she'd attended medical school. A neurology resident at UT, Dawa gave Ulysses a quick exam and pronounced him on the mend from his concussion.

LizBeth brought toys for Amelia and Monty, including a Lego beginner set and a boxed collection of Pippi Longstocking books and the children were thrilled. LizBeth told Ulysses they still didn't have definitive information about whose DNA they found in the dormitory wreckage but it appeared to predate the fire and perhaps had come from more than one individual.

LizBeth was consumed with what she and her boss were considering the major security lapse at LANL that allowed plastic explosives to go missing. Amanda Holt and several others had been called in to the Bureau to testify on their oversight and heads were expected to roll.

On his break Ulysses called in daily to check with Angela, who served as interim sheriff during his absence. She had her hands full with the regular business of domestic violence, break-ins and DWIs, but nothing more exotic. When it was time to go back to work, Ulysses felt ready for the mundane aspects of law enforcement.

On the morning of his first day back Ulysses drove the familiar roads into Taos feeling calm and resolved. He was determined not to get into the politics swirling around the Downs murders, especially the blame game that was already in full play in the press. He arrived at the station and pulled into his parking place. No sooner had he gotten out of his car than he was approached by three reporters and a press photographer.

"Sheriff Walker," a young man asked as the photographer snapped rapid-fire pictures, "did you know that Ràmon Trujillo is calling for you to step down?"

"No, I didn't," Ulysses answered. "I know Sheriff Trujillo was a close friend of the Archbishop, so I'm sure he's upset at his death. But I won't be stepping down."

"Why does Governor Montaño want to meet with you?" the same reporter asked.

"I guess I'll find out next week when I see her in Santa Fe," Ulysses answered.

Another reporter yelled, "Do you believe Archbishop Sullivan was complicit with clergy sex abuse?" Ulysses lifted his eyebrows and took a deep breath but didn't reply. He ducked inside the building. *Here we go*, Ulysses thought to himself, as the familiar smells and sounds of his workplace rushed up to greet him.

•

A week into the new year, Jo McAlister walked down the road from Tomàs's house to Sleeping Tiger. It was a cold, overcast day with low-hanging clouds and a stiff wind. Snow was predicted. Tomàs was still asleep when Jo left so she wrote him a note that read, "Gone to pack a few things, back soon, J." She brought along a suitcase and a backpack, which she expected would hold most of her earthly possessions. Whatever didn't fit she planned to leave behind.

Since the murders Jo and Tomàs had fallen in love. She was surprised at how this man, older, so different from her, seemed to know her mind, body and spirit. When Jo looked for the sad familiarity of Tim's memory, she found that it was gone from the dry, musty place he'd occupied in her mind for three years. She could no longer remember his face or how he smelled before he got sick. Instead, in her mind and her dreams, she found Tomàs, smiling, holding her in his bearlike embrace, his kind, dark eyes so often turned toward her.

But how on earth could she make a life with him and what kind of life would it be? It was impossible to imagine, which was why she was flying out tomorrow to spend two weeks with her father at Anandaville. But before she left, she had to move out of her cabin at Sleeping Tiger.

Since the night Downs broke into Tomàs's house a lot had happened. Tomàs had gotten sixteen stitches in his abdomen where Downs just missed nicking the large intestine. He was recovering surprisingly quickly. Carmen had come by to offer Jo a place to stay and to give "auntie advice" when Jo elected to remain at Tomàs's.

"You two have been through a lot," Carmen said. "Of course you want to cling to each other. But don't make any decisions you might regret."

"Okay, Tia," Tomàs had said. "I'm a big boy now."

Carmen looked at Jo as if worried about her and then embraced her suddenly and fiercely. "You be careful," she said. "He's very persuasive, that one!"

"Don't worry, Carmen," Jo said seriously. "We're taking things slow." Of course, that was the exact opposite of what was actually happening.

Jo arrived at her cabin, retrieved the key from under the front step and opened the door. The cabin was ice cold, no fire having been lit there in weeks. It smelled of creosote and ashes. She checked the faucets and found them in working order, thanks to the insulated tape Tomàs had put on as soon as they were allowed back on the property. The cabin, once a homey refuge for her, looked shabby in the gray winter light. Dust had settled on every surface. It was as if she'd never lived here.

Jo placed her suitcase on the bed and emptied the dresser of its contents—underwear and bras, a pair of red flannel pajamas and a pink summer nightgown, wool socks, blue jeans and yoga pants, long-sleeved shirts and sweaters she'd brought from California and a rain slicker she'd never worn. She took her toiletries from the bathroom, her birdwatching binoculars from the bedside table and her favorite mug from the kitchen, a piece of blue Japanese pottery she'd drunk her morning coffee out of for years. She wrapped the cup in a piece of long underwear, placed it carefully in the arms of a grey Icelandic sweater, then zipped her suitcase closed.

Jo remembered when she'd first moved in on a late summer afternoon that felt like ages ago. Melanie had picked her up at the Santa Fe airport and brought her directly to this cabin. The place was spotlessly clean and a huge bouquet of freshly picked sunflowers stood in the sunlight that pooled onto the kitchen table. Jo had been enchanted.

After Melanie had left that afternoon Jo picked through the old abbot's bookcase and found some jewels: Thomas Kelly's *A Testament of Devotion*, an anonymous monk's masterpiece, *The Cloud of Unknowing*, and surprisingly, *The Way of Zen* by Alan Watts. Jo had felt sure that she had come to the right place, home at last after wandering in the wilderness of grief.

She felt different today. A few tears rolled down her cheeks as she pulled her own books from the shelves: *Sibley's Guide to Birds*, Mosby's *EMT Basics*, a poetry anthology, *News of the Universe* and the book of koans she'd almost finished, *The Blue Cliff Record*.

Jo heard steps on the front porch. Panic rose in her until she saw through the window that it was Melanie. Jo took a deep breath and opened the door.

"I thought I'd find you here," Melanie said.

"I didn't know you were around," Jo said.

"I just got back. I was in California for Christmas with Lynne and Gary. Anne came back with me. She's at the house." Melanie looked around and saw the suitcase and backpack.

"Are you moving out?"

"I thought it best. I'm going to visit my dad for a few weeks."

"Carmen told me you were moving in with Tomàs."

"Not exactly. I have been staying there, but frankly I don't know what my future holds." Jo put the books in her backpack. Melanie sat down in the rocker. There was an awkward silence.

"You must be disappointed in me," Melanie said softly.

"I'm pretty confused, to tell the truth." Jo avoided Melanie's eyes.

"Not surprising," Melanie said. "I let you down." She paused and shifted in her chair. "I let everyone down including myself. I'm taking a year's sabbatical from roshi duties."

"Really?"

"Yes, well, it's such a mess. Alan insists we sell Sleeping Tiger. We'll be lucky if we can pay off our creditors. And now there are two lawsuits."

Jo buckled the flap of her backpack and said nothing. She was surprised at how angry she felt.

"There are other reasons, of course," Melanie continued. "I need a time of reflection after all that's happened. I have to get clear myself before I return to teaching." She paused and looked at Jo. "If I do."

"What are you going to do?" Jo asked.

"Gary has offered me their spare room for the time being. He needs help with Lynne. She's dying, you know."

"I thought she was. It's good you can be there for them."

"Yes, and I'm lucky he can take me in."

After another awkward silence. Jo finally spoke up. "I had heard the police were questioning you."

"They were. When they searched my office they found a letter I was writing to Gerald. It showed I suspected some of what he was doing, both his embezzling and more interactions with a high school student. I didn't actually know the age of the boy but I thought he might be underage. Turns out, he was seventeen, kind of borderline. They didn't charge me with anything." Melanie paused and looked at Jo. Jo nodded but said nothing. That must have been the letter she's seen on Melanie's desk the morning this whole nightmare began. She remembered the lines, "You lied to me!"

Melanie sighed and continued. "It's hard to face all of this—all the ways I've been so...*wrong*."

"How did you find out about Gerald's embezzlement?" Jo asked.

"I hadn't been in the habit of looking at the books," Melanie said. "You know me and numbers. At Thanksgiving when Gerald was gone I decided I needed to take a look. I realized something was going on and started that letter to Gerald. But I had no idea he was being blackmailed."

"It must have been hard to keep so many secrets," Jo said, trying to hide her emotions.

Melanie nodded. "It has been. I've struggled with his secrets, and my own, for years."

Jo stood up and began closing empty drawers and looking under the furniture for anything she might have left behind. She wanted to calm her feelings and give Melanie plenty of time to collect her thoughts. Finally, she turned and faced her former teacher. "What secrets, Melanie?"

"Well, for starters there was Skip, the boy Gerald molested," Melanie said. "Jon Malvern. He was only fourteen when he started having sex with him. I was seeing Gerald in therapy then and I should have called child protective services, but I didn't. I didn't want to see Gerald go to jail and I thought I could make him stop. I did make him stop but I still should have reported the crime. I have karma there."

Jo, shocked, said nothing. *You bet you have karma*, she thought. How could she have stayed silent about this?

"If I had exposed Gerald, a lot would be different. But I convinced myself I was following the dharma by avoiding actions I might later regret."

"You were lying to yourself," Jo said. "In fact, you kept lying and he kept molesting." Jo paused and took a deep breath aware that her anger was white hot. "He manipulated you. He *and you* manipulated all of us."

Melanie, who had begun to cry, said nothing.

"I wanted so much to believe in you," Jo continued. "I wasn't really following my own path so much as I was following you. I've learned my lesson. I'll never do that again." Jo looked away and swallowed hard, fighting back tears.

Melanie wiped her eyes and nose with the back of her hand. Jo went to the bathroom and came back with a tissue.

"You were my best student, Jo," she said.

"Right," Jo said with uncharacteristic sarcasm.

"Maybe I can make amends. I am going to try," Melanie said, looking up at Jo.

Jo finally decided to ask the one question she'd not been able to ask before. "Melanie, why was it that Gerald so special to you? I never understood why you put up with him."

Melanie rocked in silence for a few moments. "I'm not sure I completely understand myself," she said. Jo waited for her to continue.

"I had a child when I was 17 and gave him up for adoption. I found him years later but he wanted nothing to do with me. It was the hardest thing I'd had to face at that point in my life. I think it drove me to spiritual practice."

How is this related? Jo wondered, searching the older woman's tear-streaked face.

"In therapy Gerald told me he was adopted. His adoptive parents were older and not cut out for raising a child. He had a lot of childhood and young adult trauma."

"Did you know then that he was a predator?" Jo asked. She felt impatient with Melanie's story.

"No. You don't understand. Yes, he lied to me a lot and our relationship became unhealthy. But for many years he filled a void in my life. Of course, I was too emotionally involved to be his therapist."

"Or his Zen teacher?"

"Or his teacher. But I honestly hoped that the dharma would save him. For a few years it looked like he was better, but then…well, you know how it turned out."

Jo sighed and sat down on the couch, feeling disgusted and confused. It was very quiet in the cabin. Outside, several crows cawed from nearby trees. Melanie's remorse reminded Jo of her mother's remorse about leaving the family to be with Ananda. It made sense, it could be understood, but the harm was done and it left a bitter taste. It took years to forgive. "Why didn't you tell Roshi Akira about all this?" Jo asked. "Or go into therapy yourself?"

"I kept it secret for Gerald's sake at first, the whole confidentiality thing," Melanie said, drying her tears. "And I didn't want to believe he was unable to change. I think I was also hiding a lot of shame at my own cowardice. "

Jo felt her anger dissolve into pity for her wounded old teacher who sat before her now, unmasked.

The two women sat in silence for a long time. Jo remembered how much she had trusted and revered Melanie for her kindness and commitment to her spiritual path. Perhaps Jo could see the good in Melanie again if only she could forgive her. That would take time if it could even happen, Jo knew.

Jo put on her backpack, and picked up her suitcase. She touched Melanie on the shoulder and walked out, quietly closing the front door. A blue patch had opened in the grey clouds and sunlight sparkled on the snow. As Jo started down the path for the last time, she saw Tomàs standing by his truck waiting for her. He walked toward her smiling and took her heavy suitcase.

"Let's go home," he said.

·

The day they were to meet with the governor, Ulysses and Ray drove to Santa Fe in the Expedition. Rosemary packed a thermos of coffee for each man and sent a bag of fresh bran muffins to share during the two-hour drive. The Expedition was warm and quiet as they drove through the wintry Rio Grande Valley and up to the high-altitude capital city.

Ray seemed preoccupied with his own thoughts. Ulysses was also quiet, keeping the emotions he'd been feeling over the past month to himself. He'd benefited from the time off recuperating but all his soul-searching hadn't resolved the dilemmas posed by his job. At least Monty and Amelia seemed to have recovered from the trauma of the Deer Dance.

"You nervous about meeting the governor?" Ray asked, pouring himself a cup of coffee.

"Not really. I just hope she won't chew us out." They drove in silence while Ulysses ate a muffin.

"You'll probably get some kind of medal." Ray said at last.

"I sincerely doubt that. People are too stirred up about the archbishop."

"Yeah, well, some people think he got what was coming to him. I'm not one of those, mind you. It's a little harsh. But he won't be greatly missed."

Ulysses cleared his throat. "Hey, let's review some stuff, shall we? We might face reporter questions."

"You *are* nervous, man," Ray said, "But go ahead."

"Okay, thanks. Let's start with what we think about Archbishop Sullivan's death," Ulysses said. "We believe Downs killed Sullivan at his residence before coming to Picuris for the Deer Dance. Downs tried to fake a suicide by hanging, just as he probably did with Silvia Duràn, but the forensics show Sullivan was strangled by hands rather than a rope and traces of Downs' DNA were found on Sullivan's neck."

"And Downs exchanged Ulibarri's truck for Sullivan's Mercedes," Ray said. "But why did Downs kill Sullivan? What was the motive?"

"That's easy. Downs saw Sullivan as an enabler. Eduardo Santos told Sullivan what Miller was doing at the summer camps and Sullivan told him to be quiet. But I don't know of any evidence that Sullivan himself abused children."

"Maybe the governor's commission will uncover something," Ray said. "Go on."

"Okay. Other murders. Downs confessed to me that he killed Luis Duràn in revenge for Luis killing his cousin Elías. His account was consistent with Luis's postmortem. Downs also confessed to killing Beatty and told details about the death he couldn't have otherwise known. We think he killed Gerald because he had procured boys for Miller at the summer camp."

"He didn't know about Beatty's other bad deeds," Ray said.

Ulysses continued, "Downs also confessed to killing Randolph Miller. He told me that he abducted Randolph Miller by 'offering him something he'd always wanted but never had.' God knows what that was. Sex, probably. Anyway, Downs says he caused Miller to die of thirst somewhere out on Comanche Mesa. No trace of him has ever been found though so we don't have certainty about Miller's death either."

"Still, I think we both believe he killed Miller exactly the way he told you," Ray said. "Whew, what a way to go."

Ulysses nodded, his eyes on the road. "And, it is established that Downs attempted to kill Benjamin Duràn, who had molested Silvia Duràn."

"Abused her along with Downs, right?"

"Right. Though Downs denied it."

"And Downs killed Silvia Duràn, right?" Ray sipped his coffee.

"Well, I think he did, using the same method he used with Sullivan. But there is no way to prove it."

"And what about Astrid Berg? How do we know Downs killed her since he didn't admit it?"

"Well we can be pretty sure, I think. Did you know the FBI guys found a scapular in the sheets of her bed at Sleeping Tiger?"

"No, I hadn't heard that."

"Yeah, Tallichet told me."

"How was her body found?"

"Some hikers found her, or to be exact, their dogs found her. On New Year's Day, no less. She was buried in a snow bank in the woods just to the north of Melanie Hirsh's house at Sleeping Tiger. It had finally got warm enough her body was close to the surface and I guess the dogs got the scent. I was still on leave, thank God. Angela handled all of it."

"That girl is good," Ray said.

"She is very good," Ulysses said.

"How did Berg die?" Ray asked.

"We presume that after having sex with her, Downs somehow drugged her unconscious and then exposed her to the very cold night. When they dug her out of the snowbank she was naked but there were no bruises on her body. The cause of death was hypothermia. We got some labs back last week. In addition to recent sexual activity, she also tested positive for high levels of dilaudid for which she had a prescription. We'll know more when we get the DNA on the semen back."

Ray sighed. "What a sick dude. I hate this shit."

Ulysses bit into a second muffin. "Here, try one of these," he said to Ray. "It'll cheer you up." Ray took a muffin and bit into it. "Once again, Downs made murder look like a natural death—more or less," Ulysses continued. "Like she just happened to be wandering out naked on a cold night and froze to death."

"It's being treated as a homicide, right?"

"Yes, and when we get the DNA back we'll likely close the case."

"Why would Downs kill Astrid Berg?" Ray asked.

"Downs told me openly about killing Luis, Gerald and Randolph Miller. He was proud of those kills. He said things with Astrid Berg didn't go as planned. Maybe he simply had to kill her because she tempted him. He hated women and sex, apparently. He'd had sex with her and maybe that was enough to make him want to kill her."

"What about the rumors of her cover ups for her previous boss. Wouldn't that make him feel justified? He left the scapular and all."

"Yeah, probably. She was an enabler for Junsu Ito, I guess. But I think he felt guilty about Berg. He said he wasn't 'following orders' with her so it didn't fit in with his overall mission. Berg's family has descended, by the way, loaded for bear. I heard they are suing Sleeping Tiger. I hope they don't find reason to come after me. Evidently they've got a lot of expensive lawyers."

"Why would they come after you? Ulys, relax, you're the sheriff, remember?"

Ulysses laughed and finished his coffee. "You're right, Ray, I do need to chill." They drove for a while in silence.

"Sleeping Tiger got hit with another lawsuit too," Ulysses continued. "Marci Kelly, remember her? She's suing for damages over the trauma she suffered at the retreat."

"Whatever," Ray said, shaking his head. "More lawyers. Hey, what happened to the man who pulled a gun on Melanie Hirsh?"

"Jon Malvern? He was hospitalized several nights for that whack on the head—a fractured skull," Ulysses said. "When he was released from the hospital, he was arraigned on assault with a deadly weapon. He made bail and went home to California. His trial is in a couple of weeks. Angela told me Melanie Hirsh didn't want to press charges, but Angela told her, 'Ma'am, it doesn't matter whether you want to file charges or not. The State of New Mexico will be pressing charges.' "

"Have they been able to identify the remains found in the dormitory?" Ray asked as they approached Santa Fe.

"Not definitively," Ulysses said. "They think they are from two separate persons, but they weren't able to extract much DNA from either sample. Since it's part of an arson crime there's a federal mandate to investigate. They are supposed to let us know what they find. The remains could be more than fifty years old, they said."

"Skeletons in the closet of the Holy Mother Church," Ray suggested. "Hey, how is your head doing?"

"I'm better," Ulysses said. "It's slow. I'm tired a lot. I get frustrated really easily. Rosemary says I'm more forgetful but she's always said that. She's got me on various supplements and herbs. I'm trying to take it seriously."

"It's a good thing you're young," Ray said. "You'll recover. I don't have that much confidence in my ability these days."

"Are you kidding me? Ray, I wouldn't be here without you. You and Matt. I think about it every day."

Ray said nothing but patted Ulysses' shoulder. "Listen, Ulys, I was standing right next to Benjie when Downs shot him. I saw how much blood he lost. The bullet nicked his femoral artery and he very nearly died. Whew. It really got to me."

Ulysses arrived in Santa Fe and headed toward the New Mexico Round House, the legislature building near downtown.

"Ulys, I want you to know I'm retiring from the war council come May."

Ulysses looked at his old friend. Ray was staring straight ahead. Ulysses was not surprised, but the announcement made him sad. "When did you decide?"

"It's been coming awhile," Ray said, "but I was sure after the New Year. I guess this whole adventure was a bit much for me and Clarice."

"I know the feeling," Ulysses said. They drove in silence for a few minutes. "I'm going to miss working with you, my brother."

"Yeah, me too. But not the rest of it." Ray laughed. "The whole tribe is upset about all that happened during the Deer Dance. I say, 'How could we have stopped that?' But everyone has their ideas." Ray shook his head. "I don't know how we could have stopped it."

"Who's going to take over for you?" Ulysses asked.

"Not sure yet," Ray said. "Maybe Matt."

"Seems like you aren't too happy about it?"

"Not yet," Ray said, with a sly smile, "but I will be."

•

Ulysses's fears of criticism from the governor turned out to be unfounded. When they came in the front doors of the Round House, a gathering of local luminaries broke into applause and Governor Sharon Montaño, who to Ulysses looked both smaller and older than her pictures, came forward and shook hands with both men while press photographers took pictures. "I'm so glad to meet you guys," she said, "I've got some public words to say but before I do, I just wanted to say thank you, personally, for all you did during this crisis!" She went immediately to the lectern set up for the occasion and made her brief speech praising them as heroes. Her chief of staff presented both men with medals for "meritorious service in the line of fire" and then the governor and her entourage rushed out to another meeting.

Ulysses felt a weight lift off mind as the meeting he'd feared would become a grilling turned into a lovefest. Ulysses and Ray took punch and cookies they didn't want and said hello to those gathered including quite a few old friends. Ray disappeared to the men's room as reporters gathered around Ulysses to ask questions about the case, one of the biggest homicide investigations in recent history. Their main focus was on what Archbishop Sullivan knew of child sex abuse by the Catholic clergy in New Mexico. Ulysses was guarded in his answers, suggesting they wait for the governor's task force scheduled to begin in the spring. It seemed like they'd already forgotten about the rest of the story.

Pictures in the *Taos News, Santa Fe New Mexican, Taos News, Rio Grande Sun* and *Albuquerque Journal* later showed both Ray and Ulysses looking tired and grave under headlines that read some variation of "Northern New Mexico Law Enforcement Cited for Bravery."

THE END

Glossary

bodhisattva: An enlightened being who renounces nirvana to work for the liberation of all.

bonsho: A large outdoor bell used in Buddhist temples to call the monks to meditation.

bizcochito: Crisp butter or lard-based cookies flavored with cinnamon or anise.

calabacitas: A traditional New Mexican dish of squash, corn, tomatoes and peppers.

carne adovada: A traditional New Mexican meat dish, usually pork, marinated in chile, vinegar and spices.

crozier: The stylized staff that is symbolic of the governing power of a bishop.

descanso: A homemade roadside memorial common in Northern New Mexico.

dharma: The nature of reality embodied in the teachings of the Buddha.

doan: One who rings the bell.

Dōgen (1200-1253): A leading Japanese Buddhist during the Kamakura period (1185-1333).

dokusan: A private interview between a student of Zen and a teacher.

dona: Gifts given to a sangha to support a sesshin or a teacher.

eightfold path: The path to enlightenment as revealed by Sakyamuni Buddha.

empanadas: Baked or fried turnovers, often with fruit filling.

farolitos: A 'little lantern" or luminaria made out of a paper sack with candles placed in sand and set out at Christmas in Northern New Mexico.

horno: An outdoor adobe oven devised by Native Americans and adopted by Spanish settlers in New Mexico.

jisha: The sesshin manager of a dokusan.

kinhin: Walking meditation, which typically takes place for ten minutes between twenty-five-minute sitting meditations (see zazen).

kiva: A round underground chamber used for religious ceremonies among the Puebloan people. A fireplace, adobe or stucco, designed to harmonize with southwestern architecture.

koan: A paradoxical story or riddle designed to provoke enlightenment.

kyosaku: The stick carried by a senior student of Zen and administered to sleepy or fidgety meditators by either a touch or a sharp tap.

latillas: Peeled bark twigs used as decoration between beams of a ceiling.

Mara: The demon who brings illusions to those seeking Enlightenment.

pobrecita/pobrecito: Spanish, meaning "poor little thing."

portal: A porch in southwestern architecture.

retablos: Small devotional images of saints or deities painted or carved on a panel of wood.

Rohatsu: The December day set aside to celebrate the enlightenment of the Buddha.

roshi: Japanese, a venerable teacher of Zen. Literally, "old teacher."

samu: Work done in service to the sangha.

sangha: The spiritual community in Buddhism.

scapular: A holy necklace or garment worn by Catholic devotees or members of monastic groups.

sensei: An assistant teacher in Zen.

sesshin: Japanese, literally "to touch the mind;" a Zen retreat lasting from five to ten days.

shikantaza: Japanese, "just sitting;" a type of meditation practice that is characterized by simply observing the mind.

soji screen: A traditional Japanese rice-paper room divider.

sopapilla: Deep fried Mexican pastry bread.

sutra: A short teaching of the Buddha and his followers.

tanto: Sesshin staff; Japanese for "head of the line;" often the most senior student.

teisho: A formal dharma talk.

transmission: The teaching succession from an elder to a younger teacher or roshi establishing a lineage.

viga: A large exposed roof beam in southwestern architecture.

zabuton: A square mat of fabric-covered cotton batting used for meditation seating. Often used with a zafu.

zafu: A round pillow traditionally filled with buckwheat hulls and used for meditation sitting.

zazen: The practice of sitting meditation.

Zen: A school of Mahayana Buddhism that originated in China.

zendo: A meditation hall for Zen practice.

ABOUT THE AUTHOR

C. R. Koons is a well-known speaker, teacher and consultant on the practice of mindfulness-based psychotherapy. Koons worked for many years leading a team of experts treating suicidal and self-harming adult and adolescent patients. She has published many academic articles and book chapters and a self-help book on the use of mindfulness to improve mental health. Koons lives and writes in Dixon, New Mexico, a small agricultural village on the Rio Embudo, not far from Taos. This is her first novel.

CPSIA information can be obtained
at www.ICGtesting.com
Printed in the USA
LVHW090054250323
742437LV00002B/14